"YOU MUST MAKE A BIRTHDAY WISH, CLEVE!"

"Well, since I'm not getting any younger, I wish that someday soon the woman of my dreams will come walking through that door and tell me she wants to marry me."

Cleve leaned over the cake, drew a deep breath, and blew out the candles. He raised his head, and his jaw dropped as he beheld a startling apparition: a beautiful woman wearing a wedding gown stood in the doorway.

At least he thought that's what he saw!

Blinking several times, he cast a quick glance at the others. They, too, were staring in stupefaction.

The moment of shock past, Cleve recognized her as the girl in the plaza: the delicate chin, straight nose, and beautiful, liquid brown eyes—the face he had envisioned in his fantasies. Her figure was slim but rounded sufficiently to fill out the low neckline of the wrinkled wedding gown, its lavishly embroidered pearls dulled by a coating of dust.

"So we meet again," he said.

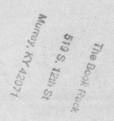

THE MACKENZIES:
Cleve

ANA LEIGH

LOVE SPELL   NEW YORK CITY

A LOVE SPELL BOOK®

December 2001

Published by

Dorchester Publishing Co., Inc.
276 Fifth Avenue
New York, NY 10001

ISBN 0-505-52464-3

The name "Love Spell" and its logo are trademarks of Dorchester Publishing Co., Inc.

Printed in the United States of America.

Visit us on the web at www.dorchesterpub.com.

I dedicate this book to Ellen Edwards,
a consummate teacher and discriminating editor,
in gratitude and appreciation for her guidance, vision, and assis-
tance in giving The MacKenzies *breath, soul, and essence.*

Her voice was ever soft,
Gentle and low. . . .

—William Shakespeare

Chapter 1

⁓᧡⁓

San Antonio, Texas
1870

Adriana saw her chance to escape.

They had left her alone for a few minutes and were outside in the enclosed patio. She quickly reread the letter Antonio had covertly sent her. He was in Fort Worth! Shoving the letter back into the envelope, she tucked it into the bodice of her gown and slipped out of the bedroom. Cautiously, she stole down the back stairs, pausing at the foot of the stairway when she heard a low murmur of voices coming from the nearby kitchen. Her pounding heart sounded like the thud of drumbeats in her ears. She had to get past the kitchen door without being seen—beyond it was the open door to freedom.

Despite the heat of the day, the adobe felt cool beneath her fingertips as she inched along the wall. With a quick glance, she peeked around the door. The two people in the kitchen were turned away from her, so she darted past the doorway.

Outside, the drone of voices from the patio carried to the rear. Fearful that at any moment someone would come walking around the corner of the house, she glanced about in desperation.

"¡Santa Maria!" she exclaimed gratefully when she

1

spied several horses tethered in the shade of a nearby cottonwood. Adriana dashed over to a huge black stallion and led it to an open portal in the stone wall surrounding the house.

With trembling fingers, she raised her skirt and unhooked the stiff crinoline at her waist, kicking aside the cumbersome bustle with its puffed flounces. She gathered up the folds of her gown and swung onto the stallion's back. Then, with a firm grasp on the reins, she goaded the horse to a gallop. Every second was precious; it would only be a matter of minutes before they discovered she was gone.

Trees whizzed past in a blur as the horse raced across the countryside. After riding hard for thirty minutes, Adriana reined in on the top of a steep rise and scanned the valley below. In the distance, the San Antonio River flowed through the sleepy town that bore its name. With luck, she might reach the town before her pursuers could intercept her.

Suddenly she caught a movement on the road below. Raising a hand to shade her eyes from the sun's glare, she recognized the northbound stagecoach.

She swung an anxious glance behind her and saw a rising cloud of dust—telltale evidence that she was being pursued—then returned her gaze to the swaying coach below. Dare she attempt to descend the steep hillside? If she fell or the horse lost its footing, she could be killed. The urgency to escape dispelled any further consideration.

Drawing a deep breath, Adriana patted the horse's neck and felt the stallion's strength as she hugged her slim legs tighter against its girth.

"*Santa Maria,* please don't fail me now," she murmured, in a quick plea to her patron saint. Then, with fearless daring, she started down the steep hill.

At breakneck, uncontrollable speed, the powerful animal half-galloped and half-slid down the treacherous declivity. Adriana skillfully managed to keep from being tossed out of the saddle and offered a quick prayer of thanks when the horse skidded to a stop at the bottom of the gorge. To her relief, the plucky animal still had the mettle to keep going as she veered it to the right. The stallion stretched out its neck and raced toward the coach.

When Adriana stopped in the path of the stage, the astonished driver pulled the rocking coach to a halt.

"Hold up there, sir. You have another passenger," she shouted. Ignoring the startled looks from the driver and the shotgun rider on the seat beside him, Adriana dismounted. "*Gracias, mi querido,*" she whispered affectionately to the sweating animal. "*Vaya a su casa.*"

Still gaping, the driver asked, "What about your horse?"

"It will find its way home, sir," she said confidently.

With a loftiness worthy of the royal court, Adriana tossed the bulky folds of her gown over her arm, climbed into the stage, and closed the door, only to flop back into the seat when the stage suddenly lurched forward.

Indignant, she leaned her head out the window. "In the future, please be a little more considerate, sir," she shouted to the driver. Then she offered a wide smile to the startled passenger in the seat opposite her. "Good morning, sir."

Flabbergasted, the man tipped his hat. "Good morning."

Adriana drew a deep breath. She had gotten away. They would never catch her now.

Smiling with satisfaction, Adriana Adelina Paloma Maria Fuente y de Elbertina adjusted the lace mantilla that had slipped askew on her head, and settled back in the seat. In folds of glossy satin, the pearl-encrusted skirt and train of her wedding gown billowed around her legs like fluffy white clouds.

Chapter 2

Fort Worth, Texas

T_he young fool is too damn dumb to realize he's beaten!_ Through the haze of cigar smoke, Cleve MacKenzie studied the man who had just raised the pot. The kid couldn't be much older than his early twenties and looked out of place in the smoke-filled, dingy saloon. From his coloring and attire, Cleve figured the young man was probably the son of one of the wealthy Spanish *criollo* ranchers scattered throughout Texas.

The young Spaniard was small in stature, with features more pretty than handsome. His jaw, high cheekbones, and straight nose were delicately formed. A moustache and neatly clipped beard were the only characteristics that lent an element of masculinity to his face.

Well, his rich papa shouldn't have left his little boy on his own, Cleve thought with a tinge of sympathy. The young man had lost continually throughout the evening, mainly to the man in the striped vest who had just thrown in his hand. All the others had folded, too. Now only Pretty Boy and himself remained in the card game.

Glancing around at the faces of the other men at the table, Cleve could feel the tension as everyone waited for the outcome of the hand. There was already over two thousand dollars in the pot. A frizzed-haired

4

blonde stood with her hand on Pretty Boy's shoulder. Whatever she was thinking remained concealed behind her impervious, green-eyed gaze.

He had hoped this showdown would be between him and Striped Vest. He sure as hell hated to see the kid lose any more money. But the day hadn't dawned when Cleve MacKenzie would throw in a hand holding four aces.

Removing the cigarillo from his mouth, he tossed it into a nearby claw-footed cuspidor. "I'll see you and I'll raise a thousand." He was nearing the end of his money. If Pretty Boy raised the pot again, Cleve might not be able to cover the kid's bet.

Cleve waited with a steady gaze as the young *criollo* mopped away the sheen of perspiration that glistened on his forehead. *First rule of poker, Pretty Boy—don't sweat.*

"I have no more money, *señor*."

This disclosure came as a relief to Cleve. It also produced a round of whispered murmurs from the few patrons in the saloon, now drawn to the table.

"I'm sorry," Cleve replied. "You know the rules."

The young man reached into the pocket of his coat. With lightning speed, Cleve drew his Colt. "No card game's worth dying over, friend."

The man raised his hand in the air. "Please, *señor*, it is not what you think. I only wish to get a paper out of my pocket."

"Very well, but nice and easy."

The man slowly extracted a folded paper and put it on the table. Cleve slipped his pistol back into its holster.

"I will put up the saloon."

"You're the owner of this place?"

Surprised, Cleve picked up the deed and read it, then looked around at the run-down establishment. Once, a long time ago, the saloon might have been grand, but now the paint was peeling from the walls, glass chimneys were missing from many of the lamps, the copper cuspidors were tarnished green, and the tables and chairs looked on the verge of collapse. A worn stairway led to the floor above, and the mahogany railing and balustrades appeared not to have seen a coat of polish since the saloon opened. The only redeeming thing in the place was a long, oak bar, which was worn but still sturdy. He figured the building must have been standing even before Mexico claimed the territory from Spain.

"Friend, this place doesn't look worth the money that's in the pot," Cleve said, leaning back. The chair creaked under his weight and he sat up again, grimacing.

What in hell should he do? What did he want with this run-down flea trap? From what he observed, it was nothing more than a whorehouse. As useful as he found them, he sure didn't want to own one.

On the other hand, practically all the money he had was riding on the four aces. But he was too proud to win any pot by default—especially from a wet-nosed kid who had no business at a poker table. He'd let the kid play out the hand. When it was over, he'd give the damn dive back to him. Maybe Pretty Boy would realize he still had a lot to learn about playing poker, and think twice before sitting down at his next game.

With an indifferent shrug of his wide shoulders, Cleve nodded. "All right."

Relief glittered in the young man's eyes as he grinned and turned over his hand. "Four kings," he announced cockily. "Or as you *Anglos* say, 'four cowboys.' You should have taken the pot when you had the chance, *señor*." He pulled in the pot and began to divide the money into piles.

"Appreciate your stacking up my winnings for me, friend," Cleve said in a calm voice. He turned over his hand.

The smile melted slowly from the young man's face as he stared in shock at the four aces. He shifted his frenzied glance up to Cleve, then back down to the cards.

Cleve saw the blonde's hand slide off the young man's shoulder. Her impenetrable stare had changed to amusement when several of the men began to laugh.

"Reckon you wuz too fast pullin' in that pot, *amigo*," one of them taunted. Another man and the blonde snorted along with him.

The young man's expression changed from shock to embarrassment. Mortified, he shoved back his chair and hurried up the stairway.

After pocketing the money, Cleve stood up and walked over to the bar.

Grinning, the bartender shoved a glass in front of him. "Name's Roy Burton. Congratulations, boss."

"Cleve MacKenzie." Cleve reached out and shook his hand. "Well, Roy, give everybody a drink on me."

Cleve had just downed his shot of whiskey when the young Spaniard descended the stairway. He was carrying saddlebags. Without a backward glance, he walked out the door.

Cleve hurried after him. "Hey, friend, wait up a minute."

The young man continued to tie the saddlebags onto a sorrel horse tethered to the hitching post. "What is it you wish?"

"Look, son," Cleve said kindly, "I don't want your saloon." He tried to hand him back the deed.

The man knocked Cleve's arm aside. "You insult me, *señor*," he lashed out angrily as he mounted the horse. "You seek to mock me more."

Cleve had no desire to argue with him. He could see how the young fool's pride had been damaged, and realized he should have let the fellow lose by default. That way the man's pride might have been bruised, but not destroyed.

"I apologize. I never intended to—"

"It is too late for apologies, *Anglo!*" He rode off before Cleve could say more.

"Goddammit." Cleve watched the rider disappear into the darkness.

Cleve considered himself an easygoing guy and did not lose his temper easily. He preferred reasoning out a situation before resorting to a fight—unlike his quick-tempered brothers, Luke and Flint. Well, maybe he could cut Luke a little slack, he reconsidered, but Flint would never take shoving from anyone. Just thinking about his brothers changed Cleve's frown to a grin.

Nevertheless, until he could straighten out this saloon mess, it looked like he was stuck here. Unhitching his dun gelding, he headed for the livery stable.

A short time later, his saddlebags slung over his shoulder, Cleve reentered the saloon. The few patrons who had been there earlier were gone. The bartender was washing glasses in a tub of dirty water, and the blonde stood at the end of the bar chatting with a long-legged, black-haired woman.

Cleve was very partial to long-legged, black-headed females. Since this part of the country abounded with brunette *señoritas*, he figured Texas was as close to heaven as he'd ever get.

"Roy, do you know where that hotheaded young Spaniard lives?"

"Upstairs."

Another surprise as far as Cleve was concerned. "I figured he was probably from one of the ranches around here."

Roy set a glass in front of Cleve and poured him a drink. "Couldn't prove it by me. The guy kept to himself. Never talked to anyone 'cept some rancher who'd come in now and then."

"What was his name?"

"The rancher or the kid?" Roy asked.

Chuckling, Cleve winked at the two ladies at the end of the bar and gulped down his drink. "Suppose we start with the kid."

Roy shrugged his beefy shoulders and refilled

Cleve's glass. His mouth curled with contempt. "Said we was to 'address him as *señor.*' Little punk—expectin' us to call him *sir*, and in that Spanish lingo of his on top of it. Told you he was uppity."

Based on his own encounter with the young man, Cleve certainly agreed with Roy's assessment of the Spaniard. "What can you tell me about him?"

"He bought this place a couple weeks ago from Ben Darvis. The kid knew nothing about running a saloon, but he wasn't the kind who asked for advice."

"What do you mean?" Cleve asked.

"Like I said. Kinda uppity. Acted like he thought he was too damn good to rub elbows with the likes of us."

"Well, this Darvis must know the kid's name."

Grabbing a towel, Roy swatted a fly crawling on the bar. "Probably did." He brushed aside the squashed remains.

Cleve made a mental note of Roy's actions but continued to question him. "What do you mean? Did Darvis leave town?"

"Nope." Roy grinned nastily. "He lives six feet under in the cemetery. Somebody slit him from ear to ear the same night he sold this dump."

Roy had a macabre sense of humor, if nothing else. "What about the rancher you mentioned? You think he was related to the kid?"

"Wouldn't know. He'd sit over there," Roy said, nodding toward a table in a darkened corner. "Always decked out in fancy duds. Went upstairs once with one of the gals."

"Which one?" Cleve asked, casting a hopeful glance toward the two women.

"Gal's name was Blanche, but she cleared out of here. People don't tend to hang around this place too long."

Understandable, Cleve thought, with another sweeping look at the decrepit surroundings. "How long have you been here, Roy?"

" 'Bout a month."

Figuring he was sticking his spurs into a dead horse, Cleve picked up the whiskey glass for a final drink. "Well, I'm tired. Which room did the kid sleep in?"

"Rear room upstairs. He liked his privacy."

"Want any company, good-lookin'?" the blonde asked, sidling up to him. With her green-eyed gaze locked on his, she grasped his hand, raised his glass to her mouth, and took a sip of whiskey.

"This here's Roxie," Roy said.

"Well, hello, Roxie." Cleve said slowly and intimately, handing her the glass.

"The other gal's Jeannie," Roy added.

Offering a friendly smile, Cleve tipped his hat at the dark-haired gal who had moved up beside him. "How do you do, Jeannie?"

"Roxie and Jeannie work the rooms upstairs," Roy grumbled.

Cleve loved women—was genuinely in awe of them. He considered a woman to be the greatest gift God had bestowed on earth: the gentlest of creatures, yet the one possessing the greatest inner strength. No matter who or what she was, he never passed judgement on a single one. Whether she was a lady or whore, he treated each with charm, courtesy—and absolute adoration.

"As much as I appreciate your gracious offer, Roxie, I've got to turn it down. I wouldn't be good company tonight."

Roxie batted her eyelashes and slid her hand down his arm. "Well, let me know when you feel . . . up for it," she said throatily.

He flashed an appealing grin that most women claimed could charm a snake out of its skin. "You bet I will!" Turning to the bartender, he asked, "Where do you live, Roy?"

"Jeannie and I share one of the rooms."

"Oh, so that's the way it is."

"Yeah." Roy smirked. "You ain't got a problem with that, do you, boss?"

"None of my business what you do on your off-hours, Roy. As for me, I'm heading to bed." Kissing Roxie's hand, he managed to ease himself from the grasp she held on his arm, then tipped his hat. "Good night, ladies."

After climbing the worn stairway to the landing above, Cleve glanced around in disgust; this floor looked as neglected as the one below. Passing two closed doors, he continued down the corridor to a room at the end of the hallway.

Pretty Boy had left the lamp burning. Dropping his saddlebags on the floor, Cleve glanced around, pleasantly surprised. Although sparsely furnished, the room was neat and tidy. The floor had been scrubbed clean, and the bed was covered with a counterpane. He lifted up the mattress and was relieved to see that it was not infested with bedbugs.

"At least Pretty Boy liked an orderly room," Cleve mumbled. In no mood for any uninvited visits, Cleve closed and locked the door. After hanging his gunbelt on the headboard, he sat down on the bed and removed his boots. Deep in reflection, he paused with a boot in hand.

"What in hell have you got yourself into, MacKenzie?" Shaking his head, he dropped the boot, blew out the lamp, then stretched out on the bed.

Cleve lay mulling over his troubled thoughts. He had come to Fort Worth following a tip from a Texas Ranger that the Charlie Walden gang might be active in Texas again. If the rumor was true, it hadn't taken Walden long to form a new gang. Cleve and his brothers had wiped out the old one in Kansas the previous year; unfortunately, Walden had gotten away.

Maybe winning this dump would be a Godsend after all. Walden was a legend in Texas, and there was always talk across a bar. He might be able to pick up some word on the bastard.

Cleve began to drift off to sleep. Yeah, it might work

out all right. But if he did hang around this place, there'd have to be some drastic changes made. And fast!

Bright and early the next morning, Cleve assembled Roy and the two women in the barroom. When they were all seated at a table, he made his first announcement.

"I intend to make several changes around here that will affect you. I'm gonna clean this place up, and there'll be no more whoring allowed."

Roxie and Jeannie exchanged amused glances. "How'd you expect us to make a livin'?" Roxie asked.

"By just standing and looking as pretty as you are. I'll pay you to talk to the men, have a drink with them if they ask, maybe even dance with them—but that's as far as it goes. If you want to whore, you'll have to do it elsewhere. Not at any place I run."

"You got some'n against whores, good-lookin'?" Roxie asked in a sultry voice.

"Nothing personal, Roxie," Cleve said, his sapphire eyes glowing with warmth. "I thank God for them every day. I'm just not interested in peddling flesh. Those are my rules if you want to remain at The Full House."

"We ain't got many customers as it is," Roy complained. "Without whores, you ain't gonna draw nobody in here."

"It's no wonder. Look around at this dump. But with a little cleaning up and a few additions, I'm going to turn this dive into a gambling casino."

Hand on hip, Roxie stood up and sauntered over to him. "Figured a good-looker like you, sugar, would know that men want more action than just gamblin'."

"If they do, they'll have to look elsewhere. You staying or leaving, Roxie?"

"I'd like to stick around out of curiosity, but I've known too many gamblers with big dreams like yours. Always dependin' on the turn of a card." She pointed her thumb at herself. "Well, not this gal." She strolled over to the stairway. "Look me up sometime, good-lookin'."

"What about you, Jeannie?" Cleve asked.

"Think I'll head out with Roxie."

"It's your choice, ladies. I thought I was doing you a favor."

"You don't have to do us no favors, handsome. We can take care of ourselves." The faint trace of wistfulness in Jeannie's voice sparked a feeling of regret in Cleve; he'd have liked to see her remain.

"Come on, Jeannie. Let's pack up and get out of here," Roxie declared.

"How you figure you're gonna get anybody in here without gals around?" Roy scoffed.

"I'll worry about that when the time comes."

"You've got another worry, MacKenzie."

"What's that?"

"Findin' a new bartender." Roy snorted. "Figure I'll leave with the gals before I choke on all the clean air you're plannin' on lettin' in here."

"I understand. Good luck, Roy." Cleve hoped his relief didn't show. The bartender had saved him the trouble of firing him. Roy's cleanliness left much to be desired.

Cleve was outside nailing up a "Closed for Repairs" sign when the two women and Roy came out of the saloon carrying carpetbags. Roxie paused at his side. "Don't forget to look me up sometime, good-lookin'. You'll find me down at the Pigeon Hole or the Alhambra."

"Sure thing, Roxie. You gals take care of yourselves," Cleve said, tipping his hat.

He went back into the empty saloon and sat down to count his money. He figured he had enough to give the place a new look. First, he'd have to hire someone to help him clean up the joint. Then he'd need a bartender and at least one gal to serve drinks—and if he had any luck at all, she'd be long-legged with black hair that hung down to her hips.

He'd always had a yen to own a gambling casino, but
his heart would be more into the challenge of turning
this place around if he'd been able to track down
Charlie Walden. Until they found the man who killed
their mother and Sarah, neither he nor his brothers
would have peace of mind.

And since Flint and his wife, Garnet, had had a baby
earlier that year, and Luke's wife, Honey, was expecting soon, neither of his brothers could leave their
families to pick up the chase. At the moment, the onus
of finding Walden was on his shoulders alone.

Glancing around at the run-down saloon, he wondered if he was doing the right thing. Should he stop
the search long enough to get this place in shape? Once
he did, he could leave it in somebody else's hands and
then continue to hunt down Walden.

Well, if he intended to do anything at all with the
dump, he wasn't getting it accomplished by sitting
there just thinking about it. With his usual optimism,
Cleve grabbed his Stetson. No time like the present to
get started, he decided.

A rumbling in his stomach reminded him that he
hadn't eaten. If nothing else, he needed a cup of coffee.
Plopping his hat on his head, he headed for the kitchen.

The room smelled of cigarette ashes. One look at the
table and sink, cluttered with cups of stale coffee and
dishes caked with the remains of food and cigarette
butts, convinced Cleve he'd rather eat elsewhere. Locking up, he went down the street to a nearby diner.

After a satisfying breakfast, Cleve found himself
alone in the diner except for the woman who served as
cook and waitress. He lingered over a second cup of
coffee as he gazed out the window and watched three
Mexican boys pitching pocketknives at a circle drawn in
the dust. Cheering and applauding would follow whenever one of the youths embedded his knife in the ring.

Recalling his own childhood and the many times he
and his brothers had engaged in the game, Cleve

plunged heart-first into a wave of homesickness. For a moment he thought of chucking aside The Full House, saddling up Swifty, and riding back to the Triple M and the family he loved.

"More coffee, *señor?*"

Jarred out of his musings, he looked up to see the waitress standing beside his table.

"Think I will," he said.

Glancing out the window, the woman suddenly exclaimed, "Oh, that boy!" She put down the coffeepot and hurried to the doorway. "José!" she shouted.

Two of the boys picked up their knives and raced off while the third remained, hanging his head.

"I told you to chop the wood for the stove," she declared.

"I tried, *Mamá*, but my arm is too sore," the boy explained. He made a feeble attempt to raise his arm, then looked up at his mother, his round, dark eyes welling with tears. "See, *Mamá*, I can't even lift it," he said sorrowfully.

Cleve kept an impassive expression as he shifted his glance to the woman to see if she'd swallow the boy's act.

"Oh, *hijo*, I am so sorry you are in pain," she said sadly. Grasping her son's face between her hands, she kissed each of his cheeks.

Well, I'll be damned! Cleve thought. *The kid's gonna get away with it.*

"My heart aches, *querido*, thinking of how much sorer your arm will be by the time you finish chopping the wood." Then her tone changed to sternness. "And when you are through, go to confession for trying to lie to your mother."

"*Sí, Mamá*," the boy said in defeat. Picking up his knife, he headed for the woodshed.

Shaking her head, the woman returned to Cleve's table. "Forgive me, *señor*. That *pequeño!* Always he tries to fool his *mamá*," she said, refilling Cleve's cup.

"But I bet he doesn't get away with it too often,"

Cleve said with admiration. Rising to his feet, he pulled
out a chair. "Come, *señora,* join me in a cup of coffee.
You've been working hard. It's time you sit down and
relax."

For a moment the woman's eyes flashed with indecision; then she nodded. "*Sí.* I think I would like that."

"I'll get you a cup." He grabbed one from the
sideboard and, once seated, filled it for her. "You
remind me of my mother. She had her hands full
raising me and my brothers, but she, too, was always
wise to us whenever we tried shirking our chores."

"I have not seen you here before, *señor.*"

"My name's Cleve MacKenzie."

"And I am Rosa Martinez," she said.

"It's a pleasure to meet you, Rosa."

By the time he left the diner, they had become good
friends.

Before returning to the saloon, Cleve stopped at the
general store for some cleaning supplies. He was in the
kitchen and had just finished scraping and stacking
the dirty dishes when a young Mexican, grasping the
handle of a small wooden box in one hand, appeared in
the entrance of the doorway.

"*Señor* MacKenzie?" the man asked.

Cleve nodded. "What can I do for you?" A short
distance behind the man stood a woman holding a girl
in one arm and a young boy's hand with the other.

Struggling with English, the man said, "I am Paulo
Guerra. My cousin Rosa Martinez said you are seeking
for the help. I am a *carpintero.*"

"A carpenter!" Cleve exclaimed, unable to believe his
luck.

"*Sí, señor.*" Holding up the wooden box, he said, "I
have the skill with the tools. And my wife, Magdalena,
she has much skill with the cleaning and cooking."

Cleve stepped aside. "Come in. Come in. Let's sit
down and discuss this." He quickly pulled out a chair.
"Here, take this seat, *Señora* Guerra."

"*Gracias,*" the woman said shyly as she sat down with the little girl in her lap.

Cleve smiled at the child. He figured the dark-eyed little charmer couldn't be much more than three years old. "Hi, there. What's your name, angel?"

The youngster giggled, then buried her head against her mother's chest.

"Bonita," Magdalena Guerra replied.

"Yes, she certainly is," Cleve said agreeably.

Tittering in amusement, Magdalena said, "No, *señor*, that is her name."

"You've named her well, Magdalena; she's as pretty as her name implies."

"And this is our son, Juan," Paulo said.

Cleve squatted and shook hands with the youngster. "My pleasure, Juan. How old are you?"

Curling an arm around Paulo's leg, the young boy looked up in confusion at his father.

"Juan no speak the English good like me, *señor*," Paulo explained apologetically. "He has five years of the age."

"I'm sure he'll soon get the hang of it," Cleve said.

"Hang of it?" Paulo asked, confused.

"Just an expression, Paulo. He'll soon be speaking English as well as you do," Cleve said. "Now, let's sit down and see what we can work out here."

By the time the conversation ended, Cleve had found his work crew.

Chapter 3

What a change a few weeks can make! Smiling with satisfaction, Cleve paused on his way out the door to take a look around at the casino. It had taken almost every cent he had and two weeks of hard work to get The Full House remodeled, but the transformation was remarkable. The casino now smelled fresh and clean; the repaired floors, balustrades, tables, and chairs glistened with varnish; the walls gleamed with paint; several ornate chandeliers with crystal pendants had been added to the ceiling lamps, which sparkled with new chimneys; and the copper cuspidors were shiny and bright. Red velvet drapes adorned with gold tassels, sewn by several of Magdalena's cousins, formed the entrance to a secluded alcove for dining.

With shrewd bargaining and a promise of unlimited free drinks, he had purchased a used roulette wheel and several mirrors from a merchant—although the wheel was inactive because he hadn't as yet found someone he trusted to operate it. He wanted no crooked gambler in The Full House. And he needed a bartender, too. Paulo had been filling in temporarily, but because of his faulty English the carpenter had no desire to attempt the job permanently.

Despite these unresolved problems, all their hard work had not gone for naught, Cleve thought with satisfaction. In the past week since The Full House had reopened, business had increased steadily. The risk he had taken was beginning to pay off. Already the casino had begun to attract the merchants and businessmen who preferred a quiet night of gambling without the distractions that other places offered.

Stepping outside, he flashed his most charming smile and doffed his hat to the three sign-toting women in front of the casino. For the past week, the preacher's wife and the women's auxiliary of the nearby Methodist church had spent an hour a day picketing the reopening of The Full House.

"Good morning, ladies. How are all of you today?"

"Humph!" their dour leader exclaimed, when the two other women tittered in reply.

"It certainly is hot today, isn't it, Mrs. Parker," he said amicably. "I've told Magdalena to bring out a pitcher of cold lemonade to you charming ladies."

"Oh, thank you, Mr. MacKenzie. You're so thoughtful," Matilda Merryweather gushed.

"Matilda!" Prudence Parker declared in disgust.

The censured woman covered her mouth in embarrassment, but her bright blue eyes twinkled above her hand as she peeked at Cleve.

Winking at her, he replaced his hat. "Now, don't you ladies exhaust yourselves in this heat," he cautioned. "If you get tired and want to rest, just tell Paulo to bring you out some chairs."

As he continued down the street, he couldn't help smiling. Today was his thirty-fourth birthday, and he felt good. This was going to be a great day—he could feel it in every one of his thirty-four-year-old bones.

Exhausted, Adriana spied a bench across the plaza and started toward it.

A cowboy who had been leaning against a wall suddenly stepped into her path. "Where you hurryin' to, little lady? Late for your wedding?"

When she tried to move around him, he sidestepped

in front of her again. "Please, sir, let me pass," she demanded with false bravado.

He winked at a nearby companion. "Don't you fret, little lady. If that guy leaves you waiting at the church, you can count on me to take his place."

Both men broke into loud laughter; then her harasser removed his hat and stepped aside with a sweeping bow.

Adriana crossed the street and, feeling on the verge of collapse, plopped down on a bench. Since arriving in Fort Worth that morning, she had been traipsing all over the city looking for a saloon called The Full House. No one she asked had ever heard of the place. Now all that was left were these few remaining blocks.

At least this section of the town appeared less hectic than the others, she observed, but it definitely lacked the quaint charm and the peace and quiet of San Antonio.

Whatever had drawn her brother to such a place? she pondered in dismay. She certainly didn't like Fort Worth, even if it was famous for being the start of the Chisholm Trail. The city was dusty, noisy, and over-crowded. People shouted loudly to each other, rowdy cowboys galloped up and down the streets, and acres of cattle pens were filled with milling steers, mewling heifers, and bawling calves.

She wanted to rip off the satin wedding gown she'd been wearing for the past three days. The dress was hot, heavy, and cumbersome. To add to her discomfort, everyone she passed stared at her as if she were *loco*, and she had had to endure uninvited comments such as the kind just suffered from the cowboy.

"Oh, Adriana, you are such an *estúpida!*" she mumbled in disgust. Why hadn't she grabbed a blouse and skirt when she ran away? *"¡Estúpida! ¡Estúpida!"* she reiterated.

Now she was desperate. The three-day journey to reach Fort Worth had cost every cent Antonio had sent her; she no longer had one coin to rub against another.

Feeling the rise of panic, Adriana closed her eyes and drew a deep breath. She had made it this far, hadn't she? Now was no time to give up.

As she tried to relax, she noticed a Catholic church at the opposite side of the plaza. After resting a few more moments, she would go and speak to the priest. Perhaps he knew the location of The Full House.

Hearing youthful shouts and laughter, she turned her head and saw a group of older boys tossing stones. Her eyes widened with horror when she saw that their target was a scruffy-looking puppy. When several of the stones found their marks, the poor animal yelped with pain.

"Stop that! Stop that!" Adriana bolted from the bench, her exhaustion forgotten, her mantilla falling to the ground as she dashed across the plaza.

Shaking her fist at the scrambling boys, she shouted, "Shame! Shame on all of you!" Then she sat down in the dust and cuddled the trembling dog in her arms.

"Poor little *perro*," she cooed affectionately. "Are you looking for a home, too, *pequeño*?"

"Is the dog all right, miss?"

"I think so," Adriana said. Tears misting her eyes, she glanced up at the speaker—and stared, speechless.

He was easily the handsomest man she had ever seen. A dark mustache rested over a wide mouth with a sensual lower lip, and a crook in the bridge of his nose, most likely caused by a fight, gave his face a rugged appearance. The way he held his head conveyed an aura of self-confidence that indicated he had nothing to prove to anyone.

His shirtsleeves were rolled up to the elbows of tanned and muscular arms. She suspected the shoulders and chest under the shirt were equally strong.

Adriana could not break her gaze from his. She felt as if she were drowning in the depths of his sapphire eyes and continued to stare at the handsome stranger until he broke the spell.

"Is this your dog, *señorita*?" he asked. His hand on her

arm felt warm, the touch stimulating, as he helped her
to her feet.

"No, but I had to stop those boys from harming the
poor little thing."

"Well, you dropped this, *señorita*," he said, handing
Adriana her mantilla.

"Thank you, sir."

"MacKenzie. Cleve MacKenzie." Then he smiled—
an engaging smile of straight, white teeth, and the
warmth of his expression carried to his incredible eyes.
"And good luck, miss. You make a beautiful bride."
Tipping his hat, he walked away.

Her gaze followed the tall, broad-shouldered stranger until he disappeared into the crowd. Sighing, she
murmured, "Well, little one, I must go and talk to the
priest." She carried the dog with her.

As Cleve hurried back to the casino, he couldn't stop
thinking about the young woman in the plaza. What a
beauty! Even looking harried and disheveled from her
efforts in rescuing the dog, the young bride had the face
of the woman of his dreams. Until now, even though he
had often spoken of love at first sight, he had never
quite believed in it. But the woman was about to
wed . . . too late now to put the theory to the test.

She had a heart as beautiful as her face, too, Cleve
reflected. This was one of the most important days of
her life, yet the selfless little sweetheart had given no
thought to either her vanity or her wedding gown,
racing to the rescue of a stray dog.

Lord! The guy she was marrying was damn lucky!

When he reached The Full House, Cleve saw that
Pontifical Prudence Parker and her two apostles, the
name he had affectionately dubbed the trio, had left for
the day. He shook his head in amusement as he entered
the casino.

He poured himself a drink and had just raised the
glass to his lips, when he looked up and stared in
surprise at the woman who stood in the doorway.

Tall and slim, she had brown hair shoved up under a large black hat adorned with a huge red plume. Cleve noticed that her dress did little to conceal a well-rounded bosom. He bet the legs under that gown would go on forever. A white boa was draped casually around her shoulders, the ends of the feathery scarf drooping from her elbows. With fluid grace, she walked over to him.

"Are you the owner?"

Her voice was pleasant, with enough natural throatiness to stroke a man's spine like a velvet glove.

Quaffing the drink in a single gulp, he put the empty glass on the bar. "That's right. What can I do for you?"

"Name's Lily LaRue."

The name had a familiar ring, but Cleve could not place her face. He was certain he had never seen her before.

"I just arrived in Fort Worth today, and I've been looking for a job. One of the women at the Alhambra said you might be hiring."

"What is it you do, Miss LaRue?"

The woman's face curved in a smile. "I think you've already figured that out."

"You've got a lovely smile, Lily. Let's sit down and discuss it."

"My smile or the job?" she asked.

Cleve chuckled. He liked this woman on sight—and it had nothing to do with her having dark hair and, most certainly, a pair of long legs.

Leading her over to a table, Cleve pulled out a chair. "Sit here, Lily. What can I get you to drink?"

"Coffee, if you have it," she said.

"Be right back." Hurrying to the kitchen, he returned with two cups.

After taking a deep drink from the cup set before her, Lily took a long look at the man who sat across the table. He was devilishly handsome, she reflected—*tall, dark, and handsome*. From her experience with men, she figured him to be in his mid thirties, possibly four or five years older than she was.

His eyes were the most incredible feature of his face. They were dark blue, the color of sapphires, and heavily fringed with long, dark lashes that most women would envy. She had seen such eyes on only one man before.

"In truth, I'm looking for a good woman, Lily."

Lily arched a brow. "Oh, I'm a *very* good woman. But it would be pretty hard to get recommendations from my clients—most of them can't write."

They both broke into laughter.

He sure liked this gal. Despite a candid, tough veneer, her femininity shone through. But her name continued to tease his memory. He was convinced he had heard it before. "So where are you from, Lily?"

"Here and there. Mostly California, though, Mister . . . I never caught your name."

"MacKenzie. Cleve MacKenzie. Just call me Cleve. I don't stand on—" He paused when he realized she was staring intently at him. "What is it?"

"Did you say 'MacKenzie'?" When he nodded, she asked, "Do you have a brother?"

"Yeah. Two of them: Luke and Flint."

"Well, I'll be! No wonder you look so familiar. I knew Luke when he was the sheriff of Stockton."

Then it hit Cleve like a punch to the jaw—Lily LaRue! He'd heard her name from Luke and Honey.

"Lily!" He jumped up, pulled her to her feet, and smothered her in a bear hug. "So I finally get to meet the woman who helped save my brother's life. Honey told me what you did."

Her mouth curved into a tender smile. "How is she?" Lily asked. After adjusting the hat that had been knocked askew, she sat back down.

"Very much with child," Cleve said, also sitting. "Expecting a baby in a month or so."

"That's wonderful. And Luke? Did he fully recover from his wounds?"

Cleve nodded. "Limped for a while, but he's fine now." He grasped her hand. "Lily, we MacKenzies are beholden to you. We never had a chance to thank you for what you did for my brother and his family. If it weren't for you, Luke and Honey would be dead—and most likely my nephew Josh, too."

Lily shrugged off the compliment. "Don't give me all the credit. You should have seen Honey that night. Believe me, Cleve, I'm not exaggerating. She was a she-wolf protecting her young." The red plume bobbed in the air as Lily shook her head. "I can still see her, sitting on the floor with those two Colts pointed at the doorway. Anyone would have had to kill her to get near Luke and Josh."

"I don't doubt that for a minute," Cleve said, chuckling. "She even pulled a Colt on me and Flint when we showed up." He reached across the table and grasped her hand. "But that doesn't lessen the role you played that night, Lily. The MacKenzies are indebted to you—and we always pay our debts."

"So, maybe I can have that job after all."

"You can have more than a job. How'd you like to run this place, Lily?" Cleve asked, suddenly inspired. "It would free me to deal one of the tables." The more he thought of it, the more excited he became. "Having a woman in charge would be a great draw. We could change the name from The Full House to The Queen's Palace, or . . . maybe just Lily's."

"What do you mean by 'run the place'?" Lily asked, perplexed. "I'm a whore, Cleve. That's what I do."

"Not anymore, Miss Lily. Those days are behind you. You've been around enough to know how to operate a gambling casino. But gambling only—a place where a man can come and enjoy an honest game of cards in peace and quiet. Where his wife won't have to worry that he's sneaking upstairs with a woman. The rooms upstairs are to live in—not work in. I need someone I can trust to run this place, and I can't think of anyone I'd trust more than you." He smiled persuasively.

"How about it? I'm afraid, though, you'll have to double as a bartender for a spell until I can hire one."

Lily was too astonished to answer. No man had ever offered her anything other than a price for her services—a price for which she had often borne the indignities and pain that many men chose to inflict on her.

Even Luke MacKenzie had paid for her services, until he fell in love with Honey. But Luke was different. He had always been considerate, even tender, when he came to her bed. And she, like many other women in her profession, had been foolish enough to fall in love with a man who had paid for her services. Luke had never suspected her true feelings for him, and it had taken her a long time to get over her love for him.

Even so, Honey had been a true friend to her. Honey had not passed judgement on her like the other women in town had. Those good, respected women had treated her just as cruelly as their husbands who sneaked up to visit her.

For a brief moment, Lily felt the rise of tears as images from Stockton flashed through her mind: Luke, Honey, Pop O'Malley, Charlie Walden. It seemed so long ago.

Honey had once tried to convince her to start a different life somewhere else, and Lily had scoffed at her well-meaning friend. Now, Cleve MacKenzie was offering her the same chance. Dare she try? Could she really escape her past, or would she only be deluding herself?

"Well, how about it, Lily?" Cleve asked, jarring her out of her reflections. He pulled her to her feet and grasped her arms.

Lily looked up into Cleve's eyes and saw more than the sapphire blue of his brother's eyes; the same kindness and trustworthiness she had seen in Luke's were in Cleve's, too.

Smiling, she nodded. "I'm willing to give it a try if you are. Cleve MacKenzie, you've just hired yourself a manager. And, boss, there's no need to change the name on that sign out there. The Full House sounds just fine to me."

"It's gonna work, Lily." Cleve hugged her, and she yelped as he raised her off her feet and spun her around.

When he put her down, she stepped back, tossed aside the boa, and unpinned her hat. "Well, when do I start?"

He picked up her carpetbag. "We've got a couple extra rooms upstairs. Let's get you settled in before you change your mind. Then I'll introduce you to Magdalena and Paulo."

A short time later, after Lily had met the Guerras and been given a tour of the establishment, Cleve and Lily returned to the barroom to discuss business. They had just sat down when Magdalena and Paulo came in carrying a cake ablaze with candles.

"Happy birthday, *Señor* Cleve!" they shouted.

"Well, I'll be damned! I sure didn't expect this."

"Happy birthday, Cleve," Lily said, as surprised as he was. "Had I'd known, I'd have brought you a gift."

"Honey," he said solemnly, "your arrival was a bigger gift than I could ever have hoped for."

Glancing around at the small party gathered at the table, Cleve cleared his throat. "Well, my fairly new but very dear friends, since I know myself to be a well-meaning, friendly sort of guy, it comes as no surprise to me that we've assembled here to celebrate this momentous day, marking the thirty-fourth anniversary of my birth."

"Hey, boss man, you better save some of that hot air for blowing out the candles," Lily said, winking at Magdalena.

Cleve's gaze, full of affection, lingered on Lily. From their first meeting just a short hour earlier, an irrevocable bond had formed between them. The role she had played in his brother's past made her sacrosanct to

Cleve: he and Lily would never be lovers, but they'd always be friends. And he sensed that Lily felt the same.

"Okay, since our new boss lady is anxious for us to get to work, I'll shut up now. I just want to thank you all for making this a special day for me."

"But your wish, *Señor* Cleve!" Magdalena exclaimed. "You must make the wish."

"Well, since I'm not getting any younger, I wish that someday soon the woman of my dreams will come walking through that door and tell me she wants to marry me."

Cleve leaned over the cake, drew a deep breath, and blew out the candles. He raised his head; then his jaw dropped as he beheld a startling apparition: a beautiful woman wearing a wedding gown and holding a small puppy stood in the doorway.

At least he thought that's what he saw!

Blinking several times, Cleve realized she was not a figment of his imagination. He cast a quick glance at the others. They, too, were staring in stupefication.

The moment of shock past, he recognized her as the girl in the plaza. Cleve stood and slowly walked over to her. For a long moment, he remained silent, gazing at a face as exquisite as he remembered: the delicate chin, straight nose, and beautiful, liquid brown eyes—the face he had envisioned in his fantasies.

Under a lace mantilla, her dark hair hung in dishevelment past her shoulders. Her figure was slim but rounded sufficiently to fill out the low neckline of the wrinkled wedding gown, its lavishly embroidered pearls dulled by a light coating of dust.

"So we meet again," he said, awestruck.

"You are the man from the plaza," she said, surprised.

"Yes. How can I help you?"

"*Señor*, can you direct me to Antonio Fuente?"

Still amazed by this woman's reappearance in his

life, Cleve continued to stare at her. The sudden flare of irritation in her brown eyes jolted him out of his fantasy. "Sir, I wish to speak to Antonio Fuente."

"Antonio Fuente? I'm sorry; I've never heard of him."

She put the dog down and pulled a letter out of her bodice. Cleve could see that the document had been handled many times. "But the priest told me to come here. This is The Full House, is it not?"

"Yes, it is," he replied.

"Is not Antonio Fuente the owner?"

"No. I'm the owner here."

She clutched the letter to her bosom. "How can that be? Antonio said he owned this place." Her voice rose in accusation. "Antonio would not lie to me." She stuffed the letter back into her bodice.

"I'm sure he wouldn't," Cleve said, trying to calm her rising panic. "Why don't you sit down and we'll discuss this, Miss . . . ah—" Cleve grabbed her as she suddenly weaved and pitched forward.

Lily hurried over as he shifted the unconscious girl into his arms. "What's wrong with her?" she asked.

"I don't know. She came in here looking for some guy named Antonio, and then she passed out. Let's take her upstairs to the spare room. Paulo, you go and get Doc Anderson."

Lily and Magdalena scurried ahead of Cleve as he carried the girl up the stairway. "Put her on the bed," Lily ordered, falling easily into her role of command. "Magdalena, there's a pitcher of water in my room—"

"I'll get it," Cleve said. He hurried away and was back a minute later, carrying a pitcher and glass.

"We'll take care of her, Cleve," Lily said. "Why don't you go downstairs and wait for the doctor?" She put a firm hand on his chest and shoved him out the door, closing it behind him.

For several seconds Cleve stared at the door; then he spun on his heels and went downstairs.

He saw the dog waiting at the bottom of the stairway. With its ears perked alertly, the puppy fixed his quizzical look on Cleve.

Bewildered, Cleve spread his arms. "Hey, why look at me, fella? I'm just as baffled as you are."

Chapter 4

A driana opened her eyes to discover a gray-haired stranger holding her wrist. Confused, she found herself lying in an unfamiliar bed—and to her horror, all her clothing had been removed except for a camisole and drawers! When she started to struggle, the man said calmly, "Just relax, miss. I'm Dr. Anderson and I'm just taking your pulse."

As Adriana glanced around the room, she saw two women whom she recalled seeing earlier. "What happened? Where am I?" she asked.

The taller of the two stepped up to the bed. "You're still in The Full House, honey. You fainted, so we brought you upstairs. This is Magdalena, and I'm Lily."

"I'd like to talk to the young lady alone," the doctor said, releasing her wrist.

"Of course," Lily replied.

As soon as the women left the room, the doctor pulled up a chair and sat down at the bedside. "Everything appears normal on the surface, Miss . . ."

"Adriana Adelina Paloma Maria Fuente y de Elbertina," she answered hastily.

"Miss . . . ah . . . Adriana, are you recovering from a recent illness?" he asked.

"No. I have not been ill, Doctor."

"Well then, when was the last time you had something to eat?"

31

"Yesterday," she said.

"I see," he said. "And drink?"

"This morning."

"I see."

I see! I see! she thought impatiently. He didn't see anything! She didn't wish to answer any more of his questions. "I'm fine now. Thank you for your help, Doctor."

"Do you faint often?" he asked.

¡Santa Maria! More questions! "No, I have never fainted before." Her dismissal of him appeared to have very little effect on the man. She had to get away from this doctor and his prying questions.

"My dear, I realize a bride is nervous on her wedding day, but one does not faint for no reason."

"Yes. It is as you say, Doctor," she said, jumping at the excuse. "I am nervous about my wedding."

"Is that why you ran away?"

Adriana jerked up her head in surprise. "How did you know?"

"It's rather unusual to find a bride alone on her wedding day, Adriana. Let me notify your family or the expectant groom. I'm sure they're waiting at the church and are worried about your disappearance."

For a moment she had feared that he knew the truth about her flight from San Antonio. Then she realized this doctor thought it had just happened today. She was desperate—she needed an ally but knew Antonio would prefer that their personal affairs remain private. Uncertain how to proceed, Adriana finally spoke up.

"Dr. Anderson, I need your help, but what I tell you must remain between us."

"Of course, my dear. A confidentiality always exists between a doctor and patient."

"What you suspect is true, Doctor. I did run away from my wedding—but that was three days ago. My home is in San Antonio, not Fort Worth. I came here looking for Antonio Fuente. He told me in his letter that

I would find him—'' She suddenly sat up in panic, clutching at her bosom. "His letter! Where is Antonio's letter?"

"Here it is," the doctor said, picking up the wrinkled piece of paper from the bed table.

Adriana snatched the envelope from his hand. "You read it!" she accused.

"I did not mean to pry, Adriana," he said kindly. "I had hoped to get your name in order to notify your family."

"Do you know Antonio? Or where I can find him, Doctor? Since you've read the letter, you know he once owned this place."

"I'm afraid I've never met him, my dear. Are you in love with this Antonio Fuente? Is that why you ran away?"

"Doctor, Antonio is my brother—my twin brother. I came here as soon as I got his letter."

"But I noticed that the letter was dated a month ago, when this place was a . . . well, it doesn't matter." He rose hastily to his feet and grabbed his black bag.

"What were you about to say, Dr. Anderson? What kind of place was this?"

His face reddened as he hurriedly began to shove his instruments into the black bag. "Nothing, my dear. Nothing." Obviously changing the subject, he said, "I suggest you eat and rest before you attempt any further search for your brother. In the meantime, I'll make some inquiries and let you know if I discover his whereabouts."

"Thank you, Doctor."

Dr. Anderson paused at the doorway. "Remember, rest and get some liquid and food into you, or you'll most likely faint again."

"I will," she said.

Adriana lay back. What should she do now? She certainly was in a fine fix. She hadn't paid any attention to the date on Antonio's letter when Maria had slipped it to her. She'd barely had time to get away. Now she didn't know where to find Antonio, and he didn't even know she had come to Fort Worth.

Adriana, you are such an estúpida!

One thing was certain—she would not return to San Antonio and the marriage her father had arranged. She closed her eyes and crushed the letter to her breast. *Where are you, Antonio?*

"How is she, Jim?" Cleve asked when the doctor joined Lily and him at the bar.

"The young lady needs rest and a good hot meal. Then she'll be fine."

"Well, we can fix her up something to eat real quick," Cleve said.

"Would it be inconvenient for her to remain here?" the doctor asked.

"Here!" Cleve exchanged a startled glance with Lily. "Doesn't she live in Fort Worth?"

"No."

"I don't follow, Doc. If she doesn't live in Fort Worth, how come she's running around in a wedding gown? Did she come here intending to get married to this Antonio she's looking for?"

"Hope not, because my guess is that Antonio doesn't live here anymore," Lily murmured with a twisted smile. "She wouldn't be the first woman who was left standing at the church." Lily put a glass down in front of the doctor and filled it. "How about a drink, Doc?"

The doctor raised it slightly in a toast. "Thank you, Miss . . ."

"Lily LaRue. But just Lily will do, Doc."

As Lily and the doctor continued to chat, Cleve only half-listened to their conversation. His thoughts were on the woman upstairs and the young Spaniard who had once owned the place. He must have been Antonio, the man she was seeking. Where had the bitter young fool ridden off to that night? He hadn't returned since.

"If you can get her to eat something, I'm sure it will speed her recovery," Dr. Anderson said.

Lily nodded. "I'll go and fix her a tray right now."

"Good-looking woman, Cleve," the doctor said, after Lily left.

"Yeah, beautiful, isn't she?" Cleve agreed, his thoughts on Adriana.

"She mentioned she's going to manage the casino. Sounds like a pretty good idea."

"Oh, you mean Lily?" Cleve said, jolted back to awareness. "Yes, Lily's a good friend of the family."

Finishing his drink, Jim Anderson picked up his black bag. "I better get back to my office. I've got more patients than just this mysterious woman."

"Who is she, Jim? What are her plans?"

"I can't say," he said.

"You mean you don't know, Jim, or you won't say?"

"Both, Cleve. I can't violate doctor and patient confidentiality, you know. I'll tell you this much: there's been no wedding. Thanks for the drink."

Cleve started to reach into his pocket. "How much do I owe you, Doc?"

"Forget it, Cleve. I've enjoyed the drink and the company. We'll call it even. Besides," Jim added, "you'd just win the money back from me on Friday night anyway."

As they walked to the doorway, the doctor glanced over at the forgotten cake on the table. "Whose birthday?"

"Oh, yeah. Mine," Cleve said.

"Well, happy birthday."

"You know, Doc, I think that's just what it is." Slicing off a piece of the cake, he wrapped it in a napkin. "Be sure and give this to that beautiful wife of yours."

"What about me?"

"You? God, Doc, you're as ugly as hell!"

"You better hope you never have the occasion to fall under my knife, Mr. MacKenzie. I shall see you Friday."

"Good-bye, Doc," Lily called out as she came downstairs.

He waved on his way out the door.

"I took her up a cheese sandwich and glass of milk, Cleve," Lily said. "And I dug through my things and found something else for her to wear instead of that wedding gown."

"You're a real sweetheart, Lily." Pulling out a chair for her, he said, "Miz Lily, let's sit down and have a slice of my birthday cake."

The woman upstairs was momentarily forgotten as their conversation returned to the business of running The Full House.

As soon as they finished, Lily pushed away from the table. "Well, if I'm going to start work, I better go up and get ready. I'll check on Adriana, too, and see how she's doing."

"Never mind; I'll check on her," Cleve said. "I want to find out what our patient's plans are."

"The poor kid. Thought I understood men, but I sure can't figure why a guy would leave someone like her waiting at the altar."

"Can't say the same thought hasn't crossed my mind, too, Lily my love," he said, slipping an arm around her shoulders as they climbed the stairs.

As soon as Lily disappeared into her room, Cleve continued down the hall and tapped lightly on the next door. "Miss . . ." What the hell was that long name that had rolled off her tongue? He couldn't remember anything beyond Adriana. He tapped again. "Adriana, may I come in?"

When she didn't reply, Cleve opened the door enough to poke his head inside. Then he stepped into the room and walked over to the bed. His gaze devoured her sleeping face as it had earlier. How often had he boasted to his brothers that he would recognize the woman he'd marry the moment he saw her? Now, he had the peculiar feeling that he had found her.

For a brief moment, he couldn't help feeling a tinge

of sympathy for this elusive Antonio. If, indeed, this was the hand of Fate, not only had Antonio lost The Full House to him, but the young Spaniard would soon lose this woman to him as well. "Tough luck, friend, but I'm not throwing in this hand any more than I did those four aces."

For a long moment Cleve continued to stare down at her. "Sleep well, my lovely," he whispered, before slipping out of the room.

Adriana opened her eyes, yawned, and stretched. Aware that it was not her bedroom, she sat up. After several seconds, she finally acclimated herself to the strange surroundings and remembered how she had gotten there.

She lay back again. Knowing the predicament she was in, Adriana couldn't believe she had fallen asleep. Her situation called for some serious thinking. First, she had to find a place to stay until she located Antonio. Obviously, not here.

Whom did she know in Fort Worth? One name came to mind: Elena Montez! Of course! She could go there. It might be that Antonio had even contacted her friend. Relieved to have solved her dilemma, she got out of the bed.

But what if Elena's father, Don Francisco, contacted her *papá*? The Spanish *criollos* in Texas were a close-knit society: Don Francisco and her father were old friends, and Adriana had known the Montez family since childhood. What was even worse, the family had attended the wedding and would know that she had fled before having to wed Miguel Castillo.

Sighing, she sank down on the edge of the bed. No, Elena wouldn't do at all. Until she found Antonio, she mustn't let anyone know she was here. It would be wiser to keep her identity a secret.

As she glanced around with a feeling of hopelessness, she saw the pile of clothing that Lily had brought her earlier.

"Thank you, Lily. Thank you," she murmured when her hurried inspection resulted in the discovery of a white bodice, a blue tiered skirt splashed with bright flowers, a shawl, and a pair of flat, thonged sandals. At least she wouldn't have to put the wedding gown back on.

She found several articles for bathing and grooming as well. Locking the door, she stripped off her drawers and camisole. After cleaning her teeth, Adriana gave herself a sponge bath, which helped to refresh her and raise her spirits. Then she put on the bodice and skirt.

In the corner, beside a battered chiffonier that looked to be at least a hundred years old, was an oval mirror mounted in a chipped, rococo frame embellished with gold paint. By shuffling from foot to foot, Adriana was able to get a full-length view of herself, despite the wide crack running diagonally from the top left corner of the glass to the lower right. Satisfied with the fit of the clothing, she released the few strands of hair that still remained in the once-thick chignon at her nape and, after a firm combing, tied back her long hair with a piece of fringe from the shawl.

Hands on hips, she studied her reflection. "Adriana Adelina Paloma Maria, is that really you?" Dressed as she was, she now could pass for any one of the maids on her father's ranch. Leaning forward for a closer inspection, she broke into laughter. "I think your brain must be as cracked as this mirror!"

With rising spirits, Adriana unlocked the door and grabbed the knitted shawl on her way out. She glanced down the length of the unfamiliar hallway and saw two stairways: the one nearer her door appeared to lead down into the barroom, and a drone of voices drifted up from the narrow one at the end of the hallway.

At the moment Adriana didn't wish to talk to anyone, so she descended the stairway into the barroom.

Luck was with her—the room was empty. She could leave without anyone knowing. Not that she wasn't grateful to these people. She'd come back later and thank them properly.

As she headed for the door, she passed a table and saw a partially eaten birthday cake covered with a thick, creamy frosting. The cake looked too tempting to resist. After a quick glance around her, she cut off a slice and took a bite. The sweet confection tasted as delicious as it looked, so she sliced herself another piece.

"Feeling better?"

Adriana grew rigid and didn't have to turn around to recognize the voice of the handsome owner of the place. Where had he come from? Embarrassed at being caught pilfering a piece of cake, she glanced at the glaring evidence in her hand and quickly shoved it into her mouth.

Unable to talk with a mouth crammed full of cake, Adriana turned around, nodded, and smiled.

Cleve walked up to her. With her hair tied back, and dressed in a white blouse and bright-colored skirt, she could pass for a young girl. *An adorable young girl,* he thought affectionately. Her eyes were shining and round—and she looked as guilty as a child caught with her fingers in the cookie jar.

"Well, you're looking better, Adriana. You must be feeling better, too," he said.

"Mm-hmm." She nodded, her frantic gaze darting to the door.

"Do you need any help? Is there something I can do for you?"

"Uh-uh," she grunted through the mouthful of cake, shaking her head. "I'll be back."

"All be what?" he asked. "I'm sorry; I didn't understand you."

"I'll be back!" she mumbled.

"All—"

"I'll . . . I'll!" Her eyes were now bulging as much as her cheeks.

"Oh, *I'll!*"

She nodded her head vigorously.

"I've got it now," he said triumphantly. "I'll be bad!"

"I'll be back!" She gulped and began to cough.

"Are you all right?" he asked. Coming to her aid, he started to pound her back.

"Water," she gasped when she stopped choking and was able to draw a deep breath.

He had already grabbed a pitcher from the bar and poured her a drink. "Not too fast," he warned when she gulped down the water. "I'd advise small sips."

"I'm fine now." She handed him the empty glass.

"Would you like some more water?"

"No, thank you. I must be going now. I'll be back."

He started to chuckle. "Are we going to start that again?"

The sound of his warm laughter was as devastating as his grin. She tried not to smile, but failed. "You knew all the time, didn't you?"

"I just couldn't resist."

"Well, good-bye. Thank you. You've been very kind."

"Hey, not so fast."

Startled, she stepped back when he reached out a finger and gently swiped at the corner of her mouth. "You wouldn't want to leave with this, funny face." Grinning, he held up his finger, now coated with icing.

"Oh . . . thank you." She looked so appealing, he had to fight to keep from hugging her.

Suddenly he no longer felt like laughing. She looked so innocent and vulnerable; he didn't like the thought of her being alone and unprotected.

"Adriana, where are you going?"

"To find Antonio, of course. As soon as I locate him, I'll come back for my wedding gown."

"And you expect to find him by wandering the streets?"

She looked up at him with a determined gleam in her eyes. "I suspect if I ask enough people, Antonio will hear of it. If I don't find him, he will find me."

"This is a rough town for a young woman alone. Do you have any money? Any family or friends to turn to?"

"I have the Good Lord, *Señor* MacKenzie. Good day, sir, and thank you again for all you have done for me."

Lily came into the room in time to see her depart. "So our patient is leaving us," she said.

Cleve walked over to the bar, reached under it, and retrieved his gunbelt. "I've got some business to take care of, Lily," he said, grabbing his Stetson.

She smiled. "You gonna play guardian angel, Cleve?"

"Thought maybe I'd kind of keep an eye on her."

"Ain't gonna do you much good, boss man. The little gal's in love with someone else."

"Miss Lily, we MacKenzies have a serious flaw in our natures," he said as he strapped on his gunbelt. "We tend not to give up a battle until we've first tried fighting it." He winked at her. "See you later."

Wearily, Adriana sank down on a bench in the plaza. Since leaving The Full House three hours earlier, she had checked the hotels and boarding houses, had gone to the stockyards thinking Antonio might have taken a job there, and had even gone to the hospital, although she was certain he wasn't hurt.

She would have sensed that. Throughout their lives, she and Antonio had always been empathetic. Whenever one or the other had been in need of help, frightened, or even happy, the other had felt it also. Two separate beings, yet they could transfer thoughts, communicate with their minds.

Hear me, Antonio. Where are you? I need you. Why aren't you listening? What is preventing you from coming to me, Antonio?

She felt a tug on her skirt and looked down to discover the puppy. "So you are back, little one." Playfully, she held the dog up to her face and looked into its inquisitive, round eyes. "You would tell me if you knew where to find Antonio, wouldn't you, little one?"

Sighing, she lowered the dog to her lap. "I just don't know where else to look for him." Absently, she began to stroke the pup. "I hope you have somewhere to go tonight, because I can't help you out. I don't know where I'll stay myself."

As she sat dejectedly watching an old man feeding corn to the pigeons, she heard the bell in the nearby church begin to toll the vesper service. With a guilty start, she realized she should go to church and pray for guidance. Putting the puppy down, she drew the shawl over her head, then hurried across the plaza.

The dog followed and stretched out near the church door.

She had found little solace for her grave situation, Adriana thought, as she left the church a short time later. Shading her eyes from the glare of the setting sun, she stepped into the street.

Preoccupied with her problems, she only gradually became aware of a dog's frenzied barking and an increasingly thunderous rumble. She looked up in time to see a herd of cattle racing toward her under the whistles and stinging lariats of a group of drovers. Stunned and horrified by the imminent danger, she opened her mouth in a scream.

Suddenly a firm arm grasped her waist, snatched her off her feet, and pulled her back against the wall of the church. Her ears became deafened by the stampeding cattle. Closing her eyes, she clamped her hands over her ears to muffle the cacophony of noise—whistles, shouts, and thundering hooves. The pungent stench of cattle and horses stung her nostrils, and she began to choke on the swirling dust that invaded her mouth.

Glancing up at her rescuer, she recognized Cleve MacKenzie. An eternity seemed to pass while she huddled in the safe haven of his embracing arms. Molded to the contour of his warm, strong body, she felt a tingling in her stomach that had more to do with the intimate contact than her deliverance from danger.

Gradually the dust settled around them, and the noise narrowed down to just a barking dog.

But still she trembled—all the fears and frustrations of the past few days were manifested in this one frightening moment. Finally, she looked up into the calm of his sapphire eyes.

"You're okay now, Adriana," he said.

She wanted to cry out in protest when he released one of his arms and gently wiped away the tears and dust that streaked her face.

The puppy padded over and stared up woefully at her. "It was *you* doing all that barking!" She looked up at Cleve with wonderment. "He tried to warn me."

"Yeah, he tried to warn you," Cleve said tenderly. Sweeping her up in his arms, he whispered in her ear, "You're safe now, Little Raven. I won't let anything happen to you."

Chapter 5

Returning to The Full House, Cleve sat Adriana down in the dining alcove and ordered a solid meal for them. As he ate the steak and potato Magdalena had prepared, he watched Adriana devour her food. She didn't talk but glanced up occasionally at him.

His food was forgotten when his gaze fell on her hair, following the flowing mass to where it fanned out over her shoulders. He wanted to bury his hands in its dark silkiness.

"Why are you looking at me like that?" she asked.

"I was admiring your hair. It's as black as a raven."

"My father thought as much, for I am named Adriana Adelina Paloma—" She suddenly stopped. "Uh . . . freely translated, it means—"

"A dark-winged dove," he said.

"You are familiar with my language, *señor?*"

"Cleve. Please call me Cleve, Adriana Adelina Paloma," he said, nodding. "What a beautiful name, *Señorita* Paloma. But since I've never seen a dove so black, I think I prefer 'raven.' Where's your home, Raven?"

She appeared to hesitate again before replying. "Why, the sky, of course," she said, gracefully fluttering her hands like the wings of a bird.

He chuckled in response. It appeared she had a sense

of humor after all. "And when do you intend to fly away, little bird?"

"Oh, I shall nest here in Fort Worth. I know my beloved Antonio will eventually come back."

She was either the most naive woman he had ever met or just too stubborn to admit the truth. "Look, honey," he said gently, "your 'beloved Antonio' left here almost four weeks ago and hasn't stuck his nose back in the door since. I think he may have skedaddled, Adriana, and has no intention of returning."

"You must not blame Antonio. He didn't know exactly when I would arrive."

Damn this evasive boyfriend of hers! Cleve could not understand why this stubborn little fool continued to defend a man who would put her life at risk. What sort of bastard would lure an innocent like her to this kind of town and then disappear, leaving her to fend for herself?

"Please, *Señor* . . . uh, Cleve, do not concern yourself."

"Honey, you can never tell what I might be concerned about." He grinned. "For one thing, I wonder why this Antonio would not be here to greet his beautiful bride when she showed up in a wedding gown."

"But Antonio is not—"

Before she could finish, Lily poked her head into the alcove. "Sorry to interrupt. Cleve, will you be opening your table tonight? Several men have asked about a game."

"Yeah, thanks for reminding me. Tell them I'll be there shortly."

Cleve shoved back his chair and stood up. "Thank you for your company, Raven. You're welcome to stay here until . . . Well, feel free to stay." He raised her hand to his lips. "Good night, *Señorita* Adriana Adelina Paloma."

"Good night, *Señor* Cleve MacKenzie," she responded, smiling coquettishly.

Cleve walked across the room, pausing to offer a quick welcome to customers seated at one of the tables, then continuing on to the bar.

"How's it going, Lily?"

"Fine. This is the easiest job I've ever had, even though I'm on my feet instead of my back," she joshed lightly.

"Lily, I need some advice."

"Oh, oh!" She poured a drink and shoved it at him. "Sounds like you could use this."

"Lily, you're a wise woman of the world," Cleve said.

"Oh, yeah! I sure am, boss man. They asked me to be the Queen of England, but I turned down the offer to become a whore instead."

"Do you believe in destiny, Lily?"

"Sure. I figure I won't live forever."

"I mean in the destiny of love at first sight."

She cast a quick glance at the alcove. "You've got it that bad, huh, boss man?"

Cleve picked up the drink and downed it. "I don't know, Lily. I always said I believed it would happen to me. Now, I can't tell if I'm kidding myself just to say I was right."

Disgusted, she shook her head. "Cleve MacKenzie, I figured you for a guy with a head setting square in the middle of those broad shoulders of yours; never thought it'd slip down between your legs."

"Is that your way of saying it's just a physical attraction, Miz Lily?"

"I figure love at first sight is the same as buying a pig in a poke. You gotta peek in that bag to see what their character's like—if they're mean in the mornings, what makes them laugh—'cause those features ain't splashed all over the face like freckles." Her expression was purposeful as she said, "And those are the traits you've got to end up loving in a person. Until you do, it ain't love, boss man—it's just that ole tricky Nature tugging at your . . ." She grinned askance at him. "Appetites."

"I suppose you're right, Lily." Absentmindedly twirling the empty glass between his fingers, Cleve gazed thoughtfully into space. "Well, whoever said that love is blind must have met Adriana."

"The poor kid wouldn't be the first fish that swallowed a line. That's why I've always viewed the opposite sex as pure business—monkey business on their part, cash-on-the-line on mine."

"You don't fool me, Lily. You're not as tough as you'd like people to believe." He slipped an arm around her shoulders. "From what you just said, I figure you've been in love."

"Only once."

"What happened? Did the damn fool ride off and leave you behind?"

"Nope. I never told him how I felt, because it wouldn't have worked out anyway. He was too good for me."

Cleve tipped up her chin and looked into her eyes. "Lily, there are a lot of men I regard with high esteem. But there's not a man alive who's too good for you, honey. Don't ever believe otherwise."

He glanced toward the alcove and then back at her. "What do you think we should do about our impulsive little would-be bride?"

"I think that's your call, boss," Lily said, amused.

"Well, I hate to think of her wandering the streets. She almost got herself killed today. Is there anything we can find for her to do around here? She's determined not to return home until the boyfriend shows up. What about having her help Magdalena with the cleaning or some such thing?"

Lily shrugged. "We can try."

"Well, come up with something to keep her busy. I better open up that table or we'll lose some customers."

He joined the men at the table, greeting them each in turn, and began to shuffle a deck of cards.

* * *

From her vantage point in the alcove, Adriana watched Lily and Cleve. The couple looked too intimate with each other to have just a business relationship. When she saw him tip up Lily's chin and look into her eyes, Adriana was convinced she was right; they were in love. Instantly, she felt a twinge of envy. Confused, she shook off the odd emotion.

The woman had been very kind to her, Adriana reflected, glancing at Lily. She certainly didn't appear to be anything like what her father had led her to expect from such a woman—*una prostituta*.

Then she looked at Cleve MacKenzie. She didn't know what to think about him, either. The gambler was a very handsome man—charming and mannerly, too. Even *Papá*, who was offended by most *Anglos*, would appreciate the man's attributes.

She didn't like lying to Cleve—about either her name or his impression that she had come here to marry Antonio. But she was glad Lily interrupted them when Andriana had started to correct his misconception. Despite the *Anglo*'s kindness and concern for her, she dare not trust anyone. She would hold to her earlier decision not to reveal her true identity until she located her brother. But at the moment, her only choice was to accept the *Anglo*'s charity.

Having finished eating, she left the alcove to return to her room. Pausing at the foot of the stairway, she turned her head and looked back. Cleve MacKenzie's dark-eyed stare was fixed on her. For several seconds, their locked gazes shut out the presence of all others in the room. She felt a heated blush, recalling the sensation she had experienced when he held her in his arms earlier—the exciting male scent of him! Never had she known such impressions. Turning away, she hurried up the stairway.

Long after retiring, Adriana lay in bed thinking about the recent events in her life. How soon would it be before her father caught up with her? If only she could find Antonio before it happened. And what of this mysterious Cleve MacKenzie? Remembering the look in his dark eyes, she felt a surge of warmth again. The man was exciting, even if he was nothing more than a gambler.

She quickly chastised herself for such thoughts. The *Anglo* meant nothing to her. Why think about him? She must concentrate on Antonio—and *Papá*. They were her real worries.

She listened to the drone of voices from below. Strange as it seemed, the sound comforted her, made her no longer feel alone and desperate.

You're safe now, Little Raven. I won't let anything happen to you.

The words Cleve had whispered to her echoed in her ears like a soothing lullaby. Gradually her eyes began to droop, and she slipped into the tranquil stage between sleep and wakefulness—until there was only sleep.

When Adriana went downstairs the next morning, she found Cleve and Lily seated at the table, drinking coffee.

"Good morning, Adriana. Come join us," Cleve said. "I hope you slept well."

"Yes, very well, *Señor* MacKenzie."

"Cleve," he corrected.

"Well, I am most grateful for your hospitality, Cleve."

"That's the very thing we've been discussing, honey," Lily said. "You see, everybody has to kinda share the work around here. We were wondering what you'd be interested in doing. How about helping to keep the place cleaned?"

"What do you mean?" Adriana asked.

"Why, maybe doing some scrubbing and dusting . . . simple jobs like that."

Shocked, Adriana looked at Lily. "My *papá* had *criadas* to do such menial tasks."

"Had what?" Lily asked.

"*Criadas* . . . or what you call 'maids.' Servants," Adriana replied haughtily.

"Oh, I see." Lily paused. "Well . . . ah . . . tell me, Princess Paloma, can you play the piano?"

Adriana shook her head.

"Can you sing?" Lily asked hopefully.

"I think not, Lily," Adriana said. Suddenly her eyes brightened. "I can cook."

"Cook?" Cleve said. He and Lily exchanged skeptical glances. "Did you do the cooking for your father?"

"Of course not! *Papá* had a *cocinera* . . . a cook."

"I bet all those *criadas* and *cocineras* must have been bumping into each other right and left," Lily mumbled.

"Not at all," Adriana replied naively. "Our *hacienda* was very large."

"I didn't doubt it for a moment, Princess," Lily remarked.

"So, do you wish for me to cook?" Adriana asked.

"No, that won't be necessary!" Cleve said hastily. The woman probably had a tough time just boiling water. Fearing he might have been too obvious, he quickly softened his tone. "Uh, maybe some other time. That's Magdalena's job. You know how two cooks spoil the broth . . . or however that saying goes."

Quickly finishing his coffee, he shoved back his chair. "Well, much as I hate to leave you two lovely ladies, I have an appointment. I'm sure you can resolve the problem, Lily."

Deliberately ignoring Lily's distressed look, Cleve hurried off before she could say another word. He paused outside only long enough to wish the church ladies a good morning.

"He is a very kind and generous *hombre*," Adriana remarked after Cleve's departure. "You are most fortunate to have such a man."

"Have such a man?" Lily almost choked on her

coffee. "Look, Princess, you've got it all wrong. Cleve and I aren't lovers. We're good friends who care deeply for each other. It's a long story and concerns something that happened in the past. But I'll warn you, I care too much about him to let any woman hurt him."

Upon hearing Lily's revelation, Adriana felt an instant flush of pleasure, although it was clear that Lily had directed the last comment toward her.

"Well, I'll try you out serving drinks." Lily stood up to leave. "You should be able to do that."

"Why not?" Adriana asked with a weak smile.

As soon as Lily was gone, Adriana propped her elbows on the table and clutched her head between her hands. What had she agreed to now? *¡Santa Maria, Adriana! You are such an estúpida!*

She just prayed her father would not hear of it. Perhaps she shouldn't have deceived these people about her true identity. A barmaid might be a proper position for Adriana Adelina Paloma; however, it was inconceivable that Adriana Adelina Paloma Maria Fuente y de Elbertina—the daughter of Don Alarico, one of the wealthiest *criollos* in Texas—had been reduced to serving drinks in a casino.

She stepped outside, and the little mongrel puppy immediately stood up and trotted over to her. "Good morning. So you have come back to me again, little *pequeño.*" Sitting down on the ground, she picked him up. "I never thanked you for trying to save my life, little one. You saw the danger and tried to warn me." She hugged him. "But I suspect you would rather have something to eat than listen to my thanks."

She had just given the puppy a plate of food when the Guerras arrived, accompanied by their children. As soon as Juan and Bonita saw the puppy, the youngsters squealed with pleasure and rushed over to it. Adriana and the children spent the rest of the morning playing with the dog and deciding on a name for it. They finally agreed upon Pepito.

* * *

The Full House had already opened for the evening by the time Adriana garnered enough courage to go downstairs. Before leaving her room, she stopped for one final look at herself.

"Oh, my!" she exclaimed, peering into the cracked mirror. Her delicate olive coloring was a vivid contrast to the red satin gown. The tight corset shoving her breasts together made her look quite bosomy, and a few nips and tucks by Magdalena had altered the flashy gown to Adriana's slim form so that it now hugged her waist and hips, flaring out in ruffled tiers below her knees. As an added touch, Lily had pulled Adriana's hair to one side and tucked it behind her ear with a large white silk rose.

"¡Santa Maria!" Adriana exclaimed. Squaring her shoulders, she left her room.

"Looks like we're in for a busy night," Cleve told Lily as he glanced around the room. A few of the tables were filled with a rougher element that he hoped to discourage. Not that he had anything against rough and shaggy cowpokes: on any given day of the week, any one of them could look better than Flint usually did. He grinned just thinking about his brother. How could Garnet ever have tamed that grizzly bear?

Then the smile drained from his face when he saw Adriana coming down the stairs. He felt as if he'd been punched in the gut. She was gorgeous. The most beautiful woman he'd ever seen. And he wanted her so goddamn bad that he ached.

"What in hell's going on here, Lily?" There was no way he'd let a lot of leering, lascivious men see her like this. Antonio or not, she was his—*his* Raven.

Lily glanced up to see what had caught his attention. "Oh, you mean the princess. I thought I'd have her serve drinks. You told me to find her something to do."

"I meant mop the floor or something. She's going to start a riot in that dress."

"Well, well!" Lily said, leaning back on her elbows

against the bar. "It didn't take long to be put to the test."

"What are you talking about?" Cleve asked.

"Now we know who's running this place. For a while, boss man, you had convinced me that I was."

"You are. It's just . . ." Cleve stammered. "I don't think she . . ." Lily's gaze remained fixed on his face. "Goddammit, Lily, you are in charge."

He pivoted and walked away.

Throughout the evening, Adriana felt awkward and out of place in the crowded, noisy, and smoky casino, but she did the best she could in the situation. She was relieved when the crowd began to thin out.

"Hey, redbird," a voice shouted out from the corner. "How about some service over here?"

Wiping up a drink she had just spilled on the bar, Adriana paid no attention.

"Look, Princess," Lily said, taking the cloth from Adriana, "I'll clean it up. Go see what the guys at the corner table want."

As Adriana approached, the four men at the table stopped their card game to ogle her. "Well, look what we have here, boys," the big man chewing on a cigar said lewdly. "Hey, Joe, did ya ever see a real live redbird in a saloon before?"

Adriana winced as Joe slowly looked her up and down, finally resting his gaze on her bosom. "Nope, can't say as I have, Pete. Looks more like a soiled dove to me."

As the men snickered, Adriana became exasperated and blurted out, "*Señores*, what is it you want?" Guffawing loudly, the men nudged each other and whistled rudely.

Pete took the cigar out of his mouth and said with mock politeness, "Don't give 'em no mind, little redbird. You just hustle along and get us some whiskey." Then, brushing the ash off his pants, he added, "That's what we want . . . for the time being, anyway."

Adriana turned toward the bar, but before she could move a step, she felt a stinging pinch on her derriere. Spinning on her heel, she raised her hand to slap the offender, but instead halted, her arm in midair at the sight of four grinning faces. Befuddled, she put her hands on her hips and was about to give them a tongue-lashing when Pete shrugged his shoulders and extended his open palms. The other three men followed suit.

"See, little *señorita*, there ain't one red feather among us. Now, how about them drinks?"

Incensed, Adriana returned to the bar. Disgruntled, she put her elbows on the bar and leaned her chin on her fists. *How dare such low vermin lay a hand on me!*

"What do they want?" Lily asked.

"Whiskey, I think."

"You think!" Lily said, puzzled.

"Yes, whiskey. But these *Anglos* talk so strange, sometimes I don't know what they mean."

Adriana stared into space. Then, as Lily set the drinks on the tray, she asked suddenly, "Lily, what is a soiled dove? My name means 'dark-winged dove.' Is that what they mean?"

Smiling, Lily shook her head. "No, but don't worry about it, Princess. Just serve the drinks and pay no attention to what they say. Mind you, though, if anyone gets grabby, just slam him on the head with the tray. Cleve wants to clear out the riffraff that's used to coming in here."

Too chagrined and embarrassed to tell Lily she had already been pinched, Adriana picked up the tray and turned around to find Cleve standing behind her.

"How's it going, Little Raven?" he asked, smiling.

Her eyes flashed. "What is it with you *Anglos*? Ravens! Redbirds! Doves! You're all loco . . . *imposible!*" She walked away in a huff.

Cleve looked helplessly at Lily. "I don't know what we have here, Lily. Do you think that dress has changed her disposition?"

"Ah, come on, Cleve. Surely you've noticed she can be a lost little girl one minute and a haughty spitfire the next. Give her time. She'll calm down."

He looked askance at her.

"Well, maybe," she added.

Both amused and unconvinced, he shook his head as he watched Adriana approach the corner table.

Adriana braced herself when the big man looked up from his cards. "Well, it's about time."

Whiskey splattered in all directions as she slammed the tray down on the table. With arms akimbo, Adriana declared, "The boss said that doves are *not* on the bill of fare, and he wants me to clear out the riffraff!"

Taken aback by her aggressive manner and jumbled insult, Pete half-rose from the chair, his mouth agape. His glance darted past her as Cleve advanced toward them. Grabbing the cigar hanging loosely from his mouth, he said abruptly. "C'mon, boys, let's get out of this dump."

"Cowards," she shouted, tossing her head. *"¡Vaya con el diablo!"* she called after them, stamping her foot in the belief that she alone had settled the score.

"What's the trouble here?" Cleve said at her shoulder.

"Nothing."

He looked down at the dumped glasses of whiskey. "I don't suppose they paid before they ran out?"

Still inflamed with victory, she said haughtily, *"Señor* Cleve, I am not accustomed to the petty details of collecting money. Furthermore, they did not steal one drop of your whiskey. See? It is all on the table."

"What?" he asked, bewildered.

Adriana ignored him and picked up the tray. Mystified, he watched the jaunty swing of her hips and the bouncing blur of red ruffles as she walked away.

At least the evening had not been a total loss, Adriana reflected later, as she finished wiping up a drink she had just spilled on the floor. Returning to the bar, she picked up the tray of drinks and headed for the table where Cleve was playing cards with four men.

Managing to reach the table without incident, she circled to place a drink in front of each man. Just as she reached Cleve, she skidded on a patch of wet floor and suddenly pitched forward. The drink spilled into his lap, and the tray crashed to the floor.

Cleve shoved back his chair and tried rising to his feet, but Adriana sank to her knees, picked up the fallen napkin, and began to wipe him off. "Oh, I'm so sorry."

"That's not necessary. I'll do it, Adriana," Cleve said, pinned between her and the chair.

"No," she insisted, increasing her efforts to dry him off. Trying to cover up her embarrassment, she turned her head and smiled up at the man in the chair beside Cleve. "I do apologize, señor. Usually, I am not this clumsy."

Cleve's hand clamped around her wrist. "Adriana, I said I'll do it!"

Startled by his tone and firm grasp on her arm, she looked back at him and found herself at eyeball level with the most intimate part of his body, which she had been vigorously rubbing. Horrified, she stared at the new—but very visible—crisis that had arisen. Her cheeks flamed with scarlet. "Oh, my! Oh, I'm so sorry . . . I didn't mean . . . oh, dear!" she lamented. Panicked, she shoved him down in the chair and threw the towel over his lap. Jumping to her feet, she jerked her arm out of his grasp, and her elbow knocked over the drink of the man in the next chair.

"Oh, no!" she wailed pitifully when a stream of liquid saturated the cards in front of Cleve. Hastily, she turned the cards over and tried to wipe them off with her bare palms.

Throughout Cleve's plight, the men at the table had been choking on their laughter, their bodies shaking as they tried not to laugh out loud. Now, with the four kings Cleve had been holding lying in plain sight on the middle of the table, they erupted in laughter and tossed in their cards.

"Looks like a joker slipped into this deal," Cleve said good-naturedly. With an amused glance at Adriana, he tossed the towel back to her. "Here, try using this."

"I'm so sorry," Adriana apologized again.

"I'm not, my dear," one of the players said. "You just saved the rest of us a lot of money."

"Hey, Lily, will you bring us another deck and a towel to wipe up this whiskey?" Cleve said. "Adriana's drowning kings by the bucket over here."

Unaware that Cleve, not she, was the butt of their laughter, Adriana's temper flared. "I said I'm sorry. And as for your precious wet cards, you can . . ."

She had raised her fist at him, and suddenly dropped it when she saw the amusement in his eyes. Being upset with him for her own clumsiness made her feel like a fool. No, she would not let an outburst reveal her humiliation nor signal defeat.

Changing her tone, she smiled sweetly. "As I was saying, *Señor* Cleve, you are . . . most kind and thoughtful. I guess being a lowly barmaid is a little harder than I thought. Don't worry, though; you shall soon see that I, Adriana Adelina Paloma, will become the best barmaid in all of Fort Worth."

The irony of her remark could hardly escape him.

"Well, good," Cleve said with a suppressed smile. "Now that that's settled, we can get back to our game. Gentlemen, while I take a couple minutes to run upstairs to change my trousers, I suggest you move to a different table."

Still laughing among themselves, the men began shifting to a far table.

"Lily, give them all a drink on the house," he said as he passed the bar. "Boy, what a muddle!"

"Well, I'm glad to see you were up for it."

He stopped in his tracks and looked back at her. "Lily LaRue, was that a bawdy . . . Did you mean—" He shook his head. "Naw, you wouldn't."

Wide-eyed and innocent, Lily glanced at him. "Wouldn't what, boss man?"

As soon as he returned, Cleve headed for the corner table but held back for a moment when Adriana passed him. "Honey, may I make a suggestion?"

"Of course," she said warily.

His breath was a tantalizing warmth at her ear when he leaned over and whispered, "Better check the looking glass. Your flower's sagging." Then he left her side.

She straightened her disheveled dress and adjusted the flower dangling in her hair. *What did he expect? I'm not accustomed to waiting on people. People wait on me!* "Do I look all right?" she asked, turning to Lily.

"Beautiful, Princess. But I gotta tell you something. Beauty is as beauty does."

"What do you mean?"

"Well, you sure have been the star attraction here tonight, but I've been noticing the till ain't as full as it oughta be. I figure you've been neglecting to collect any money. Princess, these men are customers, not guests. A drink costs twenty-five cents; we don't give them away."

"Oh! Yes, I see. As you wish, then," Adriana said. "But you must understand that I have never had to concern myself with such things before." Just then, she saw Cleve coming toward them. Fearing he had more to say regarding her clumsiness or appearance, she left Lily abruptly.

"Lily, will you get us another round?"

"Sure, boss. How's the game goin'?"

"Could be better." His eyes wandered over toward Adriana.

"Our gallant *señorita* could be doing better, too."

"I noticed. I'm thinking she isn't going to last the night. Any bets?"

"Not from me. You know I only bet on a sure thing."

"Which is?" he asked.

"Myself."

"Yes, I know," he said affectionately.

"Besides, boss, that gal doesn't seem to have any earthly sense about collecting money."

"Lily, I reckon we'll just have to figure out something else for her to do in the morning. Anyhow, that red dress is too . . . Well, get us some drinks, will you?" He walked away with a secret smile.

As the evening continued, Adriana was a constant distraction to Cleve. He couldn't keep his eyes off her to concentrate on the card game. He lost continually.

As it neared closing time, Adriana carried a drink over to a man sitting at a corner table. She picked up the gold coin he put down and started to walk away.

The man grabbed her arm. "Hey, ain't I gonna get more than a drink of whiskey for that gold eagle?"

"I'm sorry, *señor*; what do I owe you?"

"How 'bout you and me discussin' it upstairs?"

"I don't understand," Adriana said.

"Ah, come on, brown eyes, don't play innocent with me. It ain't gonna get you another cent. I'll take my change in trade."

"Just what are you suggesting?"

"Don't act so wide-eyed and innocent, sister."

"How dare you! Take your hand off me." Indignant, she tried to pull away, but his grasp held. Raising the tray, she banged it down on his head. When he clutched his head, she spun around and ran.

In a display of anger entirely out of character, Cleve shoved back his chair and jumped to his feet. He covered the distance in a few steps and yanked the man out of the chair. "Get out of here, pal, and stay out."

"I gave that little hustler ten dollars. I want my change."

Digging a gold eagle out of his pocket, Cleve slapped it into the man's hand. "Here—the drink's on the house. I don't want to see you back in here again. You'll find the kind of action you're looking for down the street." He waited until the man disappeared out the door, then went over to Lily. "Where'd she go?"

"She was a little upset, so I sent her upstairs for the night."

"Good place for her. I need a drink."

"Cleve, it could have happened to anyone." Lily filled his glass.

Cleve gave her a disparaging look and gulped it down.

"Okay, I'll try her at something different," Lily added, trying to stifle her laughter.

"Please do, before I go broke!"

The Full House was silent and dark when Cleve climbed the stairway. Seeing a glow from under Adriana's doorway, he paused and tapped lightly on the door.

When she opened it, he sucked in his breath. The flashy red gown had been replaced by a white cambric nightdress with only an embroidered tucked yoke to distract from its plainness. Long hair, brushed to a silky sheen, flowed down her back. She was barefoot, adding to her look of vulnerability.

"Hi," he said, smiling down at her like a lovesick swain.

"What is it you wish, *Señor* Cleve?"

"I saw your light, so I thought I'd stop and say good night."

"Good night, *Señ*—"

"Cleve. Please, Adriana?"

She looked up with liquid eyes ringed with long, dark lashes, and his gaze melted into hers. "Good night, Cleve." He stepped back, and she started to close the door.

"Raven."

The gap in the door widened, and he was diving again into the liquid pools. "Yes?"

"I'm sorry about tonight."

"Yes. I know I was clumsy and awkward. I—"

"No." Covering her mouth with his hand, he felt her warm breath fan his palm as she gasped in surprise. He slid his hand away and began to slowly trace her cheek with his finger. His touch felt like a caressing trail of kisses, and she shivered with pleasure.

"No, that's not what I meant. I know tonight was hard for you. I'm sorry to have put you through it." Dropping his hand, he smiled. "But I'm proud of you. You toughed it out, angel face."

She swallowed with difficulty and returned his smile. "I was so bad."

His smile slowly faded. For a long moment, he stared at her lingering smile. "You were great." Leaning down, he lightly kissed her cheek. "Good night, Raven."

"Good night, Cleve."

This time she waited until he continued down the hall before closing the door.

Chapter 6

The next afternoon, after they finished lunch, Lily told Adriana that she no longer had to serve drinks. "I know you said your father had maids to do the cleaning, Princess, but I guess you'll just have to learn. Unless there's something else you think you can do."

"No," Adriana said. "I know of nothing except cooking."

"Oh, yes! But we ruled that out yesterday," Lily added hurriedly. "I guess it will have to be cleaning. How about it?"

Since she had no other choice, Adriana swallowed her pride and agreed.

"The main stairway is in need of a scrubbing. Do you want to try that? All it takes is a pail of water and a scrub rag. I'll show you."

"I've seen how it's done, Lily," Adriana said tersely. "It is not necessary to show me."

"Well, good. You can start whenever you're ready."

"First I must take Pepito for a walk."

"Good idea. You might try losing him while you're at it," Lily said lightly.

"Lose him!" Adriana looked at her aghast.

"Look, Princess," Lily said patiently, "we've all got a lot of work to do around here, without having to clean up after that dog the way we've been doing."

As if to reinforce the point, Cleve suddenly burst into the kitchen from the barroom. "Dammit, Lily! I just stepped in another puddle of—" He cut off his words when he saw Adriana.

"Let me guess. I bet it's another memento from our little four-legged friend over there." Lily glanced toward the corner of the room where the dog was busily occupied trying to chew through a bone.

"I'll clean up the puddle," Adriana said, jumping to her feet.

"I already have," Cleve said. "But this can't go on, Adriana."

"I understand," she said quickly. "I'm just taking Pepito for a walk right now." She grabbed the dog and hurried to the door, anxious to leave before more could be said on the matter.

"Wait, I'm on my way out, too. I'll walk with you," Cleve said.

Once outside, as soon as Adriana put Pepito down, the puppy raced ahead. "Sure is a lovely day, Miss Paloma. Shame to be wearing such a worried look."

Suddenly he stopped in his tracks. Shoving her behind him, Cleve reached reflexively for the Colt on his hip. "What the hell is that?"

He stared warily at the big orange cat that had jumped out from between the buildings. Hissing and spitting at him, the cat blocked the path, its back arched, ready to spring.

The cat was large and bony, its fur scruffy and ragged, with several missing patches that had been either ripped or chewed away, along with part of its left ear. The right eye was crossed, and the eyelid of the other drooped.

When Adriana tried to step past Cleve, he held her back. "Don't move, Raven; it could be rabid."

"That's nonsense. It's not rabid. I fed it a bowl of milk this morning."

"You fed it!" He shoved up his hat. "Adriana, you'll

never get rid of it now. You don't ever feed a stray cat unless you're prepared to keep it."

She bent down and petted the cat. "You were hungry, weren't you, my little Gatito?"

Relaxing its stance, the cat purred, rubbed a cheek against her hand, and dashed back into the shadows.

"Gatito! You're calling that thing a kitten? That's about the biggest, meanest, ugliest-looking tomcat I've ever seen."

"Well, from the way Gatito reacted just now, he must have had the same impression of you, *Señor* MacKenzie." She walked on.

Cleve slid the Colt back into its holster, adjusted his Stetson, and hurried after her.

"I would like you to know, *Señorita* Paloma, I have never had a problem with animals or children; they usually warm up to me very readily."

"I'm sure they do." She caught a glimpse of Pepito chasing pigeons in the plaza, so she hurried over to one of the benches and sat down.

Cleve followed her. Propping a boot on the bench, he shoved his hat to the top of his forehead and leaned forward, an arm resting casually on his knee—and a very devilish grin on his face. "So, you think I'm big, mean, and ugly."

"No, I did not say that," Adriana quickly denied, too aware of his nearness for comfort. "I said that *may* have been Gatito's impression of you."

He leaned closer, and her gaze became locked with the mesmerizing draw of his blue eyes. "Well," he said in a husky timbre that sent a shiver of excitement streaking down her spine, "I guess I'd be more interested in hearing what *your* impression of me is, Raven."

"Why should it matter what I think?" she asked nervously.

"It matters very much to me."

Adriana drew a deep breath. Much to her relief, he broke his gaze and shifted it to her mouth.

"I think you're handsome."

"And I think you're beautiful, Raven."

"Please, Cleve, it's not necessary to flirt with me."

"And if I told you I'm sincere—"

"I wouldn't believe you," she said hastily. Her heart had begun beating so rapidly, she could barely breathe.

Suddenly, she heard her name being called repeatedly. Cleve had heard it, too; he straightened up and turned to look. The shouts were coming from a short, chubby girl hurrying toward them.

Recognizing her childhood friend, Adriana jumped to her feet. "Elena!" she exclaimed. The two girls hugged and kissed.

"I can't believe you're here, of all places," Elena said. "Shame on you, Adriana. We've all been so worried about you!" She glanced with interest at Cleve, who had stepped aside.

"Oh, forgive me," Adriana said awkwardly. "*Señor* MacKenzie, my friend, *Señorita* Montez."

Cleve tipped his hat. "A pleasure to meet you, *señorita*. Do you live in Fort Worth?"

Adriana slumped back down on the bench, glad for the opportunity to recover from the devastating effects of Cleve's nearness; his sexual magnetism was overpowering. However, her friend's unexpected appearance was another threat: Elena Montez was sure to tell her father.

Adriana glanced at them and became disgusted. Elena had already fallen victim to his charm. With only a few sentences, Cleve had the enthralled girl hanging onto his every word, giggling and blushing at whatever he said.

"*¡Santa Maria!*" she mumbled. Folding her arms across her chest, she leaned back.

"Well, I'll leave you young ladies to your reunion," Cleve said. "Good-bye, *señoritas*." Ignoring Adriana's glare of disgust, he smiled charmingly at Elena. "It's been a real pleasure talking to you, Elena."

"Who is that handsome *Anglo*, Adriana?" Elena gushed as soon as he walked away.

"Who do you mean?" Adriana asked nonchalantly.

"*Señor* MacKenzie, of course! He is so *magnífico!*" she exclaimed, clasping her hands together.

"You think so?" Adriana asked. "I hadn't noticed. *Señor* MacKenzie is an acquaintance of Antonio's and is trying to locate him for me," she added, in an attempt at an explantion. "Elena, have you seen Antonio?"

"No. Why do you ask?"

"He sent me money to come here and join him."

"You mean that's why you ran away from your wedding?"

Adriana grasped her friend's hand. "Elena, I couldn't marry Count Castillo. I don't love him."

Elena gaped in astonishment. "How could you not love him, Adriana? Count Castillo is so handsome." The young girl's eyes gleamed with adoration. "And so charming." She sighed ecstatically. "And so rich!"

"I told you, Elena. I can only marry a man I love. That's why I ran away and came here to Fort Worth. What did *Papá* say?"

"Oh, he was very angry when he discovered you were gone. He told all the guests to return to their homes."

"Elena, you must not tell your father you have talked to me. I do not wish my father to know where I am, or he'll force me to return to San Antonio and marry Count Castillo."

"I cannot lie to my *papá*," Elena protested.

"Am I asking you to lie, Elena? I am only asking you not to tell him you saw me. That is not lying. If Don Francisco knows I am here, he will contact my father and tell him where to find me."

"But what if *Papá* asks me?"

"Why would he ask you?" Adriana said, exasperated. She tried to suppress the irritation mounting within her. Elena was a dear, sweet girl, but her friend was petrified of her own father and feared doing any act that might incur his disfavor. "Please, Elena. Promise me?"

"I'll try, Adriana. But I will not lie to *Papá*." Elena glanced anxiously at the church. "There is my *dueña*."

"She must not see us together. If Antonio contacts you, tell him I am at The Full House."

"What full house?" Elena asked.

"Just tell him, Elena. He'll know."

"I will," Elena said. "Oh, Adriana! I shall worry so much about you. Go home where you belong."

"Do not worry about me. I'm in good hands," she said.

The girls kissed, and, dabbing at her tears, Elena dashed across the square.

Disheartened, Adriana returned to The Full House.

The casino was empty, but she heard voices coming from the kitchen. Adriana was not in the mood to talk to anyone, so she climbed the stairway and went to her room.

Depressed, she threw herself down on the bed.

Adriana awoke to a darkened room. Having no idea of the time, she stepped into the hall and glanced down the stairway. The casino had opened for the night and appeared to be busy, but subdued. Clearly, she had slept the day away. How could the others not wake her when they ate their evening meal! Hungry, she hurried down the back stairway. Adriana discovered that even Magdalena and Paulo had left for the night, so she set a kettle of water on the stove. At least she would have a cup of tea.

Seeing no sign of Pepito, she opened the door and peeked out. The dog was lying at the back door.

"*¡Hola, amigo!*" she greeted him affectionately. "I bet you are hungry, my little one. Come; let's see what I can find for you."

Discovering a chicken leg in the icebox, she sliced off part of it for Pepito and was nibbling on the rest when Lily entered the kitchen.

"So you finally decided to get up," Lily said.

"Yes. I seem to have missed the evening meal."

Lily shook her head in disgust. "You also seem to have forgotten about scrubbing down the stairway. I did mention, Adriana, that we all pitch in around here. If you had no intention of doing it, I wish you would have said so." She took a bottle of whiskey out of the storage room and left.

"I can't see what's so important about scrubbing down the stairway," Adriana complained aloud. "Tell me, Pepito, do you see what difference it makes when I do it?"

The dog cocked its head and wagged its tail, then returned to eating.

"Well, I can see you don't much care when the stairs are scrubbed, but since Lily is angry about it, I suppose I could do it now. Besides," she remarked, "how long does it take to wash down a stairway? Ten or fifteen minutes at the most, and that wouldn't disrupt the gamblers." She rolled her eyes. "¡Santa Maria! Heaven forbid that I disrupt any of them, Pepito!"

Firmly resolved, Adriana realized she had a problem: what to wear? She glanced at her skirt. "I hate to soil this scrubbing a floor, Pepito, but it's all I have."

Pepito followed her into the storage room where she found a bucket and scrub rag. "Let's go," she said to him, grabbing both items.

Her gaze fell on a shirt and a pair of Paulo's pants hanging on a hook. Since he was a small man, Adriana thought they might fit her. Shedding her skirt and petticoat, she tried on the pants. They felt tight and a little short-legged on her, but they would surely do to scrub a floor. However, when she pulled the shirt over her head, it dropped down past her hips.

"Paulo clearly has a long torso and very short legs, Pepito," she said, tucking the shirttail into the pants. Grabbing an old hat from a hook on the door, she plopped it on her head, and the large sombrero dropped past her ears and covered her eyes.

"I can see this is not going to work, Pepito." Then she giggled, "Or you might say, I can't see to make it work." She took off the hat, swept her long hair up under the crown, and replaced the hat. The mass of hair now held up the hat.

"Well, I *can see* that's better," she exclaimed in delight. "If anyone notices me dressed as I am, he'll never guess I'm not a boy." Picking up the bucket, she skipped gaily to the stove in the kitchen, Pepito bounding at her heels.

Adriana hummed lightly as she poured the heated water from the kettle into the bucket. Then she grabbed the pail, raised a hand in the air, and declared to the dog at her feet, "*Papá* may be a tyrant, but his honor cannot be disparaged, Pepito. Am I not my father's daughter?" she asked.

When the dog responded with a wag of its tail, she went on to say, "Adriana Adelina Paloma Maria Fuente y de Elbertina honors her word."

Water splashed over the top of the bucket as she tossed the scrub rag into the pail, and with fierce determination she started to march up the back stairs. She stopped to glance back at the dog trailing her.

"Go back, Pepito!" she ordered, pointing her finger. "You must stay here until I return. I shall not be long, *pequeño*."

Ears drooping, the dog returned to its water bowl.

With pail in hand, Adriana sallied forth to do battle.

Upon reaching the main stairway on the floor above, she got down on her hands and began to back down, vigorously scrubbing each step as she descended.

Studying the cards in his hand, it took Cleve a long moment to realize the room had quieted down to a hushed whisper. When he looked around, he saw that everyone's attention, even that of the men at his table, was fixed on a young boy scrubbing the stairs.

At least, at first glance, that is what he thought he

saw. As the boy lowered himself step by step on his hands and knees, the outline of the young man's posterior was clearly defined in the pants stretched tautly across his rear end. Staring at the figure, Cleve suddenly realized that *he* was a *she*—and that *the she was Adriana!* Having spent the last couple days admiring that same fetching little bottom, he had no doubt in his mind.

What in hell was she doing scrubbing the stairs at this time of the night? And in those pants! He didn't need this kind of distraction in his place.

"Lily!" he shouted in desperation.

Startled by Cleve's yell, Lily glanced in his direction but was immediately distracted by shrieks and yelps coming from the kitchen.

"Oh, damn!" Putting down a bottle of whiskey, she grabbed the bar towel and headed for the kitchen.

Flinging open the door, she saw Pepito frantically skidding around in a fruitless effort to escape the hissing, clawing Gatito, who was riding on the hapless puppy's back.

"Scat! Scat, you mangy critter!" Lily shouted, as she attempted to swat the cat with the towel.

When the cat failed to yield its perch, she grabbed it by the scruff, yanked it off, and then in self-defense dropped the jabbing, spitting animal to the floor.

"How did you get in here?"

At that moment, the freed puppy made a dash up the back stairs, and before Lily could react, the cat streaked past her in pursuit of the dog.

"Lily, what's going on in here?" Cleve asked, bursting through the door. But Lily had already run up to the second floor, so, taking three steps at a time, Cleve followed the ruckus.

Hearing the clamor of meowling, barking, and shouting coming from the hallway, Adriana dropped her scrub rag and looked up in time to see Gatito pounce on Pepito.

"Get off him, you ornery one-eyed jack!" Lily muttered, in pursuit, attempting to grab the cat's orange tail.

"Stop! Help!" Adriana screamed just as the cat sprang loose and leaped into the air over the railing.

Instantly, the casino customers came running to Adriana's aid, only to find her staring upward at the swinging chandelier where the crafty cat swayed back and forth, its paws splayed on the fixture's wooden base and its shaggy head poking out between the glass-covered candles.

"Adriana!" Cleve rushed past Lily, managing to sidestep the water pail. Then he let out a whooping holler as he stumbled over the unseen scrub rag, fell backward, and slid down the remaining few stairs on his rear end.

"Oh dear! Are you all right, *Señor* Cleve?" Adriana cried, extending her hand to help him up.

Ignoring her, he leaned back casually on his elbows and turned to Lily, who had run down the stairs to kneel beside him.

"Lily, what say we clean these varmints out of here?" Winking, he said, "Time to get out my squirrel gun."

"Oh no, you wouldn't—" Adriana's wail stopped short as Gatito suddenly flew from the clanking chandelier, landing on all fours on the bar.

Hesitating, the pathetic creature looked toward them, its sad eye drooping while the other seemed to glow with the glass-eyed stare of an angry demon.

Pepito jumped into Adriana's arms and began to yap furiously—whereupon the cat raced down the bar at lightning speed, leaving spilled glasses in its wake and sending a full whiskey bottle smashing to the floor. Reaching the end of the bar, Gatito leaped into the kitchen, slid across the floor, and bolted out the back door.

"Good riddance!" Cleve shouted, picking himself up and joining in the laughter of his customers.

"Now just look at what you've done!" Adriana said, angrily stamping her foot.

"Who, me?" Cleve asked in disbelief.

"Yes, you! You've probably scared away my poor kitty forever with your talk of varmints and guns!"

"Watch out, mutt," Cleve said, playfully tapping Pepito on the nose. "Mean ole Cleve's gonna be gunning for you next time Miz Paloma's occupied." Then, shifting his gaze to Adriana, he gestured toward the bar. "Speaking of being occupied, looks like there's a bit of a mess to clean up."

She opened her mouth to launch a tirade.

"Uh-uh," he warned. Putting his thumb under her chin, he gently closed her mouth, then leaned down and whispered in her ear, "But first, cover up that distracting little derriere of yours, pronto!"

Then he calmly walked away, figuring his final word on her menagerie—and her enticing, curvaceous little butt—could best wait until morning.

Chapter 7

❧⚬⚬❧

A steady downpour of rain added to Cleve's gloomy mood as he assembled Lily and Adriana in the kitchen the following morning. Although he was not comfortable in the role, he felt that he had no choice but to lay down the law to Adriana, particularly after the previous night's fiasco. The animals had to go.

Cleve had no more begun his lecture than she folded her arms across her chest and glared belligerently at him. "Do you have something you wish to say, Adriana?"

"You don't have to worry about it any longer. Gatito did not return this morning," she declared with hostility, as if it were his fault the damn cat hadn't come back.

"We should be so lucky," he remarked.

"If you look, you'll see that the bowl of milk I put outside for the poor little thing this morning is still untouched."

"You've got a bowl of milk setting out there? I can't believe it! What are you trying to do, attract others? We're running a business here, Adriana, not a shelter for every stray animal in the town. Although I think the word's already been passed among them—head for The Full House; they'll put you up for the night! It's got to end right now—no more milk bowls are to be set outside the doorway."

"Does that mean Pepito must go, too?"

73

She now looked stricken and on the verge of tears. He felt like a bastard, but if he buckled under to that sad look, he'd defeat his purpose.

"Adriana, I just spent a lot of money remodeling this place and that dog's turning it into a . . . privy!"

"It just takes time to train him. I've always tried to clean up after him," she defended weakly.

"You! What about me? Lily? Magdalena and Paulo? We've all been cleaning up the messes that dog's been making."

"Very well," she said in a faltering voice. "I'll . . . I'll send him away."

Dammit! he groaned inwardly. He couldn't go through with it. There was no way he could stand there and witness her misery when he was the one causing it.

"Well, I guess you can continue feeding him, but you better hope, little girl, that I don't step in another puddle of pee or pile of . . . Well, you just better hope."

So that the situation did not become a complete rout of his manhood, he further stated, "And from now on, when we're open for business, I don't want to see you or that dog anywhere near the casino. Is that clear?"

Adriana glanced at Lily, hoping the woman would intercede on her behalf. Lily sat holding her head in her hands, not looking at her. Adriana would have to defend herself.

"I wish you'd let me explain what happened last night. I fell asleep and when I awoke, I remembered that I had promised Lily I would scrub the stairway. Unfortunately, I left the back door open, and Gatito must have slipped in. What was so wrong about that?"

"Wrong time—and *wrong* clothes."

"Did you expect me to scrub the stairway in my only bodice and skirt?"

"I did not expect you to be scrubbing the stairway at eight o'clock in the evening. And I'm sure Lily didn't intend for you to do it then, either. Especially in those pants."

"What did the pants have to do with it? I'm sure in all

the excitement, no one paid any attention to the pants I was wearing," she declared.

"Everyone paid attention to them! And from where I was sitting, I can tell you why—they had the same view that I did!"

Then, as if she weren't even present, which only irritated Adriana more, Cleve said to Lily, "Explain it to the little girl, please."

Throwing his hands up in hopelessness, he walked out of the room.

After finishing breakfast, Adriana went into the casino and sat down at a table near the window. The rain had continued all morning, and the downpour only added to her dejection as she stared out the front window at people scurrying around, as if trying to run between the drops would keep them from getting wet.

Cleve sat in a corner of the room playing solitaire; Lily was taking inventory of the supplies; and the Guerras had stayed in the kitchen. Nobody seemed interested in talking—especially not to her.

She sat with her chin in her hands. The heavy rainfall even prevented her from continuing her search for Antonio. Cleve glanced over at her and suddenly began to chuckle. She looked down at herself. Nothing seemed to be out of place.

"What is it you find to laugh at me about?"

"I'm not laughing at you, honey." Shifting over to her table, he sat down. "It's just that you look like you've lost your best friend, Raven."

She ignored his ridiculous nickname for her. "I have. If only I could find Antonio."

The smile left his face. "Adriana, give up that hope and go back to your home. I'll buy you the ticket."

"If you wish to get rid of me, I will leave," she said. "But I will not return home to an unwanted marriage. I cannot live the rest of my life with a man I do not love."

"Unwanted marriage!" In the flicker of an eye, his look of surprise changed to one of comprehension. "I get it now. *Papá* has different plans for his little girl, so you ran away and came here to marry the fellow you *do* love. Is that right?"

¡Estúpida! ¡Estúpida! ¡Estúpida! she raved silently. *¡Adriana, you are such an estúpida!*

How could she have made such a slip of the tongue? And to Cleve MacKenzie, of all people! His mind moved with the speed of lightning. Already, he had guessed most of the truth. The only thing he didn't suspect was that Antonio was her brother—but given more time, he'd probably soon figure that out, too.

"Why ask me, Cleve? You seem to have guessed all the answers."

"Well, at least this restores my faith in my fellow man; I never could conceive how any man would leave you waiting at the altar. That still doesn't mean you should be running around Fort Worth alone, the way you've been doing."

"I appreciate your concern, but if I return home, *Papá* will insist I go through with his plans for me to wed Count Castillo. I have no choice but to continue my search for Antonio."

"How old are you, Adriana?"

"Twenty-two. Which, among my people, is considered quite old to be unwed."

"Well, among my people, twenty-two is old enough to stand up for your own rights. Simply refuse to marry this count your father has chosen for you."

"Hah!" she said, with a toss of her head. "If you knew *Papá*, you would not make such a foolish statement. No one defies him!"

"You apparently did, or you wouldn't be here."

"Yes. But maybe it will all be in vain. If I went home, I could not delay the marriage any longer. My father and Count Castillo would insist."

"Admittedly, I don't know your father, Raven, but I am anxious to meet him."

"I think not. *Papá* doesn't like *Anglos*. He is very suspicious of all of you."

His expression hardened. "I don't intimidate easily. He could never stand in the way of anything I wanted."

Cleve continued to stare at her, and once again she felt the irresistible draw of his dark-eyed gaze. Suddenly he grinned. "I'm sorry I shouted at you this morning. Believe me, I rarely lose my temper."

"I seem to cause you much grief, Cleve. That is not my intention."

"I know you mean well, Raven. That's why I was wrong to say the things I did. Everything will work out fine." He stood up. "I intend to see to it."

Just what did he mean by that?

Puzzled, she watched him walk over and pick up a deck of cards. Somehow, she had the impression that what he meant was not so much for her good, as for his own.

He came back, sat down, and began shuffling the cards. "Let's see what kind of poker player you are, Raven."

His gaze was open and direct—but she knew very well that something other than a card game had begun to formulate behind those damn blue eyes of his.

"Not as good as you are, I'm afraid," she murmured in response to his remark.

And he was the one dealing the cards.

Adriana had not budged from her room the whole evening, and now sat gazing out the window. Only a steady drizzle and distant flashes in the sky remained of the thunderous rainstorm that had struck the city. The deserted street was the quietest she had ever seen it at this time of night. Even the few patrons who came in to play cards had left early, and Cleve had closed and locked up the casino. He and Lily had retired to their rooms hours ago.

The all-day rain left her with a feeling of melancholy. She missed her home. She missed Antonio. The dreary day had dredged up memories of the past, had made her recall similar days on the ranch: days when she,

Antonio, and their dear friend Pedro had climbed up in the hayloft and talked of their dreams for the future, or often lain in the sweet smelling hay and listened as Antonio read aloud the poems and novels he loved so dearly.

Closing her eyes, she could again hear Antonio's vibrant voice as he brought the passages of Cervantes or Shakespeare alive, the infectious warmth of Pedro's laughter when one of the excerpts amused him. Before she became aware of it, the words of one of their oft-shared favorite stanzas slipped past her lips.

"'When shall we three meet again? In thunder, lightning, or in rain . . . ?'" Her voice faltered, unable to continue the passage. *Oh, Antonio! Pedro!* Turning hurriedly away from the window, she wiped away the tears that had begun to slide from the corners of her eyes.

This will not do, Adriana! She decided a cup of tea would help her get a firm grip on her emotions. Quietly slipping out of her room, she hurried to the rear stairway.

Adriana was surprised to find the kitchen fully lit and stripped of all furniture except for the large oaken icebox against the wall. Magdalena was on her hands and knees, preparing to wax the floor.

"I didn't expect to find you here, Magdalena."

"I think because *Señor* Cleve close early, it is a good time to put on the wax. As soon as I finish, I go home."

"Are you here alone?"

"*Sí*. Paulo, he is not feeling so good in the stomach, so he go home."

She had no more uttered the words than the door burst open and little Juan Guerra rushed in, crying. "*¡Madre! ¡Madre! ¡Venga pronto!*" he shouted, wiping his eyes.

Magdalena hurried over to her distraught five-year-old son and picked him up. After a hurried conversation, she grabbed her shawl. "Juan say his *papá* is very sick and my little Bonita fall and hurt her leg. I must go."

"Of course," Adriana said. Putting her arm around the anxious woman, she led her to the door.

"¿Pero el piso?" Magdalena asked, glancing back helplessly.

"Don't worry about the floor. Go to your family, Magdalena. I will explain it to Señorita Lily." Adriana guided the woman through the door and watched her hurry away. The Guerras were a precious family, and she hoped that nothing was seriously wrong.

Once outside, she checked for Pepito before remembering that after Cleve's lecture that morning, Paulo had taken the puppy home with him to play with his children. Sighing, she went back inside, this time making sure to close the door and lock it.

Adriana put on a kettle of water and sat down on the stairs to wait for the water to boil. As she did, she looked around the room and spied the keg of beeswax intended for the floor.

Why couldn't *she* wax the floor? She had seen it done often enough at home. She would show Cleve and Lily she wasn't as useless as they thought. And how surprised they would all be in the morning!

Determined to prove herself, her hunger forgotten, Adriana once again donned Paulo's shirt and trousers. Then she picked up the keg of wax and cloth, got down on her hands and knees, and set to the task.

She was amazed at what a simple labor it turned out to be. The floor soon took on a shiny, wet gloss as the result of her efforts. She laid her cheek against the surface to make sure she hadn't missed a single spot, then smiled with pride when her inspection revealed not one streak or blemish.

Too late she discovered that in her enthusiasm, she had forgotten the most important rule of waxing a floor: don't squeeze yourself into a corner—which was exactly where she now found herself.

To her further dismay, she'd forgotten the tea kettle. Now, the water boiling away, the kettle let out a shrill whistle.

Desolately, she slumped down and looked at the glistening floor. She had no idea how long it would take for the wax to dry. How could she have been so dumb! It was true—she was as useless as they claimed.

Adriana jerked her head toward the back stairs when she heard the light tread of footsteps. As if the Lord wanted her shamed, she looked up and saw Cleve standing on the bottom step.

"What's going on here?"

With a quivering chin, she blurted out, "I just wanted to surprise you. To show you I wasn't useless." Much to her further embarrassment, she felt tears sliding down her cheeks. "Now I'm trapped in this corner." Tossing the rag into the keg, she sobbed, "I can't do anything right." She buried her head in her hands and wept in earnest.

Oblivious to the wet wax, Cleve walked over and removed the kettle from the stove, then picked her up in his arms. "Honey, honey. It's nothing to cry about." He carried her over to the stairway and sat down on a step, cradling her in his lap.

Adriana continued to sob against his chest. When she finally stopped crying, he tipped up her chin, and she was forced to look at him.

His touch was tender as he wiped away her tears. "Honey, you're not the first person who ever backed himself into a corner."

It felt so good being in his arms. Warm and secure. She made no effort to get up but, instead, leaned her cheek against his chest. "I feel so stupid, Cleve. Everything I do is wrong."

Maybe she shouldn't have impetuously run away from home. But if she hadn't, she'd be married to Miguel Castillo now. She drew away and looked him in the eyes. "Cleve, was I wrong in coming to Fort Worth?"

"Raven, you were right not to marry a man you didn't love."

"But you think I was wrong in coming here to find Antonio?"

"Honey, I'm going to say this as kindly as I know how. I believe that if Antonio wanted to be found, he would be."

"What are you suggesting? That he's hiding from me? No, Cleve, Antonio wouldn't do that. He cares for me too much." Her voice had begun to rise in denial. "I have his letter. He asked me to come. He sent me the money to come." She started to struggle out of his arms. "You don't understand."

His arms tightened. "No, you're the one who doesn't understand, Raven. He lured you here, then abandoned you." Cupping her cheek in the palm of his hand, he said gently, "Forget Antonio. You need a man who'll take care of you—keep you safe."

She leaned back into the curve of his arms and stared into his eyes, mesmerized by the desire in them and the husky seductiveness in his voice. "You weren't born to be on your hands and knees scrubbing floors. You need a man to spoil you, to dress you in fine silks and furs."

A rising excitement tingled up her spine as he wove his fingers through her hair. "Do you have any idea what this beautiful hair of yours would look like against a white ermine cape, Raven?"

His finger slowly traced the curve of her upper lip as he lowered his head and whispered, "And you need a man to love you. The way you should be loved."

She watched the inexorable descent of his mouth and closed her eyes when his lips covered hers.

The touch of his mouth was a divine sensation. His moist, firm lips devoured hers, demanding a response. She drew in a breath and he slipped his tongue between her parted lips, tantalizing the chamber with warm, exploratory probes until her mouth burned with the fire of passion.

Shocked at her reaction to his kiss, she knew she should break it off. Was he not holding her, kissing her—treating her like a common *puta?* No lady would allow herself to be handled in such a fashion!

Ah, but she gloried in the feeling. She did not want to bring an end to the delicious heat creeping through her body like an erotic flame.

The sweet sensation continued after his mouth drew away. She slowly opened her eyes. Mutely, she stared into his dark gaze and saw the kindled desire.

She *had* to escape from the temptation!

This time she met no resistance when she sat up. His arms slipped away from her as she got to her feet. On trembling legs, she started to climb the stairway, not daring to look back lest she be lured to savor again the rich taste of sheer passion.

Frightened by her own weakness, she broke away and rushed up the remaining stairs.

Chapter 8

For the first time since arriving in Fort Worth, Adriana deliberated over someone other than Antonio: she spent a totally restless night thinking about Cleve MacKenzie. Assailed with confused questions for which she had no answers, her treacherous thoughts continually returned to the memory of his kiss. Blushing with guilt, she remembered how much it had thrilled her.

Finally, at daylight, she gave up trying to sleep and got up to look out the window. At least the rain had stopped. After dressing, she went down to the kitchen and hung Paulo's clothes back up where she had found them.

Despite her previous night's misgivings, she couldn't avoid inspecting the floor. The keg was gone and the corner had been waxed. Even Cleve's footprints had been touched up. So he had finished the job. Looking at the shiny floor in the morning light, she realized her attempt had not been as disastrous as she thought. As a matter of fact, the floor looked very good! She was proud of herself, and her spirits lifted.

Hearing a knock, Adriana thought the Guerras had arrived, and hurried over to unlock the door. She opened it to an old man instead. Small in stature, the stranger doffed his hat to reveal a full head of salt-and-pepper hair that matched the grizzled beard on his chin.

"Mornin', ma'am, Burt Waverly's the name. Come to bring ya your milk and eggs." He handed her a basket.

"I'm not the cook here, Mr. Waverly." Glancing into the basket, she saw that it contained several trays of eggs.

"I knowed you're not, little lady. I deliver here every mornin'. Been talkin' to Miz Guerra, and she told me to tell you folks she ain't comin' for the next day or two. Seems her little gal broke her leg, and she'll be stayin' home with her."

"I'll tell Mr. MacKenzie," Adriana said.

"If you give me your milk jug, I'll fill it," Waverly said.

Adriana handed him the jug, and he carried it out to a donkey-pulled cart. Holding it up to the metal tap of a large milk can on the cart, he filled the jug and carried it back into the kitchen.

"Where do ya want this?"

"Just put it over there on the drainboard, señor. Is Paulo feeling any better?" Adriana asked.

"Got over what wuz ailin' him, but he ain't comin' either," Waverly said, putting down the heavy jug. "Had to take his ma up near that army fort at Jacksboro 'cause his sister's havin' a baby—" He stopped, removed his hat, and scratched his head. "Or was it she had it already? Married to one of 'em Yankee soldiers, you know. Reckon he'll most likely be gone for the next day or two."

"Well, I'm glad Paulo's feeling better, at least," Adriana said.

"The Beechum gal's doin' fine, though. Her ma said the little gal's fever broke durin' the night, and she was able to keep down some milk toast this mornin'."

"Mr. Waverly, you certainly are a wealth of news. I wonder if you know the whereabouts of Antonio Fuente?"

"Fuente? Ain't he the guy what owned this place before?"

"Yes, that's right," Adriana said excitedly. This man was the first person who'd actually recognized Antonio's name. "Do you know where I can find him?"

"Can't say that I do."

"Well, if you hear of him, I'd appreciate it if you'd let me know."

"Sure will, little lady."

When he started to leave, she asked quickly, "Oh, Mr. Waverly, would you give me a hand moving the table back into the kitchen?"

"Reckon I could do that," he said, following her into the storage room.

They carried back the heavy table and placed it in the center of the room.

"Mr. MacKenzie sure has made a lot of changes," Waverly said as they returned to the storage room. "Hard to believe it's the same place." Picking up one of the chairs, he carried it to the kitchen. Soon all four chairs were around the table.

"I do thank you for your help, sir," she said sweetly, "I just wish the coffee was ready so I could offer you a cup." She sensed that this gossipy old man probably knew more about everyone's business in town than the priest and doctor combined. If anyone could find out about Antonio, it would be Burt Waverly.

He walked over to the corner of the kitchen and lifted the cover on the tall, varnished oak box. " 'Pears like your ice is almost all melted. I'll be deliverin' ya more as soon as I finish my milk run."

"Thank you again for your help. And remember, be sure to keep your ears and eyes open for any news about Antonio."

"I'll do that." He departed with a wave.

Since Magdalena would not be coming, Adriana decided to make her own breakfast. As soon as she had a fire going in the stove, she reached for a black-lacquered coffee box on the shelf above it. Scooping some beans into the coffee mill on the wall, she ground them up and set a pot of coffee to brewing.

As she put the trays of eggs into the icebox, she discovered a slab of bacon and some beef on one shelf and an assortment of vegetables on the other. Realizing she might very well have the makings for one of her favorite dishes—a Spanish omelet—Adriana grabbed a red pepper and several tomatoes out of the icebox, then checked the condiments on a kitchen shelf. To her delight, she found all the ingredients she would need.

She had just finished chopping up the vegetables when Cleve came downstairs.

"Good morning," he greeted her.

"Good morning." She wanted to look at him but was too embarrassed. All she could think of was the way she had responded to his kiss. It had been a mistake, and she had to put it out of her mind. She stole a surreptitious glance when he came over and stood beside her as he poured himself a cup of coffee.

Adriana could feel his steady stare as she stirred the sauce that had begun to bubble on the stove. Bringing the spoon to her mouth, she took a sip, then added more paprika to the pot.

"Where's Magdalena and Paulo?" he asked.

"They won't be in today. Magdalena had to stay home with Bonita. The child broke her leg last night, and Paulo went out of town. Something about taking his mother to a sister who's having a baby." She glanced at him askance, "Married to one of them Yankee soldiers, you know."

"His mother?"

She couldn't help grinning. "No, his sister." He did not react. "Too bad about little Bonita Guerra, though."

"Yeah, too bad." His voice lacked sincerity.

Surprised, she looked at him. "You don't believe me, do you?"

"Why wouldn't I?" Leaning against the sink, cup in hand, he continued to sip the coffee. "So, what are you up to?"

"I'm making an omelet."

"*You're* making an omelet," he parroted, amused.

"That's my intention. Would you like some when I'm finished?" She cut several slices of bacon off the slab and began to chop them up into small pieces.

Cleve began to chuckle. "You and Magdalena set this up, did you?"

"I don't know what you mean. I told you, Magdalena won't be coming today."

"Yeah, that's what you told me," he replied with undisguised amusement. "Has this got anything to do with last night?"

"I don't know what you mean."

"Let's say, I can put two and two together."

His expression was so smug and self-assured, she found it hard to bear—especially on an empty stomach. "Can you really? My, oh, my, seems like I learn more about you every day." Smiling, she said, "Matter of fact, it does have something to do with last night."

"I thought so!"

"Last night was when poor little Bonita broke her leg." She poured garlic oil into a cast-iron skillet, and as she waited for it to heat, she picked up a wooden-handled wire whisk and began vigorously beating the eggs. "Do you want your omelet flat or folded?"

"How long are you going to keep up this show, Raven?"

"What's this about a show?" Lily asked as she entered the room. She walked over to the stove and poured herself a cup of coffee, then sat down at the table.

"Adriana is making breakfast this morning, Lily," Cleve said, tongue in cheek. With raised eyebrows, Lily cast a wary glance over at the skillet.

"I wish you'd get out of my way, *Señor* MacKenzie," Adriana complained. "It's difficult to cook with you crowding around the stove."

"I need a closer view, *Señorita* Paloma. Sure wouldn't want to miss one moment of this inspiration."

"Are you two going to let me in on your joke?" Lily asked. "And where's Magdalena?"

"I suspect she's going to pop up here very soon," Cleve said with a meaningful wink at Lily.

"Lily, Magdalena will not be in today." Adriana paused to pour the eggs into the hot skillet. "Her daughter broke her leg," she added as she sprinkled the chopped vegetables on the eggs.

"If this is a joke, the humor's lost on me," Lily remarked. "Did Magdalena's daughter really break a leg?"

"I wouldn't bet on it," Cleve answered, grinning. "The two women have no doubt just cooked up that little story." He put a hand to the side of his mouth. "Oh, Magdalena," he called out in a light mocking voice. "Come out, come out, wherever you are."

Putting a hand to the side of her own mouth, Adriana mimicked his tone. "Oh, Cleve, you're making a fool of yourself."

"Well, you can't trick me. This *is* about last night! You didn't need to do all this to get even."

"Even for what?" she asked, preoccupied.

"For kissing you."

"You kissed her!" Lily exclaimed. "When did this happen?"

"After she waxed herself into that corner over there."

Lily looked totally perplexed. She got up and headed for the storage room. "I guess I need something stronger than coffee this morning." She came out seconds later, holding up Adriana's white nightdress. "I know this is mine, but the last I saw of it, you were wearing it, Princess. There must have been a lot more than kissing going on around here last night."

"Oh, Lily, there's a perfectly logical explanation for that nightdress's being in the storage room. I took it off when I changed into Paulo's shirt and pants in order to wax the floor."

Since it was clear that poor Lily could not distinguish

where truth ended and fiction began, she merely nodded and put the gown aside. "Of course you did."

Adriana was too engrossed in preparing the omelet to make any further comment on the subject. "Last chance. Which will it be—flat or folded?"

"It doesn't matter. You're the cook." Cleve went over and sat down.

"Then it's going to be flat," she said, working the eggs away from the sides of the skillet. "Ah, there . . . the eggs are set perfectly," she cooed with pleasure.

Glancing at the two stunned spectators, Adriana decided to get as much out of the situation as she could. They needed to be paid back for doubting her cooking skills.

With a theatrical flourish, she took a plate, placed it over the pan, and flipped over the heavy cast-iron skillet. Then, with a deft flick of her wrist, she slid the omelet off the plate and back into the skillet. After letting it cook for a few more seconds, Adriana flipped the omelet back onto the plate, picked up the sauce pan, and scooped the paprika sauce over the omelet.

Triumphantly, she carried the dish to the table.

"Well! Where are the plates and forks?" she asked in a crisp command. "Do I have to do everything around here?"

Both Cleve and Lily jumped up quickly. Cleve spread out three plates on the table while Lily hastily brought the forks. After dividing the omelet onto the plates, Adriana sat down.

"Breakfast is ready." She smiled smugly, picked up a fork, and began to eat.

Cleve and Lily each cautiously took a bite of the egg. Their heads popped up, and they exchanged startled glances.

"She can cook!" Cleve declared.

Lily was too busy devouring her food to reply.

Following Lily's lead, Cleve soon finished his egg and shoved aside his plate. "That was delicious, Raven. Who taught you how to cook like that?"

"Carmelita Moreno." A wistful smile softened her face. "She was the cook on the ranch. I spent a lot of time with her."

"In the kitchen?" Cleve asked.

She frowned at him. "Why is that such a surprise to you?"

"Why shouldn't it be? Good God, Raven, you're totally inexperienced at ordinary household duties, yet you can cook. Why didn't you tell us this sooner?"

"I tried to tell you. Besides, I never cooked as a household chore. It was *sólo por divertirse*. Even Carmelita agreed that cooking can be fun . . . if you don't have to do it for a living."

Lily patted her hand. "Believe me, Princess, I felt the same way about my previous profession." She glanced at the uneaten remains on Adriana's plate. "You gonna finish that?"

"No, I've had enough. You're welcome to it, if you'd like."

"I don't know when I've had anything that tasted this good," Lily said, accepting the plate Adriana offered her.

Smiling with pleasure, Adriana settled back in her chair. She felt good about herself: she'd waxed the floor and cooked the breakfast.

But more importantly, for the first time since her arrival, she felt a camaraderie with them. Glancing up, she met Cleve's gaze.

He winked and grinned broadly.

Her good spirits lasted only until Cleve and Lily left the kitchen. By the time Adriana finished cleaning the dishes, her thoughts dwelled heavily on the ranch and the good times she'd spent with Carmelita Moreno. Since Adriana's own mother had died giving birth to her, the cook had been the nearest person to a mother Adriana had ever known. She remembered the many happy hours passed in the kitchen with the kindly woman, and Carmelita's calm smile as she patiently explained many of her special secrets in preparing food.

But she couldn't think of Carmelita without rekindling memories of Pedro Moreno, Carmelita's son. Once again the image of his face filled her mind, the sound of his laughter filled her ears—the laughter her father had silenced forever. Dear Pedro. Dear sweet, sensitive Pedro. The memory was like a knife thrust into her breast, and tears slid down her cheeks.

As soon as she sensed another presence, she grabbed a nearby onion and began to peel it, then turned. It was Cleve, staring at her with concern.

"Are you okay, Raven?"

She smiled falsely. "Of course." She quickly held up the onion. "Onions always make me cry."

"Oh, I see. You sure you're okay?"

"What do you want, Cleve?"

"I'm on my way to the Guerras. I thought you might like to come along."

"Oh, I'd love that."

Hastily, Adriana pulled up the hem of her skirt and wiped her eyes.

Chapter 9

Even though the Guerras lived nearby, Cleve insisted on making a detour to the general store. He stood mulling over which selection to make between the only two dolls on the shelf: one a rag doll with black yarn for hair, the other with red yarn.

"Tell me, Raven, if you were a little three-year-old girl with black hair and big brown eyes, which of these dolls would you prefer?"

"Hmmm," she said. "I vaguely remember a similar child in my past."

Chuckling, he lightly tousled her hair. "By chance, her name wasn't Adriana, was it?"

"How perceptive of you," she teased.

"So okay, Miz Paloma, which of these dolls would you have wanted?"

"Hmmm," she said, stroking her chin as if in deep thought. "Since the selection is so varied, it is a very difficult choice to make, *señor.* I believe my choice would be this one." She picked up the black-headed doll.

"A wise choice, madam. And the one I would have made," he said.

"You are *loco,* Cleve MacKenzie! Plain *loco.*"

Laughing, he clasped her hand and they moved on to another shelf. "We can't forget Juan. He may not have a broken leg, but little boys like gifts, too." He stopped when he caught sight of a red ball on the shelf. "How about a ball?"

"Well, tell me, *señor*, if you were a five-year-old boy with black hair and dark eyes, which color ball would you prefer?"

"Hmmm," he said, stroking his chin. "Description sounds like one of my brothers. Reckon I'd like this one." He picked up the ball.

"Wise selection, *señor*, inasmuch as that is the only ball."

He groaned and grabbed her hand. "Let's go, Miz Paloma."

"I'll take a bag of that marzipan, and throw in a half dozen of those peppermint sticks, Ben," he said to the storekeeper.

"'Pears like you've got a sweet tooth, Cleve," the store owner said.

Looking pointedly at Adriana, Cleve said, "I do, but my hankering's not for candy."

"Can't fault your taste there, son. She sure is sweeter-lookin' than any peppermint stick."

When the old man walked away to fill the candy bag, Adriana, outraged, turned to Cleve and kicked him in the shin.

"Ouch! What'd you do that for?" he asked, rubbing the injured spot as she flounced away.

Headed for the open door, she looked back at him, her eyes flashing angrily. "That's to show you just how *sweet* I am," she declared through gritted teeth.

Adriana spun around and slammed into a man who had just entered the store. She blushed, recognizing the doctor.

"Good morning, Adriana." He doffed his hat.

"Good morning, Dr. Anderson. I'm sorry. I didn't realize you were there."

"Well, I'm glad to see you're looking much better than the last time I saw you."

"Hey, Doc, you're just the man I want to see."

Carrying an armful of parcels, Cleve hurried over.
"What's the condition of the little Guerra girl?"

"She'll be fine. It's a minor fracture of the tibia. It
should mend quickly."

"Broken shinbone, huh, Doc? I might have one
myself." He cast a pointed look at Adriana. "Well, I
want to take care of their bill. How much is it, Jim?"

"Normally, I wouldn't take your money, Cleve. But
since you have no conscience about taking mine, I'll
only charge you five dollars."

"Five dollars! Sounds like a pretty stiff fee for that
witch doctorin' you practice."

"The price of fame has its rewards, Cleve. Hey, Ben,"
he shouted to the store owner. "This good fellow here
has volunteered to buy me five of those imported dollar
cigars of yours."

Ben reached under the counter and pulled out a
humidor. Cleve walked back, picked up the cigars Ben
put on the counter, and slapped down five gold dollars.
"Can't wait for next week's game, Jim," he said pleasantly, handing the cigars to the doctor.

"I'm sure you can't," Jim Anderson said.

Chuckling, he pocketed all but one. "But do allow me
to bask in this small moment of triumph." He slowly
passed the cigar under his nose and took a deep,
lingering sniff of the tobacco. "Ah, sheer delection!
Nothing like the smell of a good cigar, my boy. I'd offer
you one, but they're too expensive." He extracted a
small gold clipper from his vest pocket. "By the way,
Cleve," the doctor said, snipping the end off the cigar,
"Caroline sends you belated birthday wishes and
thanks you for the piece of cake." He raised his bushy
brows in triumph and said smugly, "She gave me half
of it."

Returning his attention to Adriana, he smiled. "Tell
me, my dear, have you had any luck in locating your
br—"

"Antonio," she interrupted quickly, cutting him off.
She stole a hasty glance at Cleve to see his reaction to

the near miscue. He appeared not to have noticed. "I haven't found him yet, Doctor, but I intend to keep on trying."

"Good for you. Well, I can't say this hasn't been a pleasure," he said, following with another deliberate sniff of the cigar. Then he doffed his hat. "Adriana. Cleve. Enjoy your day."

"He's a nice man," Adriana said, once they were outside.

"Yeah, Doc's a good sport. I like him."

When they reached the Guerras' small domicile, all the morning's painful memories were shoved to the back of Adriana's mind as her puppy came bounding up. She lifted him into her arms.

"Pepito! My little Pepito!" she exclaimed, smothered under a torrent of slavering kisses.

"Oh, *señor* and *señorita!*" Magdalena greeted. Signs of strain played on the young woman's usually serene face. "Come in and sit down. I will get you a cup of *café.*"

Slipping an arm around her shoulders, Cleve hugged her to his side. "No, don't you go to any bother, Magdalena. We came just to see how Bonita is feeling."

"Is no bother, *Señor* Cleve. It gives me much pleasure," she said shyly.

"Then we'd be glad to." He pulled out a chair for Adriana, and they sat down.

Cleve glanced over at Juan Guerra. The five-year-old was standing silently against the wall. "*¡Hola, Juan!*" Digging into the bag from the store, he brought out the candy and held up a peppermint stick.

The youngster hung his head, the corners of his mouth tugged into a smile he was trying to conceal. Cleve winked and motioned to the boy to come over, and Juan approached slowly.

"*Gracias, Señor Cleve.*" He grabbed the candy stick out of Cleve's hand and backed away.

"Hey, not so fast there, *muchacho*. You forgot something."

Reaching again into the bag, Cleve pulled out the red ball. Juan's eyes bulged with wonderment. Smiling with pleasure, he took the ball.

"I'd think that should be worth a hug or a handshake." Cleve opened his arms.

The little boy hesitated for a moment, then threw his arms around Cleve's neck and hugged him tightly.

"*Venga, Pepito,*" Juan shouted as he ran outside.

Adriana felt a momentary stab of resentment when the puppy leaped from her lap and scurried after the boy.

"You have made my Juan very happy, *señor*," Magdalena said, placing cups on the table.

"I have to see how my little girlfriend's doing before we have coffee." Cleve stuffed the rag doll in his pocket and grabbed Adriana's hand. They went into the bedroom.

Bonita Guerra lay on the bed, her tiny left leg encased in a plaster cast. At the sight of Cleve, the three-year-old broke into a bright smile. "*¡Tio Cleve. Tio Cleve!*" Squealing joyously, she raised her arms to him.

Cleve lifted her up, and her little arms wrapped around his neck, squeezing him with all her might as she kissed him on the cheek.

Adriana stared in disbelief; the child's reaction to the sight of Cleve had been instinctive and uninhibited. When he glimpsed Adriana's startled expression, Cleve smiled broadly with unabashed pleasure. "We're in love."

"So that explains that enthusiastic greeting!" Adriana leaned over and kissed Bonita's cheek. "Poor *pequeña*," she whispered in the child's ear.

Holding Bonita on his knee, Cleve sat down on the edge of the bed. "Matter of fact, Miz Paloma, if you don't marry me, this here beauty is my next choice." He turned his attention back to the child and missed Adriana's astonished reaction to his light remark.

Marry him!

"Does it hurt, sweetheart?" he asked woefully.

Bonita nodded. Her little face puckered and her round dark eyes filled with tears.

"Ah, angel," he murmured, hugging her again. "Soon it will all go away."

He pulled the rag doll out of his pocket. "Look what I've got. This little one is looking for someone to take care of her—just like your mama takes care of you." He gently wiped away the child's tears. "How about it, angel? Will you take care of her?"

Bonita nodded.

"Trouble is, her leg's hurting, too. Do you think we can make it feel better if we wrap it up like yours?"

Bonita nodded.

He dug into his pocket and pulled out a white handkerchief. Soon the two of them had their heads together as they bandaged the doll's leg.

Since her presence appeared forgotten by both of them, Adriana walked back and sat down at the table with Magdalena. "I never realized how much he loves children."

"Es un hombre de buen corazón, señorita. De compasión. Much heart. Much sympathy," Magdalena declared fervently.

"I think you may be a little biased, Magdalena," Adriana said, patting her hand. "But I guess you're right. He does seem to like almost everyone except . . ." She thought of Cleve's very vocal and adamant dislike of Antonio. "I guess he'd have to believe a person was really deep-down rotten before he'd dislike him."

Cleve came out of the bedroom and put a finger to his mouth, motioning them to speak softly. "She's sleeping." Magdalena quickly moved to pour him a cup of coffee.

"When do you expect Paulo to return?" he asked, leaning back, relaxed.

The seed now planted in her mind by Magdalena, Adriana took a long look at Cleve. He always appeared

totally comfortable with whomever he was with—
never drawing a social distinction between a doctor or a
humble cook.

She cast her eyes heavenward. *¡Santa Maria! Next I'll
have him deserving enough to be up there with you!*

"Paulo say he be back maybe two days. Then I can
come and do my job, *Señor* Cleve. I am so sorry that I no
can come sooner." She hung her head in shame.

"Hey, none of that," Cleve said. He knelt down in
front of her and clasped her hands between his own. "I
don't want to hear any more of that kind of talk,
Magdalena. You and Paulo take all the time that's
necessary. My little girlfriend needs you more right
now than we do. I want you to stay home until Paulo's
mother returns to watch your children."

"But, *Señor* Cleve, she will not be back for many
weeks!"

"Well, your job will be waiting for you whenever she
returns."

"You are such a good man, *señor*. Every night, I say a
special prayer for you."

"So I have you to thank for all the good luck I've had
lately!"

"Oh, *Señor* Cleve," she said, giggling. "Now you
make the joke like you always do."

Adriana watched, transfixed, as Cleve wove his mag-
ic with Magdalena, and by the time they rose to leave,
the look of anxiety she had worn when they arrived had
been replaced by a smile.

"I've taken care of the doctor, so you don't have to
worry about that."

"Oh, no, *Señor* Cleve. You are very generous, but my
Paulo is a proud man. He will not take what he has not
earned." She shook her head. "Paulo will not accept
your money."

"Who said anything about money?" Cleve shrugged
innocently. "The doctor owed me a favor, so we made a
trade. Now Paulo owes me the favor instead. Maybe he
can build us a little doghouse or something like that."

He kissed her on the cheek. "If you need anything before Paulo gets back, send for me. Do you understand?" He hugged Magdalena and kissed her cheek.

"And I'll take Pepito back with me," Adriana said after giving Magdalena a hug and kiss herself.

"Pepito can stay here. My Juan——"

"I won't hear of it," Adriana declared. "You've got enough to do as it is without having to take care of a puppy." As they left, Adriana scooped up Pepito in her arms.

When she looked back, she saw Juan Guerra standing alone in the street, holding the red ball, his sad gaze following them.

Upon arriving at The Full House, Cleve stopped to greet the three churchwomen. "How are you lovely ladies doing today? Raven, I'd like to introduce you to Mrs. Parker, Mrs. Adams, and Mrs. Merryweather," he said, smiling at each of the women in turn. "Ladies, this is *Señorita* Paloma."

The women remained reserved, but from their looks of disapproval Adriana knew they were thinking the worst of her—undoubtedly believing from the manner of her dress that she was a common *puta*. She did not have to hang her head to anyone. Was she not Adriana Adelina Paloma Maria Fuente y de Elbertina?

Drawing herself up to her full five feet, six inches, Adriana lifted her head and met their disapproving looks full-faced. Humble clothing could not disguise the aristocratic dignity of generations of Castilian nobles.

"How do you do, *señoras*."

She vanquished them with the single sentence.

At that moment Pepito chose to make his appearance known also, and began to sniff at the feet of Mrs. Parker.

"Oh, get away from me, you nasty little thing," she declared indignantly.

Stepping aside, she tripped over the picket sign she

had lowered to the ground. Shrieking, she threw up her arms as she started to fall. Cleve dove to grab her, but momentum and her appreciable bulk made it impossible to prevent the fall. They both tumbled backward, his body cushioning her when they hit the ground.

"Oh! Oh! Oh!" Prudence cried, mortified to find herself sprawled over him.

A series of repeated "Oh, mys!" and "Oh, dears!" came from her two companions, who were fussing and hovering over her, their hands fluttering in agitation. Adriana finally managed to shove past them and help the fallen woman to her feet.

"Oh, dear Prudence, are you hurt?" Matilda Merryweather cried, agitated.

"Oh, you poor, poor dear." Henrietta Adams sympathized.

Prudence Parker adjusted the bonnet that was dangling in her face. "Well, I never!" she exclaimed.

Brushing the dust off himself, Cleve climbed to his feet. "Are you hurt, Mrs. Parker?"

His concern was so genuine that even the sour-faced preacher's wife could not remain impervious to it. "I must thank you. That was a most courageous and noble deed, Mr. MacKenzie. I do hope you aren't injured."

"What matters is that you aren't, Mrs. Parker. Won't you please come inside and sit down?" he asked with an appealing smile.

"Oh, I'm afraid I can't do that," she said. "Forgive me for saying so, but don't you realize that is a den of iniquity, Mr. MacKenzie?"

"Well, then, will you at least allow me to assist you home?"

She smiled in gratitude. "That's most kind of you, sir. But it won't be necessary. My friends will help me. I can't wait to tell the reverend. Come, ladies."

"Are you sure you're okay, Cleve?" Adriana asked, as he finished brushing off his Stetson, which had fallen in the dust.

"Yeah, no damage done."

"I'll say there's no damage done. Cleve MacKenzie, you wrapped those women around your finger. I just can't believe how you charm women!" She shook her head. "I guess I better get inside and make your dinner. We must keep up your strength. All that charm you exude has to be a tremendous drain on your energy."

Cleve remained outside and watched the three women walk up the street, their signs hanging loosely from their hands. He hoped this wouldn't be the last he'd be seeing of Pontifical Prudence Parker and her two apostles. He really liked those ladies.

Later that evening, still sated from the evening meal Adriana had prepared, Cleve stood behind the bar and looked around at the crowded room. It had been risky to take a chance that the promise of an honest card game and the absence of whores would attract a clientele more interested in a quiet game of cards than a hot night on the town. But that belief had paid off. Business far exceeded his expectations, and in the past couple weeks since he had reopened The Full House, he'd already recovered more than double his investment.

Further, he had just hired a retired Texas Ranger to operate the roulette wheel. Now Cleve would have more time to spend at the poker table—where the big money could be made.

He glanced down to the end of the bar, where Lily was talking to Judge Raymond. What a Godsend she was. Her presence offered enough femininity to please a man's senses without distracting him from his purpose in coming to the casino.

Feeling he had the overall situation in hand, Cleve realized he still had one serious problem—that bewitching little minx upstairs who would be his bride!

Ever since he had been foolish enough to kiss Adriana, he couldn't keep his mind off her—and she couldn't keep her mind off that goddamned, missing Antonio!

Where in hell was the bastard? In an effort to locate the guy, he'd even done some questioning of his own. He wanted to deal with Pretty Boy face to face.

When he saw a tall, rawboned man entering the casino, Cleve smiled, thinking someone had just read his mind. The new arrival approached him with the stiff gait of a man more comfortable on horseback than on foot. Cleve reached out and shook hands with him. "Glad to see you, Buckwheat."

"Same to you, Cleve."

Lily sauntered over to them, and Cleve slipped his arm around her shoulders. "Buckwheat, I'd like you to meet Lily LaRue. She manages the place. Lily, this is an old friend of mine, Buckwheat Flour. He's with the Texas Rangers."

Buckwheat brought a finger up to the brim of his battered Stetson. "My pleasure, Miz Lily."

"How about a drink, Buckwheat?" Lily asked.

"Sounds mighty fine."

Lily glanced at him as she poured the drink. "How'd you get the name Buckwheat?"

"Name's just Buck, but the fellas always call me Buckwheat. Reckon it would have been that or Flapjack. One's 'bout as bad as the other."

"And how about the gals?" Lily asked. "What do they call you?"

Buckwheat grinned. "Reckon not often enough to keep me happy."

"Well, I sure don't understand why that should be," she teased.

Breaking into the light flirtation, Cleve asked, "Did you find out anything about Antonio Fuente?"

Buckwheat shook his head. "Sorry, Cleve. Nobody's heard of him."

"Dammit! How in hell can a man just vanish into thin air?"

"Ain't hard in these parts. Lot of space out there for him to do it in," the ranger said. "I did hear some news that should interest you, though. Talk is that Charlie Walden's back here, raiding right in these parts."

"Whereabouts, Buckwheat?" Cleve asked, his face grim.

"Between here and the Brazos. He's been hitting a lot of the ranches and stages."

"Are you sure it's Walden?"

"Hell, Cleve, I ain't sure of anything 'cept that one day I'll end up at the wrong end of a Colt." Buckwheat suddenly peered intently at a figure across the room. "Say, ain't that old Waco Donniger over at that wheel?"

"Sure is," Cleve said. "Just hired him."

Buckwheat shoved his hat to the top of his forehead. "Well, I'll be damned! Ain't seen old Waco since we fought them Comanche at Julesburg in sixty-eight. Think I'll go over and say hello." He tipped a finger to his hat. "Thanks for the drink, Miz Lily. Sure been nice meeting you."

Cleve remained deep in thought. Now he had two problems to consider: Charlie Walden and Antonio Fuente. Which one should he pursue first?

A few hours later, still pondering the burning question, he locked the front door.

"Lily, go to bed. I'll finish up here."

"If you're sure you don't mind. Good night, boss man."

"Good night, honey," he said as she climbed the stairway.

Cleve loosened his tie and opened the top buttons of his shirt. Then, after rolling up the sleeves, he began to stack the chairs on the tables.

Unobserved, Adriana stood in the darkened doorway of the kitchen. She had come downstairs to make a cup of tea but became distracted by seeing Cleve. He was so undeniably masculine! She wondered if he was aware of his sexual magnetism. He didn't appear to be; he wore his good looks and dynamism with the same nonchalance as he did his clothes.

His every movement fascinated her. The fabric of his white shirt stretched and tightened across his shoulders as the muscles beneath it bunched and then expanded when he lowered the heavy chandelier. Silky, dark hair on his head and forearms glistened under the bright lights as his hands reached out to extinguish the lamps on the fixture. Even that simple act had a disturbing, virile energy to it that made her blush and reminded her of the strength of his hands when he held her, of the gentleness of their touch against her cheek.

She felt a tingling begin in the pit of her stomach and spread through her with an inner excitement. Fighting the overwhelming temptation to go to him, to feel his touch again, to taste his kiss, she turned away, and after a guilty backward glance, she stole up the darkened stairs.

Chapter 10

Feeling the effects of the previous day's fall, Cleve tried to shake the stiffness out of his back and shoulders as he came downstairs. He was hurting. Hitting the ground with two-hundred-pound Prudence Parker on top of him had felt about the same as getting tossed from a horse and having it roll over you. He hoped she didn't feel as sore as he did this morning.

As if his aches and pains weren't bad enough, he'd spent another restless night thinking about Raven. Although he prided himself on being a patient man, that patience was wearing thin: the provocative little beauty was driving him crazy.

He found Lily alone in the kitchen, her head behind the pages of a newspaper. "Good morning."

"Morning." Her eyes never budged from the printed page.

"What's so interesting in that newspaper?" he asked, pouring himself a cup of coffee.

"I'm just reading about an election in Wyoming Territory—first place women in this country were finally given the right to vote. Three cheers for Wyoming! You ought to move there, boss man. Considering your charm with women, you could probably end up running the territory."

"Hey, Lily, I can't help that women fall for me," he said, mildly amused.

"More like 'fall all over you,' from what I hear."

"Oh . . . Adriana told you about yesterday."

Lily lowered the paper long enough to grin over the top of it. "I can't believe you finally won over that prune-faced minister's wife."

"Where is Adriana, anyway?"

"Out front."

"What's she doing out there?"

Lily's blue eyes disappeared behind the paper again. "I suggest you see for yourself." She returned to her reading.

Cleve went into the barroom and glanced out the window. "Oh, no!" he groaned. Putting aside the coffee cup, he went to the door.

"Adriana, what are you doing?" he asked, calmly.

She lowered the sign she carried. "Gambling is the Devil's diversion" was painted in bold, black letters.

"Good morning, Mr. MacKenzie."

He nodded to the speaker. "Good morning, Mrs. Merryweather. Mrs. Adams," he added, to the other beaming woman.

Leaning against the building, he crossed his legs and folded his arms across his chest. "Well, let's hear it," he said to Adriana.

"Poor Mrs. Parker is feeling really achy today, Cleve. I'm sure you wouldn't want her to have to carry around this big sign. And since I feel indirectly responsible for her fall—"

"You offered to carry it for her."

She glanced sheepishly at him. "I thought it's the least I could do."

"To say *the least*," he agreed. "You are aware, Adriana, that what you are doing is bad for business. Especially since you work here."

"I only intend to do it until she's feeling better."

"And you are aware, Adriana, that the intent here is to force the closing of The Full House."

All three women nodded.

"Thus driving me into financial ruin."

"Cleve, I really think you're taking this too personally," Adriana replied.

"Oh, my, yes!" Matilda Merryweather sputtered, her hands fluttering in agitation. "We would never wish to see anything like that happen to such a dear man as you, Mr. MacKenzie. Would we, Henrietta?"

"Good gracious, no," Henrietta replied, appalled. "That was never our intent, dear Mr. MacKenzie."

"But, ladies, intent or not, that very well could happen."

The two confederates exchanged confused glances. "Henrietta, I think we should go and discuss this further with Prudence," Matilda said.

"And I think we should do it right now, Matilda!" Henrietta agreed.

"Wait up a minute, ladies," Cleve called as they started to walk away. He went over to Adriana. "Excuse me." Taking the sign out of her hand, he ambled up to the two waiting women. "I think you forgot this."

Adriana wisely spent the afternoon visiting with Magdalena, returning in time to prepare dinner and then retire to her room.

In one of the rare nights since Adriana's arrival, The Full House passed a peaceful evening.

Cleve was proud of her. For three nights in a row, Adriana had managed not to cause a disruption in the casino—a good sign that she was genuinely making an effort to listen to him. That's why he dreaded what lay ahead, and now paced the floor awaiting her return. He had put off this meeting for the past couple of days and the time had come to bite the bullet.

"Hi," he said, when she entered the barroom. "Any luck?"

She shook her head. "No, it is always the same; neither the priest nor the doctor have had news of Antonio."

"I'm sorry, Raven." He hated to see her so sad, but

were he totally honest, he'd admit he really wanted Antonio found so he could get his hands around the bastard's throat.

"You got a minute, honey? There's something we have to discuss."

"It's about those five kittens, isn't it?" she said, sitting down.

"Five kittens! What five kittens? I haven't heard anything about kittens."

"Doesn't matter. I found a home for them anyway."

"Since you raised the subject of animals, do you mind telling me just what you had intended to do with a rabbit?"

"Just feed it. The poor little thing was hungry."

"Raven, the rabbit had gotten away from Rosa Martinez's diner. All you did was fatten it up for her rabbit stew. Which, I should add, was very tasty."

"You ate it!" She brought a hand to her mouth and stared horrified at him.

That did not make what he had to say any easier.

"Actually, I didn't know it was the same rabbit until after I ate the stew. But that's beside the point. You can't keep attaching yourself to every stray animal that shows up at the back door, Raven. Which leads me to the subject at hand: we have to talk about Pepito. He's been up to his old tricks. If you remember, a few days ago I warned you that—"

"But you told Magdalena that you'd have Paulo build a doghouse. Didn't you mean for Pepito?"

"Honey, I just said that so they wouldn't be embarrassed about the money," he said.

"Well, why can't Paulo build one anyway? He's back now."

"Even if he did, that would only provide a place for the puppy to sleep at night. We'd still have the same problem during the day."

"Once he's trained—"

"Raven, he'd have this place ruined before then. You've got to give him up."

She looked at him, stunned. "I can't do that. I just can't turn him away. Where would he go?"

"I spoke to the Guerras. They're willing to take him. The puppy is very attached to Juan."

"Pepito is attached to me, too," she cried out.

"Of course he is," Cleve said gently. "And I'm sure he always will be. But you see, there's a natural chemistry—an instant love—between little boys and dogs. They think alike. They're pals. They like to romp together, roll around on the ground, explore, splash through mud puddles—do all the things a little boy and dog like to do. They kind of belong together like salt and pepper . . . bread and butter . . . flapjacks and syrup . . ." He paused for the briefest of seconds. "You and me."

"Oh, Cleve, why do you make jokes? This is not a laughing matter. I love him, too," she said pitifully.

"I know you do. And I know how it hurts to lose a dog. I was eight years old when our dog was killed. We'd had him since before I was born. I cried myself to sleep every night for a month."

Her eyes were misted with tears as she leaned across the table and patted his hand. "Oh, that is so sad, Cleve. How you must have loved him."

He nodded. "I thought my heart would break when we lost him."

"I understand. And did you ever get another dog?"

"Well, sure."

"So you see, no matter who it is or what it may be, we must never forsake loving in the fear of losing."

Cleve put his elbows on the table and cradled his head in his hands. *My God! Had anything I said gotten through to her?*

Smiling, Adriana got to her feet. "It is time for Pepito's walk. You see, I have him on a schedule."

He had failed miserably. Maybe she was right after all. He could be all wrong about the dog. Maybe he should give the little guy a couple more days.

Stupefied, he watched her leave, the puppy trotting

obediently at her heels. Pepito slowed and, in passing, raised his hind leg against a chair near the door—then followed Adriana outside for his "walk."

Cleve had cleaned up Pepito's parting gift to him by the time Adriana returned and tied the dog outside the kitchen door. Obviously unhappy with the arrangement, the puppy set up a steady barking, which continued for the next ten minutes until Paulo showed up with Juan.

The youngster giggled with delight as the dog hopped around at his feet, and as soon as Juan sat down, Pepito leaped onto his lap, smothering the youngster under a burst of wet kisses.

After a short conversation with Cleve, Paulo called to Juan that they were leaving. Stretching at the rope that restrained him, Pepito whimpered as he watched his playmate walk away. The little boy turned his head and waved pathetically at the puppy.

Cleve's gaze fell on Adriana. For a long moment they stared at each other, saying with their eyes what neither could speak. Adriana walked slowly over to Pepito and sank down on the ground beside the puppy. Hugging him, she whispered, *"Adios, pequeño. Yo te amo."* Then she set him free. Yapping, the little puppy chased after the boy, its tail wagging furiously.

Cleve gave her a moment to herself before walking over to her. He lightly stroked her head. "You okay, honey?" When she nodded, he grabbed her hand and pulled her to her feet. "I think you need some cheering up. How about a little stroll around the town?"

"I don't think it would cheer me very much, Cleve. This town's noisy and smells of cattle."

Plopping his hat on his head, he tucked her arm in his. "You just haven't been to the right spots, lady."

After several blocks they reached a plaza abounding with carts, booths, and stalls. Tiny houses in colorful shades of pink, blue, and yellow surrounded the marketplace. Beaming with pleasure, Adriana hurried over to the sunny square, tugging Cleve after her.

Hand in hand, they strolled leisurely through the dozens of shops that lined the plaza, vivid displays of colorful serapes and sombreros hanging from the doors and facades of the adobe buildings. Against her protests, Cleve bought her a red cotton peasant skirt and a white ruffled blouse to add to her limited wardrobe.

"There is no reason for you to buy me clothes, Cleve."

"Think of them as a uniform to wear when you scrub down the stairway again."

With typical female curiosity, she stopped to investigate a display of perfume. Cleve took a bottle from her, and after a few discerning sniffs, he set it aside. "You smell much nicer without it."

While Adriana stopped to admire a tasteful piece of ironwood sculpture, a youngster of six or seven, carrying a boxed tray suspended from a rope draped behind her neck, approached Cleve. "*Buenas tardes, señor.*"

Cleve doffed his hat. "And good afternoon to you, pretty brown eyes."

The little girl smiled shyly. "*¿Quiere usted comprar una peineta para la señorita?*"

"Gotta say that smile of yours is very persuasive, little one, so let's just see what these combs of yours look like." He squatted and began to rifle through the box, finally selecting a black comb with tiny red and white flowers painted on the crown. "*¿Cuánto?*"

"*Veinticinco centavos, señor.*"

He drew back with feigned shock. "Twenty-five cents! How about ten cents? *Diez centavos.*"

The little girl's face puckered with a concentrated frown. "*Veinte centavos,*" she finally said, doubling his offer.

"Hmmm," he said, stroking his chin. "I tell you what, I'll raise my offer five more cents. *Quince centavos.*"

This time there was no hesitation on the tiny girl's part. "*Veinte centavos, señor,*" she said, standing firm.

Grimacing, Cleve wiped his brow and slapped his

Stetson back on his head. "Phew, you sure drive a hard bargain, brown eyes. Okay, twenty cents it will be." Grinning, he tugged lightly at one of her dark braids and tossed her a silver dollar. "*Gracias, querida,*" he said, standing up.

"*¡Oh, gracias, señor!*" the girl exclaimed. She skipped away, pausing to look back with a demure smile.

Standing aside watching Cleve's interplay with the little girl, Adriana's heart melted like butter. What a wonderful father he would make one day. He was so patient and understanding with children—even to the way he'd squat down to their level, rather than intimidate them with his own height. But *¡Caramba!* How a daughter would be able to wind him around her finger!

Shame on you, Adriana, she scolded herself. *You are just resentful because you did not have such a father.*

Cleve came up to her and stuck the comb in her hair. "There, now you have something to remember me by," he said, stepping back to admire her. "Beautiful!"

Turning his head, his gaze searched out the youngster moving through the crowd. "I bet you looked just like her when you were a little girl," he said softly.

"You must stop buying me these gifts, for I have no money to buy something for you to remember me."

For a hushed moment, he stared into her eyes. "I won't need anything, Raven."

To elude his penetrating gaze, she moved hurriedly to a counter of fans.

"What do you think I should get for Lily?" he asked, moving up behind her.

"How about one of these, *señor?*" She turned to him and, with an adroit flick of her wrist, parted the pleated folds. Her long, dark lashes fluttered over warm, brown pools of enticement peeking seductively above its rim, as she gracefully drew the fan across her face in a slow rotation. Then she lowered it just enough to unmask the faint curve of a mysterious smile.

Cleve grimaced. "Mercy, my lady," he pleaded,

clutching at his chest theatrically. "Better you drive a stake through my heart."

Adriana giggled and lowered the fan.

As they continued to explore every booth and stall, they stopped at a vendor to sample savory tamales wrapped in dried corn husks. Moving on, neither was able to resist the tantalizing aroma of fresh bollos. The rolls, still delectably warm from the oven, were soft and sweet, and seemed to melt in the mouth. Laughing like children, they ate pieces of watermelon, the succulent juice running down their chins. Finally, unable to sample another ware, they sat down in the shade of a copse of cottonwood.

While Cleve stretched out beside her with his Stetson over his face, Adriana leaned back against a tree and relaxed. Within moments, her attention was drawn to a bird fluttering on and off the limb of a nearby tree. "Oh, it's going to hurt itself, Cleve," she said worriedly.

He lifted the hat off his face and raised up his head. "What is?"

"Look at that little bird over there, on that tree limb. It's trying to fly."

Finally, after several more false starts, the bird fluttered away.

"Do you think it will be okay?" she asked.

"Sure. It probably flew back to its nest." He lay back. "I'm afraid you will one day, too, Little Raven."

"Are you really afraid, Cleve?" She smiled down at him. "I would think you'd be glad to see me fly away. I cause you so much trouble."

"No, I don't ever want you to fly away, Raven," he said in a husky voice.

In the mere second of a heartbeat, the air had become charged with a tension that increased with every drawn breath and lingering stare. "Might have to try clipping your wings, or . . ."

A tremor of anticipation tickled her spine. "Or what, Cleve?" she whispered.

"Or see if this works."

He hooked a hand around her neck and slowly drew her head down to his. His mouth covered hers, and Adriana parted her lips to accept his kiss, melting into the sweet hunger of it.

When they separated, she stood up quickly. "You mustn't kiss me, Cleve."

"I know—your precious Antonio," he said, disgusted. Rising to his feet, he slapped his Stetson on the back of his head and picked up the packages. "Damn shame that the man you love isn't here to fight his own battles, instead of you having to do it for him."

They walked in silence back to The Full House and went upstairs.

"It'll soon be time to open, so I better get ready." He dumped the packages on her bed.

"Thank you for everything, Cleve; I had a wonderful time," Adriana said as they parted at the door.

Cleve strode down the hallway to his own room. If he could have kicked himself, he would. So he shouldn't have kissed her! But why did she keep believing in a man who had abandoned her? Why wouldn't she forget him? Well, he'd be damned if he'd listen to any more of her endless declarations of undying love for the bastard.

"What in hell has gotten into you, MacKenzie?" he said to his reflection in the mirror. "You've always considered yourself a smart man. You sure as hell aren't acting like one!"

You know why you're acting this way. You're jealous. You're jealous because she never puts the man out of her thoughts.

"I can't fight someone whom I can't see."

Facing off with his own image, he saw the pain in his eyes. "Goddammit! She's got me talking to myself!" Disgusted, he turned away, realizing he was obsessed and he was acting like a fool!

* * *

Cleve was setting up chairs when Adriana came down the stairs dressed in the bright red satin dress.

"Adriana, I thought it was clear that it's no longer necessary for you to work in the casino—particularly in that dress!" he barked.

"That's not why I'm here, Cleve. It's obvious that I'll never hear any word of Antonio upstairs in a room. Down here, I might have a better chance of speaking to someone who knows of his whereabouts."

"You can't sit around here in that dress. You'll look like a cheap bar-girl hustling drinks. People will get the wrong impression."

His attitude was unjust, and she resented the implication. "All I intend to do is ask them about Antonio. Nothing more," she quickly defended. "You and your precious others have filthy minds to think otherwise."

"Just the same, I don't want you in the bar annoying my customers with your persistent questions about your *beloved Antonio*—the same man who doesn't give a good goddamn what happens to you!"

How dare he speak to her in such a manner! Who did he think he was, to tell Adriana Adelina Paloma Maria Fuente y de Elbertina what to do! Had she not proven that she wouldn't tolerate that, even from her own father?

And she had thought they were getting along so well! In fact, from the time he had first kissed her, she knew she felt more for him than just gratitude. And his effort to dominate her hurt her, for her anger concealed a feeling for him that went deeper than physical desire— a feeling that confused her as much as it thrilled her.

"If I wish to do so, you cannot stop me. I am not breaking any law. And if you do not want me here, there are many other bars in this city."

The determined little fool would probably try it, Cleve reflected. She would actually walk into the Alhambra or Pigeon Hole wearing that goddamned red dress! If he had a mite of common sense, he'd let her do it, let her find out what she'd be getting herself into.

Well, he'd put an end to it once and for all. No more talk about Pretty Boy. He wasn't going to let that bastard's name cross her lips again.

He swept her up, trapping her arms against his chest, and carried her up the stairway. Entering her room, he kicked the door shut behind him and dumped her on the bed.

Snarling like a wildcat, she was off the bed in an instant. "How dare you terrorize me like this, you blustering bully!" She delivered a stinging crack to his cheek. "Get out of this room at once!"

Her slap to his face was like pouring fuel on the fire she had already stoked to a blaze. He wanted to shake her until her teeth rattled.

"I'll get out of here when I've said what I came to say."

"You'll get out of here now!" She lifted her chin in fearless determination. "I'm not interested in anything you have to say."

"Of course you aren't! An addle-brained little fool like you—who's been spoiled and pampered all her life—wouldn't be interested in what *anyone* has to say. You should have been put over a knee and spanked years ago."

She put her hands on her hips. "I suppose you think you're the one to do it?"

"No, lady, I'm not going to spank you, but I'd sure as hell like to give you a swift kick in the rear. I've been trying to keep you from getting hurt, but you're hell-bent on destruction."

"If I am, that's my choice. You've got nothing to say about it." She started to turn away. "Once I **find** Antonio, I'll—"

At the mention of her lover's name, he lost control. Grasping her by the shoulders, he swung her around to face him.

"Take your hands off me," she ordered. She attempted to hit him again, but this time he grabbed her hands.

Pulling her against him, he forced her arms behind her back so that their bodies pressed together, their mouths inches apart. "I don't want to hear that name again."

"Or you'll what?" she challenged, glaring defiantly. Both had gone beyond the bounds of caution in their battle of wills. "Antonio! Antonio! An—"

His lips plummeted down on hers in a hard, punishing kiss. As she struggled to free herself he increased his hold, pressing her even tighter against the length of him. She whimpered under the assault of his bruising lips, and he raised his head, glaring down at her.

"Before I leave this room, I'll hear my name pass your lips with the same fervor as you say his."

He frightened her, but she refused to cower. "Never!"

"We'll see about that." Reclaiming her lips, he released her arms, crushing her to him.

Trying to push him away, her efforts faltered as she became overpowered by the pure manliness of him: his strength, his male scent, the pressure of his lips. Blood pounded in her brain and ears, throbbed at her pulses. She drew a deep, shuddering breath when his mouth left hers to trace a moist trail down her neck.

"Say it, Raven," he whispered against the pulsating hollow of her throat.

When he slowly pulled the dress off her shoulders, she felt a rise of excitement. "My beautiful, beautiful Raven," he whispered, trailing warm, moist kisses across the swell of her breasts.

The heady sensation was making her dizzy. Before she could cry out in protest, his mouth returned to her lips and his tongue explored the recess of her mouth, sending erotic shivers shooting to her spine. Surrendering to the divine sensation, she lost all awareness of when she ceased the struggle—of when anger no longer was the issue, of when passion left reason behind.

"Oh, God, Raven, say it. For the sake of our sanity, say it," he murmured in a hoarse plea.

Opening her eyes, she gazed into his tortured face. What would be gained by denying it any longer? The mere nearness of him excited her. She longed for his touches—the arousing warmth of his palms felt as powerful an aphrodisiac as his kiss.

"Cleve." The word came out in a loving sigh, dredged from the depth of her heart and the throbbing demand in her loins.

This time his kiss was tender, caressing. She melted into the sweet hunger of it, succumbing to the drugging effects of its promise as his hands roamed over her, impatiently shoving the gown and petticoat past her hips.

I must stop him; this was wrong—improper. No lady allows a man such intimacies before marriage.

She raised her hands to shove him away just as he released her corset and dipped his head. His tongue tantalized the nubs of her breasts, and he took one into his mouth. Charged currents of sensation shot through her, and she clung to him as he gave her other breast the same erotic concentration. It felt divine, the most sublime feeling she had ever known. God forgive her, but she never wanted it to end.

Adriana's escalating passion far outweighed reason. She dropped her arms and threw back her head.

Cleve picked her up and carried her to the bed. Laying her down gently, he quickly shed his vest, yanked off his tie, and started to unbutton his shirt.

The wait had become unbearable; she reached up to him with outstretched arms. He couldn't resist the invitation. Lying down, he slipped his arm under her back and drew her against him. His kiss was long and arousing as he filled his hand with her breast.

"Cleve," she sighed.

His name on her lips was music to his ears, an elusive melody that had played in his head from the first time he saw her. Raising his head, he gazed down into her eyes, slumberous with desire. "Are you sure you're ready for this, Raven?"

"Yes, Cleve. Yes."

He rained kisses on her cheeks, her eyes, her parted lips, returning to her breasts to tug a hardened nipple into his mouth. Raising his head, he murmured, "No more talk of Antonio . . . or flying away, Little Raven."

His words thrust into her mind like a wedge driven between them, accomplishing what her earlier reservations had not.

"Cleve, wait," she said breathlessly. "There is something I have to tell you."

She couldn't go through with this without being completely truthful with him. It would only lead to more trouble. If she gave in to her desires, they would have to be married. And how could she do that, when she had deceived him with one lie after another? She had to tell him now—explain about Antonio, and her father's prejudice toward *Anglos*. Her *papá* would never accept an *Anglo* gambler for a son-in-law, instead of the wealthy Count Miguel Castillo.

"Cleve, I can't let you do this. We must stop." This time she had the moral determination to shove him away.

Oh, God! Don't do this to me, Raven! He looked at her, experienced enough to know that the thought of making love had become the farthest thought from her mind.

"I'm sorry if I've offended you, Raven. I understand why you—"

"Cleve, stop. It's nothing you did. It's me. I haven't been honest with you. Antonio is not my lover. He's my brother—my twin brother."

Cleve sat up, too stunned to say anything. He didn't try to stop her when she got out of bed and hastily pulled on her nightgown and robe. By the time she had picked up her strewn clothing, he found his voice.

"Why didn't you tell me? You led me to believe—"

"I know. I thought it best at the time not to reveal my

true identity. I didn't want word of my whereabouts to get back to my father."

"Why in God's name did you come here in a wedding gown?"

"I told you that my father had arranged for me to marry a man I do not love. Shortly before the ceremony, I received Antonio's letter telling me to come here. I had to make my escape when I had the chance. You assumed that I came here to marry Antonio; I never said I did."

"I'm not the only one who made that assumption, Adriana," Cleve said, exasperated. "You sure as hell didn't try to clear up the confusion."

"I told Father Allegro the whole truth."

"Good for you," he scoffed. "At least you didn't lie to a priest."

"I didn't lie to anyone!" she exclaimed. "I found that it was convenient not to deny all your misconceptions, that's all."

"You lied to me about your name. You said it was Paloma."

"It is—Adriana Adelina Paloma Maria Fuente y de Elbertina."

"Kind of dropped part of it, didn't you?"

"I've already explained my reason for doing that." She looked at him beseechingly. "Cleve, my father can be very ruthless. And I have defied him. He won't hesitate to use his influence or power to get what he wants."

"You should have trusted me enough to tell me all this sooner."

"In the beginning, I didn't know who I could trust." She looked at him beseechingly. "You? Lily? Magdalena? I just had to keep on perpetuating the deceit, and hope I would find Antonio before my father found me."

Walking over to her, Cleve grasped her by the shoulders and said gently, "I feel bad that you had to fight this all alone, Señorita Adriana Adelina Paloma Maria Fuente y de Elbertina." He tilted up her chin and kissed the tip of her nose. "What do names matter anyway?" Pulling her into his arms, he murmured, "I meant it when I said I care about you, Raven."

"I think you should leave, Cleve," she said, stepping out of his arms. "I must think. We came so near to making a dreadful mistake. There's still my father to consider . . . and Antonio. I must find him, Cleve."

"All right. I understand." He didn't, of course. He wanted to tell her that what was growing between them was of greater importance. But he was a patient man. Aching at the moment, but patient. He couldn't see how her father or brother had anything to do with his making love to her. His only consolation was knowing that the elusive Antonio was not his rival after all.

"We'll find your brother, Raven. But it's not over between us—it's just the beginning. You know that as well as I do." He pulled her back into his arms. "So are you sure you want me to leave?"

Adriana nodded.

"You know, I intend to keep on trying to make love to you," he warned with an endearing grin.

His charm was too infectious to ignore. "I know you do. But now I'll be prepared for it. You can bet on that."

Cleve picked up his vest and tie. "I can see, brown eyes, where you and your brother have a lot in common—you both tend to raise the pot against a guy holding all the aces."

Later, as Adriana lay in bed thinking about Cleve, she couldn't help smiling. It had taken a quarrel to make her admit to both him and herself how much she cared about him. And they had come so close to making love. She felt a hot flush, recalling their passion in those fervid moments. She had been shameless! How would she ever be able to resist him when it happened again? And it would happen—he had warned her as much.

So this was what being in love was like.

His touch, his kiss, the feel of his hands and mouth on her body! It had all felt so divine.

Why had she allowed anybody to stand in the way of her happiness? She certainly hadn't when she fled from her wedding and jumped on the stage to Fort Worth.

Did she love Cleve MacKenzie enough to forget any other considerations?

Chapter 11

Adriana waited nervously for Cleve to join her in the kitchen. She knew it would be difficult to look him in the eye after last night. Since there was no avoiding it, she just wanted to get the embarrassing moment over with.

As she prepared breakfast, Burt Waverly arrived with the milk and eggs. "Got some news for you, little lady," he said, carrying the milk jug to his cart.

Adriana followed him outside as he filled the jug. "You mean about Antonio?"

Burt nodded. "Met a fella who said he saw a man what fits your brother's description with a rancher named Carlos Valez."

"Where can I find this Valez?" she asked, dogging his heels as he lugged the milk back inside.

"Seems this fella's got a spread due west of here, 'bout fifty miles or so." He pulled a folded paper from his pocket. "Fella drew me this map. He don't know the exact whereabouts of the ranch, but he said there's a tent town near it called Devil's Dip. Somebody there oughta be able to tell ya."

"I can't thank you enough, Burt," Adriana said, ecstatic.

As soon as he departed, Adriana sat down at the table to study the makeshift map. At last she had a possible lead to Antonio's whereabouts! Tucking the letter into her skirt pocket, she returned to preparing breakfast, but she could barely keep her mind on the task at hand.

Lily had already joined her by the time Cleve came downstairs. Adriana avoided looking at him.

"Good morning, lovely ladies." He lightly kissed each of them on the cheek. "Beautiful day, isn't it? The sun's shining, the birds are singing . . ." He trailed off with a sweep of his arm toward the outside.

"What's got into you?" Lily groaned. She leaned her head in her hands. "This is pretty hard to stomach so early in the morning."

"Sounds like our Miss Lily may have overimbibed last night."

"No, I didn't overimbibe, boss man. My head aches; that's all. And I'd sure like to know the reason you're so chipper this morning." She grinned with a knowing smile. "Something happen that you're not telling me?"

Adriana almost dropped the pan she was holding. "Well, I have something to tell you," she quickly remarked. Before she could tell them the good news about Antonio, she was interrupted by a knock on the door.

Lily opened it and was greeted by Buckwheat Flour. "Mornin', Miz Lily."

"Good morning, Buck."

"Sorry to be botherin' you folks this time of day, but I'm lookin' to talk to Cleve."

"He's right here. Come on in."

Buck stepped in and doffed his hat.

"Morning, Buckwheat," Cleve said. "I don't believe you've met Miss Fuente."

"My pleasure, ma'am," he said to Adriana.

"So what brings you around so early?" Cleve asked.

"Mind steppin' outside a minute, Cleve? Got somethin' I think you should know."

"Will you join us for breakfast, Buck?" Adriana asked.

"Appreciate the offer, ma'am, but I'm short on time."

Cleve left the kitchen with him. "What's on your mind, Buckwheat?" he asked as soon as they were outside.

The ranger unhitched his horse. "Thought you'd want to know that some of the Walden gang's been hangin' around a town west of here near the Brazos. A few of us are headin' there to round 'em up."

Cleve's eyes lit up. "I'm coming with you."

"You best take that up with Capt'n Wolf. This is Ranger business, and the captain don't want no civilians trailin' along. I've gotta get goin' now." The ranger climbed up on his horse. "If Walden's among 'em, I'll let you know."

"Good luck, Buckwheat. And you take care."

Cleve stared after the ranger until he was out of sight; then he went inside. Adriana and Lily had already sat down to eat. He joined them but barely spoke. After observing his preoccupation for a couple of minutes, Adriana figured he had no idea what he was eating. She looked at Lily, who arched a brow and shrugged.

"What are you thinking about, Cleve?" Adriana asked. When he didn't answer, she repeated, "Cleve?"

He looked up. "I'm sorry. What did you say?"

"Just what did that ranger tell you, boss man?" Lily asked. "Since you talked to him, you seem to have something on your mind."

"Buckwheat said some of the Rangers are going after the Walden gang. I'd like to be in on it." He shoved away from the table. "Think I'll go speak to that Ranger captain."

He was out the door before Adriana could tell him the news about Antonio. She thought it wouldn't have mattered much anyway, since Cleve was so interested in that gang. She'd just have to check out Mr. Waverly's lead herself.

"Lily, do you have any money?"

"A little. Why?"

"I need enough to rent a horse."

"I have enough to do that, but why in the world do you want to rent a horse?"

"Oh, Lily, Mr. Waverly brought me the most exciting news this morning. He knows where I can find Antonio."

Lily looked at her reflectively. "So you've finally located your Antonio." She gave Adriana a guarded look. "Uh, where does that leave Cleve? He's crazy about you, you know."

"Lily, Antonio is my brother."

"Your brother! Wow, you sure had us fooled!"

"Forgive me for not being honest with you, but it's very complicated. I'll tell you the whole story when I get back."

"Does Cleve know the truth?" Lily asked, grinning.

"Yes. I told him last night."

"No wonder he was so chipper this morning!"

Adriana could hardly contain her excitement. "But I just can't wait to see Antonio."

"I'm happy for you, Princess."

"I have to get ready to leave." Adriana hurried up to her room. Since she had no riding skirt, she'd have to make do with the skirt she was wearing. After tying back her hair, she grabbed the shawl off a hook and dashed from the room.

"As soon as I find Antonio, I'll pay this back to you," Adriana promised when Lily gave her the money.

"I just hope Burt Waverly isn't getting your hopes up for nothing," Lily said. "I'd hate to think this is a wild-goose chase."

Adriana kissed her cheek. "*Gracias*, Lily. You are a good friend. I must leave now."

"You tell that old busybody to take care of you, honey," Lily warned.

"Oh, Mr. Waverly isn't going with me," Adriana said, already halfway out the door.

"Hey, wait a minute. Get back in here. Who is going with you?" Lily demanded.

"I'm going alone. Mr. Waverly drew me a map." She dug the paper out of her skirt pocket. "You see, Mr.

Valez's ranch is located near a town called Devil's Dip." She refolded the map and returned it to her pocket.

"I didn't realize you intended to go alone, Adriana. You can't ride off by yourself. You're not familiar with this territory. At least wait for Cleve and see what he thinks."

"Lily, I'll be fine."

Lily's distress escalated. "I don't like this at all. Why can't you wait until Cleve gets back? I'd never have given you the money if I knew you were going to ride off on your own like this."

"Dear Lily, are you not on your own?" Adriana said, trying to console the agitated woman. "You take good care of yourself, don't you?"

"What I do is no example for any girl. Besides, I'm not as impetuous as you are, Princess. I stop and think of what's best for me before I do anything. And the one thing I don't ever have to think about is riding around the countryside alone. I'm too smart for that."

"You're not going to convince me to stay, Lily," Adriana said affectionately.

"You could at least stay long enough to clean up all these messy dishes you made, instead of expecting me to do it."

"I'm not fooled for a moment, Lily. You're just trying to stall."

"Well, I don't understand why you won't wait for Cleve to get back. He only went to speak to some ranger."

"That could take all day. Who knows?"

Lily sighed in resignation. "Cleve's sure right about one thing. You're a stubborn little fool, Adriana Adelina . . . and whatever the rest of it is. You be careful, Princess," she warned.

"I will. Besides, what could happen? I've been riding for almost my whole life."

Lily went to the door and yelled after her, "I ain't talking about falling off any horse."

Adriana practically ran the few blocks to the stable. The old livery man, Pete Behlings, looked at her strangely when she asked him about the trail to Devil's Dip. "You ridin' out that way by yourself, lady?" She nodded. "Pretty lonesome country out that way for a lone gal."

Adriana had often ridden alone in the area around San Antonio. Much of that terrain was desolate and treacherous. She'd seen no evidence that this part of Texas was any different.

"Sir, it has been my observation that most of Texas is bleak."

Apparently the remark did not sit well with Behlings, who looked old enough to have ridden behind Sam Houston at the battle of San Jacinto. A spray of tobacco juice narrowly missed splattering her foot. "Sounds like some of that there sedition talk to me."

With a disapproving glance at the damp stain near her feet, Adriana stepped aside and ignored his comment. "Are there hostile Indians in the area?"

"Ain't heard of none for a couple of years."

"Then I see no cause for concern."

"All right, lady, I'll saddle up that bay mare over there. Reckon she's gentle enough."

"Sir, I've been riding since I was a child," she informed him with haughty disdain.

"That long, huh!" the old-timer said. "Reckon that was 'bout last year." Adriana's natural instinct for survival enabled her to dodge another missile of tobacco juice.

Behlings walked over and grabbed a canteen off a hook. "While I saddle up the mare, go out to the pump and fill this up. I'd hate to see ole Blondie here goin' dry."

"Sir, I can assure you, I will take proper care of your horse." She snatched the canteen out of Behlings's hand and did as he asked.

Five minutes later, Adriana rode west.

* * *

For the past half hour, Cleve had managed not to lose his temper. After all, a calm argument got better results than a shouting match. He kept hoping that he could convince the Ranger captain that he wasn't just a hothead out for revenge. But so far, his arguments were falling on deaf ears.

"Sir, all I'm asking is for your authority to join your Rangers in capturing Charlie Walden."

"I'll be glad to swear you into the Texas Rangers, Mr. MacKenzie, if that's what you want."

"I'm not interested in becoming a Ranger, Captain Wolf. I just want to assist your men on this mission. Charlie Walden led the gang that raped and murdered my mother and sister-in-law six years ago."

"Mr. MacKenzie, please believe that I sympathize with you, but Walden's behind many other crimes as well. If we allowed every man who has a grievance against Walden to go gunning for him, we'd be condoning murder. Let the Texas Rangers handle it."

"The issue is more than just holding up a stagecoach or rustling a few cattle, Captain Wolf."

"I understand that. Even if it were permissible, though, it's too late. I've already dispatched four of my men."

"Four Rangers against the Walden gang?"

"We have no idea how large a gang it is. Some witnesses have said six; others swear it was ten. You can see, Mr. MacKenzie, that without knowing for certain what we're dealing with, I can hardly risk the life of a civilian."

"I'm willing to take that risk, Captain Wolf, and it sounds like your men could use an extra gun."

"I'm sorry, Mr. MacKenzie. I won't consider it. I insist you stay out of this matter. Now, if you'll excuse me, I have some business to attend to."

Cleve had no choice but to leave.

It was almost noon by the time Cleve returned to The Full House. After pouring himself a cup of coffee, he sat down at the table. For a morning that had begun so brightly, the day sure had gone sour. He glanced up glumly when Lily came into the kitchen.

"Oh, you're back!" she said. "I was beginning to think you went with those Rangers."

"Naw. Swifty threw a shoe on the way back. I ended up walking about ten miles; then I had another hour's delay waiting to get the horse reshod."

Lily sat down. "You have any luck at the Ranger office?"

"Yeah, but it was all bad. I was told to either become a Texas Ranger or butt out. I'd have been better off just following those Rangers without asking permission. Now, I'm officially ordered not to get involved. Dammit!" he swore. "My brother Flint would have followed his own instincts and got there ahead of those Rangers. I was a fool to try and do it legally."

"Cleve, I hate to tell you this when you're feeling so down, but there's something else that I don't think you're gonna like."

Cleve glanced across at her. "What is it?"

"It concerns Adriana."

"Yeah. What about her?" His look and voice were guarded. "Where is she anyway? Upstairs?"

"No, she went in search of her brother."

"Think I'll go find her. Did she say she was going to the doctor's office or the church?"

"I'm afraid it's neither, Cleve. She rented a horse and is on her way to some ranch. Burt Waverly told her that a man matching her brother's description was seen with this rancher."

"What's the rancher's name?"

"Carlos Valez."

"I've met most of the local ranchers, but that name's not familiar to me."

"I'm not sure he's a local rancher, Cleve. At least, the map she showed me didn't look like he was."

Cleve began to get a sinking feeling in his stomach. "How far away do you think it is?"

"I don't know. It looked quite a distance on the map."

"Where in hell did she get the money to rent a horse?"

Lily looked sheepish. "From me."

"Dammit, Lily, I thought you had more sense."

"She didn't tell me the whole story until after I gave her the money. Give me credit for that much, Cleve."

"Did Waverly go with her?"

"No, she went alone."

"Sonofabitch! That woman is impossible! The only one I know who goes looking for trouble more than she does is my brother Flint. What was the name of the nearest town?"

"It was Devil something. Devil's Ditch or—"

"Devil's Dip!"

"Yeah, that's it," Lily said.

Cleve jumped to his feet. "How long ago did she leave?"

"Right after you did."

He took the back stairs two at a time and dashed to his room. Within minutes, he had shed his black frock coat and trousers for a pair of jeans, shirt, and vest. Then, after strapping on his gunbelt, he grabbed his rifle and hurried back down the stairs.

"Will you please tell me what in hell is going on?" Lily demanded.

"Adriana's riding right into a gunfight between the Texas Rangers and the Charlie Walden gang! I'm checking at the livery and then heading out to try to catch up with her. You're on your own tonight."

She followed him out to the hitching post. "We'll take care of it, Cleve. I'll get Waco to help." When he swung up into the saddle, she said worriedly, "You be careful, boss man."

Cleve reined up his horse in a cloud of dust at the livery.

"What's your hurry, Cleve?" Behlings asked. "You got a posse on your trail?"

"Pete, did a young woman rent a horse from you this morning?"

"You mean one of 'em uppity Spanish *criollo* gals that look down their noses at ya?"

"Then she's been here?"

"Yep. Rented a horse and asked about the trail to Devil's Dip. I told her not to go, but she 'peared like the kind who weren't partial to takin' anybody's advice."

"How long ago did she leave?"

"Reckon four or five hours. Why? You goin' after her?"

When Cleve started to ride away, the old man said, "She's ridin' a bald-faced bay, son. But Blondie gets winded easy, so that gal ain't gonna get there too fast."

"Thanks, Pete."

"And tell her to remember to give the old gal a drink. Hate to think of Blondie bein' thirsty," Behlings shouted after him.

Goading his dun to a full gallop, Cleve sprinted down the road.

Chapter 12

"**S**o your name is Blondie," Adriana said as she sat in the shade of a large oak tree, staring at the winded horse. "Well, Blondie, I don't think we have too far to go. Then you'll be able to rest longer."

For several hours, she had been riding along the narrow trail. It meandered through the rolling flatland of tall grass, broken by an occasional stretch of woods abounding with towering oak and leafy sumac. Although it was not a scenic route, it was easy to follow, and she anticipated the end when she would ultimately find Antonio.

Thinking about the half-eaten omelet she had left on her plate that morning made her mouth water. How good that would taste now, instead of the pecans she had gathered from a nearby tree. Adriana picked up a rock and cracked several more shells. Leaning back, she dug the meat out of the broken halves.

Why hadn't she brought along something to eat? As Lily had said, she was too impetuous. In the future, she had to plan things out instead of acting so hastily.

Rising to her feet, Adriana brushed off her hands and clothes. "Well, Blondie, I think you've rested long enough. This time, old girl, let's try to get at least ten miles without having to stop again." Climbing on the back of the horse, she continued on her journey.

Adriana reached Devil's Dip near dusk. From what

she could observe, the town consisted of several dozen tents and a few wooden buildings. At least a half dozen of them appeared to be taverns or bordellos.

After eating a plate of horrible-tasting stew, made from Lord knows what, Adriana asked the waiter for directions to the Valez ranch. He assured her there was a trail leading to the ranch house.

She was disappointed to find out she still had another hour's ride ahead of her. Convinced she could reach the ranch before nightfall, though, Adriana started on her way again.

Unfortunately, Blondie appeared to have no such intention. Despite Adriana's constant prodding, the stubborn horse would not allow herself to be hurried. Adriana had covered only half the distance by the time the sun set. If not for the full moon, she couldn't have followed the trail.

Suddenly the sound of gunfire broke the stillness. Adriana reined up in alarm. There seemed to be a heavy gun battle going on somewhere ahead of her. She was at a loss to know what to do. Her common sense battled with her instinct, torn between turning around and going back to the town, or riding forward to reach the ranch and the protection of Antonio.

After what seemed an eternity, but in truth was only a few moments, the firing stopped. She strained to listen, but all was silent. Peering ahead through the dusky shadows, she could see nothing but the deserted trail. She started off at a slow trot, her heart pounding in rhythm with the measured thud of her horse's hoofbeats.

After about a quarter of a mile, she approached the edge of a wooded grove. As she drew nearer, she thought she heard a sound. Reining up, she looked toward the obscured shadows and listened intently. Soon, she distinctly heard a low moaning. Then it stopped. She waited, looking around for any sign of movement. Giving Blondie a gentle prod, she proceeded cautiously.

All of a sudden the mare reared, and Adriana jerked in fright as a riderless horse trotted out of the shadows. Seeing that the animal was saddled, she knew it wasn't a stray—the horse and the gunfire were related, and instinctively, she realized the pooled stains on the saddle were blood. Looking around and hearing nothing, she rallied her courage, climbed down, and walked over to the trees.

"¡Dios mío!" she murmured, quickly crossing herself as she stared in horror at four bodies on the ground. Dazed, she moved from one to another, checking for signs of life. Finally, she felt a heartbeat in the last man. He was bleeding from the shoulder. Her hands trembled as she removed the bandanna from around his neck, made a compress, and stuffed it into his shirt. The face of the unconscious man looked familiar, and she recognized him as the Texas Ranger Cleve had introduced her to that morning. Stunned, Adriana glanced around and realized the dead men around him must be Rangers, too. Who could have done this to them? That gang he'd mentioned?

"Adriana!"

Startled, she spun around and stared in stunned disbelief at the man before her, then collapsed gratefully into the arms of Cleve MacKenzie. "Cleve! Oh, thank God, it's you."

"Raven!" he whispered. "When I heard the shots, I was afraid that something had happened to you." He hugged her tighter against him. "What went on here?"

Adriana drew a shuddering breath. "I don't know. I just got here myself. These dead men must be Texas Rangers. Buck Flour is still alive, but he's wounded."

"Buckwheat!" Cleve released her. He knelt over the body of his friend. After a cursory examination, he said to her grimly, "He's sure lost a lot of blood. Buck, can you hear me?" The wounded man groaned softly and moved his head. "Raven, get the canteen from my saddle."

She ran to do his bidding and hurried back.

"Buckwheat, can you hear me?" Cleve asked. He poured a few drops of water on the man's face.

The ranger opened his eyes. "That you, Cleve?"

"Yeah. Don't try to move, Buck."

"What about . . . the others?" Buck asked.

Cleve shook his head. "Sorry, Buckwheat. What happened here?"

"We were bushwhacked. Rode right into their trap." He sighed and looked at Cleve wearily. "Let me sit up, Cleve. Don't cotton to lyin' here waitin' to die."

"You're too ornery to die, you old coot, but you're bleeding pretty badly. We've got to get you back to that tent town." He folded his own bandanna over the one Adriana had already put on the wound. Then he helped the ranger to sit up and drink. "You feel strong enough to ride, Buck?"

"Reckon so."

"Then let's get you back to that town."

Adriana brought the horses over. Seeing the chestnut gelding next to Adriana's mare, the Ranger managed to chuckle. "Figured you wouldn't leave me, Strawberry."

"He's too weak to ride alone. Let's get him up on my dun," Cleve said to Adriana. "You can lead his horse."

After they helped Buck into the saddle, Adriana mounted her horse and Cleve tied the reins of Buck's chestnut to her saddle horn. Climbing up behind Buck, Cleve enfolded the wounded man in his arms and took the reins.

"We ain't gonna leave the others, are we?" Buck asked in a weak voice.

"I'll get a wagon in town and come back for them, Buckwheat."

"I'd appreciate that, Cleve," the ranger said, then slumped forward in the saddle.

"He's passed out. Let's go, honey."

They rode in silence back to Devil's Dip.

There was no doctor in town, but with the help of a midwife, Cleve removed the bullet from Buckwheat's shoulder. The ranger was soon sleeping peacefully.

At dawn, while Cleve drove a wagon back to the grove to recover the bodies of the slain Rangers, Adriana fell asleep on a chair near the wounded man's bed. By the time she woke up, Cleve had returned. Adriana washed her face and prepared to leave.

"Where are you going?" he asked.

"Now that it's daylight, I'm riding out to the Valez ranch to find my brother."

"Oh, no, you're not," Cleve declared. "It's too dangerous."

Adriana shook her head. "I don't want to quarrel, Cleve. I intend to go, and you can't stop me."

"I suppose not," he said, but his grin said otherwise. He sat down in the chair and pulled her down on his lap. "Sweetheart, I don't want to quarrel, either." He kissed her lightly, then traced a moist path to the sensitive hollow behind her ear. Erotic shivers raced down her spine. "I just want you to think clearly about this," he whispered, his warm breath fanning the hair at her ear.

"How can I think clearly when you're doing what you're doing?"

"What am I doing?"

"You know what. You're deliberately trying to distract me by what you're doing with your lips," she replied breathlessly.

"What I'm doing with my lips is kissing you, my love, because I enjoy kissing you. And I'd want to be kissing you whether we were having this discussion or not. I'm trying to persuade you to kiss me back. It's even more enjoyable then." He claimed her lips in a long, drugging kiss. Finally he drew away. "See what I mean?"

"I haven't changed my mind, Cleve," she declared breathlessly.

"Raven, sweetheart, it's too dangerous at this time. That gang is probably still around."

"But Antonio is only an hour's ride away, Cleve. I'm too close to turn back now. Won't you come with me for protection?"

"Don't you think it's more important right now to see that Buck gets proper medical attention, and that we get those Rangers' bodies back to Fort Worth? Then we'll come back, Raven."

She closed her eyes in despair. Everything he said made sense, but she was so close, she hated to turn back. He tipped up her chin, and she opened her eyes. His gaze was warm, his smile persuasive.

"Hey, sweetheart, I know what you're thinking. But you don't even know if your brother can be found at this Valez ranch. Waverly told you it was someone who fits Antonio's description. No one specifically identified your brother."

She couldn't quarrel with the logic of his argument. And when he looked at her the way he was now, she couldn't resist him. Conceding, she sighed deeply. "I suppose you're right."

Leaning her back, he cradled her head in the crook of his arm. "These gangs never stay around one place too long. As soon as it's safe, we'll come back and find your brother."

"Promise?"

"Promise," he murmured just before his mouth closed over hers.

"Sure glad you two settled your differences," Buck said.

They broke apart and looked at the ranger.

"How are you feeling, Buck?" Cleve asked, releasing Adriana.

She sat up, and they both went over to the bed.

"Reckon it ain't my time to cash in," he said. "Sure feel bad about the others, though. We rode a lot of trails together."

"How'd you let them bushwhack you, Buckwheat?"

"Reckon we all had our heads on crooked and just weren't thinkin' straight. When we didn't find any of 'em in town, we figured we'd take a look around. Didn't think nothin' of it when we rode up to this fella drivin' a wagon in plain sight, headed to town. Should have guessed it was a trap. Looked like their own man even got cut down in the crossfire."

"I didn't see any wagon tracks, Buckwheat," Cleve said.

"Well, there was one there all right, and I saw that driver take a bullet."

"Maybe he wasn't one of the gang?" Adriana suggested.

"Oh, he was one of 'em all right, or they'd have left him behind like the rest of us. I'll know him if I ever see him again. Good-lookin' fella. Young Mexican or Spaniard. I ain't gonna forget his face."

"Did you say he might have been a Spaniard?" Cleve asked.

"Mex or Spaniard. I can't tell 'em apart. But I'll sure as hell know him when I see him again."

"Well, we better think about moving out of here. The wagon's loaded," Cleve said. He didn't envy the wounded man, having to lie in the wagon bed with the bodies of his dead comrades. "It's not gonna be a pleasant ride for you, Buckwheat."

"Reckon not. But we rode out together. It's only fittin' we ride back together, too."

Tears glistened in Adriana's eyes as she leaned over him and kissed his cheek.

Buck grinned weakly. "Man don't need no better healin' medicine than that."

The livery man helped Cleve carry Buck to the wagon. Cleve thanked him and tipped him for his help. "I'll see that the Rangers return your wagon and team," Cleve told him.

He tied Swifty and Blondie to the back of the wagon, and they rolled out. To keep Buck as comfortable as possible Cleve kept the team moving slowly, so they didn't reach the town until nightfall. By the time they stopped at the Ranger office, said their good-byes to Buck, and stabled Swifty and Blondie, it was past midnight.

Covering her mouth to stifle a yawn, Adriana could

barely keep her eyes open. *The poor kid,* Cleve thought with affection. She had come upon that bloody massacre and then had only a few hours' sleep, sitting up in a chair. With still a three-block walk to The Full House, he picked her up. Adriana didn't protest, but merely slipped her arms around his neck.

Expecting that Lily would have closed up for the night, Cleve was surprised to see an amber light glowing from the front window. Cleve entered the casino with Adriana snuggled asleep against his chest, and stopped in his tracks, staring in surprise at what greeted him.

Lily was standing behind the bar. After observing the six *vaqueros* who were sitting at tables or leaning against the wall, Cleve's gaze came to rest on the two Spaniards seated at a table in the center of the room.

One of the men jumped to his feet and stood in an angry stance, staring at him. Lean and short, the man appeared to be in his late fifties. He looked imperious, from the European cut of his expensive suit to his neatly trimmed gray hair and beard. The man's black eyes were as cold and hard as marbles.

The younger man with him rose slowly to his feet. Possibly a decade or two younger than his companion, the tall, handsome man had dark, wavy hair and a short, impeccably groomed goatee. His expensive Spanish-style gray jacket and fitted trousers complemented the man's lean and sinewy body. His manner was arrogant; the look in his eye was one of disdain.

Before Cleve could say a word, Lily spoke up. "Cleve, this is Adriana's father, Don Alarico Fuente." She arched a brow. "He arrived last night."

The older man asked with concern, "Is my daughter—"

"Fine, sir; she's just sleeping. I'll take her upstairs and put her to bed."

"You will do no such thing, *señor,*" Don Alarico declared.

Cleve took another sweeping perusal of the eight

men staring at him. He lightly shook Adriana. "Wake up, honey," he said softly in her ear. The intimacy of the gesture set a muscle twitching in the don's cheek.

Adriana slowly opened her eyes. "Are we home yet?" she asked sleepily.

"Yeah, sweetheart, we're home. And we've got company."

Chapter 13

A driana lifted her head and looked around. Her eyes rounded with shock when she recognized the *vaqueros*; then her gaze came to rest on the face of her father.

"*Papá!*" she exclaimed, slipping out of Cleve's arms. "How did you find me?"

The older man regarded her with a grimace of displeasure. "Thanks to my dear friend Don Francisco, it was not difficult."

That damn Elena! Adriana thought. She should have expected it. The little toad never could keep a secret.

Her father shifted his cold glare to Cleve. "Your name, *señor?*"

"Cleve MacKenzie, sir. I'd like to explain—"

"Do not offend me with your explanations, *Señor* MacKenzie."

"I feel one is in order, sir. However bad this may look, I can assure you the circumstances are perfectly innocent."

"*¡Silencio!*" the don roared in a sharp command.

The man beside the don walked over to Cleve and Adriana. "My dear Adriana," he acknowledged with a curt bow of his head.

"Count Miguel," she said.

He then looked at Cleve and abruptly gave him a light slap in the face with his glove. "The Count Miguel

142

Enrique Felipe Castillo y de Rey at your accommodation. You may choose the weapon, *señor*."

Astonished, Cleve looked at Adriana and then back to the count. The man had actually slapped him in the face! "I may *what?*" he exclaimed.

"I demand satisfaction, *señor*. Since I have made the challenge, you may choose the weapon."

"You mean a duel?" Cleve began to chuckle. "You're challenging me to a duel!"

"You laugh in the face of death, *Señor* MacKenzie. I admire your courage, if not your integrity," Count Castillo said. He looked down his nose at Cleve. "Are you so primitive that you presume to offend a lady's honor and expect not to pay for the affront?"

"Well, now, I'd hate to offend anyone's honor and all that, but I don't deal in duels, Castillo. Too *primitive* for me. I have no intention of fighting any duel with you."

"Is that so?" the count remarked. He slapped Cleve again. "Perhaps I can convince you to change your mind."

"You keep that up, mister, and I'm going to beat the hell out of you," Cleve said through a clenched smile.

"I take that to be a refusal, *señor*. I can only assume you are a coward, as well as a cad. I withdraw my hasty opinion regarding your intrepidness."

"You know, Castillo, ordinarily I don't let myself get goaded into shooting down foppish, loudmouth idiots. But you keep this up, and I just might have to reconsider." As though pondering the thought, Cleve paused for a split second. "Tell you what, Castillo," he continued. "Since you're so game for a duel, I've decided to give you as much satisfaction as you can handle."

The count raised a brow in interest. "I am listening."

"Here's the deal," Cleve said in good humor; then the smile left his face. "Touch me one more time, and I'm going to wipe up this floor with that fancy suit of yours—and you'll be in it when I do."

The count didn't blink an eye. He glanced at Adriana's father. "What is your wish, Don Alarico? This coward refuses to settle this like a gentleman."

"What more can you expect from these *Anglos,* my dear Count? Leave the matter in my hands; I shall settle this," the don said.

"Don Alarico, my dear Count," Cleve said, mocking their pretentious manner. "You two are long on reminding each other of your titles and importance, but you're both sure short on common sense."

"*Señor,*" the don exclaimed, "I am—"

"Jumping to conclusions and challenging people to duels that could get you killed before you find out the facts," Cleve interrupted. "Now, if you *gentlemen* will excuse me, I intend to take Adriana upstairs. She's had a very terrifying and exhausting experience in the last couple of days."

"No, Cleve," Adriana said. "I wish to remain."

"Leave the room, Adriana," Don Alarico ordered.

"*Papá,* Mr. MacKenzie has been—"

"You heard me," he declared.

When she made a motion to move, Cleve put a restraining hand on her arm. "I believe the lady prefers to stay, sir."

"Her preference is of no importance to me," the don said impatiently.

"It is to me," Cleve said calmly. He looked around him, assessing the six *vaqueros* who were standing alertly, waiting for a command from their leader.

"What you wish, *Señor* MacKenzie, is of little significance to me."

"With all due respect, sir, this is my establishment. I don't take your orders. And I would do an injustice to my mother's memory were I to permit you to continue vilifying a lady's name under its roof."

"Your actions with my daughter speak for themselves. You have destroyed my daughter's reputation and treated her like a common *puta!*"

"That's not true, sir. She has done nothing shameful."

"Has she not just spent the night alone with you? What of the other nights she has been here?"

"Miss LaRue can vouch for the fact that we all have separate rooms."

"You expect me to accept the word of a common—"

"Hey, watch it, Pop," Lily objected. "As long as I keep my opinion about you and your dandy friend to myself, I expect the same courtesy!"

Anger blazed from the don's dark eyes. "Enough has been said on this matter," he said impatiently. "You have blemished my daughter's honor and reputation. There can only be one proper end to it."

Don Alarico issued a sharp command to one of his *vaqueros*, and the man left the casino. Then the don addressed Cleve. "You and Adriana will wed immediately—this night. I have summoned a priest." He walked back to the table and sat down. His bearing proclaimed the issue closed.

Cleve glanced at Adriana. She looked pale and confused, and had remained silent throughout the conversation. It was clear to him that she was still intimidated by the arrogant man. "I believe Adriana has a say in this matter, sir."

"My daughter has nothing to say. She is responsible for creating the situation."

Cleve squared his shoulders and faced the overbearing *criollo*. "I don't agree. From what I've observed of your attitude, I'm inclined to believe that *you* may be the one responsible. Perhaps this situation is best discussed in private, Don Alarico. Will you join me in the kitchen? You have my word I will not harm you or make any attempt to leave."

The don smirked. "The word of a—"

"MacKenzie, sir."

The restrained anger in the response must have finally gotten through to the don; after a brief hesitation, he nodded.

"And tell your *pistoleros* to relax. The games are over for tonight."

Once Cleve had closed the kitchen door behind them, he faced the imperious man. "Don Alarico, I want to make several things clear to you, the first being that there is not a power on earth that could force me to marry Adriana if I didn't want to. But I am in love with your daughter, so I am willing to wed her as you wish. Furthermore, despite what you believe, she has not been dishonored. She came here looking for her brother, and we took her in to keep her off the streets. As for last night, she rode off to Devil's Dip alone yesterday morning. I followed in the hope of protecting her. I'm not a cad who takes advantage of a helpless female, sir."

Don Alarico broke out in mocking laughter. "Then you must be a fool, to believe my daughter is a helpless female. She is a spoiled, headstrong young woman who never considers anything except her own wishes. Both she and her brother have always been a source of great disappointment to me. But this time, she has gone too far. She has dishonored her family's name and insulted Count Castillo by running away on the day they were to be wed."

"Obviously, she is not in love with the count."

"That is of no importance. The marriage had been arranged for years."

"Where I come from, we let the woman make up her own mind about who she'll marry."

"You *Anglos* do not understand our culture, and I have no inclination to explain it to you. I grow impatient, *señor*. Do you have anything else to say?"

"Yes, I do. From the first moment I met her, it has been my intention to wed Adriana."

"No doubt. The daughter of a wealthy rancher would hold great appeal to one in your profession," Don Alarico said with scorn.

"There you go again—jumping to conclusions. I knew nothing of Adriana's background. But you and I are not at cross-purposes; I am perfectly willing to marry the woman I love. If she is agreeable, we will wed tonight. If not, there will be no marriage."

The two men's gazes locked. For a moment, Cleve thought he saw a fleeting look of respect in the don's eyes.

"Furthermore, you and the count have pushed my good nature a mite close to the edge. You rave on about how you and the count have been insulted, yet the method you chose to *welcome* me into your family is an insult—to Adriana, to yourself, and to me. Believe me, Don Alarico, whether or not you would sanction our marriage is of no concern to me."

"I can assure you, *Anglo,* that if you had not compromised my daughter, I would never consider this marriage. I have no desire to see her wed to an *Anglo* gambler. However, considering my daughter's actions, I cannot expect Count Castillo to wed her. If you are the man of honor you claim to be, it is your obligation, *señor.*"

"This has nothing to do with my honor or obligations, Don Alarico," Cleve said, shaking his head. He realized the man was simply too arrogant to comprehend the situation. "Tonight I'll do as you wish, but only if it's agreeable to Adriana. And, if so, this will be the last time you will interfere in her life."

Cleve spun on his heel and returned to the barroom.

As soon as Cleve and her father left the room, Adriana slumped down in a chair at one of the tables. Miguel Castillo walked over to the bar and ordered a drink.

"I'd like to see the color of your money first," Lily declared.

Count Castillo looked down his finely shaped Castilian nose and regarded Lily with a look of contempt. "I beg your pardon, madame."

"Just call me Lily," she said. "Two bits, Count." She held out her hand for the money.

"Are you implying you will not serve me until I produce a coin? Madame, I am the Count Miguel Enrique Felipe Castillo y de Rey. I come from one of the oldest and finest families in Spain."

"Yeah, yeah, I'm real impressed," Lily said. She continued to hold out her hand. "Two bits." Indignant, the count slammed a gold dollar down on the bar.

Lily poured him the drink. "Have you been in Texas very long, Count . . . whatever?"

"Miguel Enrique Felipe Castillo y de Rey," he repeated.

"We don't stand on formalities, Count. So, have you been here long?"

"Not at all. Fortunately." He downed his drink.

She shrugged her shoulders. "Then I reckon I don't have to waste time asking how you like it here. So you're from Spain. Pretty far away, isn't it?" She refilled his glass.

"Yes, it is, besides being a civilized country."

"You speak pretty good English for being in Texas only a short time."

"I seem to be the only one in Texas who does," he said with a supercilious smile.

"No need to apologize, Count." Lily appraised him. "You sure had me fooled. Who'd have thought you were hiding humility under that tight jacket and pants you've got on."

"Perhaps some day, I'll have the opportunity to prove to you just what else I have under these tight pants," he said with a suggestive smirk. "In the meantime, permit me to buy you a drink." He picked up the bottle, poured her a drink in the glass she handed him, then refilled his own glass again.

"You know, Count, in my business, I've observed that it don't much matter where a man comes from or what he does. Rich or poor alike, they seem compelled to prove their worth with the same kind of . . . ruler."

The count threw back his head in laughter. "Rulers

may be designed similarly, my dear Lily, but such devices can have different *attributes*."

She smiled. "Sounds like some of our tall tales might have rubbed off on you after all. Exactly how long have you been in Texas, Count Miguel?"

"Six months."

"Then you really don't know much about Texans, do you?"

"Much to my credit, that is true."

When he reached for the bottle again, Lily picked it up. "Sorry, your money ran out." She leaned over the bar and whispered, "Confidentially, Count, let me tell you something about Texans. You made a big mistake when you slapped Cleve MacKenzie in the face."

She walked down to the other end of the bar.

Unable to hear what they were saying, Adriana watched the exchange between Lily and Miguel, wondering what they had found to talk about so intently. And when Lily walked away, Adriana noticed how Miguel's lingering look followed her.

Waiting nervously for Cleve and her father to return, Adriana listened to two of the *vaqueros*, who were spinning the wheel at the gaming table and pretending to make bets. While everyone appeared to be relaxed, she could feel the tension that hung in the room.

Suddenly the kitchen door opened, and her heart leaped to her throat when Cleve came out. Her father followed a few steps behind, which was uncommon for him: Don Alarico never played the role of follower. She wondered what Cleve had said to cause this. Whether invited or not, she now wished she'd gone with them into the kitchen, because whatever Cleve had had to say most certainly would have concerned her.

Glancing at him, she saw that his hair was rumpled and his chin was covered with a dark stubble of whiskers. He looked tired, and she realized he had not slept for two days. But he still walked tall, she thought with admiration.

What did he think about being forced into marrying her? He clearly wanted to bed her, but only once had he ever even joked about marrying her.

She shifted her glance to her father. He looked stormy and ill-natured—a look she had often seen when things did not go as he had planned. What could Cleve have said to him? Could he have talked her father out of this forced marriage? She was the only one who did not have a say in the matter.

With a wary eye, she watched Cleve approach. "I have to talk to you, Adriana." He took her hand and led her into the curtained alcove.

"Honey, your father insists your reputation has been compromised, and demands we marry tonight. I told him I would marry you, but only if it's agreeable to you."

His last words caught her by surprise. "What if I said I don't want to marry you?" she challenged.

"Then we won't go through with the ceremony."

"Will that be acceptable to my father?"

"I doubt it."

"What can he actually do if we both refuse?"

"Adriana, whatever you're thinking, I won't be a party to your being forced into doing something you don't want to."

"So, you'll resist. Does that mean there'll be bloodshed?"

"What do you think? You know your father better than I do."

The images of Antonio, of Pedro Moreno, and the faces of others who had tried to resist her father flashed through her mind. Many innocent people had been hurt or destroyed by his oppressive dominance. She couldn't allow Cleve to become his next victim. "Yes, I know my father," she said sadly. "We'll wed tonight."

Cleve cupped her cheeks in his hands and gazed down into her eyes. Lowering his head, he kissed away the tears that had begun to slide down her cheeks.

"You ready, honey?" She nodded.

When they stepped out of the alcove, she saw that Father Allegro had arrived and was in deep conversation with Don Alarico. Cleve took her arm and led her over to the two men. "Adriana has agreed to wed, but she would like to freshen up first."

"I grow weary of these delays," the don said.

"It's my wedding, *Papá*. Surely you wouldn't deny me the small privilege of preparing for it," she accused.

"Don't try one of your headstrong schemes, Adriana," her father warned. "Others will suffer if you do."

She looked at him with loathing, then climbed the stairway. Lily hurried after her.

"Look, Princess, there are a lot worse things than being forced to marry Cleve MacKenzie," Lily said as soon as they were alone. "There are dozens of women who would love to be in your place right now." When Adriana didn't reply, Lily added, "I know you don't like being forced into marriage, but at least it's not to that arrogant count!"

Still Adriana remained silent as she shed her bodice and skirt, then scrubbed the trail dust off her face and hands.

She sat woodenly on the edge of the bed and let Lily unwind the braid in her hair. "Princess, I wish you'd say something," Lily said as she began to brush out Adriana's long hair. "You're acting downright spooky."

"No matter where I go, there's no escape, Lily. His power is everywhere," she murmured in a dull voice, as Lily helped her into the voluminous folds of the white wedding gown.

Finally, Adriana put on the mantilla, replacing the expensive, pearl-encrusted comb intended for the lacy headpiece with the cheap comb Cleve had bought for her at the marketplace. At the last minute, Lily dashed out of the room and returned carrying a blue garter. "Here. Lift your foot and let me slide it on you. You gotta wear something blue for luck."

When Lily finally finished, Adriana surveyed her reflection in the cracked mirror. "You're a beautiful bride, Princess," Lily said.

"Yes, a beautiful bride," Adriana repeated numbly. She turned away and walked from the room, her body held stiffly.

All eyes stared up at her when she paused at the top of the landing. Cleve moved to the foot of the stairway, smiling at her as she descended. As she neared the bottom, he reached up and clasped her hand—firmly, protectively.

Then he led her over to the priest.

Throughout the ceremony, Adriana remained rigid and stared ahead as if in a trance, somehow managing to answer on cue. But for the most part, Father Allegro's voice was only a soft drone in her ears.

When the ceremony ended, she felt Cleve's hand enfold her icy fingers in his warm grasp. Glancing down, she stared dazedly at their entwined fingers. Then she looked at her father. His expression was inflexible—not one sign of remorse or compassion.

"I shall never forgive you for this, *Papá*," she said impassively. Then she turned away and walked up the stairs.

Chapter 14

Cleve waited until he heard the door above close; then he walked over to the bar. Lily poured each of them a drink. "May I be the first to congratulate you, Cleve. It is what you wanted, isn't it?"

"Yes, but not under these circumstances. My bride is on the reluctant side right now."

Glancing at the door, he saw Don Alarico and his *vaqueros* departing without so much as a backward glance. Turning back to her, he picked up his drink. "Pleasant chap, isn't he?"

"Takes all kinds, boss man," Lily said wisely. "Hate to tell you, but one of them is coming back."

Miguel Castillo reentered the bar. "You forget something, Count?" Lily asked. "You better hurry or your friends will leave without you."

Castillo extended his hand to Cleve. "*Señor* MacKenzie, I believe it is customary to congratulate the groom."

Cleve looked at the count, quizzically.

"Since the bride was my betrothed, it appears the better man did win, as they say. I, myself, would never have accepted damaged goods."

Ignoring Castillo's outstretched hand, Cleve put down the glass. "And I recall, Count Castillo, you told me I could choose the weapon." He drew back and punched the man in the face.

The force of the blow knocked the Spaniard off his

feet, and Miguel Castillo landed on his rear end. He sat stupefied as Cleve walked away and climbed the stairs.

Lily went over to the dazed man, who was clutching his right cheek. Kneeling beside him, she lifted his hand and examined the injury. She shook her head and put a cool cloth on Castillo's reddening jaw. "I warned you it was a mistake," she said with a knowing smile.

"Come in," Adriana said, when the light rap sounded on the door. She glanced up impassively when Cleve entered.

"They're gone." Cleve came over and sat down beside her on the edge of the bed. When he picked up her hand, she quickly withdrew it.

"Please don't touch me."

"Are you blaming me for this, Adriana?"

"No, it is not your fault. I just want to be alone. I hoped you'd understand."

"I'm not sure I do. I don't understand what's going on between you and your father, but I'm not stupid. It's easy to see there's a hell of a lot more to it than just a shotgun wedding. Since I'm involved, I'd like some answers."

Adriana stood up and walked away. "I don't want to talk about it. I'd be grateful if you'd leave me alone right now."

"You want me to leave! Good God, Adriana, I'm your husband now. This is our wedding night!" He followed her and put his arms around her, drawing her back against him. "Sweetheart, there's nothing to be nervous about," he said gently and traced a trail of light kisses down her cheek.

Adriana remained impervious to his touch. From the time they returned that evening, and she had looked across the room into the unrelenting eyes of her father, she had felt a continuous rise of this troubling emotion. Was it anger? Resentment? Confusion? She couldn't distinguish it. She only knew she felt stripped of her dignity and self-respect. Didn't she have anything to say about her own destiny? Who were these others who could decide her fate: her father, who considered his own wishes over anyone else; Miguel Castillo, interested only in restoring his honor; Cleve MacKenzie, this man who was now her husband, presuming to declare his conjugal rights?

What of *her* rights? When in the course of the evening had her rights been made a consideration? Oh, yes! Cleve had implied the marriage was her decision to make. That was laughable! If she had refused, most likely Cleve would have been killed, and she herself banished to a convent.

Oh, Antonio! Antonio! If only I could have escaped like you. Why didn't you take me with you?

"I know the events of the last couple days have been disturbing to you." The hum of Cleve's voice penetrated her musings. How long had he been speaking? Why didn't he just get out and leave her alone as she had asked? She needed privacy—time to think. She lunged out of his arms.

"Yes, they've been very disturbing, Cleve. I need to be left alone, so please go."

"I'll leave, Adriana, if that's what you wish. But we're man and wife now. Whatever is bothering you, we should be talking about it and trying to work it out together."

"My father's been doing this type of thing as long as I can remember," she cried out in frustration. "Not only to me, but to others. Forcing his will upon people by threatening their lives."

He grasped her shoulders, turning her to look at him. "I realize we weren't married under the best circumstances, but that doesn't mean we can't build a good marriage out of it. Whatever your father's done in the past, he can't hurt you anymore."

Clasping her hands between his own, he led her over to the bed and they sat down. "Raven," he said in a softened tone, "in all the madness of the last couple days, at last we're being given the chance to create some measure of sanity. Your father's out of it. Whatever happens from now on is between you and me. I believe we can build on what we have."

"You don't understand at all," she lashed out defensively and stood up, starting to pace the floor. "You sound as narrow-minded as my father. Don't you see that the issue here is choice? *I never had a choice!* My life. My future. If those things didn't matter to me—were not even worthy of considering—I could simply have remained in San Antonio and married Count Castillo!"

"I suppose you could have. Instead, you're married to me. Like it or not, that's how the cards were dealt. But I'm a gambler, Raven. I don't believe in throwing in a hand unless it's a losing one."

"What makes you think this one isn't?" She looked away from him to gather her courage. "Why not have the marriage annulled?" she asked hopefully. "After all, we haven't consummated it."

"Don't even think it."

"I don't need your permission, Cleve."

"Maybe not. But I don't cotton to it." He walked over to her. "Besides, I've got a much better idea," he said gently, putting his hands on her shoulders.

Realizing his intent, she shook her head. "No, Cleve. It's no good. I really want this marriage annulled. It can't ever be what it should be."

"Try giving it a chance, sweetheart," he said, beginning to run his fingers through her hair.

Perplexed, she stared into his earnest gaze for a few seconds, and then her temper flared. "You haven't understood one thing I've said. First *Papá*, now you— you're both only interested in forcing your will on me!"

Cleve dropped his hands. "I'll tell you what, Raven. I'm prepared to wait until you're comfortable with our arrangement. You forget your talk of annulment, and I will agree to be a very patient man. Do I have your word on it?"

"Very well," she said, exasperated. At the moment, as usual, she had no choice.

Cleve released her arms. "Then you have my word I won't touch you until you're ready. I can't say this is how I planned to spend my wedding night, Mrs. MacKenzie." Despite his derisive tone, she could tell he was relieved that they had reached an agreement.

"Be assured this was not how *I* envisioned my wedding day, either."

"I guess this evening's been one disappointment after another." He walked to the door.

"Cleve," she called out softly. He stiffened and paused with his hand on the doorknob. "I'm sorry. I know this isn't your fault. I just need time to think out this situation."

He turned around slowly and looked at her. "Well, since I'm sitting in on this game, Raven, I figure the deal's gotta pass to me sometime."

As soon as the door closed behind him, Adriana knew she had made a mistake. She threw herself down on the bed, battling with her own conscience. Cleve was not to blame. She had just pointed a finger of guilt at a man who had shown her nothing but kindness. And in so doing, she had again played right into her father's hands—allowed him to interfere in her life. By making Cleve an involuntary accomplice, her father was driving a wedge between her and Cleve.

Santa Maria, please help me. What am I to do? I'm so confused.

Returning to his room, Cleve plopped down on the bed, bunched up the pillow, and lay with his hands tucked under his head. He needed time to think about his so-called marriage. What a laugh his brothers would have if they knew of his predicament. Oh, he had been so sure of himself. Had all the answers! He'd know that *right* woman the moment he saw her, the moment she walked through the door. Had he really fallen in love with Raven at first sight, or had he just convinced himself that he had?

In his confusion, he was certain of only one thing: he

sure as hell wanted her, and since they were married, he intended not to delay that moment too long. But for now, he'd try and make the best of the situation. That meant not issuing her orders and ultimatums. The poor kid had had enough of that from her father.

At the moment, the best bet was to put the whole thing out of his mind and get some sleep. Tomorrow morning he'd approach the situation with a clear head.

Sitting up, he hung his legs over the side of the bed and pulled off his boots, glancing up when the door opened. Raven stood in the doorway dressed in only a thin nightgown. A rush of hot blood shot through him from brains to loins.

She stepped in and closed the door, leaning against it for support. "I have something to say before I lose my nerve."

"Your nerve about what?"

"About our marriage. About you and me."

"If it's about an annulment, I think I made myself pretty clear."

"I'm not clear about anything, Cleve. How I feel about you. My father. Our marriage. I'd like to believe that you love me, and that I love you. But I'm not clear on that either. The only thing that I know for certain is that my father dragged you into this against your will. Instead of being grateful to you, I took it out on you. I was wrong to do that."

"No harm done," he said, trying to sound more nonchalant than he felt. His stomach had started to flip-flop.

She faced him guilelessly. "I thought about us, Cleve. I want to be your wife. That means sharing your bed, too. And I wish you'd kiss me before I lose my nerve altogether, because I don't know what else to say."

He was at her side in an instant, pulling her into his arms. Her body tingled from the contact. His hand on her cheek was gentle, his eyes warm with tenderness.

"You don't have to say any more," he told her.

"That's all I have to know right now—that you're here because you want to be. Anything else, we can work out later."

His mouth covered hers possessively, the feel of his lips a delicious sensation that coursed through her like a hot tidal wave. Instinctively, she parted her lips in response to the firm pressure, and his arms tightened around her, drawing her closer. Her thin nightgown was a flimsy barrier against the heat and hard outline of his body, and his exciting male scent added to the assault on her senses.

"Raven, I don't understand what caused this change of heart, but at the moment, I don't care," he whispered against the pulsing hollow of her ear. "I just want to love you."

"I want you to, Cleve," she murmured. She eased her head back, giving him a freer access to her neck, and he responded to the enticement with a slow tantalizing sweep of his mouth and tongue. Releasing the buttons of her gown, he slid it off her shoulders and down her arms. It dropped in a heap at her ankles.

She blushed as his torrid gaze swept her body, and with maidenly modesty she shifted her eyes downward.

"Sweet heaven, Raven, you're even more beautiful than I imagined."

The husky murmur buoyed her courage and brought a resurgence of desire. She slipped her arms around his neck, inviting a kiss. He devoured her mouth hungrily until they were both breathless. Then, as if she were weightless, he swooped her up in his arms and placed her on the bed. The tantalizing pressure of his body followed.

"Raven."

She gazed momentarily into the warmth of his sapphire stare before spilling her love in a smile. Drawing a quick breath, she waited for the slow descent of his mouth. This time his kiss was harder, more demanding, his tongue exploring the recess of her mouth and sending shivers of desire spiraling through her. She responded openly, mindful only of him and the thrill of his kiss.

Raising his mouth from hers, he slid his lips to her ear. "You're so beautiful, Raven."

"You make me feel that way, *querido*."

He reached out and cupped her breasts, then slowly skimmed his hands along her sides. The sensation was sublime, engulfing her in a feeling of delirium.

Lowering his mouth to her breasts, he teased the sensitive peaks with his tongue. When he took a nipple into his mouth, she arched against him, sucking in her breath at the feel of the slide of his warm hand across her stomach.

"Cleve!"

Continuing the sensuous torture on her breasts, he began to massage the sensitive chamber of the most private part of her body, and his probing fingers sent jolts of erotic sensation spiraling through her. She whimpered beneath him and wanted to cry out for him to stop, but feared that if she did, he would. The exquisite furor in the core of her sex tightened like a coil and continued to build until it burst, flooding her with waves of mindless tremors.

She burrowed against him, and he held her in his arms until her rapid breathing ceased. Then, raising his head, he covered her mouth in a passionate kiss, and she felt the quickening within her begin again.

"Don't stop," she pleaded when he pulled away. She reached out to him in protest. "Please don't stop."

Cupping her cheeks in his hands, he gazed down tenderly at her. "Sweetheart, I have no intention of stopping. I couldn't if I wanted to. I've thought about this from the first moment I saw you." Finally able to release the passion he had fought to control, he moved just far enough away to quickly shed his remaining clothes, then returned and stretched out alongside of her.

The wide, muscular brawn of his body was a magnificent sight to her. Cleve made no effort to stop her when she curled her fingers over his broad shoulders and followed their slope into his firm chest. Feeling the rapid surge of his heartbeat, she grew bolder and began to toy with his nipples; then, curious, she licked the tip of one nub.

The quick intake of breath broke his silence. Glancing at his face, she saw he was watching her intently. A faint sheen of perspiration glistened on his forehead, but he remained silent and motionless. Suffused with desire, only his eyes revealed the effect she was having on him as she licked the other nipple. This time, his groan was all the invitation she needed to continue. She tugged at the nipple with her teeth, just as he had done to her.

His body felt taut under her touch as he held himself in check. Sliding her fingers along the curve of his waist, she traced them across the flat plane of his stomach, feeling his muscles jump beneath her fingertips. Then she halted, unable to rally the boldness to lower her hand any farther.

"Finish what you started, Raven," he whispered hoarsely. "It's just another part of my body, sweetheart."

"I don't know if I can."

He took her hand and curled her fingers around his organ. It felt hard and hot, and pulsated in her hand. The strength and the feel of him excited her, intensified her own arousal.

"Gently, honey," he warned when her grasp tightened.

She released him, and he rolled over on top of her. "Oh, Lord, sweetheart, I want to learn every inch of you," he said, lowering his head to her breast.

Within minutes her breath was reduced to ragged gasps. Barely able to think, she gripped the cold, hard grill of the brass headboard as her throbbing body writhed under the mastery of his kisses and touch.

"Raven, I can't hold out any longer. Open for me,

love," he murmured, as his hand sought the pulsating chamber at the junction of her legs. "I'm sorry, love, but this will hurt you for just a few seconds," he whispered apologetically.

Suffused in passion, she was beyond caring. "Cleve, I came to your bed as a woman. Don't talk to me now as if I'm a child."

He kissed her deeply as, raising himself, he eased into her. Adriana stiffened, and cried out when he ruptured the thin membrane. Smothering her outcry with a tender kiss, Cleve finally felt her relax, and he knew the pain had ceased. Instead of resisting, she tightened around him.

"Now our wedding waltz begins, my love," he whispered.

With their bodies linked together, his hands and mouth reignited the rapturous ecstasy, until the tempo of their dance escalated into a driving impetus. Adriana felt a glorious release at the instant his body vibrated with rapid tremors. And as his hot liquid filled her for the first time, she faintly regretted that she could never know this sublime moment again.

Fighting to regain his breath, Cleve lay back and closed his eyes, his chest rising and falling in rapid rhythm. In the afterglow of their loving, Adriana's gaze worshipped his handsome profile. Lily was right, she reflected; Cleve was the handsomest man she had ever seen.

As if he felt her stare, he turned his head to look at her. "What are you thinking about, Raven?"

"How handsome you are," she replied honestly.

Rolling over, he cupped her cheek in his hand and stared down into the full measure of her adoration. Then, lowering his head, he pressed a gentle kiss on her lips and each of her eyelids.

"We'll have a good marriage, my love. I promise you. Your father may have forced you to wed me, but I'll never give you cause to regret it."

"I have no regrets, Cleve. I worry more that you do."

"No regrets, Raven, but we've got a lot of plans to make. I've got to figure out what to do with you, my little wife. We can't keep living here."

She raised her head and looked at him. "Why not? It doesn't matter to me, Cleve."

"Well, it does to me. This is no place for you." He kissed the tip of her nose, then pulled her down beside him. She settled against him with her head on his chest.

"First off, though," he said, "I want to take you home to meet my family."

"Where is home, Cleve?" she asked, sighing as his hand stroked her back and spine.

"Farther upstate, northwest of here, near a little town called Calico."

"Was that where you were raised?" she asked, pressing a kiss to his chest.

"Yep. My brothers and their families live there now. Luke and Honey have an eight-year-old son, Josh, and they're expecting a baby in a month or so. Flint and Garnet have a son, Andy, who just turned a year old a short time ago."

"Do you think they'll like me, Cleve?"

"They'll love you, Raven."

She suddenly sat up. "I'm so happy! But before we leave, we must go to the Valez ranch. I cannot abandon my search for Antonio." She suddenly stopped and said in a soft voice, "That is, if you agree, my husband."

Cleve chuckled and tousled her hair. "Raven, my love, there's no need for you to play the docile wife. I don't want you to change. I love you just the way you are."

Her eyes glowed with delight. "Do you, Cleve? Do you really love me?"

For a moment, he stared at her, startled by his own words. They had flowed out of him naturally—and, he realized, they were heartfelt. All his previous doubts vanished with the uninhibited release of those few simple words. He had been right; he'd loved her from the beginning. Smiling up into the anxious look in her brown eyes, he pulled her head down until their breaths mingled. "Yes, sweetheart, I really love you," he murmured right before his mouth claimed hers.

His lips felt warm and exciting. But everything about him excited her. His mere touch sent a shiver down her spine, and when he gathered her closer, a delightful, tingling sensation coursed through her. Breathless, they parted, and their gazes locked as they breathed as one.

"We know so little about each other," she murmured, enthralled. "Cleve, have you been married before?"

"No," he said, covering her face with slow, tantalizing kisses.

"Why not?" she managed to ask, despite the provocative toying of his tongue at her ear.

"Dunno. Reckon I never felt a shotgun barrel at my head before," he teased, shifting his mouth to her neck.

"Oh, Cleve, you know . . ."

Her words fell away as his tongue and teeth on her neck raised magical, erotic sensations. Under the heated flush of renewed arousal, she managed to ask him one burning question in a quivering whisper, "Have you ever been in love before?"

Raising his head, he smiled down at her. "I've loved you all my life."

He knew she didn't understand, but some day he would explain it to her. Before she could ask, he sealed off the query with his mouth.

Chapter 15

"**G**oddammit, Lattimore, I told you never to come here!" Charlie Walden cursed. "And then you ride right up to the ranch. Why didn't you just bring the Rangers with you?"

"Aw, boss. I ain't that dumb. I checked my trail before I rode in here."

After looking around to make sure they hadn't been observed, Charlie closed the barn door. "What the hell did you come here for, Lattimore?"

"Lopez is hurt real bad, boss. He was drivin' the wagon when we ambushed them Rangers, and he needs a doctor. We can't take him to that vet doc in Devil's Dip 'cause the town's full of Rangers."

"Really! Now just why do you suppose the town's full of Rangers, Lattimore? Do you suppose it's got something to do with your gunning down four of them?" Disgusted, he turned and walked away.

"Well, Lopez needs help right away."

"What do you expect me to do about it?" Charlie snarled.

"Thought you'd want to know. He's hurtin', boss, and he'll die soon if we don't get him to a doctor," the outlaw said.

"So shoot him and put him out of his misery."

"I can't kill him," Lattimore whined. "Lopez and me are friends. We've been ridin' together a long time."

"Then have one of the other boys do it for you. If you weren't so damn stupid, Lattimore, you wouldn't be in this fix. Killing those Rangers is going to bring a dozen of them roaming these parts. Why didn't you just draw them a map and invite them to dinner?" Charlie said angrily. "I've spent a lot of time and money setting up this cover. You've probably ruined it all by killing those Rangers."

"We didn't have no choice, boss. They came gunnin' for us."

"And if you'd kept on riding, they'd have gone back to Fort Worth. Instead, you get in a gunfight practically right on top of the ranch." Charlie shook his head in frustration. "I swear you were born without a brain. Thanks to your stupidity, in the next couple weeks the Rangers crawling around these hills are gonna be thicker than ants."

"You got no call to be talkin' to me like that, boss. You would have done the same thing if you'd have been there."

Charlie slapped him across the face. "Shut up, you stupid fool! I'm trying to think." He began to pace the floor nervously, kicking at the straw in his path. "Where are the rest of the boys now?"

"At the hideout."

"Well, get back there and pick a half dozen to stay here as ranch hands, or it'll look too suspicious. The rest of you head south to Nellie's. You go along to keep them in check." He stopped pacing to glare at Lattimore. "That means 'stay out of trouble!' Since we've been operating north of here, the Rangers'll probably start looking there first—unless you were obliging enough to lead them to the hideout."

"We didn't leave no trail," Lattimore declared.

"Get rid of Lopez's body after you kill him. Don't leave it lying where the Rangers can find it. I'll get word to you at Nellie's as soon as it's safe to come back."

As Lattimore started to leave, Charlie gave him a final instruction. "I want you all to stay out of trouble and keep your mouths shut. Tell the boys to forget they ever heard my name. If anyone asks, you all just got back from taking a herd to Kansas. Got that?"

Lattimore looked at him, confused.

"What?" Charlie asked.

"What if someone asks who we rode for?"

Charlie threw his eyes heavenward. "Make up a name, you damn fool!"

"Gotcha, boss."

"In the meantime, I'm going away for a while, too. I'll probably head for Dallas or Fort Worth and pretend I'm on a cattle-buying trip or something."

"Oh, that's smart, boss."

"Thank you. I'm flattered you think so." If the idiot didn't get out of there, Charlie was afraid he'd shoot him himself. "Get going, Lattimore, and remember what I said."

After Lattimore left, Charlie waited for a few minutes, then left the barn and returned to the house. He went into his study and opened his ledger books. Thanks to the shootout with the Rangers, he had to think about moving on, and the sooner the better. Those kill-crazy fools! They didn't even know you might get by with shooting a rancher or stagecoach driver—but you don't kill a Ranger! It'd be best to get out of the state altogether. But where to? Maybe completely out of the country—like England or France. There'd be little chance of anyone having heard of Charlie Walden in London, England, or Paris, France!

But he just couldn't pack up and ride away. He had too much money invested in the ranch. Disposing of his herd and livestock would be no trouble, but finding a buyer for the ranch could take longer.

People were getting uneasy in the area because of an outbreak of raids and killings by the Walden gang. Too bad he couldn't reassure a prospective buyer that all the bloodshed would stop as soon as he left the state. He grinned at his own witticism. That was funny. He sure had a sense of humor!

Charlie went back to studying the ledgers. To avoid suspicion, he'd have to draw his money out of the bank gradually—before he robbed it. He chuckled again. Goddamn, he was a funny man! Too bad the incompetents he dealt with continually put him in a bad mood.

Now he had to formulate a new plan. He'd claim his herd was rustled. That would set up an excuse for leaving. But the thing to do at the moment was to go away for a short time. If he wasn't around, he wouldn't have to answer any questions.

He felt the rise of anger again. All this trouble because of the blunders of a few louts! Why did he have to pay for their mistakes? Despite their incompetence, though, he needed them for the time being. Once he was away from the ranch, whoever the Rangers hadn't killed, he would. He hoped Lattimore would manage to stay alive until then—he wanted the pleasure of putting a bullet into that idiot's head himself.

At the sound of approaching footsteps, Charlie relaxed, his frown disappearing into a serene smile. "Come in, my son. Come in," he called out. "I've just been thinking about you." A master of dialects, he had replaced his normal soft Southern drawl with a Mexican accent. Lately he had been using this accent so often that his Southern speech pattern came out more as imitation than natural.

"Good morning, Carlos." Smiling, Antonio Fuente entered the room.

Chapter 16

"**H**ow long will you be gone?" Adriana asked as she sat on the bed, watching Cleve shove items into his saddlebags. Waking up after her wedding night to find her groom packing to leave town, had left her feeling quite stunned.

"I should be back tomorrow. Sweetheart, when I agreed to meet Captain Wolf at Jacksboro, I had no idea I'd be getting married last night."

"Why can't I go with you?"

"Jacksboro is just an army post. There'd be nothing for you to do while I'm tied up with business."

"There's not much more for me to do here," she lamented.

"I left you money on the dresser. Go shopping; you need clothes. Get yourself fitted for a couple of ball gowns and whatever else you need."

Her eyes brightened at the prospect. Then, recalling the delightful day they had spent shopping together in the plaza, her spirits drooped. "I'd rather do it with you."

"If you don't want to go alone, have Lily go with you." He strapped on his gunbelt. "As soon as I get back, we'll start making some permanent plans."

Pulling Adriana to her feet, he slipped his arms around her waist, his gaze worshipping her. "I'll be thinking about you every minute, honey." His mouth covered hers in a deep, drugging kiss. Savoring its sweetness, she wanted it to go on forever.

When they separated, he grinned down at her. "Remember, stay out of trouble while I'm gone. No stray dogs, cats, rabbits, or birds. And no protest signs! I told Lily to close the place if she wanted a night off."

"You leave me no choice except to go out and spend your money," she teased.

"I thought of one thing you can do for sure. Move your clothes into my room." Despite their night of loving, she blushed when he added, "The sleeping arrangements aren't the most convenient."

"But, Cleve, it's highly improper for a husband and wife to share a bedroom."

He cocked a brow. "Mrs. MacKenzie, in a MacKenzie household, it's improper *not* to."

He slung the saddlebags over his shoulder and grabbed his rifle. Then, hand in hand, they went downstairs.

His good-bye kiss made her miss him before he had even cleared the door.

Despite Cleve's absence, Lily opened The Full House that evening. One of the first to come through the door was Miguel Castillo.

"And how are you tonight, my charming Miss Lily?" Miguel inquired.

"Well, well! Count Castillo!" Surprised to see he had returned to the casino, Lily poured him a drink. "I thought you'd be on your way back to San Antonio by now." Strange as it seemed, she was rather pleased to see him—not that she would inflate his overlarge ego any further by telling him so.

"No, I did not leave with Don Alarico. I have developed a fondness for your city and decided to remain here for awhile," the handsome Spaniard said.

"I thought Texas was too primitive for your tastes, Count Castillo. Are you sure you won't need an interpreter?"

He picked up her hand. "Ah, Lily, I don't need anyone to interpret what is between us."

Momentarily disarmed by his sudden move, Lily glanced nervously at him. Desire gleamed in his dark eyes.

"Well, I sure need one, because I don't know what you're talking about." When she tried to pull her hand away, his fingers tightened around hers, and she felt an unexpected warmth from the contact.

"Please release my hand, or I'm going to have to call Waco over here. I'll warn you in advance: he used to be with the Texas Rangers, so you're liable to end up on your rear end again, with a new bruise on your face to match the one you're already wearing."

"Oh, but it will be worth the ache, *querida mia,* just to feel your gentle touch minister to my needs again." He kissed her palm and released her hand.

"That's a smooth line, Count, but you're wasting it on me. Try the Alhambra, down the street. You'll find plenty of gals there who'll be happy to offer you their 'genteel touch to *meeneester* to your needs.' "

"Now you mock me. Ah, you have a cruel heart, *querida mia.* But I will forgive you."

"Let's set the record straight once and for all. I am not your '*querida mia,*' Count Castillo. I know what you're after, and I'm not selling. Okay? Take your money elsewhere."

He clutched at his heart dramatically. "How you wound me, Lily. I would think a woman of your experience would be amenable to such an offer. Especially from a man of my rank."

"Your rank, all right. And I'd think a man of your experience would know when he's wasting his breath, Count."

"Miguel. You may call me Miguel, *querida.*"

The smirk on his face convinced Lily he was not taking her seriously. The swaggering peacock actually believed she'd be flattered by his proposition and would willingly lead him to her bed.

"Well, this is the way it is, Mike—"

She drew blood; he actually flinched. "Miguel," he corrected.

"You're in Texas now, Mike."

"Ah, you taunt me again, my dear Lily," he replied, his self-assurance restored. "But you do not fool me."

"About what?"

"You can't deny that last night a flame ignited between us."

"Well, thanks to you and your friends, there were a lot of sparks flying around here last night, but I figured I dodged all of them."

"I think not, Lily. I think you remember exactly what passed between us."

"I certainly do. It was a gold dollar for the drinks."

"Why do you pretend? You and I are both adults. We understand what passes between a man and woman, do we not, Lily?"

"We sure do. So how about you passing me twenty-five cents for the drink, Mike."

Smiling, he put down a twenty-dollar gold eagle. "Leave the bottle, *querida mia*," he said as she started to walk away. "I shall have to drown my disappointment in alcohol . . . for tonight."

She glanced back in response to the challenge in his last words. Miguel raised his glass in a salute.

After spending several hours at the couturier, getting pinned and poked to distraction, Adriana spent the rest of the day with the Guerras. Nightfall had descended by the time she returned to The Full House. Slipping in the back door, she decided to say good night to Lily, and peeked into the barroom. When she recognized the figure standing at the end of the bar, she drew back in surprise. Whatever was Count Castillo doing back at the casino?

Adriana glanced around the room to see if her father had accompanied the count. Seeing no sign of him or the *vaqueros*, she stepped into the room, suspecting that

Miguel had brought her a message from her father. "Count Castillo, what are you doing here?"

"Ah, Adriana," he said with a proper bow of his head. "I did not expect to see you. I would have thought you and your husband would be on *una luna de miel.*"

"How dare you speak of husbands or honeymoons, when you were a party to my father's nefarious deed!"

"My dear Adriana, have you forgotten how you embarrassed me on the very day we were to wed?"

"I would apologize for my actions, Miguel, but you deserved to be embarrassed. You knew I was opposed to marrying you, yet you did not concern yourself with my wishes—only with my father's, just as you've always done."

"Adriana, your youth encourages you to jump to conclusions that aren't always true. You were too young to realize the advantages of marrying me. Now what do you have? An *Anglo* gambler who doesn't even have the grace to fight a duel properly. I would have sliced him bloody with a rapier," he said smugly.

"And he probably would have filled you full of holes with a Colt revolver," she replied. "Remember, he had the choice of the weapon."

"Any duelist knows you can fire only one shot. Surely, despite their backwardness, these Texans are aware of that!"

"I think one shot is all he would need, Miguel."

"So, you have chosen to defend him despite your upbringing. The man is a cad, you know. He did not warn me he intended to resort to fisticuffs."

"So that's how you got that bruise on your cheek." Adriana tried to stifle her laughter.

"It appears that you are amused, Adriana. I can see you have been associating too long with these *Anglos.* These are not your kind of people."

"Oh, but you forget, Miguel. Thanks to you and *Papá,* I'm married to one." She spun on her heel and returned to the kitchen.

Her conversation with Miguel had angered her,

besides reminding her how much she missed Cleve. Tomorrow, she would prepare him a delicious dinner for his homecoming. Later, she would welcome him with something more appeasing to his lustier appetite as well. She blushed at her earthy thoughts.

Adriana went into the barroom to attempt another good-night to Lily. She saw that Lily was serving drinks to two men at a corner table, and waited at the bar for her. When Lily turned to come back, Adriana caught sight of one of the men. She stared incredulously, then broke into a smile of joy. "Antonio!" With outstretched arms, she rushed past Lily. "Antonio! Antonio!"

"Adriana!" Antonio Fuente bolted to his feet, and she flung herself into his arms. After a lengthy hug, he kissed her on the cheek. "¡No creo que eres tú, hermana pequeña!" Antonio exclaimed.

"Oh, I can't believe it either," Adriana replied as they hugged and kissed again. "I've been looking everywhere for you."

He took her hand. "Come, Adriana, sit down. I wish for you to meet my patrón, Señor Carlos Valez."

"So, at last I meet you, Adriana," Carlos said, rising to his feet. "The two of you look remarkably alike, my dear."

"Señor Valez," Adriana acknowledged.

She took a long look at her brother's companion. The handsome and distinguished man appeared to be at least twenty years her brother's senior. His dark hair and goatee were neatly groomed, and his clothes were expertly tailored to his tall and slender figure. His most riveting feature was his gray eyes. They were penetrating—but cold in comparison to the warmth of his smile.

"Your brother has spoken of you often, Adriana," Carlos said in a pleasantly modulated accent. "I feel I know you as well as I do Antonio."

"That is probably true, Señor Valez, for we are twins and have always been very close," Adriana replied.

"Apart we are only halves, but together we are a whole."

"And now we are together again," Antonio said, squeezing her hand. "Oh, how I've missed you, my sister."

Adriana saw Valez surreptitiously cast his steel-gray glance several times in Lily's direction. The covert gesture piqued Adriana's interest.

"But, Adriana, what are you doing here?" Antonio asked.

Adriana turned with a big smile to her brother. "My husband is here."

"¡Santa Maria! You are married!" he exclaimed.

"Yes, but it is a long story, Antonio."

"I must hear it at once."

Just then, Lily came over to the table. "I couldn't help but overhear you. So you have found your brother, Adriana. I'm so happy for you."

"Oh, Lily, isn't it wonderful? Antonio, this is my dear friend Miss Lily LaRue."

"My pleasure," Antonio said politely, although his surprise at the close relationship was apparent on his face.

"And this is my brother's *patrón, Señor* Carlos Valez," Adriana said.

Carlos had risen with Antonio. He slightly bowed his head. "*Señorita.*"

"Sit down, gentlemen. I have to return to my duties. I'm happy for you, honey," Lily said, smiling. She walked away. Once again Adriana noticed that Carlos's cold stare followed her.

"Oh, if only my husband were here to meet you." Adriana sighed. "He's away on business and will not return until tomorrow."

"But what are you doing in this place, Adriana?" Antonio asked in surprise.

"We live here. Right upstairs. Isn't it exciting?" she replied eagerly. "Lily has her own room, too."

Taken aback, Antonio hesitated, but apparently not wanting to quell her enthusiasm, he said, "Well, at least this place certainly looks different from before, doesn't it, Carlos?" He looked around absently, as if pondering something else.

"Indeed. Your husband has spent much money to improve it."

Adriana grabbed her brother's hand and squeezed it affectionately. "Oh, Antonio, I can't tell you how happy I am to see you. I've missed you so much, *mi hermano.*"

He turned back to her, covering her hand with his. "And I am overjoyed to see you, my sister," he said lovingly. "Now tell me, when did you marry?"

"Well, as you know, *Papá* had arranged my marriage to Count Castillo."

"Of course, from the time you were sixteen."

"Antonio, my young friend," Carlos said, interrupting them. "I think I will return to the hotel and leave you and your sister alone to enjoy your reunion. I can see that you have much to say to each other. I will see you in the morning. Perhaps we all can meet for a meal."

"Oh, I'd love that, *señor,*" Adriana exclaimed. "Perhaps by then my husband will have returned, and you can meet him."

"Then I insist. Antonio, arrange it." He kissed her hand. "It has been my pleasure to meet you, Adriana. I look forward to tomorrow."

After Carlos departed, Adriana and Antonio sat down. He clasped her hand and smiled lovingly. "I've missed you, *hermana pequeña.*"

"And I you, Antonio. After you left, I thought I would die from missing you. And *Papá* . . ." She shook her head. "*Papá* has become worse than ever."

His eyes clouded with sadness. "So he finally had his way, and you married Miguel Castillo."

"Oh, no! I didn't marry Miguel. Your letter arrived on the day I was to wed him. I ran away and came here looking for you. But you were gone, Antonio. I had no money and no one to turn to. Cleve MacKenzie, the man who owns the casino, gave me a job."

"A job!" he said indignantly. "You mean as a—"

"No, no. It is not as you think. Cleve does not run a brothel, Antonio. This is a gambling casino only."

"It is still no proper place for my sister. Is this Cleve the same *Anglo* who won it from me?"

"Yes," she said hesitantly, remembering the little regard Cleve held for Antonio.

"He cheated me to win it," Antonio declared.

Adriana's eyes widened in shock. "No, you are mistaken, Antonio. Cleve would not cheat to win. He is an honorable man."

"I tell you, Adriana, the man cheated me."

Shaking her head, she closed her eyes. "No, that cannot be. Do you know this to be true? Did you actually see it with your eyes?"

"No, not with my eyes. But I know he did, just by the way the *Anglo* taunted me."

"How you sound like *Papá*, Antonio," she said sadly. "If a man is an *Anglo*, then he must be dishonest. Just like *Papá* always said."

"Why do you defend this *Anglo*?" Antonio asked.

"Because I came to know him, Antonio. Cleve is my husband."

The air hissed out of his lungs. Astounded, he stared at her. "*¡Su esposo!*"

Adriana nodded. "*Papá* followed me here and made Cleve marry me last night, even though he had done nothing. But *Papá* would not listen to the truth. He cared more about how it appeared to others."

"*Papá* is here in Fort Worth!" Antonio exclaimed.

"No, he went back to San Antonio today."

"*Su esposo*," Antonio mumbled, still having trouble accepting the fact. "It is hard to believe that *Papá* would force you to marry an *Anglo*." He drew a deep breath. "And this *Anglo*—does he treat you well, Adriana? He will have to answer to me if he doesn't."

"I think Cleve has answered to the only Fuente he intends to, dear Antonio. He did not take kindly to being forced into a marriage. He did it only to avoid bloodshed."

"To himself, no doubt."

Confused, Adriana stared at her brother. It was unlike him to be so judgmental. "No, Antonio, the bloodshed of *Papá*'s *vaqueros*. What has happened to cause you to speak so bitterly? You have changed, my brother." She leaned forward to examine an ugly wound on his forehead. "And how did you get this injury? It appears to be very deep."

Antonio raised a hand to his forehead. "Oh, it is nothing. Just a clumsy accident. Carlos took care of it for me."

"You will have a scar, because you did not have it stitched," she warned.

"That will be just as well. My face is too pretty-looking anyway. I suffer much teasing because of it. On you, little sister, the look is very fetching. But on me, I think not."

"Tell me about your *patrón*, Antonio. How did you meet him?"

"I made Carlos's acquaintance right here when I owned The Full House. He would come in on occasion, and we struck up a friendship. On the night I left here, I met him nearby. He invited me to his ranch."

"Near Devil's Dip, is that not right?"

"Yes; how did you know?" he asked, surprised.

"I tried to reach you there but had to turn back because of a gun battle between the Texas Rangers and an outlaw gang. You are very fortunate to have such a friend. He seems very kind," she said.

"He is, Adriana. Carlos is everything *Papá* is not—thoughtful and caring. He treats all men alike. No man is lowlier in his eyes than another. But more importantly, my sister, he treats me with respect and listens to my opinions. He doesn't laugh or scorn me when we differ, like *Papá* did. But we don't differ—that is what is so beautiful; our minds and souls are *simpático*. At night, we often read together and discuss the book, or we play a game of chess. He says I am the son he had always hoped for."

"Doesn't he have a family?" she asked.

"Tragically, his wife and two daughters perished in a fire."

"Oh, how sad," Adriana said.

"Carlos grieves, but he is not bitter like *Papá*, Adriana. Nor does he try to point a finger of guilt."

"So you have found happiness with him," she said, tears glistening in her eyes.

"I have found my soul mate, little sister."

"I thought I was your soul mate, Antonio, the way you are mine," she said with a rise of resentment toward his newfound friend.

"You are, dear Adriana. You are my twin. But now that you are wed, you will soon put your husband's love ahead of ours."

"Never, Antonio. What we have is special. It takes two of us to make a whole. No one can ever hold the place in my heart that you do."

"The same is true for me, too, my little sister. Carlos may take the place of the loving father that I have always yearned for, but no one will ever replace you in my heart."

"Thank God we have found each other again," she sighed. "I felt so lonely without you."

They continued to talk quietly for another hour; then Antonio left to return to his room at the hotel. He promised he'd be back early the next morning.

After saying good night to Lily and Waco, Adriana climbed the stairway to her room.

It was late by the time Cleve left the livery and walked back to the casino. He entered through the back door. For a moment he hesitated, torn between checking in with Lily or going straight up to Adriana. The choice was an easy one, since Adriana had been on his mind all day. He had even chosen to ride back at this late hour rather than spend the night away from her.

He climbed the stairs and entered the dark room. Adriana lay asleep in his bed, her dark hair shimmering in the moonlight that graced her face. His stomach twisted in a knot. He walked softly across the room, hung his gunbelt on the bedpost, then removed his boots. His shirt and jeans followed, and he sat down on the edge of the bed. Leaning over Adriana, he pressed a light kiss to her lips, and she awoke to the heady sensation of his lips against her neck.

"Cle—" His lips cut off her startled exclamation, and she felt the rise of passion.

"Cleve, I didn't expect you back until tomorrow."

"I know; I couldn't stay away," he whispered, kissing the tip of her nose and then her soft mouth again.

He ached from wanting her, and she did not resist when he pulled the nightdress over her head. Cleve drank in her nakedness. Then, with the loving touch of an artist shaping the form of a precious sculpture, his hands traced the lines of her slender neck, soft shoulders, the thrust of her firm breasts, tiny waist, and the curve of her hips.

"Oh, God, *querido!* Your touch sets me on fire."

Lowering his head, he ran his tongue across the peaks of her breasts, then he shifted his gaze higher and saw her eyes studying him with unabashed boldness.

"What are you thinking about?" he asked.

She reached for his hand and brought it to her breast. "You. Feel my heartbeat, my love. It beats for you." Sliding her arms around his neck, she pulled him down beside her, then stretched out on top of him.

As the erotic pressure of the peaks of her breasts pressed into the firm muscle of his body, his loins felt on fire. Curling his fingers into her tousled hair, he pulled down her head, kissing her hungrily. His senses devoured the sweet taste and smell of her; her muted sighs were a rhapsody to his ears; the texture of her skin, a lustrous satin beneath his stroke.

Suddenly she sat up, straddling him. "But this isn't what I planned."

"Me neither. But it can't be any better than this."

"I wanted to fix you a grand dinner, and then when we finished, we would come up here and . . ." Too embarrassed to say it, she covered her face with her hands.

Chuckling, he peeled away her hands. "And what, Raven?"

"I can't say it."

"Then don't try, sweetheart." He carried her hand to his erection. "Actions speak louder than words."

A short time later, as he began to drift off to sleep, she remembered about her brother.

"Oh, Cleve, I forgot to tell you. I have wonderful news. I found Antonio!"

"Uh-huh. That's nice, honey," he mumbled, barely awake.

"Well, I mean to say, he found me. He came here tonight with his *patrón*, *Señor* Valez. You see, I was right, *querido*. I told you he'd come back. Oh, Cleve, I'm so happy. Perhaps we can persuade Antonio to remain with us. He is coming back here in the morning, and *Señor* Valez wishes us to join him for breakfast."

"Uh-huh. That's nice, honey."

Leaning over him, she said, "Isn't it . . ."

His steady breathing told her he had drifted into sleep. Smiling, she leaned her head on his chest and closed her eyes.

Chapter 17

From the time he recognized Lily, Charlie couldn't get out of the casino soon enough. With his hair dyed black and a moustache and goatee disguising his face, he had seen that the cheap little whore hadn't recognized him, but he didn't dare risk leaving her alive. He had to get rid of her before she had a chance to think about it and spoil things even more than that stupid Lattimore had done by killing those Rangers.

He waited in the shadows. Antonio had left an hour ago, and his sister had gone upstairs to bed.

Apart we are only halves, but together we are a whole.

The little bitch! Who did she think she was? Antonio had him—he didn't need her! Lucky that her husband was not home; that made it easier. As soon as the two women were alone, he'd kill them and make their deaths look like a robbery.

Besides, he couldn't take the chance of not killing Antonio's sister, in case Lily had remembered who he was and told her. He'd lose Antonio then.

He knew how sad his young friend would feel about his sister's death. It would hurt him to see his son in such pain, but he would make it up to Antonio somehow. Besides, this sister was the last hold on Antonio's past.

I've missed you so much, mi hermano!

Well, soon there would no longer be the threat of his Antonio returning to the little bitch. How he had hated the boy's incessant talk of his sister! The jealousy he had felt when Antonio spoke of his love for her! Didn't Antonio realize women couldn't be trusted?

Oh, Antonio, I can't tell you how happy I am to see you.

Even tonight, when the two were reunited, they only had eyes for each other. At the exclusion of him! Pity the husband wasn't there after all, Charlie reflected. He and the unfortunate fellow could have consoled each other. Charlie chuckled. He was such a funny man. Despite all the adversities in his life, he had never lost his sense of humor.

Yes, it would all work out fine. Antonio had no use for his father, so with his sister gone, there would only be the two of them. The boy would then become the son Charlie had hoped for: refined and educated, someone to sit and talk with in the evening, to play chess with or smoke an occasional pipe with.

That's how it had been when he rode with Quantrill. Like it would be again once these two women were out of the way.

Women! He felt the rise of outrage he suffered whenever he thought of how they interfered in a man's life. They were all alike. Bitches and whores! *Lying, cheating bitches and whores.* Just like his mother—running away when Charlie was only twelve, leaving him and his two younger brothers to the mercy of their drunken father.

And his father! Charlie spit in contempt. Stomping around shouting orders, a bottle of whiskey in one hand and that goddamn whip of his in the other. Well, he'd shown the drunken bastard all right! His father sure had found out what the sting of that whip felt like the night Charlie used it to beat him to death.

And that goddamn captain he'd had in the army was just like his father! Always giving orders. The young fool deserved to die. Who did he think he was, ordering Charlie Walden around? He found out soon enough that Charlie Walden didn't take orders from anyone. If he'd obeyed the man, instead of killing the fool and then deserting the army, he'd be as cold in his grave as that captain was right now!

He suddenly frowned. What the hell was that captain's name? He delved deep into his memory but couldn't remember. "Oh, hell! It's not important anyway," he mumbled to himself.

For over twenty years he had been a hunted man. Now that he was willing to forsake his life of crime and go to Europe for a few years, all that stood in his way were the two useless women inside. *Bitches and whores! All alike!*

Lord knows, he'd had no choice but to kill his wife and burn down their house. She had lied to him—promised she'd give him a son. And what had she done instead? Two goddamn daughters! What in hell had he wanted with goddamn daughters? They'd have grown up to be liars like their mother. *Lying, cheating bitches and whores!*

He closed his eyes and drew a deep breath. He had to curb his anger. Remain calm. If he got mad, he could make a mistake. Everything was falling into place. Soon he'd have the son he'd always hoped for. All that stood between him and having Antonio to himself were the two women in that casino. *He had to remain calm.*

Then he'd show them. He'd prove to all of them: his father, his wife, his daughters—and especially Antonio, his son—just what a loving and caring father he could be.

Charlie stepped back, hugging the shadows deeper. He smirked with pleasure. Two women alone. A robbery. No one would find that suspicious.

No one would ever suspect him.

Nearby, a clock struck the twelfth hour. From his hiding place, he could see through the window into the casino. Only Lily and the old man at the wheel remained. Charlie saw the man put on his hat, preparing to leave.

He drew his knife. It would soon be time. He felt the exhilarating rush of blood to his head. His heart pounded, his pulses throbbed. He tightened his grasp on the knife.

The door opened, and the old man appeared in the doorway. "Good night, Lily."

Charlie shifted his eyes and saw that she had lowered the chandelier and was extinguishing the lights. " 'Night, Waco," she called out without turning around. "See you tomorrow."

He grinned. *That's what you think, bitch!*

He waited for a few seconds until the old man walked away; then he crossed the street and slipped stealthily through the doorway. The room was in darkness now except for a single lamp near the stairway. He slunk into the shadows.

He watched Lily, his stare impassive, as she raised the chandelier and anchored the chain. Then she came toward him to lock the door.

As soon as she passed him, he sprang up behind her. Clamping a hand over her mouth, he jerked her back against him and held the knife to her throat. He could feel her tremble. Her fright excited him, and he lowered his mouth to her ear.

"Hello there, Miss Lily," he whispered. "It's been a long time. I've missed you and the good times we had together."

Her body began to twitch, and he chuckled. "No sense in squirming, little fish. Won't do you any good."

She began to whimper, and he increased the pressure on the hand clamped against her mouth. "Figured out what I'm gonna do, haven't you? And as soon as I slit this pretty little neck of yours, I'm going upstairs and do the same thing to that precious little bitch, Adriana. Maybe before I do, I'll have a little fun with her. Just like I used to with you. Remember, Lily?"

When she began to struggle, hot-blooded lust surged to his loins. "Ah, that's it, Lily. You're scared, aren't you? Real scared," he murmured. "I can feel your fright. I can smell it." He closed his eyes and threw back his head. Gasping in demonic ecstasy, he released his hand. "I want to hear it!"

Chapter 18

Cleve bolted out of bed at the sound of a bloodcurdling scream. Scrambling to pull on his trousers, he heard sounds of a struggle downstairs.

Startled awake, Adriana sat up. "What is it?"

"I don't know," Cleve said, grabbing his Colt. "Could be a holdup. Lock the door after me."

"But—"

"Lock the door, Raven," he ordered over his shoulder.

The hallway was dark, except for a dim glow from the casino. He opened Lily's door, and as he feared, her room was empty. The scream had to have been hers.

Colt in hand, Cleve snuck down the back stairway and quietly made his way into the darkened kitchen. Moving to the closed door that led into the casino, he eased it open and peeked into the room. Taken back, he saw Count Miguel Castillo kneeling over Lily's body.

Cleve stepped into the room. "Get the hell away from her, you sonofabitch!"

Startled, Miguel Castillo looked up to see Cleve's pointed pistol. "Don't shoot!" Raising his hands in the air, he rose to his feet.

"Up against that wall," Cleve ordered, with a slight motion of the pistol. "And one fancy move will be your last." He hurried over to Lily, and to his relief, she began to stir. "What did you do to her?"

186

"Nothing, *señor*, I swear. I tried to help her."

Dazed, Lily sat up, holding her head. "He's telling the truth, Cleve."

"Do you need a doctor, Lily?" Cleve asked, kneeling down at her side.

"I don't think so. I'll let you know when I stop trembling."

"*Señor*, may I put down my hands?" Miguel asked.

"You sure he wasn't mixed up in this, Lily?"

"No; he saved my life, Cleve."

"Okay, Castillo, you can put them down." Holstering his Colt, Cleve stood up, still eyeing the man suspiciously.

Miguel rushed over to Lily and knelt down at her side. Grasping her hand, he kissed it. "Did he hurt you, my dear Lily?"

"No. Thanks to you, Mike."

"Let me help you to your feet," Miguel said, putting a hand on her arm.

"Is one of you going to tell me what happened here?" Cleve asked. He was beginning to feel frustrated. "You want a drink, Lily?" He walked over to the bar and lit several lamps.

"No . . . no. I'm all right now," Lily said. "I had the vinegar scared out of me, but no harm done, I guess."

"What about you, Castillo?" Cleve asked.

"I think not. Did he try to rob you, my dear Lily?"

Hesitating, Lily cast a furtive glance at Cleve. "Yeah, I guess that's what he wanted."

Breathless and exhausted, Waco Donniger appeared in the doorway. "Couldn't catch him. Chased him 'til he disappeared into one of them backstreets. Any of you folks hurt here?"

"Nothing serious, Waco," Lily said.

"So you saw it, too," Cleve said. "Did you get a look at his face, Waco?"

The old ranger shook his head. "No. I was up the block a piece when I heard Miz Lily scream." He shook

his head. "Got back here in time to see this fella runnin'
down the street. The *señor* here yelled for me to stop
him, so I chased after the guy. Sorry I couldn't catch
him. Seems like when you've been in a saddle as long
as I have, you ain't much good on foot."

At that moment, Cleve looked up to see Adriana
hurrying down the stairway. "Lily, are you okay?" she
asked, rushing over to the disheveled woman.

"I'm fine, Princess."

"We heard a terrible commotion. What happened?"

"Just some guy trying to rob the place. Fortunately,
Miguel came along before there was any harm done."

"The man had a knife, Lily," Miguel said pointedly.

"A knife!" Cleve exclaimed. He glanced at Lily. "All
right now, are you ready to tell me what happened?" he
asked impatiently.

"Well, Waco had just left, and I was closing up. I went
over to lock the door, and this guy jumped out of the
shadows and grabbed me. I tried to free myself, and as
we struggled, Mike showed up and came to my rescue.
Then the guy ran out the door."

"Came to your rescue, huh," Cleve said, with another distrustful look at Miguel. "Pretty coincidental, I'd
say."

"Not at all, *señor*, since I was on my way back here."

"Why?" Cleve asked.

"Nothing that concerns you, *Señor* MacKenzie."
Miguel glanced at Lily.

"If it involves The Full House, it concerns me,
Castillo," Cleve declared. He looked up and saw Lily
and Miguel staring intently at each other.

Never taking her eyes off Miguel, Lily shook her
head. "No chance, Mike," she said with a smile. "You
saved my life, but it's not gonna get you a free ticket
into my bed."

"Ah, Lily! Still you continue to wound me! I am only
thinking of your welfare," he said. "Wouldn't you feel
more secure with me there?"

"I don't think I want to hear this," Cleve complained.

Miguel glanced at Cleve long enough to give him a disgusted look. "You may take your leave at any time, *Señor* MacKenzie."

"I was about to suggest the same to you."

"Will you two stop that bickering?" Adriana said. "What is it accomplishing?"

Eyeing the count, Cleve folded his arms.

"*Señor* MacKenzie, I think I will have that drink now." Miguel put an arm around Waco's shoulders. "Come, join me, *amigo*."

Miguel took a swallow of the whiskey Cleve set before him, then poured the rest of the liquid over a cut on his hand.

"Miguel, you're bleeding!" Adriana cried out.

"Just a nick, my dear."

"Come with me, Miguel," Adriana insisted. "I'll clean out that nasty cut and bandage it for you."

"My mouth feels like I've been chawin' cotton," Waco said. "Reckon I need a drink of water to paint my tonsils more'n I do this rotgut." He followed Adriana and Miguel into the kitchen.

"Cleve," Lily said quietly, "there's something I haven't told you."

"I figured as much. I could tell by the look on your face that you were holding something back."

"This was no holdup. He intended to kill me. He told me so."

"Whyever—"

"He didn't say. But I know one thing for sure, Cleve. It was Charlie Walden."

"Walden! Did you see him?"

"I didn't have to. I'd know that voice anywhere."

Cleve couldn't believe it. "So Walden's right here in Fort Worth!"

"That's not all of it," Lily said. "While Walden was holding that knife to my throat, he bragged that when he finished with me, he was going upstairs and doing the same thing to Adriana."

"What!" Cleve said, glancing toward the kitchen.

"He called her by name, as if he knew her. He never mentioned your name, so he must have thought you weren't here. By the way, I never saw you come back."

"I came in the back door and went right up to my room." Puzzled, Cleve shook his head. "So, he didn't come to get me. He came to kill you and Adriana."

"That's what he said. But how would he know you were gone tonight, unless he'd come into the place? In that case, I would have seen him. It just doesn't make any sense," she said thoughtfully.

"I'd like to know the answer to that myself. You'd recognize Walden if you saw him, wouldn't you?"

"Of course," Lily said. "But I didn't see him in here tonight."

"Why would he even come here?"

"Revenge, maybe?" Lily asked.

"Well, he hates me and my brothers. But if he was out for revenge, how would he know that Adriana was my wife?"

"Someone could have told him."

"Who in hell knew about it, except the priest and the four of us?"

Lily thought for a moment. "Antonio must know. Adriana surely must have told her brother tonight. And, I suppose, that man he was with knew, too. I think his name was Valez, or something like that."

"Don't mention this to the others. We'll talk about it later," Cleve whispered as the three people came through the door. Miguel's left hand was swathed in a bandage.

"Castillo, I guess I owe you an apology," Cleve said, extending his hand. "I'm indebted to you."

"*De nada*," Miguel said as the two men shook hands. "Anyone would have done the same."

"Now, you know that isn't so. Besides, modesty doesn't become you, Mike," Lily teased.

"Miguel," he reminded her. "Does this mean I cannot anticipate a personal thanks from you, Miss Lily?"

"I've already given you that," Lily said.

Incredulous, Miguel drew up to his full six feet. "I can't believe you are sending me away, Lily," he said.

"Believe it, Mike, because that's just what I'm doing."

"He could stay the night," Adriana blurted out.

All three of them looked at her with shock.

"I beg your pardon?" Lily asked.

Adriana blushed and started to stammer. "I meant . . . well, my room's available. He could sleep there, if he liked."

Three sets of eyes turned on Miguel.

"That's not exactly what I had in mind."

Cleve had had his fill of the whole conversation. "Sounds like the best offer you're gonna get tonight, Castillo. Take it or leave it."

"I think we should leave now," Adriana said. She took Cleve by the hand and headed toward the stairway.

"I'm gone one day and all hell breaks loose," Cleve grumbled. "I'd sure like to know what the devil's going on around here."

"I'll explain it all to you upstairs, *querido*."

Lily winked at Miguel, then grinned at Cleve as he allowed himself to be led docilely up the stairway by his young wife. "It's been a long day, boss man."

"If you don't mind, Miz Lily, I'll head back home and grab some shut-eye," Waco said as soon as Cleve and Adriana left.

"Of course, Waco, and thank you for coming to our help."

"Sure wasn't much of that," Waco said. He nodded to Miguel.

"*Gracias, Señor Waco*," Miguel said, following him to the door. Reaching into his pocket, he pulled out two gold eagles. "Take this, please, as a token of my gratitude."

The old ranger looked at the twenty dollars Miguel was offering him—more money than he could earn in a month.

"Shucks, Mr. Castillo, that's right generous of you, but I sure wouldn't take money for what I did. Miz Lily is a fine lady. Nobody's gonna hurt her as long as there's breath in my body."

"Ah, a man of chivalry!" Miguel bowed at the waist. *"Tu eres un verdadero caballero, mi amigo.* You are a true gentleman, my friend." The old man's eyes gleamed with restored pride as he departed.

"Thank you, Mike," Lily said when Miguel returned to the bar.

"For what are you thanking me?" he asked.

"What you just said to Waco was very nice."

"I was sincere, my dear Lily."

"I know you were; that's why I'm thanking you. You're such an enigma, Mike. One minute you're an arrogant snob looking down your nose at all of us, and the next, you're respecting the dignity of an old man." She looked into his eyes. "I don't know which of these men to believe."

Long after Adriana fell asleep, Cleve lay awake worrying about her safety. Walden had to have known she was his wife; revenge was the only logical reason he would specifically come to murder her. Having failed, would he try again?

The next morning, Adriana was awakened by bright sunlight streaming through the window. She yawned and stretched, then turned her head on the pillow and saw that Cleve was awake and watching her.

"Good morning." His blue eyes were dark with desire.

"Good morning." Adriana wondered if she'd ever stop blushing when he stared at her like that. She turned her head away but could still feel his eyes on her.

Suddenly remembering, she popped her eyes wide open and looked at him. "Well, did they?"

"What?"

"You know . . . Lily and Miguel. Did they spend the night together?"

"How should I know?"

"Don't you even care?" she asked, nearly bursting with curiosity.

"Not in the least."

Adriana couldn't believe he could be so calm about it. "You mean you haven't looked?" she asked incredulously.

"Good heavens, no!"

"Oh, Cleve, just go and peek in my room. See if Miguel's there."

"Not a chance, Raven. It's none of our business what they do."

"Oh, you're no fun!" Her mouth had puckered into a pout.

Cleve arched a brow. "That's not what you said last night."

"That was before I found out what a spoilsport you really are. Well, if you won't do it, I will."

She jumped out of bed. Too late, she realized she was stark naked.

Immediately, Cleve's lewd perusal took her in from head to toe. "Gotta admit, no one can ever accuse you of being one." Grabbing her hand, he pulled her back onto the bed, rolled over, and trapped her beneath him, pinning her hands above her head.

"Cleve, it is not proper for us to do this in the light of day," she said, shocked.

"Not proper?" He chuckled. "Now who's being the spoilsport? Ain't me, lady." He lowered his head to her breasts.

Within minutes she was writhing beneath him in the fervor of arousal. "Oh, yes, *querido!*" she murmured through ecstatic moans. "Again! Again!"

Adriana was dressed and waiting when Antonio arrived—alone.

"Carlos is feeling indisposed this morning, Adriana.

He sends his regrets that he is unable to join us," Antonio informed her after they had hugged and kissed.

"I'm sorry to hear that. I hope he has a swift recovery. Please offer him my sympathy, Antonio," she said compassionately. "Then there is no reason to go elsewhere. I will fix us breakfast, and we can eat in the small dining nook right here. That way we can talk in private. Come, let us sit down until Cleve joins us."

"Your husband has returned?"

"Yes, last night. He will be joining us very soon. He and Lily have gone to the sheriff's office. Someone tried to rob the casino last night, and only Miguel Castillo's timely intervention prevented Lily from being harmed."

"Count Castillo is here in Fort Worth?" Antonio asked, surprised.

"Yes; he did not go back to San Antonio with *Papá*. He appears to be quite smitten with Lily."

Antonio chuckled and patted her hand. "Smitten? I think not, little sister. That romantic mind of yours is speaking again. You're naive not to recognize what the count's real interest in this Lily. After all, he is a Spanish *hidalgo*—a nobleman! And what is she? An *Anglo puta!*"

Aghast, Adriana stared at him. "Antonio, such talk is not like you. You are beginning to sound just like *Papá*. Have you forgotten about dear Pedro? Or Carmelita, who was like a mother to us?"

"Of course not, Adriana. You know I cannot forgive *Papá* for that tragedy. He is insensitive and overbearing. That is what drove me away from the ranch. No, Adriana, I will never be like *Papá*." Staring into space, he said, "I have spoken many times with Carlos on this subject. He has taught me that the gentry have a responsibility and obligation to those born beneath them. Kindness and compassion are principles of that responsibility."

"Really, Antonio, I know *Papá* never practiced those

principles, but I can't believe you needed your friend Carlos to explain *noblesse oblige*."

"That is not what I mean, Adriana. It's just that . . . Carlos understands me. He sees how deeply the suffering of others disturbs me. We talk of this often together." Antonio's eyes glowed with adoration. "Oh, Adriana, if only you knew him as I do. Carlos is such a kind man, my little sister. I have never seen or heard him raise his voice or hand to anyone on his ranch."

She clasped his hand. "Carlos sounds like a very good man, Antonio. I can see why you are so drawn to him."

She looked up to see Cleve coming toward them. "Ah, here is my husband now."

"Husband! Don't you mean the *Anglo Papá* forced you to wed?" Antonio said bitterly, rising to his feet.

"Antonio, this is my husband, Cleve MacKenzie."

Cleve recognized the young Spaniard at once. "We've met," he said. The two men shook hands and sat down. "Nice seeing you again, Antonio."

"Now, while the two of you get to know each other, I will go and prepare breakfast," Adriana said. "I won't be long." She hurried off, leaving the two men eyeing each other like combatants in a ring.

"At least we meet again under more favorable conditions than last time," Cleve said.

"I am not certain the conditions of this meeting are less unfavorable, *señor*, since I find that my sister was forced into an undesirable marriage."

"I appreciate this warm welcome into your family, Fuente. Cordiality must be a trait you inherited from your father."

"I will try to be as amenable as possible because of Adriana's unfortunate situation. But even you must be aware that she was not raised to live above a barroom."

"You ever stop to think that she might not live here if you'd been around when she arrived? I think your concern for her welfare comes a little late. Where the hell were you when she needed you?"

"I would have been here, *señor*, had you not cheated me."

Cleve took a slow, deep breath, then said calmly, "You know, Fuente, I wanted us to become friends for Adriana's sake, but you're hell-bent not to see it that way, and I've plumb given up the idea."

"Then we are in complete accord, *Señor* MacKenzie."

"I understand this Valez you're living with has a ranch near Devil's Dip."

"That is right," Antonio said.

"Pretty big shootout there the other night. Three Rangers were killed."

"So I have heard."

"And did you know that Adriana rode into that carnage right after it happened? Not only was it a nasty sight, but she could have been killed."

Antonio sucked in his breath. "*¡Santa Maria!* Why did you allow her to risk her life like that?"

"I didn't have much say on the matter. She took off on her own—in search of her *beloved brother*. Speaking of Adriana, did you happen to mention your sister's marriage to your friend Carlos?"

"Certainly! Of course, I was too embarrassed to admit to him whom she married," he said with disdain. "Since Carlos was aware of her betrothal to Count Castillo, I made no attempt to change that impression."

This was an interesting revelation. If Walden had intended to murder Adriana because she was his wife, Cleve reflected, it would appear the outlaw hadn't heard this from Antonio or Valez. Perhaps revenge had not been the motive after all. The whole mystery was mind-boggling.

Arriving with plates of spicy omelets, Adriana exclaimed exuberantly, "I have made your favorite, Antonio. Let us eat while it is hot."

Adriana's presence brought an end to the discussion. Throughout the meal, as Adriana and her brother carried on a running conversation, Cleve observed that

Antonio nervously fingered an injury on his forehead. There was something suspicious that the young man was holding back. However, one thing became clear to Cleve as he listened and watched the two together: Antonio's devotion to Raven was as great as hers was to him, which made it more confusing to Cleve that her brother had failed to be there for his sister when she needed him the most. And Adriana's joy at being with her brother again was so evident that, despite some reservations, Cleve decided to cut the young man some slack.

"I must go and find Lily," Adriana said, as they were finishing steaming cups of coffee. "She is my best friend, Antonio. I'm sure you will like her when you have a chance to talk to her."

"Lily's not here, Raven. She went to breakfast with that stiff-necked count." He glanced pointedly at Adriana to make sure she got the message. "He asked her last night before he left."

"So," she said with a sigh, "he did not remain here for the night."

"Apparently not, honey. After we left, he went back to his hotel. Sorry to be the bearer of bad news," Cleve said good-naturedly.

Antonio snorted. "I am sure Miguel will have the *puta* in bed before the day is over."

Cleve shoved back his chair and stood up. "You know, Fuente, I really don't give a damn what you think of me. For your sister's sake I've tried to like you, because I know how much she loves you, and I even let you get by with accusing me of cheating, to spare her from being hurt any more than she's been already. But I want to hear an apology for what you just said about Lily. The woman helped to save my brother's life, and no man's going to speak disrespectfully of her in my presence."

"Please, Cleve, he doesn't understand. I apologize for what he said," Adriana cried out.

"You've been apologizing for this cowardly bastard from the time I met you. It's time he fights his own battles, without your making up excuses for him."

Antonio stood up. "I do not need anyone to defend my actions, *Anglo*. And I make no apology for them."

"Then get the hell out of here before I kill you."

"No, Cleve, please. Don't say that."

"I'm sorry, Raven, but I've got no use for him. He's spineless, and runs when the going gets tough. He ran out on you and left you to face your father alone. He even ran the first time I met him. So start running again, Fuente; it's the only thing you do well."

Antonio glared at him with loathing. "As you have reminded me, we have Adriana's feelings to consider. If I have offended your Lily, I apologize. And I shall leave as you have requested." He rose to depart.

Adriana began to sob. "No, don't leave, Antonio. Not in anger," she pleaded, chasing after him.

Antonio halted at the doorway. "Adriana, *mi hermana pequeña*," he said gently. "Come with me."

"I can't. He is my husband. Please, Antonio, come back. We all must sit down and resolve this quarrel."

"I think perhaps this is not the time, little sister." He slipped an arm around her shoulders. "Come; walk me to my horse."

Seeing her anguish, Cleve felt guilty for the role he had played in causing her heartache. He stood up to go after them, then thought the better of it. Fuente was right; it would be wiser to let both their tempers cool.

But there were some questions about Antonio Fuente that needed answering.

Chapter 19

❧◦◦❧

Through the window in Adriana's bedroom, Cleve watched her tearful good-bye with her brother. His heart ached for her, but her brother was unbearable——a disgusting snob whose actions, as well, were not above suspicion at the moment. Cleve saw the two kiss and part; then Adriana dabbed at her eyes as Antonio rode away.

He sat down on the bed, bracing himself for the pending quarrel.

When Adriana entered, she drew up in apparent surprise at discovering him in her room. For an instant, she looked at him as if she were on the verge of speaking, then seemed to change her mind and walked to the window.

"I'm sorry about your brother, Raven."

Without turning, she lashed out at him. "You didn't try to understand him. Antonio is young and may appear brash, but——"

"Adriana, he's overbearing and rude. That's the long and the short of it."

"That's not true. He's just covering up his true feelings by posturing just like *Papá*. But that's not the real Antonio."

"He sure convinced me," Cleve said.

Throwing her hands up, she pivoted to face him. "Why do you make jokes? Is it funny to you that you

199

have forbidden my brother to visit me? I can't tolerate that. I won't!"

"I haven't forbidden you anything. I don't have the right. There are a dozen other places where you can meet him—or do it here when I'm gone. Just don't expect me to be around and listen to his insults."

"If you'd make peace with him, there wouldn't be any insults."

"So, you think it's all my fault?"

"No, I don't mean that."

"Then I guess I don't understand what you mean. No more than I understand why your father and brother have such contempt for me because I'm an *Anglo*. In fact, they appear to hate anyone who's not a Spanish *criollo*. This is America. Why do they live here if they hate the rest of us so much?"

"This is their country, too," she declared belligerently.

"Sure it is. So they should start appreciating it, or else go where they'll be happier." He walked over and stood before her. "Look, honey, I understand the meaning of family ties—although I haven't seen any evidence that your father and brother do—so I don't expect you to cut yourself off from them. Just don't ask me to accept them, when you know they won't extend the same courtesy to me."

He tipped her chin up and smiled at her. "I love you, Adriana. The last thing I want is to see you unhappy. But it'll take some cooperation on their part, too." He pulled her into his arms. "Now, let's dry those tears. I'm sure it'll all work out in the end."

When Cleve lowered his head to kiss her, she stepped out of his arms. "I think I'd rather be alone. If you don't mind, I'll sleep in here tonight."

Cleve gave her a disgusted look. "I see. I've been mean to Antonio, so his sister is slapping my hands. Think about what you're doing, Adriana. There's not room for three of us in the bed."

Frustrated, Cleve went downstairs hoping Lily had returned. He had to talk to her. If he ever hoped to settle down to a happy marriage, he had to put together the pieces regarding the actions of the mysterious Antonio Fuente.

He was relieved to find her behind the bar. "Lily, there's something fishy about that Valez. When I was in Jacksboro, I learned from the Rangers that they've been checking up on him since the attack. Seems Antonio's Carlos showed up about the same time the Walden gang started operating in these parts again."

"Are you thinking that Carlos's ranch is a hideout for the gang?" Lily asked.

"Well, Buckwheat talked about a young Mexican or Spaniard riding with the gang. He said he was pretty sure that the guy was either shot in the head, or that the bullet grazed him. Did you notice that fresh injury Antonio has on his forehead? It sure looks like the mark a bullet would make in passing."

Lily stared at him, aghast. "God, Cleve! Do you think Adriana's brother is a member of the Walden gang?"

"The thought's been stuck in my craw. Just a hunch, that's all."

"Why, that would break Adriana's heart," Lily said sadly.

"I haven't mentioned any of this to her. She'd never forgive me if I was wrong. Lily, did you get a good look at this Valez guy last night?"

"Just a quick glance when we were introduced. I didn't really study him. What are you getting at?"

"Don't you think it's an odd coincidence that this Valez and Walden showed up right here at The Full House on the very same night?"

"You think they came to Fort Worth together?"

"That, or Carlos and Charlie are one and the same *hombre*."

"No, that can't be," Lily said, shaking her head. "I've seen Charlie Walden many times. For one thing, his hair is light. And Charlie has a real smooth-sounding,

Southern accent. This Carlos fellow had dark hair and spoke with a Mexican accent."

"You mean like someone playacting?"

"Well, that could be," she said, pondering the idea. "But you can't disguise the eyes. This Carlos had cold, gray eyes like—" Lily looked with astonishment at Cleve. "Oh, my God! Carlos Valez *is* Charlie Walden!"

"Which is why he wanted to kill you. He's afraid you'd recognize him."

"But he intended to kill Adriana, too. He told me. How would Walden know Adriana's name, unless—"

"Unless Antonio introduced them."

Lily nodded. "Yeah, but he'd still have no reason to kill her, especially knowing she's Antonio's sister."

"That bastard would kill his own mother if it served his purpose."

Miguel Castillo came through the kitchen door, and Cleve glanced at him in disgust. "You're becoming a fixture around here, Castillo."

"Good morning, *Señor* MacKenzie," Miguel greeted him, unperturbed.

"I thought you were leaving Fort Worth."

"I've decided to extend my stay longer than I had planned. Who knows; I may decide to make Fort Worth my home." He turned to Lily. "Lily, thank you for your pleasant company," he said, kissing her hand. "I can't remember when I've enjoyed a breakfast more."

"I enjoyed it, too, Mike. Now, if you two will excuse me, I have work to do in the storeroom."

Cleve eyed the Spaniard suspiciously. "I was talking to a friend of yours this morning—Antonio Fuente."

"Oh, yes, young Antonio," Miguel said. "A very confused young man, I'd say."

"No more so than some other Spanish nobleman I've met recently," Cleve said.

With a haughty brow, Miguel eyed Cleve. "And what does that mean?" he asked.

"For one thing, your station in life is far above Lily's, is it not?"

Miguel nodded. "That is true."

"Then it would seem your obvious attraction to her is at war with the rules of nobility . . . unless you are using her for sport."

"My alliance with Miss Lily is no concern of yours."

"I'm here to tell you to leave her alone, Castillo, or you'll have to answer to me."

"So you are her champion!" Miguel said, amused. "Now, it is you who throws down the gauntlet."

"Yeah, hoping for a chance to get another crack at your jaw. Looks like the swelling's gone down, Castillo."

"*¡Viva!* An opportunity for another barroom brawl!" Miguel said caustically. "Others might find it unusual that you declined to defend the honor of your wife, but you will fight for a common barmaid."

"There's nothing common about Lily, Castillo."

"I have made the same observation, *señor.* I was referring to others' opinions."

"Just remember what I said."

As Cleve started to walk away, Miguel asked, "You are involved with her?"

Disgusted, Cleve turned around and returned to the bar. "Not the way you're suggesting, Castillo. She's a friend, and I care about her. I don't want to see her hurt."

Miguel's mocking expression changed to one of irritation. "Then why do you think the same is not true of me?"

"Who are you trying to kid? We both know what you're after."

"Perhaps that was my intent—it isn't now."

"I can't imagine what your intent is now. But for sure, she's not impressed with your rank or money."

"It appears so," Miguel conceded.

"So you think that what you can't buy with money, you'll get with charm."

"I have observed that it worked for you, *señor.*"

Cleve realized how true that had been in the past—

before Adriana. He shook his head. "Well, I'm betting on Lily. She's too smart not to see through a phony like you. Just remember my warning; I don't want to see her hurt."

The count appeared unintimidated. "At least we agree on that point, *amigo*."

"I'm not your friend, Castillo."

Lily's return brought an immediate end to the conversation. "Lily, I'll be gone for a couple of days," Cleve said.

"I know what you've got in mind, Cleve," she accused. "Don't do it."

He glanced at Miguel, who was listening with interest. "We can discuss this in private, Lily."

"No. We'll discuss it now." To Cleve's further disgruntlement, Lily proceeded to repeat his suspicions about Antonio and Carlos to Miguel.

"Damn it, Lily, I asked you not to say anything."

"Mike can be trusted," she said confidently.

Cleve rolled his eyes in response. "Well, I've decided to take a ride to Devil's Dip and look around."

"You mean alone?"

"That's the best way."

"It's too dangerous, Cleve," Lily protested.

"Perhaps you would like some company, *amigo*? Alas, I fear young Antonio is more confused than I thought," Miguel said sadly. "It is my obligation to help you seek out the truth in this matter."

Miguel's offer of assistance surprised Cleve. "I appreciate the offer, Count Castillo, but I want to take a good look at that ranch, and it'd be easier for one person to move around unobserved. But there is something you can do. Adriana said that Antonio and Valez were returning to the ranch today, but just in case Walden gets the idea to double back and finish what he started, would you stay here at The Full House and protect the women?"

Miguel grinned broadly. "*Señor* Cleve, it would be my pleasure."

"Cleve, you won't try anything foolish, like taking on Walden alone, will you?" Lily asked.

"Of course not. I just want to be sure my hunch is right. And for God's sake, both of you, don't say anything to Adriana about this. I'll tell her I'm going away on business for a couple of days."

"All right. But I don't like it. You're taking a big chance, boss man," Lily replied worriedly, as Cleve took the stairs two at a time.

Adriana followed Cleve downstairs after he told her he was leaving for a couple days. Lily and Miguel were seated at a table in the casino. After a quick good-bye to them, Cleve took her arm as they walked to the door.

"You stay close to Miguel and Lily."

"I think they would prefer to be alone," she said, with a backward glance at the couple.

His gaze lingered on her face. "I'll miss you, Raven," he whispered tenderly, and kissed her cheek. Then, with long, easy strides, he headed for the livery.

Sadly, Adriana watched his tall figure disappear into the crowd. Sighing, she went inside. Lily and Miguel hadn't moved. Talking quietly, they seemed absorbed with each other. She doubted they even knew she had returned. Every time she saw them, they had their heads together. She couldn't imagine how two people from such different backgrounds could find so much to talk about.

Poor Lily. Miguel really is stiff-necked! she reflected. His conversation was dull and usually revolved around himself. Unlike Cleve's. She smiled poignantly. Cleve was witty, and he always had something interesting to talk about.

Rather than encroach on their conversation, Adriana continued into the kitchen.

Lily looked up in time to see Adriana walk through the kitchen door.

"The poor kid," she said, her heart swelling with compassion.

"You mean our young Adriana?" Miguel said.

Lily nodded. "Mike, you know Antonio Fuente. This bad blood between him and Cleve is breaking her heart. Do you think Antonio's the kind that would get mixed up with an outlaw like Charlie Walden?"

"Ah, *querida*, I guess we all have a dark side."

Lily nodded. "You mean a demon on the back. That's what I've always called it."

"And what demon rides you, my Lily?"

She thought for a moment. "My past, I guess. The men . . . the degradation . . . the indignity." She laughed in an effort to sound flippant. "Reckon I've got more than just one demon."

She twisted and glanced at him over her shoulder. "See 'em? How about whacking a couple of 'em away, Mike?"

He leaned over the table and playfully brushed off her back. "There. The Count Miguel Enrique Felipe Castillo y de Rey has vanquished every single demon of the fair Lily LaRue."

Laughing, she turned back, and he clasped her hand. "You are free now, my sweet Lily."

"I wish I *could* rid myself of my past that easily," she said ruefully.

"The secret to reviewing the past is to do it with a forgiving eye," he said, studying her thoughtfully. "You, who are the epitome of kindness, should learn to be kind to yourself, my dear."

He began lightly stroking her palm with his thumb. The sensation was so tantalizing, she quickly withdrew her hand.

"Oh, for goodness sake, Mike," she said with a sheepish grin. "If we're gonna start trading compliments now, I have to confess that you can be a real gentleman when you want to be." Raising an eyebrow, she added in jest, "Or should I be wary of what the pompous Count Castillo might say next?"

"Not at all. Why do you ask?"

"Well, considering how some folks around here

prefer ridin' a wide path when you come by, I've
noticed that you talk mighty different when it's just the
two of us."

"Perhaps some folks, as you say, can't see beyond the
end of their noses. Whereas you, my dear Lily, listen
with understanding and look for the truth within a
man." He gazed at her intently. "I think the man who
claimed you for his own would be very fortunate
indeed."

Taken aback, she chuckled. "Whew! That's some
mighty smooth talking, Count Mike." She looked away,
all too aware of a mysterious and hopeful yearning that
began to stir inside her.

"Tell me, Lily, have you ever been married?"

She looked back at him and shook her head.

"But you have been in love," he guessed with conviction.

She barely dipped her head. "Once."

"And what happened?"

"Nothing happened. I'm afraid the feeling was quite
one-sided."

"Is that why you chose the life you have?"

Her laughter sounded harsh in her ears. "If you think
an unrequited love drove poor Lily to a life of sin, you'd
be wrong, Count Castillo. At fifteen I became a whore,
the same as my mother was."

"And where is your mother today?" he asked kindly.

"Ten years ago she was beaten to death in San
Francisco by a drunken French sailor—on my eigh-
teenth birthday."

"I'm sorry, Lily."

"So was my mother. She enjoyed life—even that of a
whore."

"And what of your father?" Miguel asked.

"I never met the gentleman," she said lightly. "Trixie
said she had no way of knowing who he might have
been. Who knows, Count Castillo, I could even be the
daughter of some Spanish *hidalgo*."

"Trixie LaRue was your mother's name?" When she

nodded, he grinned. "A delightful name. So your mother was French."

"The only thing French about my mother was the red dress she wore, given to her by the same bastard who killed her. Actually, her real name was Ernestine Boettcher, and she came from some crossroad in Wisconsin. She said she took the name Trixie LaRue because it had a happy sound that fit her personality."

"I think I would have liked Trixie LaRue," Miguel said.

Lily smiled. "She was easy to like."

"And so is her daughter, my Lily."

At the unexpected tenderness in his eyes, Lily cradled her head in her hand. "Did I just tell you the story of my life? I've never told a soul before."

"Perhaps you sense, as I do, *querida*, that there will be many more secrets you and I will share."

"Well, there's no time like the present. What about you, Mike? Have you been married before?"

"At one time."

"I'm sorry, Mike."

"She's not dead. Irena has become a nun."

"A nun! So marriage to you was that pleasurable, huh? Very interesting." She started to rise.

"No, please, don't leave," Miguel said.

"I thought we were having a serious conversation, but I see that's not your intention."

"I am being truthful, Lily. The marriage was arranged, and I opposed my father as much as Adriana did Don Alarico."

"Not quite as much. You did marry."

"Only when I could not delay it any longer. You see, being the second-born son, I was expected to go into the priesthood. That, too, I opposed."

She arched a brow. "A priest! I can't imagine you as a priest, Mike."

"Nor could I." He grinned. "Especially taking a vow of celibacy."

"So what happened?"

"I was so rebellious that the Jesuits washed their hands of me, as you Americans say. After that, I attended the University of Madrid and then Oxford University in England. While I was in school, my father betrothed me to Irena, who was only twelve years old at the time. Actually, Irena is Adriana's aunt—Don Alarico's younger sister."

"They say it's a small world," Lily said.

"I finished school at the outbreak of the Crimean War, so I joined the French army. When I returned from Russia, Irena was of marriageable age and we wed."

"Did you have children, Mike?"

"Ah, Lily," he sighed, "the whole marriage was a tragedy. Irena was a frightened, pitiful little thing, afraid of her own shadow. Her only solace was her religion. I felt like a pervert every time I touched her."

"You never grew to love her?"

He shook his head. "Nor did she love me, but she endured the intimacy. After six years, when it became apparent she was barren, Irena asked to enter a convent. My father arranged for the church to dissolve our marriage."

"Is that when you became betrothed to Adriana?"

"A year later. I had no desire to wed, so I wasn't disturbed by Adriana's reluctance in the matter. I traveled around the world and finally came to Texas six months ago."

"Well, I expect you'll be returning to Spain very soon, then."

"Not at all. As a matter of fact, Lily, I've decided not to return."

"But that's your home, Mike."

"Not anymore. My mother has been dead for five years, and my father died a year ago. Since my brother is my father's heir, there is nothing to keep me in Spain, and I can go wherever I choose. My wealth was left to me by my mother."

"If not Spain, where do you intend to settle?" she asked.

"I am not certain, Lily. Europe is constantly engaged in petty wars. One country forever invading another: Prussia—France—Italy. ¡Caramba! Now, since Isabella's abdication, these same countries squabble about who should sit on the *Spanish* throne! No, Lily, I shall not return to the intrigues of the European aristocracy and the everlasting political upheavals over there."

He smiled slyly. "Actually, I find this country of Texas to be quite interesting. I am considering making my home here."

"Texas! But Count Castillo, Texans don't even speak English. You said so yourself," she said with a laugh.

"You wound me, Lily. Using my own words against me is not a fair way to fight." He smiled and grasped her hand. "That is why I find you so refreshing."

"I never promised a fair fight," she said.

He gazed deeply into her eyes. "And I am not asking for one."

She broke the intense stare with a nervous laugh. "Uh, seriously, Mike, you are a Spanish nobleman— you can't just forsake your country and the life you've always known."

"That is the very life I wish to forsake. The world is changing swiftly, dear Lily. Yet my people still cling to the Old World traditions. Titles, arranged marriages, division of classes." He shook his head. "It is a futile way of life."

"Well, you sure put up a good show defending it."

"Old habits die slowly, Lily," he said with a slow grin. "But the patient can survive . . ." He arched a devilish brow. "With the proper nursing."

She stood up to leave. "Well, someday you'll find that nurse, Count Castillo."

"I think I already have."

Startled, she looked at him. Passion, naked and vivid, glowed in his dark eyes. A shiver of desire coursed through her—a sensuous magnetism that had been growing stronger with every moment they spent together.

She walked away. Pausing at the kitchen door, she looked back. His gaze had not altered.

As Adriana chopped vegetables for dinner, her thoughts continued to dwell on the problem of Cleve and Antonio. She had to sit down with Antonio and have a lengthy talk with him, convince him that Cleve wasn't the scoundrel her brother believed him to be.

With Cleve gone, what better time than the present? Why not ride out to the ranch now? It had not been a difficult ride, and surely there would be nothing to fear; Antonio had told her the area was safe and that the gunfight between the Rangers and the outlaw gang had been unusual. Even the Rangers believed the gang had left the vicinity.

But this time, she would rent a speedier horse and leave early in the morning, so she could reach the ranch in broad daylight. Then, if things worked out the way she hoped, she and Antonio would be back in Fort Worth before Cleve returned.

With her plan in mind, she could hardly wait until morning. That evening Adriana claimed a headache as an excuse to retire early.

As soon as Waco left that evening, Miguel locked the door and pulled down the window shade. As Lily finished washing glasses, he extinguished all the lights except for a lamp on the bar.

"There, did I not do well?" Miguel asked, pleased with himself, after stacking the chairs on the tables.

"And without a bit of help from a servant! There might be hope for you yet, Count Castillo," Lily teased.

"Which is why I am here, *querida*."

For a long moment they gazed into each other's eyes. She felt the familiar sensuous draw of his dark gaze. "It's not worth risking your life in the hope of going to bed with me, Mike."

"I think it is." His smile flashed against his olive skin, the nearby lamp casting a glimmering light on his handsome face.

"Why me? There are plenty of my kind in this town."

"You are wrong, my dear Lily. You are one of a kind."

She dropped her gaze. "I suppose you've decided that I'm what you want at the moment. And you're used to getting whatever you want."

"What you say is true. I will not lie to you, Lily."

"What earthly reason would I have to go to bed with you?" she flared.

"Because you want to. As much as I want it."

"That's ridiculous!"

"There's no better reason for two people to make love, *querida*."

"I mean, it's ridiculous for you to think I would want . . . I mean, for— Damn it, Mike, wipe that smile off your face. If I agree to go to bed, will that satisfy you? Appease your pride?"

"Or desire," he added.

"Then let's get it over with," she said, resigned. "I'm tired of this issue. Then you can go back to San Antonio, and I can get on with my life."

He took her into his arms. Strange how his tall, lean body was deceiving: his arms felt powerful. Glancing up at his face, Lily saw a mingling of victory and tenderness, and she closed her eyes as he lowered his head.

His mouth felt firm and pleasant, the kiss surprisingly gentle, even as his tongue explored the recesses of her mouth. There was a subtle sense of urgency—no forceful seduction, just a slow, persuasive pressure that lulled her into a feeling of serenity.

As he lifted his head, Lily stepped away and picked up the lamp. Walking to the stairway, she paused at the lower step. Smiling, she reached out a hand to him.

Miguel came over to her, grasped her hand, and together they climbed the stairs.

Once in her room, she put the lamp on the table.

When she was about to blow it out, Miguel stopped her. "Leave it lit, Lily. I want to see you."

He slowly undressed her, caressing her with his eyes. In a mixture of English and his native tongue, he murmured about the beauty of her naked body. Then, lifting her into his arms, he carried her to the bed and eased her down gently onto its softness.

As Miguel shed his clothing Lily made no attempt to look away but watched him with intensity, matching the dark-eyed gaze fixed on her. Then he lowered himself, covering her with the heated warmth of his body.

"What do you want me to do to you, Mike?" she asked.

"Nothing, my sweet Lily. I wish to pleasure you. Tell me your fantasy."

Astonished, she glanced up warily. No man had ever asked her such a question. As a whore, she'd done as she was told—regardless of the pain or indignity involved. Oh, once or twice with Luke, she had slipped into the fantasy that he was in her bed because he loved her—not just hired her for the night. But for the most part . . .

"I guess—"

"Yes, *querida*?" Miguel asked anxiously.

"I guess I'd hope you wouldn't hurt me, Mike."

He cupped her cheek in his hand. "Hurt you, my sweet Lily? I hope to bring you only pleasure."

He didn't hurry, but took the time to explore her with his hands and mouth until her body tingled. Much to her surprise, she felt the rise of sexual desire.

She had forgotten that a man's hand could feel so gentle, yet be so arousing. Marveling at this reawakening, she reveled in the feeling, an excitement that had nearly been destroyed by the hundreds of men who had shared her bed.

Yet under his patient, masterful touch, she felt the escalating force of passion sweep through her with a heat that soon torched the jaded wall of impassiveness she had erected through the years. Stunned by the exquisite sensation, Lily couldn't control her response. For the first time in her life, her body flooded with supreme ecstasy, and she cried out in mindless bliss.

Throughout the night, they loved and loved again—exploring, arousing, discovering—until, at dawn, she fell asleep in his arms.

Chapter 20

Adriana rose at daybreak and dressed. Then, grabbing her shawl, she stole quietly down the back stairway.

Once in the kitchen, she ate a slice of buttered bread and a banana as she wrapped up a cheese sandwich and an orange for lunch. She had learned well the imprudence of rushing off unprepared.

Before slipping out the back door, she put the letter she had written to Lily, explaining where she was going, on the center of the table. Adriana knew she would be long away from Fort Worth before her absence was discovered.

She headed for the livery stable.

Just as Adriana had anticipated, the ride to the ranch was speedy and uneventful, and she was relieved that her plans had not gone awry. The only distressful moment on the whole trip had been when three men approached her on horseback as she neared Devil's Dip. When they identified themselves as Rangers, she had relaxed once again.

Now, as she rode up to the ranch house and saw the corral with grazing horses, the sprawling barn, and the scattered outbuildings, Adriana felt a bit of nostalgia. She loved ranch life and hadn't realized how much she missed it.

When she reined in, a tall man with a heavy paunch bulging above his gunbelt walked up to her. "You lost, sister?"

"Is this the ranch of *Señor* Valez?" She glanced at several men lounging against the corral fence, watching with lewd smirks on their faces. *Papá would never permit his vaqueros to look at a lady so disrespectfully.*

"Yeah, what do ya want?" the man asked in a gruff tone.

"I am looking for Antonio Fuente."

"What for?"

"I am his sister, sir," she said haughtily. "Is Antonio here or isn't he?"

"Well, climb down. I'll take you to the boss." Rather than offer her a helping hand, he grabbed the bridle and nodded to one of the other men. The man sauntered over to them and took the reins.

Adriana was left standing on the front porch while the first man disappeared inside. Never had she experienced such ungracious hospitality! Glancing at the men, she saw they were still watching her with the same salacious expressions.

Suddenly, the door sprang open. "Adriana! What a pleasant surprise, my dear." Carlos Valez appeared shocked by her unexpected arrival.

"*Señor* Valez. I'm sorry to have come uninvited, but I must talk to Antonio."

"Please come in." He stepped aside for her to enter. "That will be all, Mel." The heavy man nodded and left.

Turning to Adriana, the rancher smiled broadly. "Antonio will be so happy to see you." He glanced past her. "Have you come alone?" he asked, closing the door.

"Yes, my husband went away on business, so I thought I'd take the time to see Antonio."

"Very clever of you, dear," he said, "but unwise. So many unfortunate accidents could befall a woman traveling alone." He smiled.

"Well, I had no problems, thank goodness. And, hopefully, Antonio will return to Fort Worth with me."

"Oh, I am afraid that is not possible," the rancher said emphatically. "No, my dear. You see, we have much work to do here right now." Opening a box on the table, he proceeded to take out five candles.

"*Señor* Valez, may I see Antonio, please?" Irritation had crept into her voice.

"Unfortunately, this is not an opportune time. He is resting at the moment, and I don't think he should be disturbed."

"Maybe you should let Antonio decide that," she said, annoyed.

"I have already made the decision, my dear. Now, if you will excuse me, I have work to do." Turning away from her, he picked up an ornate candleholder from the table and calmly began to remove the burnt-down candles.

His stalling offended her. "Forgive me, *señor*," she said, trying not to lose her patience, "but I have traveled quite a distance. Under the circumstances, I am sure Antonio would not mind my disturbing his rest."

"But, I'm afraid, I would."

Indignant, she turned toward the stairway, hesitated for a moment, then called out, "Anton—"

The sudden, stunning blow to her head sent her reeling. Stumbling forward, she fell to the floor, unconscious.

Cursing as he threw aside the candleholder, Charlie stormed to the door and flung it open. "Mel, you and Macon get over here," he shouted.

The two men hurried over and followed him inside. Charlie pointed to Adriana, lying on the floor. "Take her out to the barn and tie her up."

"Is she dead, boss?" Macon asked.

Charlie muttered a string of expletives. "If she were dead, Macon, would I tell you to tie her up?" He launched some additional obscenities regarding the man's stupidity. "Don't forget to gag her, too."

"She told me she was Fuente's sister, boss," Mel said. "Is she or ain't she?"

"She is. But there's bad blood between them," Charlie lied. "And anyway, I have to get rid of her. She's guessed who I am, and was about to get a pack of Rangers out here." Charlie figured he'd be better off letting the idiots believe she was a threat to all of them. "That's why I don't want Antonio to know. So tell the others they're not to say anything to him about her even coming here."

"Gee, boss, Fuente ain't gonna like you doin' away with his sister," Macon said.

"Mel, get this fool out of my sight before I kill him," Charlie declared.

"Why not let me finish her off right now?" Mel asked.

"I want her death to look accidental, just in case Antonio hears about it. We'll get rid of her on the road somewhere between here and Devil's Dip. I just have to plan how to do it."

The two men picked up Adriana and started to carry her out.

"Macon, you ride to Nellie's and find Lattimore. Tell him I want him and the rest of the boys back here, pronto. I'm gonna be far away when that gal's body is discovered. Now get her out of here before Antonio comes downstairs."

Thank goodness he had given Antonio a pipe to smoke just a short time ago, Charlie thought. The opium would keep the lad in a euphoric state for a while, safely out of the way.

With all the setbacks in the last week, Charlie figured he needed something to calm his own nerves. What with the shootout with the Rangers, his failure to kill Lily, and now that clinging bitch sister of Antonio's showing up right at his door, a pipe would do him good. He needed the drug.

He started to climb the stairway. Maybe it wasn't too late to join Antonio. Since the time he'd first gotten the young man to try a pipe, the two of them often sat down and smoked together.

In fact, his young friend had begun to use the drug too frequently, Charlie thought. An excessive use of anything was no damn good, and he would never allow himself that kind of self-indulgence. To lose control of your senses could be dangerous to a man in his profession.

He was a strong man; Antonio was weak. But that was fine, since Antonio was a son to him. A father's duty was to see that his son was satisfied. If smoking the opium kept Antonio happy, he would allow it.

Charlie grinned. As long as he supplied Antonio with the drug, the boy would remain with him.

The smile never left his face as he hurried up the stairway.

Over the past hour, concealed in the cover of a stand of birch about five hundred yards from the ranch house, Cleve had counted a half-dozen men besides Antonio and Carlos, whom he had caught a glimpse of earlier.

At least, he assumed the man with Antonio was Carlos Valez. The fellow fit the description Lily had given him. Despite a couple of encounters with Walden in the past, he had never seen the outlaw face to face—only from a distance, and even then it had always been in darkness.

He had spent the night in a run-down line shack that looked like it hadn't been used in years; had risen at dawn; and, after checking the ranch, was now concentrating on the ranch house.

Earlier, he had spent hours riding around the ranch and had seen plenty of hoofprints showing a lot of recent activity. But other than an occasional stray cow, there was no sign of any herd—which seemed strange, since this was supposed to be a working ranch. Carlos or Walden, whichever he was, had either sold off the herd or driven it elsewhere.

The ranch hands appeared to be doing nothing. They weren't mending fences, painting outbuildings, breaking broncos, or doing any of the dozen other chores necessary on a ranch. Besides the absence of cattle, the only horses in the corral appeared to be the outlaws' own mounts. This reinforced his belief about the place. It looked like Carlos Valez might be on the verge of pulling up stakes and clearing out.

Cleve sure wondered why the man would be leaving if he wasn't guilty of any crime.

Having seen all he could from a safe distance, Cleve had decided to return to Fort Worth and pass on his suspicions to the Rangers. At the sight of a rider approaching the ranch house, he raised his spyglass to his eye.

Adriana! What in hell was she doing here? In shock, he watched as she spoke to one of the men, dismounted, and went inside after speaking to Valez.

Nearly frantic, Cleve lowered the glass. His wife had just entered the house of the very man who intended to kill her! Dammit—it was his fault. He should have told her his suspicions about Valez! Now he had put her in jeopardy.

How in hell was he going to get her out of there? He couldn't just ride up and start blasting away. He still had no proof that Valez was Charlie Walden, or that any of these men were outlaws. Thank God Antonio was in the house. Walden wouldn't try to harm her in Fuente's presence. But Cleve knew he mustn't wait too long; every moment he delayed put Adriana in greater danger.

Minutes passed like hours as he tried to think of a way to get her out. He saw two men enter the house. Maybe he should just ride up there, but that could get them both killed for sure. He had to stay calm and figure out a way.

When the two men came out of the house, he raised the spyglass again. The hair on his neck stood on end when he saw that they were carrying Adriana. His palms started to sweat, and his heart began pumping blood to his brain so fast that he couldn't think.

They carried her into the barn, and in a short while came out. One of the men saddled up and rode away.

At least that was a good sign. If they had killed her, the man probably would have taken her body with him to dispose of somewhere.

Now the count was down to five of them, besides Walden and Antonio in the house. Cleve knew his brother Flint wouldn't even flinch at such lopsided odds! *Where the hell are you when I need you, Brother Flint?*

No matter what he thought of Antonio Fuente, Cleve felt Adriana's brother wouldn't be a party to harming her. But time was running out. He had to get inside that barn.

Cautiously, he stole forward. Working himself to the far side of the barn, he saw two men with their backs to him, leaning on the hitching post in front of the house. Two other men were at the corral, unsaddling Adriana's horse. But where was the fifth man? He had to be either in the barn or directly in front of it, which was out of Cleve's sight.

His question was answered when one of the men in front of the house called out, "Hey, Barnett."

"Whatta ya want, Mel?" The sound had come from right around the corner where Cleve was standing.

"Get over here. I've got orders from the boss," Mel yelled.

Barnett came into Cleve's view as he sauntered over to the two men. When they put their heads together and began to talk in low voices, Cleve glanced at the two men at the corral. Satisfied, he made his move around the corner of the barn and opened the door wide enough to slide through. Closing the door quickly, he peeked out through a split between the slats. To his relief, he had not been observed.

Dust motes swirled in the shafts of sunlight filtering

through narrow cracks in the walls of the damp, dimly lit barn. The acrid smell of wet hay, manure, and horseflesh permeated the air.

In one of the stalls, a huge dun gelding looked up with its ears perked attentively and eyed him suspiciously. Fearful that the animal would whinny and attract the attention of the men outside, Cleve remained motionless until the horse lowered its head and returned to chewing on a pile of hay.

Cleve moved silently across the floor, searching. In a darkened corner, he finally found Adriana. Bound and gagged, she had been tossed on a heap of old hay.

When he knelt down beside her, her eyes were round with fright until she recognized him. Cleve released the soiled bandanna that had been used to gag her, and hastily cut the rope binding her arms and legs. Then he pulled her into his arms.

"Oh, Cleve," she sobbed, burrowing against him.

"Hush, love; you're okay now. I won't let anything happen to you." He kissed her, then hugged her tighter.

"Carlos hit me and knocked me out," she said. "When I woke up, I was tied up here. I don't understand what's happening. What are you doing here?"

"There's no time to explain right now. We've got to get out of here, but there's no sense trying to go out the way I came in." He stood up. "Are you able to walk, Raven?"

"I think so." She got to her feet, then rubbed her head.

"Are you okay?" he asked, grabbing her arm.

"My head hurts and my legs feel a little shaky, but I think I can walk."

Cleve slipped an arm around Adriana's waist to support her, and they headed to the back of the barn. Glancing around for a tool, he spied a rusty branding iron and quickly used it to pry apart a couple of loose slats in the wall. Crawling through the opening, he helped Adriana out just as he heard the barn door open.

"Let's go," he whispered. He grabbed her hand and they dashed into the concealment of a nearby stand of cottonwood, then stopped to allow her to catch her breath.

"Raven, we've got to move fast. I left my horse about a quarter of a mile away from here. As soon as they discover you're gone, they'll be on our trail."

She nodded, and they raced across the countryside, speed more of a consideration then concealment. Breathless, they reached his horse, and Cleve swung her up into the saddle. Climbing up behind her, he shouted, "Get going, Swifty." The gelding took off at a gallop.

A quick glance behind them disclosed a cloud of dust. They were being pursued, and with Swifty carrying a double load, they'd never make it to town before the gang caught up with them.

Bullets were whizzing past their heads by the time Cleve reined in, grabbed his rifle, and jumped off. "Keep riding. I'll slow them down," he shouted.

"I'm not leaving you." She dismounted.

"Dammit it, Raven, there's not time to stand here arguing." Several shots kicked up the dirt at their feet and he shoved her down. "Get behind those rocks." Grabbing Swifty's reins, he followed as bullets began zinging past them and striking the rocks above their heads.

Sheltered by the granite, Cleve fired several shots at the nearest rider and saw him fall to the ground. The other four men scattered and took cover.

"All right, Raven, get back on that horse and ride like hell to that tent town. I saw Rangers there yesterday."

"I'm not leaving you," she declared adamantly. "Cleve, I know how to handle a rifle or pistol."

"Raven, you could help more if you'd go and bring back some help."

He fired off several more shots as the outlaws began to work themselves nearer. "I can hold them off alone. I'm even a better shot than my brothers, and either of them could handle four men in a gunfight. Now get going." When she continued to hesitate, he ordered sharply, "Go, Raven."

Suddenly bullets started ricocheting off the rocks, flying in all directions as the outlaws set up a barrage of shots. Cleve dove for Adriana, shielding her with his body. The very site that had offered them cover had become a death trap.

When the firing stopped, he sat up. "Goddammit!" he cursed, dropping his rifle.

She looked up. "Are you hit?"

"Yeah. One of those ricochets hit my hand. Raven, take my rifle and return their fire."

As Cleve pulled the bandanna from his neck and wrapped it tightly around his right hand, Adriana picked up his rifle and fired back at the outlaws.

"How bad is it?"

"Won't be able to fire a rifle, that's for damn sure. We've got to get out of here." He drew his Colt. "I'm not as good a shot with my left hand."

"What do you want me to do, Cleve?"

"Just keep firing with that rifle. I've got to think for a minute. Too late now for me to hold them off, and we can't outrun them with one horse. Our best bet is to try it on foot, but as soon as we stop firing, they'll be on our heels."

An idea popped suddenly into his head. "I have to get to Swifty. When I tell you, start firing that rifle and don't stop. I want them to keep their heads down for a minute."

He crawled over to the sheltered spot where he had left his horse. "Okay, Raven."

When she set up a barrage of fire, he quickly untied the saddlebags and slung them over his shoulder. "Swifty, it's time for you to do your stuff. Don't fail me now, boy." He slapped the horse's flank, and the gelding galloped down the trail toward Devil's Dip.

"Cleve, the rifle's empty," Adriana said.

"Let's get out of here." Grabbing Adriana's hand,

they dashed into the trees, then crouched down and waited. Just as Cleve had thought, the four riders galloped past.

"I figured they'd think we rode off. They'll never catch Swifty now, and while they're chasing him, we can get away." He set out walking.

"But Cleve, the town's in the other direction," she said, confused.

"I know. I haven't fought Comanche all my life without learning some of their tricks. They do the last thing you'd expect them to do—double back when they're being chased."

"But we're heading right back to the ranch."

"That's right. The last place they'll think to look for us. For the time being, we can hide out in an old line shack I found last night. With my right hand busted, I'm not much help. The shack will buy us some time 'til I can figure what to do next. Let's get going."

They started out on a run. A short time later, breathless and exhausted, they reached the cabin.

Chapter 21

Charlie was crazed with anger. He had permitted himself a few moments of pleasure, and in that short time, the idiots had let the girl escape with some *hombre* they had never seen before.

Who was he? He couldn't have been the girl's husband. Antonio had told him that his sister had been betrothed to some rich Spaniard, and according to the boys, this guy had been a white man. Probably one of those goddamned Rangers! There were so many crawling around the area, it was hard telling who belonged and who was one of them snooping Texas Rangers!

Now he had to get out fast—before the Rangers returned. Thank God he had gotten his money out of the bank earlier, because after today, he didn't dare show himself in town. He wouldn't have time to sell the ranch, or hold up the bank either!

He cursed again. How in hell had the careless fools let that damn bitch get away?

He glanced up when Antonio came down the stairs carrying saddlebags. Well, at least Antonio believed his story of having to leave immediately to go to the bedside of a dying aunt in the North. Once they got there, a simple lie would convince Antonio that this fictitious aunt had died before they arrived.

Composing himself, Charlie smiled broadly. "Are

you all packed, my son?" he asked cordially. "We have a long ride ahead of us."

"Yes, I go now to saddle my horse."

"It has been saddled," Charlie said. "I'm almost ready. I will be right out."

As Antonio crossed the room to leave, his boot made contact with an object lying on the floor. He bent down and picked up a black comb painted with red and white flowers.

"Where did this comb come from?" he asked. "Do you have a friend you kept secret from me, Carlos?" Antonio teased.

Realizing it must be Adriana's comb, Charlie hastily grabbed it out of his hand. "I bet one of the ranch hands entertained a gal or two while we were in Fort Worth. I've told them time and time again not to bring their whores into this house." He shrugged good-naturedly. "What can I do, my son? When the cat's away, the mice will play." Slapping Antonio on the shoulder, he laughed. "We must get moving."

At the sound of a knock, Charlie opened the door to see Mel standing there, hat in hand. "Boss, there's a man here who wants to talk to Antonio."

"To me?" Antonio asked, surprised. He stepped forward when Miguel Castillo entered the room. "Why, Count Castillo! It's a pleasure to see you, Miguel," Antonio said.

As Charlie watched the two men shake hands, he felt the rise of anger, fearing what would follow.

"May I introduce you to my *patrón*, *Señor* Carlos Valez."

"*Señor* Valez," Miguel said pleasantly.

"My pleasure, Count Castillo. Antonio has mentioned you often."

"Miguel, to what do we owe the pleasure of this visit?" Antonio asked.

"I am seeking Adriana. I assume she is here."

"Here? Why would Adriana be here?" Antonio asked.

"She left me a note saying she was coming to this ranch."

"What on earth for?" Carlos asked nervously.

"She said something about a misunderstanding that she wanted to speak to Antonio about."

"Well, we didn't part under the best of terms, but there were no hard feelings," said Antonio. "I don't understand where Adriana can be."

"I stopped in the nearby town of Devil's . . . ah—"

"Devil's Dip," Charlie supplied hurriedly, relieved to hear that the girl had not gotten back to town.

"Peculiar name, indeed!" Miguel commented, brushing a speck off the sleeve of his jacket.

All Charlie could think of was getting rid of the man and escaping before Antonio got suspicious. "Perhaps she changed her mind and went back to Fort Worth."

"Ah, *Señor* Valez, you are most probably correct. I, too, suspect that is what happened," Miguel said. "Well, I mustn't linger. I won't feel comfortable until I find her. Forgive this intrusion, gentlemen."

Charlie and Antonio went outside with Miguel. "I am worried about my sister, Carlos," Antonio said as he watched Miguel ride away. "It is not right that I leave when she is missing. Perhaps I should accompany Miguel to make certain she is safe. I can stay in Fort Worth until you return."

"Nonsense, Antonio," Charlie said, sliding an arm around his shoulders. "I would be devastated if you did not accompany me."

"But, Carlos, what if Adriana is injured or has fallen into foul play? I would never forgive myself for leaving."

Charlie could barely contain his anger. In a moment, he would have Antonio placed bodily on his horse.

"Didn't you often say your sister is impetuous? I feel confident she changed her mind and returned to Fort Worth. The poor count rode here on a wild-goose chase. Now, my son, we, too, must leave. My beloved aunt is dying. Every moment is precious. Mount up; I will be right out."

Torn by indecision, Antonio closed his eyes and conjured up the image of Adriana. Concentrating, he shut everything else out of his mind. If she were in danger at the moment, he knew he would sense it, feel it. After several moments, he relaxed. He had nothing to worry about. Adriana was safe and in good hands. Relieved, he climbed onto his horse.

Charlie hurriedly opened the safe and stuffed his money into his saddlebags. As he left, he glanced at the table where he had put the little bitch's comb, but it was no longer there. Puzzled, he glanced around but quickly decided to forget it. He was in too much of a hurry to waste time looking for it.

Chapter 22

After closing the cabin door, Cleve tossed his rifle and saddlebags on a broken-down table.

"Let me see your hand," Adriana said.

"There should be something clean you can use in my saddlebags," he said. He sat down on a chair and waited while she dug through the bags. She found a white neckerchief.

"I wish we had some whiskey or medicine to disinfect this," she said, removing the blood-soaked bandanna. She poured some water from the canteen on a strip she'd torn off her slip, and wiped away the blood.

"Oh, Cleve, your hand. Look at it!" Tears welled in her eyes.

"It'll be fine, Raven. It's a clean wound. Just tie it up to stop the bleeding."

"A clean wound!" Disgusted, she muttered in Spanish under her breath.

"What was that? I didn't quite catch it," he said, amused.

Her dark eyes flashed angrily. "A wound's a wound!"

"The bullet went right through. Sure hurts like hell but I can wiggle my fingers, so there's no nerve damage."

She folded the neckerchief into a compress, then ripped off another strip from her slip.

"I figure it'll be awhile before I can use this hand. I

can shoot with my other hand, but I'm not quite as accurate. Should have followed Luke's example. He draws from both hips." Cleve laughed lightly. "I always told him I can do the same job with one hand that takes him two. Good thing my big brother's not around to see me now. He'd make me eat those words."

"There, that's the best I can do," Adriana said, tying together the ends of the strip. "Does it feel too tight?"

"No, it's fine, honey."

"Thirsty?" She handed him the canteen.

He drank, then handed it back to her. "If you're hungry, there should be some jerky in my saddlebags."

"I'm not hungry right now. What about you?"

"Later's fine," he said.

"Cleve, why don't you lie down and try to rest? You've lost a lot of blood."

"Yeah, I suppose so. We're safe here. They'll never figure we doubled back."

He walked over to the bunk beds and flopped down on a thin straw mattress. "Come on over here, Raven. There's room for both of us."

"I can use the top bunk."

"Why that heavy frown?"

"What would you expect? I'm worried about Antonio."

"God! Here we are trying to stay alive; I can't use my gun hand; I haven't figured out how we're getting out of here; and all you have on your mind is your brother!"

"You know what I meant. What if Carlos—"

"There is no Carlos!" He paused, getting a grip on himself. Shouting would only widen the rift that was growing between them. "Carlos is Charlie Walden, Raven. And Walden is a cold-blooded murderer."

"Do you have proof that Carlos is this Walden?"

"Not exactly. But all the signs point to the truth. My God, he tried to kill you, didn't he? That gang chasing us was his. How much proof do you need?"

"That doesn't prove Carlos is this Charlie Walden

you're talking about. And if he is the murderer you say he is, maybe he's killed Antonio. I know my brother would never let anyone harm me—or anyone else for that matter."

"Raven," Cleve said, exasperated with her refusal to see the truth, "I watched the two of them this morning. Besides Walden, Antonio's the only other person who appeared to have free rein of that house. You're going to have to accept the fact that your brother is a member of the Walden gang."

"Never!" Her eyes flashed with anger. "You don't know Antonio."

"So you've said." He could see the argument was useless. "But I'd sure like to know what he's doing at this ranch." Cleve relaxed and closed his eyes.

"Perhaps this rift with my father has changed Antonio somehow."

"Or his association with Charlie Walden has."

"Why must you keep implying he's an outlaw?" she said, provoked.

"Birds of a feather."

"Everything has happened so fast, I haven't had a chance to sort it all out. If only I could speak to Antonio, I know that would help."

Cleve bolted to his feet and grasped her shoulders. "Goddammit, Adriana, I'm sick of hearing his name! Why won't you admit your brother is in this up to his eyeballs?"

"He's my twin, Cleve. We were always inseparable. I feel like half of me is missing right now. Can't you understand that?" she asked desperately.

"I'll tell you what I understand, Adriana: you're blinded by loyalty. Whatever this quarrel is between you and your father, your precious Antonio ran out on you and left you to face it alone. Sounds like a pretty one-sided allegiance."

"That's not true. You don't know Antonio. And you're not aware of the facts."

"Exactly! But I'll tell you what I think: he's a

coward—a lying coward who plays on your loyalty to deceive you. If he ever comes out of hiding, I'll tell him as much to his face."

The crack of her hand stung his cheek. "How dare you say such things?"

Silence hung heavy in the room as they stared at each other for a long moment. "I dare because I'm your husband, Adriana," Cleve finally said. His hands dropped from her shoulders, and he turned and walked over to the bunk.

"More reason to defend him, not malign him. I wouldn't presume to make such accusations about any one of your brothers."

He spun on his heel. "Because you couldn't if you wanted to. My brothers don't run in a pinch. We're all there for each other when the chips are down—unlike your brother, who bolts when the going gets tough. From what I saw of him, he's nothing but a headstrong young fool who seems to think that pride is a substitute for common sense. And I've got a problem with that, lady."

"Well, Antonio's not your problem, any more than your vicious accusations about him are true."

"It becomes my problem when it affects my marriage. It's time you grew up, little girl. You, your twin brother, and your overbearing father have some serious problems, but I'll be damned if I'm gonna let them into our marriage bed."

"As long as you continue to vilify my brother with your baseless accusations, we can never be man and wife. There will be no marriage bed."

"Fine with me. I'll honor your wishes. In fact, you're going to have to be the one to ask. And I should point out, Adriana, there is a name for women who use the bed as a bargaining block. But you, of course, being the fine lady you were raised to be, wouldn't see the connection, would you?"

He climbed into the bunk. "I suggest you try to get

some sleep. As soon as I feel a little stronger, we're gonna have to get out of here." He closed his eyes. Shortly afterward, he felt her climb into the upper bunk.

After a lingering silence, she asked, "Cleve, are you awake?"

"Yes."

"I think you should know what happened between Antonio and my father."

At the moment, he felt as if he'd heard all he wanted to hear about her damned father and brother. He sighed, resigned. "All right, go ahead. What is it?"

"As you may have observed, my father is a tyrant."

"I hardly noticed." He regretted the hasty remark. He'd keep his thoughts to himself and let her say what she had to say. Maybe getting it out of her system would help.

"At times *Papá* can be very ruthless—to both people and animals. My mother died giving birth to us. *Papá* often made a point of reminding us of that, and of what a disappointment we were to him. So we grew up suffering that guilt. I think that's one of the reasons Antonio and I are so close. Most of the time, the punishment *Papá* dealt out was unjust and overdone. I remember one time when Antonio was eight years old, *Papá* had given him a pony. My brother loved that little black horse. One day, Antonio went riding and he came in late for dinner. *Papá* was so angry, he shot the pony to teach Antonio a lesson. My brother was broken-hearted, and he cried all night. I did, too, because my heart ached for him."

A melancholy tone crept into her voice. "Through the years, he'd do similar things to discipline me. If I disobeyed him, he'd hand me a pair of scissors and make me cut up a favorite gown, or burn favorite toys or books. The ultimate punishment came when I was sixteen, and he betrothed me to Miguel Castillo over my objections.

"As the years passed, Antonio grew to like ranching

less and less. He began to see it as a cruel life—to both man and animal. He wanted to go to the university and become a doctor or an educator—to save lives, or to teach the beauty of the written word. Antonio even thought of becoming a priest, but *Papá* reminded him that his responsibility was not to the church, but to his father. After all, Antonio was a Fuente, and someday he would have to carry on that tradition.''

"So, you're saying Antonio was a disappointment to your father.''

"No, it's much more than a son not wishing to follow in his father's footsteps. It had to do with our beloved friend Pedro.'' She paused for a lengthy moment.

"Pedro?'' he asked quietly.

"Yes. Pedro Moreno, the son of Carmelita, our cook. As we grew, the three of us were inseparable companions, totally devoted to each other. Pedro was a sensitive boy, just like Antonio. I think that was one of the reasons the two were so close. Both abhorred violence in any form. They were gentle men. *Papá* always said that I was stronger than the two of them put together. Maybe he was right, but I wasn't proud of it.''

Cleve heard the rasp as she drew a deep, shuddering breath.

"Pedro also had a gift. He was a talented artist, and his paintings were as beautiful as his soul. They seemed to have a spirituality to them. He loved the beauty of nature. The three of us would ride out on the plain, and Pedro would paint a sunrise or a sunset . . . a deer drinking from a stream. He was in awe of such sights. We both begged him to go to the academy in San Antonio, where he could study and possibly have his art displayed. But he was too shy. He wanted to stay home at the ranch and just paint for his own pleasure.

"Then, a year ago, Carmelita became ill with influenza and had to take to her bed. The doctor told us she didn't have long to live. That's when she revealed the secret she had kept from the three of us all those years. She told us that Pedro was our half-brother.

"Antonio and I were both ecstatic to learn of this. Even though we knew *Papá* was a firm believer in the division of classes, we were angry at him for not acknowledging Pedro as his son. But Pedro said it didn't matter to him. He understood that Don Alarico was a wealthy *hidalgo*, whereas he was just a bastard born to the don's cook. What was more important to Pedro was our love—Antonio's and mine—and his mother's. He said it was all the family he needed.

"When Antonio and I went to *Papá* and told him we wanted him to recognize Pedro as our brother, he laughed at us," she said bitterly.

"Raven, maybe you should put it aside for awhile. This is upsetting you so much."

"No, I want you to hear it all. So you'll understand."

She continued on. "To get even, *Papá* had Pedro beaten bloody; then he ordered him off the ranch. He said that if Pedro came near us again, he would throw Carmelita out, too. We begged *Papá* to relent: Antonio swore he'd become the rancher *Papá* wanted him to be; I agreed to marry Miguel immediately. He laughed at us."

"Raven, you don't have to relive this."

"That night, Carmelita died. I think she didn't have the strength remaining to fight the disease and the heartache. Pedro went into the barn and . . . and hung himself. My brother and *Papá* had a terrible quarrel, and Antonio could no longer abide living under the same roof. So he left, promising that he would send for me as soon as he could. That is the Antonio I have always known and loved. I won't believe he's changed so drastically, Cleve." Her voice was full of tears. "Not my Antonio."

"I hope not," he whispered.

Long after she had fallen asleep, Cleve lay thinking about what she had said. What could have changed Antonio? Or who? Charlie Walden? But why would someone as sensitive as Raven had described ever hook up with a cold-blooded killer like Walden to begin with?

Cleve could feel himself becoming drowsy. "Just doesn't make sense," he mumbled, right before he dozed off.

The squeaking door woke Cleve. Grabbing the Colt, he lunged to a sitting position, slamming his head on the upper bunk.

"What's wrong?" Adriana asked, jolted awake.

When Cleve saw the man in the doorway, his mouth gaped open and he lowered his weapon. "Dammit, man, I could have shot you!"

Count Castillo grinned broadly. *"Buenas tardes, señor y señora."*

Adriana was astonished. "Miguel, what are you doing here?"

"Looking for you, my dear Adriana. You left this morning so abruptly that you upset Lily."

Cleve climbed out of the bunk. "Speaking of Lily, I thought you were supposed to be guarding her and Adriana. Good job, Castillo. Now I know who not to ask, if I'm ever in need again."

"At her insistence, I left Lily in the very capable hands of *Señor* Donniger."

"You left Waco to guard Lily! Good God, man, Waco's too old for that kind of work."

"You do the gentleman an injustice, my friend. The heart of a man is the measure of his worth, not his age or appearance. If I did not have faith in this man, I would never have trusted Lily's welfare to him."

"And I suppose you think my opinion of you is another injustice, Castillo."

"Obviously, my friend, for it is clear that you have underestimated the capability of the Count Miguel Enrique Felipe Castillo y de Rey."

"Is that what you came here to tell me?" Cleve asked in disgust.

"Since I was certain you would want me to track

down our dear Adriana——" He stopped to smile at her. "You are unharmed, are you not, my dear?"

"I'm fine, Miguel, but Cleve is wounded in the hand."

"Yes, I have observed that. I hope it is not too serious an injury, my friend."

"Well, why don't we have Adriana brew us some tea, and we'll sit down and discuss my health. Good God, man, will you get on with what you have to say?"

"Upon discovering Adriana's note, I rode here to speak to Antonio and this *Señor* Valez. Neither one claimed she had been there." Miguel offered one of his haughty looks. "Antonio's denial appeared genuine, but *Señor* Valez never fooled me for a moment." He reached into his pocket and pulled out a small comb. "I believe this inexpensive trinket is yours, dear Adriana."

"My comb!" she exclaimed.

"I thought it was. I remember you wore it on the night you were wed." He arched his brow in disdain. "How could one have missed it?"

"Who in hell cares about the goddamn comb!" Cleve snapped.

"You should, since I found the comb in Valez's house after he denied seeing Adriana. Much too coincidental, is it not?" He looked directly at Cleve. "I don't believe in coincidence, *Señor* MacKenzie. I also had the impression that this Valez was too anxious for me to leave. I thought it wiser to get out of there as quickly as possible, so I could look around at the ranch of this suspicious *Señor* Valez. Finally, I came upon this shack and——"

"You can stop calling him Valez. His name is Charlie Walden. He's the same man who tried to slit Lily's throat."

"I realized that. Believe me, my friend, in the face of this knowledge, it was difficult to keep my composure."

Cleve walked over to Miguel and offered his good hand. "Sorry about the left hand, Castillo, but I owe you an apology. I appreciate what you've done. You took a big chance coming here."

Miguel paused in reflection. "Yes, I did, didn't I?"

"You risked your life for us, Miguel. It was very courageous of you," Adriana added.

"Rather so, wasn't it," Miguel agreed. After another moment, he smiled and looked pointedly at Cleve. "Hey, *amigo*, that makes us comrades in arms!"

The hair on Cleve's neck stood on end.

Chapter 23

When the three came through the door of The Full House, Lily glanced up with relief, the dark circles under her eyes a testimony to her night-long vigil. "Oh, thank God, you're all safe. I've been worrying about you all night." She threw down the towel she'd been using and raised a trembling hand to her forehead. "I must've washed and dried these glasses a hundred times."

Adriana rushed behind the bar and kissed her on the cheek. "It was dark by the time we reached Devil's Dip, so we spent the night there."

Smiling, Miguel eased up to the bar. "So, you were worried about me, *querida?*"

"I was worried about all of you." Seeing the bloody bandage on Cleve's hand, she gasped in alarm. "Cleve, your hand!"

"Hey, wipe that frown off that pretty face of yours, honey. I'm fine. I caught a bullet yesterday, but it should be okay in a week or so," Cleve said, painfully flexing the fingers of his wounded hand.

"Is that what the doc said?" Lily asked.

"Haven't seen one yet. The one in Devil's Dip was out of town."

Scoffing, Miguel shook his head. "Ah, yes! The honorable *doctor* in that deplorable tent town was out somewhere delivering a horse!"

Seeing Lily's perplexed frown, Cleve grinned. "Our *Señor Hauteur* is out of sorts because the only doctor in the big Dip is a veterinarian. They're lucky to have that much."

"An animal doctor!" Miguel said indignantly, throwing up his hands in a hopeless gesture. "*¡Caramba!*"

Cleve shook his head. "Trouble with you, Castillo, is you're too used to banging your silver spoon whenever—"

"Lily's right, Cleve. I'll go with you to the doctor's office," Adriana declared adamantly. She grabbed his good hand and pulled him toward the door.

"If you don't mind, Miz Lily, seeing as how the *señor* is back, I'll head to my room and grab some shut-eye," Waco said as soon as Cleve and Adriana left.

"Of course, Waco, and thank you for standing guard last night." Lily slipped her arm through his and walked out with him.

"Glad to do it," Waco said.

Lily stood outside the door watching Cleve and Adriana head toward the doctor's office.

"You should see them, Mike," she said, returning to the bar. "They're still holding hands, but she's leading him just like he was a little boy. I sure never expected one of those MacKenzies to be hog-tied by a member of the Spanish nobility." She chuckled in delight.

"I'm not so sure he is. They barely spoke to each other on the way back. But sometimes it happens the other way around, my dear," he said quietly.

"What does that mean, Mike?" Lily asked, turning to him. Her smile faded when she saw the look in his sensuous dark eyes.

"Sometimes it is the Spanish nobility who is conquered and, as you say . . . hog-tied."

Stunned, she stared at him, unable to reply. His eyes never left hers as he stepped toward her, took her hand, and raised it to his lips.

At his gentle kiss, her heart began to pound in her throat.

"Mike, I . . . I don't know what you mean. What . . ." Too flustered to continue, she looked away from his penetrating eyes and started to withdraw her hand, but he increased his hold.

Raising her chin, he forced her gaze back to his. "My dearest Lily, as a woman who has been in love once before, you do know what I mean," he said, smiling. "But whatever has happened in your past, today you are the *conquistadora*."

"*Conquistadora?*"

"*Sí*. For I, Count Miguel Enrique Felipe Castillo y de Rey, find that my heart has been vanquished, and I stand before you in humble surrender."

Embarrassed, Lily gently pushed away from him. "Whoa there, Mike. That's a mighty pretty speech, but it really isn't necessary. This here is Lily you're talking to. Remember?"

"You don't think I am sincere?"

Struggling to control her emotions, she said nonchalantly, "Well, you already made yourself clear on how you feel about damaged goods—which don't seem to go in the same breath with vanquished hearts and such. But you don't have to sweet-talk me to get me in bed. I don't expect you to, and I don't want to hear it."

"Even after the other night, Lily?" he asked gently.

She turned away quickly, unable to face him. "Whatever your motives were, the other night was the most . . . beautiful thing that ever happened to me. I know it was a delusion, but don't spoil my dream. I shall still have it when you are far away from here."

He walked up behind her and grasped her shoulders, pulling her back against him. "It wasn't a delusion, *querida*. And I'm not leaving here. I want to be with you always."

Shrugging out of his arms, Lily turned to face him. "Let's not kid ourselves, Mike. Oil and water don't mix. You are a Spanish *hidalgo*, and your world is one of wealth and tradition." She made a sweeping gesture with her hand. "Mine is The Full House."

"My dearest Lily, my world has not been what you might suppose. Yes, I admit to enjoying the privileges of the spoiled nobility. Indeed, I have played the role of Count Castillo rather well when it served my purpose. But I have told you, even as a youth I was a renegade to my family's traditions. My only attempt to conform was a fruitless disaster."

"You mean your marriage."

"Yes. Poor Irena . . ." He paused, shaking his head. "What folly to be betrothed for the sake of strengthening bloodlines! What archaic nonsense! I know now that to marry without love destroys a man's soul."

"But even knowing that, you agreed to wed Adriana, didn't you?"

"In truth, I fear it was a selfish agreement on my part. I had fought a war, had traveled and learned so much away from Spain. I saw marriage to Adriana as a way to flee the dismally backward land of my heritage and, at the same time, satisfy my family's wishes." He paused thoughtfully. "But I found that the Jesuits were right after all."

"Right about what?"

"So often spoken that I should have learned it well: 'The end does not justify the means.' "

She looked at him thoughtfully for a moment before chuckling. "I get it. It's like I shouldn't have been a whore just because I needed the money to eat. I guess I'm as guilty as you on that rule."

He smiled at her tenderly. "No, Lily, not like me at all."

"How come?" she asked, smiling back into his dark-eyed gaze.

"Because the good fathers also taught me another lesson."

"Which is?"

"While we mere mortals had better mind the holy canons, angels are exempt from all the rules," he said, leaning forward to kiss the tip of her nose.

"Oh, for heaven's sake, Mike. There you go with that

sweet talk again. Just get on with your story," she said, pleased in spite of herself. "So, Adriana foiled your plans."

"Yes indeed, and it's well she did. I had heard that Adriana was bold and headstrong, and I thought that, being raised in America, she would not be so tied to Spanish ways. Not like Irena—afraid to love a man. Of course, I also thought Adriana would love me immediately." He laughed at the thought. "But how could she?"

"Love can't be had for the bidding, can it, Mike?" Lily asked thoughtfully.

"No, it can't. Love either grows over a period of time, or else . . ."

"Or else what?"

"It explodes in an instant. ¡La gran pasión! You do know what I mean, my dearest Lily. Do you not?"

Tears welled in her eyes, and she turned her head aside.

"From the first moment I saw you standing behind the bar, I wanted you; and I knew that because I was Count Miguel Castillo, I would have you."

Lily flinched at his candidness. "And you got what you wanted," she said, returning his gaze.

"Much more than I ever dreamed, my dearest Lily. For you have touched something within me that no one has before. And I feel that for you it has been the same. I want you with me, Lily. I will give you anything you wish. Yo te amo, querida."

She tenderly cupped his cheek. "You do now. But how long would such a love last, Mike? Until you marry? We both know you'll want to do that some day. And I couldn't bear that. I'm not proud of what I've done for a living, but I've never let any man keep me. Right now, thanks to Cleve, I have the best life I've ever known."

"Are you saying there's no place for me in your world?" He gripped her shoulders and crushed her to him, his mouth covering hers in a demanding kiss that left her clinging to him after he raised his head and gazed into her eyes. "Now tell me you're convinced there's no place for me in your life."

"I would be lying if I tried. I'll be your mistress, Mike, as long as I'm the only woman you're sleeping with. But I won't share you with another woman—not even a wife you don't love."

"Then I will remain here with you."

"Now you're talking even more foolish. You'd be as miserable here as I would be in Spain or San Antonio. We live in two different worlds, my love. There would always be times when my Mike would slip away from me to become the Count Miguel Castillo."

"And what if I told you I was beginning to prefer Mike Castillo to that pompous count?"

"It would just be another delusion, Mike. We can pretend for a while, but we can't change who we are—eventually our pasts will catch up with us. You can move between Miguel and Mike, but I can only be Lily."

"Only Lily," he said tenderly. "The Lily I adore and cherish." He pressed a kiss to the palm of her hand. "Tell me now, Lily, that you will do me the honor of becoming my wife."

"Your wife! Oh, Mike, I . . . I can't think!" she stammered. "This is all so unbelievable. All I know is I want you to make love to me," she implored. "To never stop. To pretend the arrogant Count Castillo and the shameful Lily LaRue never existed—only Mike and Lily, with a love that will go on forever."

She laughed derisively and shook her head. "Pretty naive thinking for a gal like me, isn't it? A whore is supposed to have enough sense not to fall in love—"

He put his hand across her mouth and said gently, "Love is not a matter of common sense. As the honorable Frenchman once said, 'The heart has reasons, which reason knows nothing of.' So tell me, my dearest Lily, why are we wasting all this time?"

Looking up into his adoring gaze, she cried out,

"Damn you, Mike. You're the one doing all the talking."

He swooped her into his arms and carried her up the stairway.

As the hour drew near to open the doors for the evening, Cleve gave up trying to button his vest with only his left hand. He figured the rain would keep most of the card players away, and he would be able to close up early. He needed the sleep. Ever since their argument, he'd lain awake thinking about Raven. Tucking his watch into his vest, he rushed out the door.

As he stepped into the hallway, he collided with the very person who dominated his thoughts. Reaching out, he grabbed Adriana to keep her from falling. Her body was still damp from her bath, and he felt her warm flesh through the thin nightgown.

"Are you okay?" he asked. Their mouths were only inches apart. "I'm sorry. I hope I didn't hurt you." He couldn't take his eyes off her face. Standing there wide-eyed, she looked so defenseless—and so goddamned desirable, he ached to kiss her.

"I'm fine." Her voice seemed to tremble.

Reaching out, he brushed away a damp curl still clinging to her forehead. "Looks like you just had a bath."

"Yes." She expelled the word in a released breath. "Yes, I did." She finally broke their locked gazes. "Cleve, please release me."

"Oh, of course." He hadn't realized his arm still circled her waist. He removed it.

"Ah . . . Adriana, do you mind buttoning my vest for me?" He held up his bandaged hand. "I tried. Guess I'm just too awkward."

She lowered her head and began to work the buttons. The sweet scent of lavender soap tantalized his nostrils, and he fought the urge to grab a fistful of the long black hair that hung damply down her back like a mantle.

"There. Is there anything else you need?"

"No. That should do it. Thank you."

For the length of a drawn breath, she glanced up at him. "Good night, Cleve."

"Good night, Raven." His gaze followed her until she disappeared into her room.

No matter how Adriana tried to escape the memory, the moment she lay down to sleep, her tortured thoughts ruminated over the harsh words they had said to each other in the cabin. Her heartache was like a knot slowly being tightened in her chest, cutting off her breath. The two men dearest to her were at odds—and the day might come when one would destroy the other.

Tears trickled down her cheeks. *Santa Maria, help me as you have always done*, she prayed. *I love them both so much. To have one, must I relinquish the other?*

After a long night alternating between wakeful tears and troubled sleep, Adriana dressed and went down to the kitchen. Desolately, she left the casino. She needed advice and decided to seek out Father Allegro, in the hope that he could help her.

The priest was sympathetic that she had been forced into marriage, but he reminded her that now she was Cleve's wife and she had obligations to him—one of which was the marriage bed. Exactly what she didn't want to hear at the moment. Adriana left the priest, feeling worse then she had before.

Returning to The Full House, she discovered Cleve sitting at the kitchen table. He glanced up when she entered, and she could see by his drawn look that he must have spent as restless a night as she had.

"Good morning. You're out early," he said.

"I went to speak to Father Allegro."

His eyes flashed with suspicion.

"Father Allegro wants us to repeat our wedding vows in church."

"A vow's a vow in the sight of God," Cleve said, shrugging his shoulders. "Doesn't much matter to Him where it's said." He looked at her pointedly. "I'm sure

He only cares that the vow is honored. After all, old Moses was up on a rock, not in a church pew, when he got handed the rules."

"Please be serious, Cleve. I told Father Allegro we would. Will you please do what he asks?"

"Sure. Why, old Cleve is an obliging kind of guy. You can ask him to do anything."

"I realize you are being patient about all this, Cleve. And I do appreciate it, even though it doesn't seem so."

"Is the priest implying we're not married in the eyes of the church?"

"No, he never said that. He just feels that, with the circumstances that we were married under, he'd be happier to have us repeat our vows in church."

"Why not?" he said sarcastically, standing up and stalking across the room. "That ought to make us the most wedded couple in Texas. Maybe if we marry enough times, you'll finally acknowledge me as your husband."

He slammed the door so hard, the kitchen window rattled.

"Is it safe to come in?" Lily asked as she came down the stairway.

Adriana plopped down on a chair and cradled her head in her hands. "Life sure is complicated."

Lily smiled and patted her hand, then took a seat at the table. "Now that's an understatement." She looked toward the doorway that Cleve had just stormed through. "Can't figure what could get Cleve so riled. It's not usual for him to go on a rampage. I'd sure like to be sympathetic, honey, but it's pretty hard to console a woman who's married to Cleve MacKenzie. Sort of like apologizing to a customer for giving him French champagne instead of homemade corn liquor."

"So you *are* in love with him, Lily. I always suspected you were."

Lily shook her head. "I love him, but not in the way you're thinking. I'm gonna tell you something that I've never breathed to another soul. His brother Luke is the one I was in love with—not Cleve. I've never met Flint, the other brother, but from what I know of Luke and Cleve, any woman lucky enough to marry one of those MacKenzies ought to be counting her blessings. That's all the sermon you're gonna hear from me, Princess."

"So you think I'm wrong, too." Adriana sighed. "It's not right that I was forced into a marriage, even if the man is Cleve MacKenzie."

"Well, I wouldn't much like being told who I have to marry, either. I just think as long as you were, you got lucky that it was a MacKenzie."

Despite a feeling of dejection, Adriana leaned back in her chair and smiled at Lily. "What makes a MacKenzie so special, Lily?"

"Well, for one thing, they're the handsomest s.o.b.'s a girl could hope to meet—Cleve even more so than Luke. And a couple years ago, I wouldn't have believed that possible."

"There has to be more to a man than just a handsome face."

"That's very wise. With that kind of wisdom, I don't see why I have to explain anything more to you."

"Please do, though, Lily. You seem to know a lot about Cleve and his family. Why are they so exceptional in your eyes?"

"In my line, Princess, you meet all kinds of men—and more often than not, they're the scum of the earth. I guess that's why Cleve and Luke made such an impression on me. They're a rare breed: they're men of honor who play fair."

"Cleve told me his brothers and their families live in North Texas. What about their parents? Are they still alive?"

Lily shook her head. "That's where the real tragedy comes in. His father died at the Alamo six months before Cleve was born. Luke was two, and Flint was only one at the time. Their mother, Kathleen MacKenzie, was a remarkable woman. Her sons revere her memory. She kept the ranch going and raised them alone. When the war broke out, Flint and Cleve went east and joined the Confederate army. Luke was the only one who was married, and his wife was expecting. As soon as his son was born, Luke left to join the army, too."

"I thought you told me Luke married Honey in California."

"He did," Lily said. "Honey's his second wife. His first wife, and the mother of his son, was named Sarah."

"What happened to Sarah?" Adriana asked.

"While the three brothers were at war, Charlie Walden and a gang of Comancheros raided the ranch. They raped and murdered Kathleen and Sarah MacKenzie."

"Oh, dear God!" Adriana exclaimed. She stared horrified at Lily. "And Cleve believes my brother is riding with that gang! I'm beginning to understand why he's so bitter toward Antonio." Dazed, she looked at Lily. "And Luke's son survived?"

Lily nodded. "I guess they had a Mexican who worked on the ranch; he escaped with the boy. Josh was only two years old then. When the fellows came back after the war ended, they found out what happened. Luke traced his son to Mexico and found him. That's when he went to California and became a sheriff.

"All three of the brothers have been tracking down Charlie Walden ever since. Walden and his gang almost killed Luke a couple years ago in California. I guess, according to Cleve, they almost got Flint last year in Kansas. Now, Charlie's operating in Texas again. That means Cleve's gonna be sniffing at his trail. I just wish he'd leave it to the Rangers. He might not be as lucky as his two brothers. But I can tell you, from what I know of these MacKenzies, none of them will give up until Charlie Walden is dead."

"Lily, Cleve is convinced Carlos Valez is Charlie Walden. Do you think he is?"

Lily leaned across the table and patted her hand. "I'm afraid so, Princess."

"Maybe the Rangers will find this Walden first," Adriana said hopefully.

Lily shrugged. "I hope so. Walden's a sadistic bastard! He likes to inflict pain. I know; I've had one or two experiences with him myself."

"You mean you know him, too?" Adriana asked, aghast.

"Yeah, I was in Stockton when he shot Luke in the back." Lily looked away. "I was a prostitute. Charlie would come into the bar and . . . well, you know."

She turned her head and looked Adriana in the eyes. "He's an animal! Some men, when they're paying for your services, do some pretty mean things to you. Charlie was about the meanest. That's how he got excited."

As if to shake off the memory, Lily stood up and walked over to stare out the window. "Cleve's given me the chance to put that kind of life behind me. Now do you understand why I love him?" She turned back with a sad smile. "You can put that kind of life behind you, but you can't get rid of the scars."

Adriana's heart ached for Lily. Rising, she hurried over and hugged her. "I know I sound spoiled and shallow to you. I just don't know what to do. My brother is not a murderer! If Cleve won't believe me, we'll always have this problem between us."

Lily smiled at her. "I understand how you feel, Princess. I just think you're not being entirely fair to Cleve. Trust him, honey. Cleve's a smart man—about the smartest I've ever known. He's a thinking man, too. He's not a hothead who acts out of haste. For instance, it takes a lot to provoke him into reaching for that Colt on his hip. He knows that when he does, he's got as much chance of dying as the man he's drawing against. So no matter what he thinks of Walden, if there's a way to solve this business with your brother, he will."

There was a haunted look in Lily's eyes as she drew a deep breath. "We all seem to have some kind of demon on our backs—something to complicate our lives." She gave Adriana a quick hug. "Well, I'm gonna go upstairs and take a bath before the day heats up too much."

"Lily," Adriana called softly to her. Lily paused on the stairway and looked back at her. "Thanks."

Chapter 24

Since her discussion with Lily that morning, Adriana had thought about nothing else. The more she pondered the conversation, the guiltier she felt. Lily was right: she had no excuse for treating Cleve the way she did. Everything he'd done had been to try and help her—and he had received only her condemnation for his effort. Once he returned, she would have a quiet talk with him, and if he was as honorable as Lily claimed him to be, Cleve would understand why she had been so unreasonable. After all, they were husband and wife. Between the two of them, they could work out a solution if they approached it levelheadedly—the way he had suggested.

Throughout the day she waited anxiously for his return. Where could he have gone to, and when would he come back? She welcomed the opportunity to keep busy when Lily put her to work polishing the balustrades. Although she gladly tackled the job with vigor, her thoughts remained on Cleve.

A storm that afternoon brought terrifying flashes of lightning, accompanied by the clamorous boom of thunder. She'd always been afraid of thunderstorms, and by the time the storm passed over the city, her anxiety had doubled. By nightfall, with no sign of Cleve, her uneasiness had increased even more, and she became convinced that something dreadful must have happened to him.

Lily did not share her alarm, and made light of it. "Cleve's a big boy, Princess. He can take care of himself. I'm sure he's just been delayed by the storm."

But Adriana did not have Lily's confidence. Desolately, she added another coat of wax to the balustrades and awaited his return, praying the Lord would give her the opportunity to tell Cleve how much he meant to her.

What if she never had that chance? she thought later, pacing the floor behind the closed door of her room. What if she had lost the opportunity to tell him how much she cared about him—that her feeling for him was much more than gratitude, that the sight of him set her heart to skipping—and that his kiss and touch excited her?

And what if it was too late to look into his warm, sapphire eyes and tell him she was proud to be his wife?

Finally, unable to bear the confines of the room any longer, she went down the back stairway to the kitchen, but even that change didn't help. She brewed herself a cup of tea and sat at the table, deep in thought. If Cleve wasn't hurt, where could he be? Sickened, she thought of the one thing she hadn't considered before. What if he was with a woman?

Had she spent the day worrying about him while he basked in the arms of another woman? Lily would know! Perhaps that's why she hadn't been concerned over his welfare—Lily knew he was with another woman and didn't want to tell her. Well, she had no one to blame but herself.

She returned to her room and her pacing, fretful that she would fall asleep before he returned.

The Full House had closed for the night by the time Cleve returned. He walked wearily into his room, lit a lamp, then hung his gunbelt on the headboard. Sitting down on the bed, he pulled off his boots. All day, his thoughts had been on Raven. No matter how he tried to keep his mind on other matters, he couldn't shake the thought of her. Maybe she wasn't asleep. Maybe he should go down the hallway and tap on her door—just to see her and say good night. No, he was just kidding himself.

Standing up, he hung his hat on a hook, and just as he removed his jacket, the door opened behind him.

Cleve turned around. "Hi." He turned quickly and tossed his jacket on the chair.

"Where have you been all day? I was worried about you," Adriana said softly.

"I'm sorry. I rode out with the Rangers to the Valez ranch."

"Oh!"

"It was deserted, Raven. Not a soul around. They've all pulled out, cleared out of the area completely. The bank said Valez withdrew all his money shortly after those Rangers were killed."

"Guess that takes care of that," she said with the game little smile he loved so dearly.

"On the way back, we got caught in a storm and had to hole up until it passed."

"I see," she said. "It's so late; I was afraid something dreadful had happened to you."

"I'm fine, Raven. Just tired." He turned and looked at her. "Everything's okay, isn't it?"

"It is now that you're back."

He picked up his jacket and walked over to hang it up on a wall peg. "If I didn't know you better, I'd think you missed me."

"I missed you very much, Cleve," she said softly. "I even began to think that you were with another woman."

Incredulous, he turned and looked at her. "Why would you think that?"

"Once you start worrying, your imagination can play crazy tricks with you."

"Well, that's the least of your worries." His gaze lingered on her face. "Another woman is the farthest thing from my mind."

"Even if you have a wife who's a big disappointment to you?"

"I wouldn't know. I don't have a wife who's a disappointment to me. I figure it's the other way around."

He watched hopefully as she struggled with the temptation of the moment. "Well, I guess I better let you get some sleep. Good night, Cleve."

"Good night, Raven," he said sadly.

The arrival of her new clothing the next morning brightened Adriana's depressed mood, which had carried over from the previous night. Once again, she forced aside her troubling thoughts about Cleve and Antonio, and delved into the contents of the dozen or more boxes.

"Looks like those clothes came just in time," Cleve said. "Since my hand's still too sore to deal, I got tickets for the ballet tonight."

"The ballet!" Adriana squealed with pleasure. "Oh, Cleve!" She threw her arms around his neck and kissed his cheek. "I'm so excited."

"Well, since you've got some fancy gowns now, maybe we ought to do it up right. How about my making reservations at the finest hotel for a table after the show?"

"Oh, I'm going to love it. Just think how wonderful it will be to dance to an orchestra. How often do we get to dress up and go to an actual ballroom . . . with an orchestra!"

She shoved him out of her room. "I must begin to get ready."

Cleve pulled out his watch and glanced at it. "Honey, the ballet's not until eight o'clock tonight. You've got all day to get ready."

"I must bathe and wash my hair." She closed the door in his face.

Smiling to himself, Cleve went down to the kitchen and got himself a cup of coffee, then sat down at one of the tables to do the books. A short time later he looked up to see Miguel Castillo coming down the front stairway. He couldn't believe Lily was sleeping with the guy. Even though Raven had told him earlier that the couple was in love, he still couldn't believe it. Lily was too damn smart to fall for the bastard's line.

That fool couldn't love anything except his own reflection in the mirror, Cleve thought as he watched Miguel approach. Although, he had to admit, the fellow had shown a lot of courage in riding to Walden's ranch alone. At least Castillo wasn't a coward.

"Ah, my good comrade, you are just the man I wish to see," Miguel greeted, sitting down at the table.

"Let's set the record straight, Castillo; I am not your comrade. I'm getting tired of hearing you call me one."

Miguel grinned. "Shall we concede, at least, that we have the same person's interests at heart?"

Cleve glanced up from the books. "I hope you don't mean yours." He returned to perusing the ledgers.

"I am speaking of Lily—which is why I wish this little talk with you. You appear to be the only family Lily has, so I have decided the proper thing to do is inform you that Lily and I intend to wed."

Cleve slammed shut the ledger book. "You what?"

"I hope you will not try to interfere. It would come to no good."

"Is that so? Well, I guess I have no control over what Lily does with her life, Castillo. If I did, I'd sure stop her from making a big mistake. She's only going to end up getting hurt."

"Why do you think I will hurt her?"

"Let's be honest, Count Castillo. This is just a whim with you. You're an arrogant bastard who's amusing himself. When you get tired of the game, you'll laugh it

off, ride back to your own kind, and never give Lily
another thought."

"Is that what you intend to do with Adriana?"

"What the hell are you talking about?"

"Are you forgetting that your wife also comes from
the same kind as I do? If your logic is prophetic, *Señor*
MacKenzie, then you, too, would leave Adriana because she is not of the same kind as you. Is that not so?"

"Certainly not. I'm in love with Adriana, and I
believe she's in love with me."

A glint of anger flared in Miguel's eyes. "And of
course Lily and I could not possibly be in love."

"Lily probably is, which is what upsets me. But I sure
as hell have my doubts about you."

"My friend, I would like to believe we both are men
of honor."

"Is that so? Then why would a man of honor like
yourself, Castillo, refuse to marry Adriana because he
considered her to be *damaged goods?*"

"Ah, *amigo*, you must not believe that falsehood for a
moment longer. The remark was merely a Spaniard's
attempt to salvage his pride. Just rattling the sword, as
they say. After all, Adriana ran away on the day we
were to wed. Furthermore, when we found her with
you, I did not refuse to marry her. Don Alarico assumed
that. The truth is, had I believed she loved me or even
wanted to wed me, I would have married her without
hesitation. My heart would not have been in it, but I
would have honored my word."

The revelation took Cleve by surprise. It was obvious
that Miguel was being truthful.

"Also, you did not fool me for a minute, my friend.
Don Alarico could not have forced you to wed Adriana
if you hadn't already been in love with her."

"All right, so what does all this have to do with you
and Lily?"

"Simple, my friend. I love her."

"I find that hard to believe, Castillo. You believe
strongly in your own importance and traditions. Lily,

besides being an *Anglo,* has a past. You strike me as the kind who wouldn't be able to overlook all those things."

"I have nothing to overlook, for I have found the woman of my dreams. The woman who understands me and loves me for myself. You yourself have reason to know what an extraordinary woman she is."

Cleve nodded, but said skeptically, "It just doesn't make sense to me."

"That I could love Lily?"

"No—that Lily could love you," Cleve replied quickly. "You're right about one thing: Lily is easy to love. But you, Castillo, are hard to even like, much less love."

"The strength of love can change us all, my friend—no doubt even you. Didn't Adriana give up her past and traditions when she wed you?"

"I think she was prepared to do that when she left home and refused to marry you. Are you implying you're gonna run away from home, Castillo?" Cleve couldn't resist snickering.

"For the time being, we do intend to remain in Fort Worth. It is Lily's wish. But who knows? Perhaps we will even get a ranch. Having been in this wonderful country of Texas for a while, the idea appeals to me."

"Is that what you want?"

"I want what will make Lily happy."

"Which is all I want, too, Castillo. I'm skeptical, but Lily's old enough to know what she's doing."

"As I am, my friend. And just as I always knew I did not love Adriana, so do I know I am in love with Lily."

"Well, you sound sincere enough. I hope, for Lily's sake, you believe what you're saying."

"I am not an immature adolescent, making judgements motivated by youthful, hot-blooded passion. I have had my share of women and can recognize a rose, or should I say a lily, among thorns."

Even though he was not entirely convinced, Cleve reached out a hand. "Congratulations, Castillo. You're marrying a wonderful woman. And remember, if you do her wrong, you'll have to reckon with me, or one of my brothers. So when is the happy day?"

"As soon as she agrees to marry me."

"What?" Cleve exclaimed. "You mean she hasn't agreed to all this hogwash you've been spouting?"

"Thus far, only to our being together here in Fort Worth." Miguel smiled confidently. "But I am very persuasive, my friend. I soon will convince my little countess."

"Gotta hand it to you, Castillo. You sure aren't short on self-confidence."

"I think my darling Lily will be very happy with me, don't you agree, *Anglo?*" Miguel said, adding the closing word as a final rattle of his sword.

"I think she's already been good *for* you," Cleve responded, parrying the thrust.

Grinning, the two men shook hands.

With an hour to go before the curtain went up, Adriana began to dress for the ballet. As she put on her corset, she stole a glance of pleasure at the ball gown laid out on her bed.

"Raven, I'm having trouble with these studs. Will you help me?" Cleve asked, knocking and immediately entering her room. He drew up abruptly when he saw that she was dressed in only a corset, lace-trimmed drawers, and white hose. "Oops, sorry!"

"Just a minute." After she finished hooking her corset, she hurried over to him.

"Sorry to be such a bother. My hand's too stiff to hold onto these damn studs," he said, handing them to her. "I've finally given up in defeat."

"It's no bother."

"What do you call that thing you've got on?" he asked, as she began to insert the studs.

"A French corset."

"Different."

"Uh-huh. More comfortable, too. It's shorter and hooks in the front."

"So I've noticed. It's kind of fetching."

"I'm glad you like it, because it cost you a lot of money." She finished buttoning his shirt and picked up his right hand, cradling it tenderly in her own. The wound had closed up, but it still looked red. "Does your hand hurt?"

"No, it's just difficult to manipulate anything as tiny as those studs."

She glanced up skeptically. "You wouldn't tell me even if it did hurt."

"I wouldn't say that." He grinned wickedly. "Especially if you'd promise to keep holding it."

"Well, as long as you're here, you can help me." Picking up a small crinoline hoop, she handed it to him. "Will you hook this to the rear of my corset?"

"I don't understand how you women can walk around all wired up in these gadgets."

"This is just a tiny one for the rear. Think of what they were like when we wore them from waist to ankle," she declared.

"Oh, yes! I remember them well," he teased.

She glanced over her shoulder, her dark eyes flashing devilishly. "I might have known!"

"There." He backed out of the room. "Uh . . . I better finish dressing. If you need any more help, just call out."

Adriana stepped into white satin pumps, each adorned with a black satin coquille, then donned her gown and adjusted the black satin bodice over her bosom. The bodice and skirt hugged her breasts, tiny waist, and slim hips. Thin satin straps and a décolleté neckline exposed the smooth, olive luster of her shoulders and slender arms. Panels of black velvet, split at the waist, were draped over her hips and drawn into a tiered bustle over the rear crinoline. Satisfied with the result, she brushed her hair to a shine and pinned it behind her left ear with a tiny white plume tipped with delicate black and white peacock feathers. As a final touch, she pulled on white gloves that covered the length of her arms.

Then she hurried down the hallway to Cleve's room.

"Well, how do I look?" she asked, spinning around for his inspection.

"Wow!" he exclaimed, staring at her.

"Do you really like the dress?"

"It's elegant and painfully seductive." His gaze devoured her. "There won't be a man at the theater who'll be able to keep his eyes off you," he said, awestruck. He quickly turned away and picked up a cravat.

"Let me help you with that," she said, and went over to tie it for him. "Put your head back."

He held up his chin. "So, where'd you learn to tie a cravat?"

"I always tied Antonio's for him." She paused a moment, then finished and adjusted the tie to her satisfaction. Next she buttoned his vest, embroidered with red and gold thread, and stepped back to admire him.

His tall figure was clad in a black evening suit fitted to his broad shoulders, slender hips, and long muscular legs. A white shirt provided a stunning contrast to his deep tan and dark hair.

"My, you are handsome! I'm afraid every woman at the theater will be throwing herself at you."

Tucking her hand in the crook of his arm, he grinned down at her. "The gorgeous Spanish spitfire in the black dress is the only one that matters to me, Mrs. MacKenzie."

"Why, whatever do you mean?" she asked laughingly, as she posed with her chin in the air. "This little dove is the most serene lady in these parts. Ask anybody."

Lily's eyes rounded with pleasure when they came downstairs. "Oh, you two are the handsomest couple I've ever seen," she exclaimed. "Aren't they, Mike?"

"Yes, indeed!" Miguel said, nodding with pleasure as Cleve hurried Adriana out the door.

"Did you see Miguel?" Adriana exclaimed. "He was as excited as Lily."

"Yeah! Because I was leaving. He can't wait to get rid of me to try and break down Lily."

"Oh, Cleve, you have no romance in your blood!"

Chapter 25

❦❦

❝If that's romantic, then I stand guilty as accused,'' Cleve grumbled, as they left the theater after the performance of *Giselle*.

Entranced throughout the ballet, Adriana would hear none of it. ''Oh, I could have watched it again. It was so romantic and tragic when the poor girl died.''

''Romantic! From the few operas and ballets that I've seen, it seems like if you fall in love, you're doomed. It's a sure bet that before that curtain comes down, either one lover or both will be kicking the bucket.''

''They're all bittersweet. That's the beauty of it.'' She glanced at him askance. ''Admit it, MacKenzie, despite that smooth charm of yours, you're just not a romantic.''

''I am, too. That's why I believe that when two people fall in love, they'll live happily ever after.''

''Adriana.''

Hearing her name, she turned around, her smile disappearing at the sight of Elena Montez, accompanied by her parents.

''Elena, how nice to see you.'' *You little tattler!* she thought with disgust, recalling how her friend had broken her promise by telling her father that Adriana was in Fort Worth. ''Don Francisco, *Señora* Montez,'' she acknowledged politely.

"Well, Adriana, this is indeed a surprise. Where is Don Alarico?"

"In San Antonio, I would think, Don Francisco."

"And when do you intend to return there?" *Señora* Montez asked.

"I have no intention of returning to San Antonio, *señora*."

"Have you informed your father of this decision?" the don asked.

"No. And I do not intend to, Don Francisco."

The don and his wife exchanged shocked glances. He looked at her with disapproval. "Then I shall make it my responsibility to do so."

Cleve had stood silently throughout the exchange. Resenting the man's officious attitude toward Adriana, he now stepped forward, putting his hand on her elbow.

"Are you ready to leave, Adriana? We have reservations, remember?"

Don Francisco looked at him haughtily. "And who are you?"

"Oh, excuse me. Don Francisco and *Señora* Montez, may I introduce my husband, Cleve MacKenzie," Adriana said.

"How do you do," Cleve said, offering to shake hands.

"You married an *Anglo!*" the don said, ignoring Cleve's hand as well as the introduction. "Is Don Alarico aware of this?"

"Don Alarico is very aware of it, sir. *Señora, señorita,*" Cleve said, tipping his hat to the astounded women. Grasping Adriana's arm firmly, he led her away.

Adriana was embarrassed by the way the Montezes had treated Cleve. Their rudeness and snobbery were inexcusable. These people were shallow and imperious—had they always been so overbearing? She realized that after knowing people like Cleve and Lily, she could never go back to her former kind of life.

Now she saw clearly the reason behind Miguel's decision. He must have recognized the truth, too, had decided that what he gained from a life with Lily would far exceed the life he abandoned.

Her brooding thoughts were forgotten when they entered the elegant ballroom, and the maître d'hôtel led them to their table. Once the music began, she became aware only of the desire in the eyes of the handsome man waltzing her around the floor.

It was past midnight when they returned to the darkened barroom of The Full House, lit only by an upstairs wall sconce. Adriana hummed the melody of the "Blue Danube" as she kicked off her pumps, then waltzed across the floor. Removing the plume, she tossed it on the bar and released her hair.

"Oh, Cleve, I had such a wonderful time tonight," she said. Combing her fingers through her hair's thickness, she shook it out.

"I did, too."

He came up behind her and slipped his arms around her waist. "Raven, have you ever been out of Texas?"

"No." She sighed, leaning back into him.

"Some time I'm going to take you to see New York and St. Louis." He lowered his head and slid his lips down the slender column of her neck.

She turned in his arms and smiled up at him, her eyes sparkling with excitement. "And New Orleans, Cleve! I've heard so much about New Orleans! And, oh, I want to see San Francisco, too."

He chuckled warmly. "Hmmm. I guess we've got some traveling to do. Seems like they finished that transcontinental railroad just in time to be ready for us."

"Can we afford it, Cleve?"

"Sweetheart, as long as I can find a card game, we can afford it."

"Doesn't your luck ever run out?"

"It hasn't yet. Right now, looks to me like it might be getting better. But before we leave Texas, I want you to meet my family."

Turning, she snuggled back against him again. "Do you think they'll like me, Cleve?"

"They'll love you, honey. There's no doubt about it," he whispered at her ear.

But the talk of his family brought Antonio to her mind. Stepping out of his arms, she turned to look at him, this time with despair.

"What is it?"

"Do you think I'll ever see my brother again?"

"I don't know, Raven. Especially since he's with Walden."

"If I could only find Antonio and talk to him. I'm sure I—"

"Raven, he made a choice," Cleve said firmly. "You're going to have to accept that."

Appalled, she looked at him. "Accept it? I can't just abandon my brother."

"The truth, Raven, is that he has abandoned you."

"He has not abandoned me. I don't believe it. I'll never believe it."

"Maybe that's half the problem."

"Then the other half is you!" she declared. She went to stare gloomily out the window.

"So nothing's changed. We have to continue thrashing over the same argument that neither of us has a solution for. To go on pretending we don't want each other—when we both know that's not true. And all because of an arrogant, weak sonofa—"

"Don't say it!" She spun to look at him. "Don't ever say it in my presence. You've made it clear how you feel about Antonio. Think of me for a change, and try to understand how much your dislike of my brother hurts me."

"I love you, Raven. I've never meant to hurt you. Yet you continue to hold me to blame. How about you

trying to understand how it hurts *me* that your brother
is riding with a man who murdered my mother and my
brother's wife, and you don't think he should be held to
task for it? Pretty pitiful, isn't it? Good night, Raven."

She stood stiffly at the window and listened to the
echo of his footsteps.

The next morning, as he passed the door to Adriana's
room, Cleve stopped abruptly when he heard an unusual sound coming from inside. He listened and heard
the sound repeated.

After tapping on the door and getting no response,
he opened it. Adriana sat on the floor, leaning over the
chamber pot and regurgitating.

"Honey!" He hurried over and knelt down beside
her.

Adriana raised her head. Strands of hair clung to her
forehead, and her eyes looked like black circles against
the pallor of her face.

"Have you been sick all night?" he asked worriedly.
She shakily tried to rise, and he lifted her in his arms
and carried her over to the bed.

"No. I woke up this morning, and when I stood up, I
suddenly felt dizzy and nauseated."

Cleve wet a towel and gently wiped her forehead.
"You stay in bed. I'll get Jim Anderson."

"Cleve, I don't need a doctor. I'll be okay. I feel better
already." Cautiously, she rose to her feet.

"There's no harm in resting, Raven," he said firmly,
setting her back down on the edge of the bed.

"Well, maybe you're right. I'll lie down for a short
while."

"Do you need anything?"

"No."

"I'll leave your door open. If you want anything, just
call out."

"Thanks, Cleve." She closed her eyes and he left.

Despite her show of bravado, Adriana still felt
squeamish. She soon got up and dressed slowly, and

went down to the kitchen. Cleve made her a cup of tea and a toasted muffin, which settled her stomach.

"Feeling better?" Cleve asked. "At least you've got your color back."

"I'm fine now. Maybe I was just hungry."

"Well, the little you ate sure wouldn't have satisfied a hungry appetite."

The pattern of her morning sickness was repeated daily throughout the week. Lily was convinced Adriana was pregnant, and she suspected it was true. Cleve insisted she visit Jim Anderson, and, as all three of them expected, the doctor confirmed their suspicions.

Cleve grinned broadly when she told him the news. "Do you have any idea how much I want a child?"

"Having seen you with children, it doesn't come as a surprise," she said, just as pleased as he was.

"Whew," he said, sinking down in a chair. "We've got to make some changes to get ready for the baby." He looked at her and smiled. "Start packing, honey. It's time we go home."

"Home to where?"

"To the Triple M. Lily can run this place without my help. I'll settle some business, and we can leave on the northbound stage in two days."

"I'm really happy for you, Cleve," Lily said, when he sat her down and told her his plans. "You're gonna make one hell of a father."

"I'm not putting any time limit on how long we'll be gone, Lily. Do you have any problem with that?"

"Of course not." She leaned back in her chair. "I've got something to tell you, too: Mike and I are getting married."

"Married! How soon?"

"Mike went down to speak to the priest. He said we're getting married tonight, before you try to talk me out of it."

Cleve looked at her hopefully. "Do I have a chance?"

Amused but decisive, Lily replied, "Not a prayer, boss man."

That evening, upon arriving at The Full House, the usual collection of card players received an unexpected surprise when they were invited to witness the marriage of Lily LaRue to Count Miguel Enrique Felipe Castillo y de Rey.

Radiant with happiness, Lily wore a gown of pale blue satin and long white gloves borrowed from Adriana. She carried a single lily.

Despite his sophistication, the count appeared to be a typical nervous bridegroom.

Grinning with amusement, Cleve looked around the room at the assorted guests, ranging from Judge Thaddius Raymond to Magdalena and Paulo Guerra. Even Waco Donniger had slicked back his hair and waxed his moustache for the occasion.

With champagne flowing freely, the card players finally drifted off to their game. Due to the slight stiffness in his hand, Cleve did not join them. Instead, he enjoyed dancing to the music provided by a three-piece Mexican band.

"Happy, Lily?" Cleve asked as he waltzed her around the floor.

"Oh, boss man, if this is all a dream, please don't wake me."

"You love him that much, honey?"

She nodded. "Don't ask me to explain it. I don't understand it myself. Oh, not why I love him . . . but why Mike married me after I had already agreed to be his mistress. He said he wanted me as a wife instead."

"And you're sure he's not interested in going back to San Antonio?"

"That's right. We'll stay here in Fort Worth, and I can continue to manage The Full House if you want me to."

"And do you want to?"

"Of course. I love this place, Cleve. The Full House . . . you . . . Adriana, Magdalena, Paulo, and

Waco. You've all made me feel good about myself. I'm independent for the first time in my life."

"Not anymore, Lily; you just got married."

"Oh, you know what I mean."

"Yeah. I'm glad for you, Lily."

"It's all due to you, Cleve."

"I had nothing to do with it. It was you who put your life on the line to save my brother. No, honey, you've got nobody to thank but yourself."

He took her hand and walked back to their table. After they sat down, he reached into his pocket and pulled out a folded paper. "This is my wedding gift to you."

Perplexed, Lily looked at him, then opened up the paper and read it. "Why, this is the deed to The Full House!"

"That's right. I signed the place over to you this afternoon. You own it now."

Lily stared in astonishment at him. "Why would you do this, Cleve?"

"As I told you, Adriana and I are heading north to the Triple M to meet my family, but then we're thinking of going to California for a spell."

"Damn you, Cleve MacKenzie," Lily said, dabbing at her eyes. "Now you've made me cry."

"Brides are expected to cry on their wedding day."

"I don't know what to say," Lily said. "Nobody's done anything like this for me before."

"Well, I know you married a rich man, honey, so you won't need money. But this will be something of your own. I don't want you to lose the sense of independence you have. If Mike doesn't want you running the place, find yourself an honest manager like I did."

She grabbed him and kissed him. "I love you, Cleve."

"So, what is this? I find my wife kissing another man?" Miguel exclaimed, returning to the table with Adriana.

Cleve looked up at him and groaned. "Oh, don't tell

me. Does this mean another slap in the face and a challenge to a duel?"

"Mike, look at this," Lily said excitedly. "You're not going to believe it." She handed Miguel the deed.

"It's our wedding gift to Lily. I apologize for not including you, but that would defeat the purpose. Besides, Mike, you've already gotten the best gift at this wedding." He squeezed Lily's hand.

After a quick perusal of the paper, Miguel looked at him. "Your generosity is exceeded only by your wisdom, my friend." Slipping his arm around Lily's shoulders, he said, "I thank you for making her so happy. I suppose I'd be wasting my breath if I offered to pay you for this place."

"You supposed right, Mike." Turning to Lily, Cleve said, "I might have misjudged this man, Lily. He's beginning to think more like an *Anglo* every day."

They all broke into laughter. Lily leaned over and lightly kissed Miguel. "And he's cute, too!"

"Cute!" Miguel threw up his hands. "*¡Caramba!* Only my darling Lily would call me cute!"

"Well, I sure as hell wouldn't," Cleve said.

Lily and Adriana were both claimed for a dance, and once Cleve was alone with Miguel, he said, "Actually, Castillo, I do have a wedding gift for you. I'm giving you Swifty."

"Swifty? Isn't that your gelding?"

"Yep."

Miguel's eyes widened in surprise. "You jest, my friend. He is a beautiful animal."

"You bet he is! And he can outrun any horse in Texas. So I expect you to take good care of him, Castillo."

"Why would you do this, *Señor* Cleve?"

"Adriana and I will be taking a stage, so I can't take the horse with me."

"Then let me buy him from you," Miguel said.

"I'd rather give him to you. I can tell you're a horseman, Castillo, so I know you won't mistreat him. He's smart and loyal. And he's got a good heart."

"The same could be said about you, Cleve MacKenzie." Clearly moved, he added, "My friend, I am at a loss for words."

"Hell!" Cleve said, grinning broadly. "If I'd known that, I'd have given him to you sooner."

The dance ended, and the two men rose to their feet as their wives rejoined them.

"You'll have to excuse us, folks," Cleve said. "I have an urgent need to hold my wife." Gazing down into her brown eyes, aglow with warmth, he took her arm. "I believe this is our dance, Mrs. MacKenzie."

The following morning, in a tearful parting, Adriana said good-bye to Lily, Waco, the Guerra family, and Pepito. After the two women hugged and kissed, Lily reminded her to be sure and write to them as soon as she and Cleve were settled.

"And do not be surprised if someday we meet again," Miguel added.

"The door will always be open, Mike," Cleve said. "I think I've finally figured you out."

"And I you," Miguel replied. *"Hasta la vista, amigo."*

"Until we do, take good care of her, Mike."

"I pledge it on my honor."

"Then I reckon I can quit worrying, friend."

As they grinned and shook hands, Miguel offered a solemn invocation.

"Vaya con Dios."

Chapter 26

As the stagecoach rattled and bumped along the road, Adriana tried to read, but the coach swayed and rocked so much, she soon gave up. She managed to nap most of the day, leaning against Cleve's shoulder or curled up on the seat with her head in his lap. She was relieved when they finally stopped at a stage station to change horses and spend the night.

She could barely stay awake during dinner. As soon as they finished, they went to their room to go to bed.

"I can't believe how doing nothing all day can be so exhausting," Adriana said, yawning.

"Imagine how the poor horses must feel," Cleve teased. But Adriana had drifted off to sleep.

With his elbow propped and his head cradled in his hand, he lay on his side, gazing down at her face. "Hope I never get *that* sleepy, my Little Raven," he whispered tenderly. Then he kissed her on the forehead and blew out the lamp.

The following day was worse than the previous one. The stage was full, so Adriana could only rest her head on Cleve's shoulder.

The next morning, Cleve and Adriana were the only passengers on the mail stage that headed west toward Calico. Adriana was thrilled to discover they had the coach to themselves, but Cleve was uneasy about the situation, after seeing the driver tuck a whiskey bottle in his pocket before climbing up onto the box seat. Drinking and driving a team did not mix, as far as Cleve was concerned. He figured they were in for a rough ride.

His hunch proved to be correct. The light stage bounced and swayed more severely than the previous days, as the driver sped recklessly along the countryside.

In a short time, Adriana became ill. Cleve shouted at the driver to stop the coach, and she barely had time to scramble out before she lost her meal. They rested awhile, giving Adriana's stomach a chance to settle. Meanwhile, much to Cleve's distress, the driver continued drinking.

"I should have rented a buckboard and driven this last fifty miles myself," Cleve said.

"How much farther do we have to go?" she asked, her head in his lap.

"I figure about twenty or twenty-five miles."

"I'm sorry to be such a bother." She smiled wanly up at him. "I don't remember ever getting ill like this. I think I'd rather walk the rest of the way than climb back into that coach."

"Honey, you're in a delicate condition, and this drunken sonofabitch has managed to hit every rock in the road."

"I'm not so fragile that I'll crack, you know."

"Yeah, I know; you're one tough gal, all right," he teased lightly, brushing aside the hair clinging to her forehead. "I just don't like taking chances with you and the baby."

She gazed lovingly up at him. "I hope it's a boy, Cleve." A soft smile curved her face as she closed her eyes.

He gently stroked her cheek. "And I want a little girl who looks just like her mother," he said softly, pressing a light kiss to her forehead.

"Let's get goin', folks," the driver called out.

Irritated, Cleve glanced at him in time to see the man toss away the empty whiskey bottle. "I'd like my wife to have a little more chance to rest."

"Got a schedule to follow, mister. You can rest all week 'til the next stage comes through, if you've a mind to. But I'm gettin' out of here." He climbed unsteadily up onto the box and grabbed the reins. "Get aboard if yer comin'."

"What in hell does an hour matter, one way or the other?" Cleve grumbled, helping Adriana to her feet.

"Mister, I ain't gonna argue. I'm drivin'." His speech was heavily slurred. "You folks comin' or not?"

"I don't think you're sober enough to handle that team," Cleve accused. "Why don't you let me drive?"

The driver snorted. "Mister, you're in good hands. Gus Baylor can handle a team sleepin'."

"What about drunk?" Cleve mumbled as he assisted Adriana into the coach. "Well, Gus, will you please have some consideration for my wife's condition, and take it a little slower on those turns?"

Cleve climbed into the stage, and they took off in a cloud of dust.

After another ten minutes, the terrain began to rise and the road took a series of sharp curves. Gus made no effort to slow his speed on the narrow trail. Several times the rear right wheel careened off the road. Glancing at Adriana, Cleve saw that her skin looked waxen.

"Dammit, this has got to stop!" he cursed. He leaned his head out the window. "Gus, rein in." The driver either didn't hear or just ignored him, because they continued on at breakneck speed.

As they rounded a curve, Gus veered left, trying to avoid a huge boulder lying on the trail. The rear wheel smashed against the granite wall and broke apart, and the coach slammed to the ground. The team broke free, dragging the box seat and part of the splintered axle with them.

Cleve threw his body over Adriana, clutching her

tightly as he tried to protect her, but they were tossed from side to side as the coach tumbled off the road and rolled over, coming to a stop in the ditch at the side of the road.

"Honey, are you okay?"

When she didn't answer, he raised his head to look at her. "Raven!"

Cleve managed to roll out from under her. Turning her over, he laid his ear to her heart and found that her breathing was slow, but steady. "Raven. Raven, honey."

With the coach turned on its side, it was too cramped to do anything for her. The door was sprung and wedged shut, but after several forcible kicks, he managed to break it open and crawl out. The trunks had been damaged, and pieces of clothing and mail lay scattered on the ground. In the distance, he caught a glimpse of the racing team with Gus clinging to the reins.

Cleve succeeded in pulling off the door and crawled back through the opening. Maneuvering his arms under Adriana, he managed to lift her out and carry her over to the shade of a tree. Laying her down, he checked her limbs but did not detect any breaks. She looked so pallid, however, he worried that she might have a head injury.

Cleve left her long enough to find a canteen among the scattered remains. Then, wetting a scarf, he laid it across her forehead. She slowly opened her eyes.

"How are you feeling, honey?"

"Wha . . . what happened?" she asked in a weak voice.

"The coach turned over."

"I feel like the horses trampled over me," she said, trying to sound flippant. Sitting up, she flexed her shoulders. "Ouch! I'm going to be black and blue for a month, but nothing feels broken."

"Well, just take it slow. We've lost Gus and the horses, so it looks like we've got a walk ahead of us."

"Anything's better than riding in that coach. You aren't hurt, are you?"

"No, I'm fine, Raven."

He sprang to his feet when she attempted to stand up. "Now, don't try moving too fast," he warned, putting a helping hand to her elbow. "How does your stomach feel?"

"Queasy, but the thought of not having to climb back into that stagecoach is making me feel better already."

He grasped her around the waist to help support her as Adriana took several wobbling steps.

Startled, she suddenly stopped and clutched her stomach. "Cleve! The baby!" She sagged, fainting in his arms.

He lifted her and gently placed her under the tree. Seeing large spots of blood on her skirt, he guessed the reason for her outcry. She was losing the baby. For a moment he stared, bereft, fighting back the rise of tears over the loss of the tiny life that one day would have grown to become the child they would have nurtured with their love.

The stains spread rapidly, and he knew he had to do something fast. Grabbing a couple of his shirts that were lying nearby, he ripped one into strips. Then he removed her soiled clothing, padded her where she bled, and dressed her in a shirt. He couldn't think what else to do, except try to make her as comfortable as possible. He found a couple of blankets belonging to the stage company scattered among the clothing and the mail. After hastily gathering some fallen pine needles from the stand of trees behind them, he covered them with clothing and a blanket, and managed to make her a fairly soft bed. Adriana awoke when he carried her over to it and laid her down.

"I lost the baby, didn't I?"

He nodded and reached for her hand. "I'm sorry, sweetheart. We'll have others." He brushed aside the tears streaking her cheeks. "The important thing is for you to get well now."

Feeling despair, she turned her head away. Seeing the pile of her discarded clothing, she glanced down at herself, then blushed with embarrassment. "Cleve, you didn't have to—"

"Raven, we're husband and wife."

Sobbing, she drew a shuddering breath. "It's all my fault. I wasn't strong enough to protect my own baby."

He gathered her into his arms and rocked her. "Aw, sweetheart, don't blame yourself. If that goddamn driver hadn't been drunk, this never would have happened."

He tipped up her chin and smiled at her. "All that matters now, my love, is that you get well."

"Please forgive me, Cleve," she whispered against his chest.

"Sweetheart, it's not your fault."

"I mean forgive me for how I've been acting about Antonio. Blaming you for something that isn't your fault, either." She slipped her arms around his neck. "We'll make a baby again soon, won't we, Cleve?"

"Of course, love. As soon as you're well." He kissed her lightly and smiled tenderly. "We'll have as many babies as you wish, my love." He pressed another kiss to her forehead. "Now, you get some rest while I pack up our clothes. They're lying all over the place."

Docilely, she allowed him to lay her down, but tears continued to roll down her cheeks. He held her hand and stayed beside her until she cried herself to sleep.

While Adriana slept, Cleve repacked their clothing and returned the mail to the pouch. Then he glanced around to survey their situation. He spied a narrow stream among the trees and saw that it flowed parallel to the road. Analyzing its course, he said aloud, "Bet it's the same one that runs through the Triple M. Too bad I don't have a boat."

Since it soon would be nightfall, he collected the splintered wood of the stagecoach and built a fire. Then he sat down and gazed at the face of his sleeping wife. Purple shadows had formed beneath her eyes, but the color had returned to her cheeks. He thought of how ill she had been throughout the carriage ride, and yet she had not complained. He knew her heart was aching over the loss of their baby, but one day, this whole incident would be just a faint bad memory.

Reaching out, he gently traced the delicate curve of her jaw. Adriana opened her eyes. "Hi, sweetheart."

She smiled at him. "Hi," she said softly.

"Feeling better?"

She nodded, then stretched. "Oh-h-h . . . still sore, though."

He grinned. "Well, there's something I can do about that. How about a back rub?"

"I'd love it!"

"Then roll over, Mrs. MacKenzie."

She turned over on her stomach and rested her cheek on her folded arms. Cleve slipped his hands beneath the shirt and began to knead her aching muscles.

Sighing with contentment, Adriana closed her eyes. "Oh, that feels so good. Nothing compares to the feel of your hands, Cleve. I could lie here forever and have you do that."

He worked the muscles at the back of her neck until he felt them relax. "There, how's that, honey?"

She turned over and sat up, leaning back against the tree. "It was wonderful. Aren't you sore?"

"No, I've been able to move around and work out the soreness." He covered his mouth as he yawned.

"I can see that you're tired, though. Why don't you try and get some sleep?"

"Yeah, I think I will. Do you need any help before I do?"

"No. You've done enough already. I can help myself now."

"Well, if you need anything, just holler," he said. Within minutes, he dozed off.

Snuggled together, they slept undisturbed throughout the night.

The next morning, Cleve succeeded in shooting a

rabbit. While he roasted it on a spit, Adriana slipped among the trees and gave herself a cool but cleansing sponge bath at the stream. Then, after dressing, brushing her teeth, and braiding her hair, she felt like a new woman. Returning to the fire, she said so to Cleve.

"I'd say you look like a new woman, too, Raven, but I think it'd be better if you continue to rest."

"Cleve, I'm fine. Truly I am. There's no reason why we can't leave."

"I know of several reasons. We've got a source of water and food right here. And if we go, we'd have to leave our clothes and my saddle behind. There's no guarantee they'd be here when I came back for them."

"Well, they'd most likely still be here," she declared.

"Besides, someone is sure to come looking for the stage when it doesn't show up in Calico. All we have to do is wait it out—and while we do, you'll be gaining your strength back instead of losing it."

"It's very difficult to argue with you, Cleve MacKenzie. You're too logical."

Chuckling, he held up an axe. "Speaking of logic, look what I found. Should have figured sooner that there'd be one on that stage. They bring them along in case they have to chop up tree limbs or anything that might be blocking the trail.

"Of course, a fallen tree would never deter Mr. Gus Baylor," he said sarcastically. "I wonder how he made out. The last I saw of him, he was being dragged away by his team."

"All right, you've convinced me we should stay. What can I do to be helpful?"

"Just sit and rest. That'll do fine for the time being."

Resigned to her fate, Adriana returned to the bed and sat down.

Later that day, just as Cleve had predicted, two men in a wagon arrived at the site of the accident.

"Well, I'll be goddamned! It's Cleve MacKenzie!" the driver exclaimed.

Cleve walked over to the wagon and shook hands with the driver, who had just climbed down. "How are you doing, Curly?"

"Howdy, Cleve," the other man called out.

"Good to see you, Cal." Cleve shook hands with the older man, who had remained seated. Adriana saw a badge on his vest.

"Thought for sure you'd be retired by now, Cal," Cleve declared.

"I could be if that damn brother of yours would take the job," Cal said.

"You aren't gonna get Luke to go back to being a lawman, Cal. He promised Honey he wouldn't."

"Don't suppose you'd be interested?" the sheriff asked, with a wily gleam in his eyes.

"You've got that right, you old fox," Cleve said, slipping an arm around Adriana's shoulders. "Raven, this is Sheriff Cal Ellis and Curly Gunter. Curly runs the livery stable." Both men doffed their hats. "Gentlemen, this is my wife, Adriana."

"Your wife!" Curly exclaimed. "Congratulations, Cleve. Hadn't heard you tied the knot."

"It's only been a month."

"Well, I'll be god—ah, dadblamed!" Cal Ellis said. "Figured I'd never live to see the day all three of the MacKenzie boys were married—especially that Flint. Sure a right pleasure meetin' you, Miz MacKenzie."

"The pleasure's all mine, Sheriff Ellis. And you, too, Mr. Gunter."

"Shucks, ma'am, just call me Curly like everyone else does. Sure glad to see you folks alive. Didn't know what we'd find out here when that team came trotting into Calico dragging Gus Baylor."

"Is he still alive?" Cleve asked.

"Yeah. Rode the box seat in. 'Course he's a mite banged up, and the skin's peeled off him in a place or two."

Adriana blanched when he added, "Looked like the

Comanches had gotten hold of him and had been funnin' with him. Doc said he'll be okay, though."

"He was probably too drunk to notice there wasn't a stage under him," Cleve grumbled. "Well, let's get out of here."

Within a few minutes they had loaded the trunks onto the wagon. Cleve made Adriana a comfortable pallet to sit on in the wagon bed, then climbed in next to her.

Twilight had descended by the time the wagon pulled into Calico.

Adriana glanced around with interest. The town was nothing more than several blocks of dusty road lined with wooden buildings on either side.

After dropping Cal off at the sheriff's office, they passed the livery stable and gunsmith's shop. At Cleve's insistence they unloaded the trunks at a two-story hotel, then continued down the street, passing Jenkins Dry Goods and an abandoned diner with a weather-beaten sign that read *"Maud's Eatery—Best Home Cooking in Texas"* hanging tenuously from a broken chain. Curly finally reined up in front of a white house with a doctor's shingle tacked to the front porch.

"Thanks, Curly. I'll be needing a buckboard to ride out to the ranch tomorrow," Cleve said, swinging Adriana out of the wagon.

"Sure thing, Cleve. Night, Miz MacKenzie."

"Good night, Curly, and thank you for your help."

The doctor appeared to be as old as the sheriff. Gray-haired, with a soft-looking white beard that Adriana itched to tug, he checked her vital signs and recommended she remain off her feet to avoid any possibility of excessive bleeding. After a lengthy welcome to Cleve, he told Adriana he wanted her to return in two weeks for an examination.

Hand in hand, they walked back to the hotel. Only the occasional glow of a lamp shining through a window cast any light on the street.

"So this is where you were raised?" she remarked.

"Yep," Cleve said. "As long as I can remember, the town hasn't changed, except for the addition of the telegraph office and Maud closing up her diner. Even most of the people are the same, too."

She smiled up at him. "But I can tell you love this town, don't you?"

He laughed and slipped his arm around her waist, pulling her against his side. "Yeah, I guess I do."

"It must be a good feeling to come back to something so dear to you."

He squeezed her hand. "You know, Raven, I hadn't thought of that," he said. "But you're right. It feels good to be home again."

Chapter 27

As the old buckboard creaked along the winding trail, Adriana continued to nervously twist a strand of her hair while she gazed absently at the passing countryside.

Cleve had said the ride from Calico to the Triple M was all of twenty miles—but it certainly hadn't been far enough for the butterflies in her stomach to settle down and enjoy the ride. Would the MacKenzies be as fair-minded as Lily had led her to believe? And even if Cleve's brothers were as likable as Lily claimed them to be, what about their wives? What if Honey and Garnet, whom she had heard so much about, wouldn't accept her? Ostracized her? After all, two's company and three's a crowd. And she just knew Cleve would treat her like an invalid. He'd been doing so from the time she'd gotten morning sickness. That would probably irritate his sisters-in-law all the more, especially with Honey due to have a baby soon.

And she looked terrible, too! Large purple circles under her eyes . . . Adriana shook her head hopelessly. This was the worst time possible to be meeting Cleve's family. She was certain it would turn out just as disastrously as Cleve's meetings with her father and brother.

As Cleve turned off the road and started to follow a

worn wagon path, it was suddenly too late to worry anymore. They were nearly there.

"I just know they won't like me," she said.

"You're that sure," Cleve replied, amused.

Adriana nodded. "Women usually don't like me. They think I'm headstrong and spoiled."

"Wonder where they would get that impression," he said drolly. He was looking straight ahead, so she couldn't see if he was serious or not. "And how do you get along with men?"

"I can usually get along with them."

"Then at least that's half the battle. Come to think of it," he said, "it's more than half. Josh, Andy, and Amigo are males, too."

"Amigo?" she asked, feeling a rising panic. "You've told me Josh is Luke's son, Andy is Flint's. Who is Amigo?"

"Oh, Amigo is a very important family member. He's Josh's genuine, absolutely certified, purebred mongrel." Looking glum, he shook his head. "And if he doesn't like you, I'm afraid you just won't fit in at the ranch."

"Cleve MacKenzie, you're making fun of me," she declared.

He started to chuckle. "They're all going to love you, Raven; you'll see. We're Scots, honey. We tend to be clannish."

"If anyone's clannish it's my father, *Anglo,*" she teased.

He looked askance at her. "In your father's case, any clannishness is a matter of snobbery, but in the case of a Scot, the clan means unity and loyalty."

Cleve pulled to a stop at the top of the hill, and she caught her first glimpse of the MacKenzie homestead. Below in the sage-covered valley, a stream snaked lazily past a pine-fenced corral that contained a dozen grazing horses. Nestled in the shelter of white birch and Ponderosa pine were a half-dozen buildings.

"It looks like a small village," Adriana exclaimed.

"That log house on the right was built by my father. Luke and his family live there now. Last spring, he added another room because Honey's expecting."

He pointed to another log house about a hundred yards west of the first. "Flint and his family live there. Maud Malone and Ben Franks live with them. The others are just outbuildings."

"It's a compound, isn't it? Why did they choose to live so close together?"

"They wanted to—just to be together, I guess. Better protection that way, and more companionship for the women and children. After Flint and Garnet married, we bought the neighboring spread from Ben Franks and extended the boundaries of the Triple M."

"Well, who owns what?"

"The Triple M's owned by all of us."

"But you're not a rancher, Cleve."

"So what? There's room for me anytime I want to be there."

"Who are Maud and Ben?"

"Well, Ben owned the Flying F, the bordering spread I mentioned. He's an old-timer—settled here even before my folks. When he got too up in years, his daughter wanted him to go out east and live with her, somewhere in New York. We figured it'd break his heart to leave here, so Flint and Garnet took him in."

"And who's Maud? His wife?"

"No, but talk about old-timers!" Cleve said, grinning. "Maud used to run the diner in Calico. She was a close friend of my folks. Other than Ma, Maud was the only family we knew. She even went with us last year on the cattle drive to Kansas."

"So she's not really related to you."

"Not blood-related, no, but that doesn't mean she's not family to us. Maud always kind of kept an eye on us while we were growing up."

"So now you're taking care of her."

He chuckled. "Don't ever let Maud hear you say that.

She's a tough old gal who can take care of herself. We all love her."

Cleve flicked the reins, and they descended the hill.

"Hello," he shouted, reining up in front of Luke's house. After climbing down from the buckboard, he swung Adriana to the ground.

"Anybody in there?" he called out again, tapping on the door. When he still didn't get an answer, he shoved the door open and peeked in. "It's empty. Maybe they're all over at Flint's."

He took her hand, and they crossed the yard to the other house. It was just as deserted.

"Where the hell can they be?" He began to feel worried. "They couldn't have gone to town. We would have passed them on the road."

He swung his glance to the closed doors of the barn, which made him doubt he'd find anyone inside. "I'm going to see if their horses are in the barn."

"Maybe they're all out on the range," Adriana suggested as they walked over to the barn.

"Honey's on the verge of having a baby. I'd think she'd be sticking close to the house."

When Cleve opened the barn door, a whiff of new-mowed hay drifted from the darkened building. He swung both doors wide open to let in the sunlight.

"Wait here, Raven." Slowly, he stepped into the barn, uncertain of what to expect.

Suddenly, a horrendous clamor of clanging and shouts rent the air. Cleve reached for his Colt, but just as quickly dropped his arm away.

Shouts and laughter sounded above the clamor of spoons and forks banging against pots and pans, as his family jumped out from the concealment of the stalls. Yapping loudly, and with a furiously wagging tail, Amigo raced up in his limping gait and lapped at Cleve's boots.

"Dammit, you all scared the hell out of me!"

"Uncle Cleve! Uncle Cleve!"

Grinning with pleasure, Cleve opened up his arms, and his eight-year-old nephew leaped into them, throwing his arms around Cleve's neck.

"Mama said you got married. Does that mean you're gonna stay here now? Sure hope so. How come you got married, Uncle Cleve? Daddy said you'd never settle down. But Mama said you'd find the right woman some day. Guess you found her, huh, Uncle Cleve?"

"Hey! Hey! Slow down there, Josh." He hugged and kissed his nephew, then put the boy down. Reaching out, he gently drew Honey into his arms. After kissing her, he smiled affectionately into her baby-blue eyes. "How's our little mother feeling?"

"I'm fine," Honey said. "I'm so happy for you, Cleve."

"Impending motherhood has made you even lovelier, Honey Bear."

"You're not going to get me riled with that stupid name," she said. "I'm too glad to see you."

"Congratulations, Cleve." Holding her infant son, Garnet stepped forward. After they hugged and kissed, he peeked at the bundle in her arms. "How's my godson doing? Hi there, Andy," he cooed. "Just look at that. He sure is all MacKenzie, isn't he?"

Garnet smiled down at her infant son. "I'm glad he didn't get my coloring—he'd look lost in this family."

Cleve kissed her again on the cheek. "Well, then, let's hope you saved it for a girl, 'cause that red hair and green eyes sure look good on you."

"I always knew some lucky gal would get you some day, you good-looking devil," Maud Malone exclaimed, poking him in the ribs with her elbow. She grabbed him and gave him a big smack on the lips, then stepped back and wiped away the tears in her eyes. "Now all three of my boys are married." Sniffling, she moved aside for Ben Franks to offer his congratulations.

"Thanks, Ben," Cleve said to the old rancher. "You're sure looking good, old-timer."

"That's cause I've been eatin' some decent cookin' for a change, Cleve. These gals take right good care of me."

Glancing over the old man's shoulder, Cleve saw his two brothers standing back, grinning. Having not seen them for so long, he felt both the joy of reunion and a twinge of sorrow at realizing how much he had missed them.

"So you finally up and did it, Little Brother," Flint said, walking up and shaking hands. Then, grinning broadly, the two slapped each other on the back.

"I figured if a woman could put up with an ornery coot like you, Brother Flint, I sure wouldn't have a problem." Cleve then reached for Luke's outstretched hand. "Howdy, Big Brother."

"I'm happy for you, Cleve." After they exchanged the usual backslaps, Luke said, "You gonna introduce us to your bride, or not?"

"Oh, God! Adriana!" Cleve rushed outside.

Adriana had stood silently watching the reunion. It was such an outpouring of love that her previous misgivings melted away. Cleve grabbed her hand and drew her into the group. "May I present my wife, Adriana."

Polite restraint held them in check for a moment; then their exuberance burst forth like a wild bronco in a cinched saddle. Vying for position, all talking at once, they crowded around to welcome her.

Adriana found herself hugged and kissed with the same warmth and sincerity that Cleve had received.

"Bet you sure was surprised at the shivering we just gave you," Josh said.

"Shivaree, sweetheart," Honey corrected.

"Hey, I'll tell you what surprised me," Cleve said to his nephew. "When did you learn how to pronounce 'surprised'? I kind of got attached to your 's'pised.'"

"You tell your Uncle Cleve that we've been working on it very hard for the past year," Honey said.

"The shivaree was the best thing we could think of

on such short notice," Luke explained as they walked back to the house.

"Although I wired you that I got married, how did you know we'd show up today?" Cleve asked.

"Cal Ellis rode past on his way from town. He told me you and your wife were there, so we were watching for you."

Once they were in the house, the women and Josh sat down to enjoy some fresh lemonade while the men sought a stronger drink. Adriana was finally able to catch her breath.

Raising his glass, Luke offered a greeting. "Best wishes to the bride and groom, and welcome to the family, Adriana."

"It's just not fair!" Honey blurted.

"What's that, Jaybird?" Luke asked, seeing the pout on his wife's face.

"Well, first Flint marries a woman with the beautiful name of Garnet. Now Cleve comes along with his Adriana. Listen to it. It just rolls off the tongue. And what have I got—that stupid name *Honey!*"

"Do I hear our little Honey Bear complaining about her name again?" Cleve asked, winking at Flint.

Flint never cracked a smile. "We could always call her Sugar Bear, but she just don't like that, either. Boy, Luke, how do you put up with a woman that hard to please?"

"I warned you two about teasing me with those dumb nicknames of yours."

Josh dashed into the kitchen and came back with the broom. "Here, Mama, you said you'd whomp 'em with this if Uncle Cleve and Uncle Flint kept calling you by those names."

"Tell you what, Josh: I can't do it myself because of the baby, so how about you doing it for me?" Honey said.

With broom in hand, Josh started to chase the two men around the room. Within minutes, the three of them were wrestling together on the floor.

Garnet looked at Honey and Adriana. "You think they'll ever grow up?"

"I hope not," Honey said.

Josh squealed with delight when his two big uncles began to toss him back and forth as if he were a ball.

"Be careful, you two," Luke warned. "You drop him, and I'll do more than whomp you with a broom."

"Watch out, Brother Flint," Cleve said, feigning fright. "Sounds like Big Brother is siding up with this little bronco."

"Ah, we can handle the two of 'em, Little Brother."

"Don't you wish," Luke said, grinning.

"Don't you dare!" Honey said, not grinning.

"Okay, we give up," Cleve said, flopping down on the floor and stretching out on his back. Flint plopped down beside him and leaned against the wall.

Josh ran over and made a move to climb on Honey's lap. Then, as if remembering her condition, he climbed up on Luke's instead. "I beat 'em, Daddy. Did you see?"

Luke tousled his hair. "You sure did, son."

Although Luke was only two years older than Cleve, Adriana could see why Luke was the undisputed head of the family. He radiated a sense of quiet calm and leadership. Now, having had a chance to study the three brothers more closely, she was amazed by the physical resemblance among them. All three were tall men, with not more than two inches' difference between them. Yet, despite having the same dark hair and extraordinary sapphire-colored eyes, there was a distinctive quality to each of their faces.

Cleve had a polished, casual look to him; Luke was more serious and reserved. Flint had a more rugged, mysterious look, due to a scar on his right cheek that extended to his eye, and the strip of rawhide tying back his dark hair. Regardless, she concluded, all three men were exceptionally handsome—with Cleve the handsomest, of course.

"Hey, Honey," Cleve said, "we ran into an old friend of yours in Fort Worth."

"Of mine?" Honey asked. She started to giggle. "I can't imagine who it could be. My list of old friends isn't that long."

"Lily LaRue," Cleve said.

Honey's blue eyes brightened with pleasure. "Lily!"

"Lily LaRue! Well, I'll be damned!" Luke said. "How is she? Hope you remembered to thank her for what she did for us."

"Yes, Papa, I thanked her," Cleve said with a tolerant grin.

"And very generously, I would say," Adriana added. "Cleve gave her his casino as a wedding gift."

"Casino? Wedding gift? I want to hear more of this," Luke said. "Who'd she marry?"

"A wealthy Spanish count by the name of Miguel Castillo. Adriana was once betrothed to him."

Flint scratched his head. "Is this the same gal who helped save your life in Stockton?"

Cleve nodded. "Yeah."

"I thought she was a whore."

"Well, she was, Flint," Cleve said, "but if you met her, you'd see how that doesn't make any difference. She's a wonderful person."

"Oh, I ain't saying she's not. I just didn't think those rich *criollos* married outside of their own." Flint winked at Adriana. "You're gonna have to explain why'd you toss over a rich count for our little brother, Adriana."

"Besides," Cleve continued, "Lily gave up her old profession and ran the casino for me. Castillo met her, fell in love with her—simple. We all know that falling in love can change people's ways. Hell, look at you as an example! It's still a mystery to the rest of us how Garnet could ever fall in love with you."

"I haven't quite figured it out myself," Garnet interjected.

Flint arched a brow. "Reckon I'll have to refresh your memory, Redhead."

At that moment, Andrew MacKenzie began to cry.
"Okay, sweetheart," Garnet cooed lovingly to her son.
"This little guy's hungry and needs to be changed, so
I'll take him back to the house. Oh, darn! Now I won't
hear the end of this story."

"I'll come with you and tell you the rest," Adriana
said. "I know the whole story." She sighed. "It's so
romantic. Miguel even saved Lily's life."

"Reckon I'll go, too," Maud said. "Thought I'd bake a
pie for supper."

"Bake two, and we'll invite ourselves to dinner,"
Cleve said.

"You're all invited," Garnet announced.

"Then I'll come with you and help," Honey said.

Garnet eyed Honey's rounded stomach. "There's
plenty of help, so you can sit and watch us."

"Well, I can peel potatoes or something." Honey
patted her stomach. "If I don't have this baby soon, I
think I'll burst. I'm carrying it all in front. Do you know,
I've forgotten what my feet look like!"

Ben Franks decided to go back for his nap, and Josh
trailed after the women, leaving the three brothers to
themselves.

In a short time, Cleve finished telling them all about
the casino, Adriana, and Lily, including his own wedding to Adriana.

"Sure funny, the turns life takes, isn't it?" Luke
declared. "If this Don Alarico hadn't come to Fort
Worth, you might still be trying to convince Adriana to
marry you, and Lily wouldn't be married to this count.
Ma always said that everything happens for a reason."

"Well, speaking of Ma, you've only heard half the
story. I think you'll find the rest of it very interesting."

"It's been pretty interesting already, Little Brother,"
Flint said, breaking out in a broad grin. "Especially the
part about that old guy holding a shotgun to get you to
marry his daughter."

"Wasn't any worse than you and Luke pulling out
your Colts to get Garnet to marry you, Brother Flint."

"Hey, I only drew my Colt to keep the crowd from rushing Flint and most likely lynching him," Luke said, trying not to laugh.

"Hell!" Flint grumbled. "I had the whole situation under control."

"Okay, let him have the last word, Cleve. What's all this got to do with Ma?" Luke asked.

"I ran into another old friend of ours in Fort Worth—Charlie Walden."

The smiles instantly faded from their faces. They both stared grimly at him.

"Yep, ole Charlie got himself a cattle ranch west of Fort Worth."

"You saying Charlie Walden's running cattle?" Flint asked.

"Yeah, other people's cattle. This is where the story starts to get complicated."

By the time Cleve finished telling them about Antonio and the Valez relationship, Luke and Flint sat dumbfounded. After a long pause, Luke finally spoke.

"So you think Adriana's brother is riding with the gang?"

"It sure looks like it to me. But I can't believe Antonio would let Walden harm Adriana. They're twins, and closer than hell. That's the part of this puzzle that just doesn't fit."

"You have any idea where Walden is now?" Flint asked.

"No. The ranch is deserted. He and his gang just disappeared. I've a hunch they haven't left the state, though."

Deep in reflection, Luke nodded. "You're probably right, Little Brother."

"And we've got a big problem," Cleve said, staring solemnly out the window. He turned around and faced his brothers. "I can't help feeling that some day, one of us might have to kill my wife's brother."

Chapter 28

As soon as they were settled in Garnet's kitchen, Adriana and Honey began to peel apples while Maud rolled out the piecrusts. Garnet went out to the smokehouse and came back with a ham, which she skewered on the spit to roast.

"Guess what, Adriana—Cal Ellis told Flint this morning that the town's having a wedding celebration for you and Cleve tomorrow. It'll be fun to get out and kick up my heels again," Garnet said. "We don't have too many occasions to do so around here."

"Well, at least I could dance at yours and Flint's celebration; I sure can't now. This baby hasn't learned how to dance yet," Honey said good-naturedly. "And if I tried teaching him, he'd most likely pop right out on the dance floor and start kicking up his heels."

"Oh, dear!" Adriana moaned, suddenly remembering. "I won't be able to dance, either. Doctor's orders."

Adriana glanced up to find all three women staring at her and waiting for an explanation, so she proceeded to tell them about the stagecoach accident and her miscarriage.

"That Gus Baylor always was reckless," Maud grumbled. "Riskin' people's lives the way he does. He ought'n be allowed to drive a stage."

Leaning over as far as her stomach would permit,

296

Honey patted Adriana's hand. "Well, you and I can sit and watch the others dance."

"Do you think it will look strange for me not to dance at my own wedding celebration? I'd rather no one knows the real reason," Adriana said, blushing despite being among women.

"Don't you fret, sweetie, we'll just tell them you're not feeling well," Garnet said. "Nobody has to know more than that."

"Won't they think I'm being snobbish?"

"Whyever would they think that?" Garnet asked in her soft Southern accent.

In the past, due to her father's insistence on maintaining a division of the classes, she'd often had to suffer this misconception. "Well . . . you know . . . my being a *criollo.* I'd hate to offend any of your friends."

"Shucks, gal, nobody's gonna find fault with a sweet little young'n like you," Maud said.

"Let's think of some good excuse," Garnet suggested. "Honey, you're the one with the quick mind. Got any ideas?"

Honey thought for a moment and then broke into a wide smile that produced a dimple in each cheek. "I remember once, years ago, I didn't have enough money to buy a train ticket, so I wrapped my ankle in a bandage and acted as if I couldn't walk." Her eyes flashed with amusement. "The conductor was so busy helping me to board, he forgot to ask for my ticket."

"That's a great idea!" Garnet exclaimed. "We'll pretend you sprained your ankle, Adriana. We can even tie it up to make it look authentic."

Soon the three women had their heads bent together, giggling among themselves as they planned the ruse.

"I think we should tie a big bow around her ankle as a decorative touch," Honey suggested.

"How about a cast?" Garnet said excitedly. "We could make a plaster of Paris cast, and then it would really look authentic."

"And we could draw pictures on it to make it really funny," Honey added.

Maud glanced over her shoulder at them. "Land sakes alive! I can't believe you gals would go to all that trouble just to get out of tellin' the truth. You must torment to death them fellas you're married to!"

"Well, maybe the cast is a little bit too much," Garnet conceded.

Honey cradled her chin in her hand. "I sure liked the idea of tying a bright bow around her ankle, though."

"It probably wouldn't be seen under my gown anyway," Adriana speculated.

The three women looked at each other, and all burst out laughing.

The smile lingered on Adriana's face as she resumed peeling the apples. To think she had feared meeting these women! How quickly they had made her feel welcome, had rallied around her when she had a problem. She felt as if she'd known them forever—but even more heartwarming, as if she belonged.

Later, returning to the house, Honey and Adriana went into the spare bedroom where the men had put the trunks. Honey sat down in a stiff-back rocker and chatted with Adriana while she unpacked.

She's so big-hearted, Adriana thought affectionately as she glanced over at her vivacious sister-in-law. Now she understood why, even though Lily had been in love with Luke herself, she had not resented Honey when Luke had fallen in love and married her.

"Mama! Mama!" Josh shouted as he came running into the room. The boy's eyes were brimming with excitement.

"What is it, sweetheart?" Honey asked as Josh tugged at her hand.

Seeing Honey and Josh together, it was obvious how much Luke's son loved her, too. Had Adriana not known better, she never would have guessed that Honey wasn't the boy's natural mother.

"You gotta come, Mama. Uncle Flint bet Uncle Cleve a whole dollar that he couldn't ride Ole Diablo. Hurry, or you'll miss it. You come, too, Auntie Adri—Auntie Adee." He raced out of the room.

"Adee!" Adriana looked at Honey and grinned. "No one has ever called me that before. I like it."

"Leave it to Josh. I'm sure glad I'm 'Mama' to him, or Lord knows what he might have done with Honey. But you'll probably be stuck with Aunt Adee now. Shame, too; Adriana is such a beautiful name."

Firmly planting a hand on each arm of the rocker, she hoisted herself out of the chair.

As tempted as Adriana was to rush to the corral, she matched her step to Honey's. They got there just in time to see Cleve preparing to climb onto the back of a huge black stallion.

"That horse looks like it could snort fire," Adriana said with a worried frown. "Maybe Cleve shouldn't try to ride it."

"I don't know why they don't just set that animal free," Honey lamented. "That horse is never going to let anyone ride him. But Luke and Flint aren't convinced of it."

"Is he dangerous?"

"Only if you get too near to him. If you leave him alone, he won't bother you."

They moved over to where Luke and Flint sat on the fence, shouting words of advice to Cleve.

"Since neither of you can ride him, why should I listen to you?" Cleve yelled back.

Grinning, Flint turned toward Luke. "This'll be the easiest buck I've ever made. I give him ten seconds; then he'll be eatin' dirt."

"Oh, he might surprise us. It could be twenty-five or thirty seconds," Luke said.

Garnet came hurrying over to the corral. "Don't tell me they're trying to ride Ole Diablo again," she said.

"They just don't learn," Honey said.

"You'd think they would have by now, since they're the ones who keep landing on their rear ends. Even the horse knows he's smarter than they are."

Listening to the conversation around her, Adriana's uneasiness grew. She called out anxiously, "Cleve, be careful."

"Don't worry, Raven. I use finesse, where these guys just use muscle."

Glancing at Flint, Luke said, "Twenty seconds."

"Tops," Flint agreed, nodding.

Grasping the reins and horn firmly, Cleve put his left foot into the stirrup and swung himself up, easing himself onto the saddle.

Snorting, the horse reared up on its hind legs, then pounded back to the ground, lowered its head, and instantly proceeded in a relentless flurry to buck, bend, twist, wrench, jerk, and do practically everything short of rolling over. Then, suddenly, it came to an abrupt halt. Braced tautly to withstand the fierce trouncing, Cleve was caught off guard and was thrown from the horse.

Ole Diablo trotted away.

Adriana climbed through the rails and rushed over to Cleve. He was stretched out on his back, motionless, his eyes closed.

"¡Querido! ¡Querido!" she cried out, kneeling beside him.

Flint and Luke came over and stood next to their brother's prone body. Slowly Cleve opened his eyes.

"That horse is evil! Malicious! Diabolic—the devil incarnate!" He sat up. "And downright mean!"

"You need any help getting up, Little Brother?" Flint asked, unconcerned.

"No!" He stood up and began brushing himself off.

Palm up, Flint held out his hand. "You owe me a buck."

Cleve reached into his pocket and slapped a coin into his hand. "I bet you trained that horse to do that. You set me up, didn't you?"

"Did no such thing. Ole Diablo just won't let anyone ride him. Whoever can ride him can have him."

"Who'd want him!" Cleve grumbled.

Glancing past Flint, Cleve suddenly exclaimed, "Good God, that horse will kill her! Raven, get away from him," he shouted.

His warning came too late. Adriana had stormed over to the animal. Shaking her fist in the horse's face, she ran off a long string of words in Spanish.

"What in hell is she saying?" Luke asked, astonished.

"I can't follow it all. Something about his mother being a burro and his father a son of a jackass."

As a final act of defiance, Adriana tweaked the horse in the snout, spun on her heel, and, mumbling angrily, headed back to them.

"Well, I'll be goddamned!" Luke exclaimed. "Will you look at that?"

Dumbfounded, they watched Ole Diablo following docilely behind her.

Before retiring that night, Adriana rubbed salve into Cleve's aching limbs. "I'm afraid your, ah, finesse didn't work, *querido*."

"Don't remind me. Beats me why anyone would want a horse that can outthink him. I can't believe the devious mind of that animal."

"Oh, he's just a big pussycat," Adriana insisted.

"Yeah! Maybe some witch's big pussycat!"

"Well, he was as gentle as a lamb with me. I'm sorry I said those nasty things to him."

"Pussycat . . . lamb!" Cleve murmured as he started to doze off. "Just more of his cunning. You stay away from him, Raven. He can't be trusted. If my hand wasn't sore, he'd never have gotten . . . away with it." His voice faded away as he slipped into slumber.

Smiling, Adriana covered him with the quilt, then blew out the lamp and snuggled up beside him.

* * *

The next morning, Maud and Garnet loaded up the pies and potato salad they had prepared for the wedding celebration, and everyone climbed into the wagons for the twenty-mile ride to town.

"Uncle Cleve, can Amigo and me ride with you and Auntie Adee?" Josh asked.

"If you promise to limit yourself to not more than twenty questions." Seeing Adriana's puzzled look, Cleve swung her up on the seat. "Trust me on this one, sweetheart."

"I promise." Josh and Amigo jumped on the back of the buckboard. "How come I can only ask twenty questions, Uncle Cleve?"

"That's one a mile. And you just asked the first one."

After lifting Adriana down from the buckboard, Cleve rode off to return the horse and wagon to the livery. As she waited for Cleve to come back, Honey came up and joined her, proceeding to introduce Adriana to the townsfolk who happened by. The doctor was among them.

"I thought I advised you to rest, Mrs. MacKenzie," he said gruffly.

"I didn't plan this celebration, Doctor, but my husband and I are the guests of honor."

"I understand. But don't let me see you on the dance floor of the meeting hall when those fiddles start playing. And the same goes for you, Mrs. MacKenzie," he said, addressing Honey. "We don't need a baby born today. I intend to enjoy the day without any interruptions."

"Well, you heard the good doctor," Honey said as soon as he went inside. "I guess we two old invalids better find ourselves a couple of rocking chairs and pull out our knitting."

The rest of the afternoon passed pleasantly. The people were friendly, the food was delicious, and, to the men's satisfaction, the beer flowed freely.

As soon as everyone had eaten their fill, the fiddle

and guitars appeared, and the celebrants took to the dance floor. Adriana yearned to join them, but Cleve was like a watchdog, running interference with any man who approached her for a dance.

She waved at him as he danced past, his partner a little girl standing on his boots, with her golden curls bobbing. Looking up adoringly, the youngster giggled with pleasure as Cleve hopped around the floor with her.

Adriana smiled. *How he loves children.* For a moment her face saddened, reminded of the baby they had lost. But one day, they would have their own child.

A short time later, tapping her foot to the lively beat, Adriana watched Cleve dancing with Garnet. Flint, who appeared to have been assigned watchdog duty for the moment, sat beside her. "Don't you like to dance, Flint?" she asked. "I haven't seen you on that floor one time."

"No. Reckon I just never put much stock in it."

"Oh, Flint, it's so much fun. You ought to learn for Garnet's sake. Look at her; she's having such a good time. It can't be any fun for you, just sitting here watching."

"You're wrong, Auntie Adee. I enjoy watching her."

"But wouldn't you enjoy it more if you were the one dancing with her?"

His dark-eyed gaze followed his wife as Cleve swung her around in a lively step. "If I was dancing with her, I might never see how that red hair of hers catches the light when she's whirling, or bounces on her shoulders when she's hopping. There, look at that—did you see how she smiled when she changed partners? If I was out there on that floor, I'd have missed it. No, ma'am, reckon I'd rather just be sitting here watching her."

"Why, Flint MacKenzie, how romantic!" Adriana exclaimed. "I declare, you're a poet at heart."

He grinned, and she saw how it changed his mysterious look to one of pure boyishness. "Me! A poet? 'Fraid not, Auntie Adee. I've never read a poem in my life."

He suddenly frowned. "And if you go saying that hogwash to my little brother, I'm gonna deny I ever said it."

"Oh, your secret's safe with me, you fraud. But I think you should at least tell Garnet what you've just told me. I'm sure she'd love to know."

"Nothing doin', Adee. My tongue would get all tied up if I even tried."

"Are you my guard for the next dance, too?"

Chuckling, he tipped back his chair. "When did you figure it out?"

"It's pretty obvious, isn't it? I should have a dance card so you MacKenzie men could just sign it and take away the suspense. So, who's got me next?"

"Little Brother."

"Well, your little brother is going to hear about this."

"Now, now, Auntie Adee, don't go getting yourself all riled. He just didn't want you sitting here all by your lonesome." He lowered his eyes. "Cleve told us about the accident and all. I'm plumb sorry about the baby, Adriana."

She could see how difficult it was for the taciturn man to discuss such a delicate subject.

"I know you are, Flint. And just call me Adee if you want—or Raven; that's what Cleve calls me."

"Raven fits you proper all right, with that dark hair of yours and all. But I figure it's a private thing between you and Cleve and oughta stay that way."

"Why, you really *are* romantic, Flint!"

He looked around with a guilty glance. "You gotta stop saying that, Adee. I've got a reputation to hold up in these parts. If you start spreading that kind of rumor, I'm gonna be gettin' into fights just livin' it down."

Seeing Cleve approach with Garnet on his arm, Flint stood up. "Mind your promise, now," he warned.

"My lips are sealed," she said.

Garnet came up and slipped her hand into his.

"Having a good time, Redhead?"

"Oh, yes! But it's almost time to feed the baby. I'll go and get him from Maud."

"I'll come with you," Flint said.

As they walked away, Flint put his arm around Garnet's shoulders, and she slipped hers around his waist. Observing it, Adriana smiled.

"What are you thinking about to bring on such a big smile?" Cleve asked.

She turned her head and looked at him. "Oh, it's nothing."

Cleve grinned. "You've got that mysterious woman-look about you. What aren't you telling me, Raven?"

Fortunately, a discordant screech of a fiddle caught everyone's attention. Maud had climbed up on the makeshift stage and raised her hand for quiet.

"I'm gonna make a speech," she declared.

"Who asked you to, Maud?" a voice called out from the crowd.

"I've got somethin' to say, and dadblast it, I'm gonna say it."

"Okay, say it and get it over with," another person yelled out, good-naturedly.

"Well, I ain't never made no secret of how I feel about the MacKenzie brothers. I couldn't love them boys any more if they was my very own. I only wish Andy and Kathleen was here to see this day. I know how proud they'd be of their sons, and how much the two of 'em would love the women they married." She swiped at her eyes with her sleeve.

"Best quit afore you start blubberin', Maud," one of the men yelled out.

"You just give it no mind, Sam Bates. I ain't gonna start blubberin'," Maud declared. "I said what I come to say! Now, I'm thinkin' if we all try, maybe we can coax Honey up here to sing us a song for the occasion." A clamor of clapping, whistling, and foot-stomping ensued.

Honey was appalled. "Oh, I can't." She looked down at her swollen stomach. "Not in my condition."

"Come on, gal. We all know you're in a family way. No sense tryin' to hide it. Get that good-lookin' husband of yours to carry you up here."

As if she were weightless, Luke scooped her up in his arms. "Let's go, Jaybird."

"All right, but get me a chair. At least I'll sit down and do it."

After a quick conference with the band, she sat down and, in her husky voice, began the haunting lyrics of "Beautiful Dreamer."

Her gaze never strayed from Luke, who stood beaming with love and pride. When she finished to a thundering applause, he raised his arms and lifted her off the stage.

"What a lovely voice!" Adriana whispered, spellbound.

Cleve nodded. "I'm amazed they got Honey up there to sing, because she's so self-conscious about her condition. I don't know why. I think she looks lovelier than ever."

Adriana looked at him intently. "You MacKenzie men are amazing," she said.

"What do you mean?"

"Oh, nothing."

"Uh-huh! There's that mysterious look again. Feel up to a walk?"

"I'd love it."

She drew a deep breath when they stepped outside. There was a slight chill in the air, and he slipped his arm around her shoulders, hugging her to his side. "You cold?"

"No. The fresh air feels good."

They crossed the street to a small wooded square. Adriana glanced around in surprise. "This is like an oasis in the middle of a desert. Everything else is so barren."

The park was deserted, and they sat down on a bench. As the band began playing again, the strains of a slow ballad drifted across to them.

Adriana sighed and cuddled closer to Cleve. "Why do love songs always sound so sad?"

"I reckon because the lovers know they're going to die soon," he said, tongue in cheek.

"Cleve! Are you bringing up the ballet again?"

He stood up and bowed formally from the waist. "Mrs. MacKenzie, I believe I have the honor of this dance."

"Oh, how I wish we could. But you know what the doctor said."

He took her hands and gently pulled her to her feet. "The doctor won't object to this dance, I'm sure."

He drew her into his arms and held her tightly against him. Laying her head on his chest, she closed her eyes as they swayed back and forth in the same spot to the slow rhythm of the music.

"Now, sweetheart, imagine that we're waltzing in a magnificent ballroom, and I'm whirling you around the floor. Laughing gaily, you look up at me, and as I gaze down into your beautiful brown eyes, I feel as if I'm slowly being drawn into their warm depths. Then I say to you, 'Why, Mrs. MacKenzie, you are as graceful as a *danseuse.*'"

"And I look up at you with a coy smile," Adriana said, "and reply, 'Oh, sir, you're most kind. And you glide so smoothly, I can't even tell we're moving.'"

"All evening, as I watched you in the arms of others, I waited anxiously to claim this dance. You are the loveliest woman in the room, *madame.*"

"You flatter me, *señor,* but I must remind you that you're holding me much closer than propriety allows."

"Propriety be damned, *madame!*"

"I fear you must stop, sir. You see, I have a very jealous husband."

"And a very fortunate one—who's going mad waiting until he can make love to you," he finished, with a whispered groan at her ear.

The impassioned utterance was a woeful reminder that ended their playful fantasy. Laying his cheek against the top of her head, Cleve breathed in her sweet fragrance. Slowly swaying, they remained locked together in an embrace until the song ended.

He lifted his head and gazed down into her upturned face. "I love you, Raven."

Then he lowered his head and kissed her.

Chapter 29

When Adriana awoke the next morning, Cleve wasn't beside her. There was no clock in the room, but it felt early, and she wondered where he had gone.

For a long moment, she lay thinking about the previous day. Not being able to dance had been a disappointment, but she'd still had a good time. Funny, she thought, she'd never enjoyed the *fiestas* at home. The music and dancing had been the only reasons to attend those dreary affairs, especially with her father holding court over his stuffy friends.

It seemed that whenever the MacKenzies were together, whether for a *fiesta* or just dinner, they had a good time.

Stretching, she rose from the bed and walked over to the open window in time to see Flint ride up to Cleve and Luke, who were standing in front of the barn. After a brief conversation, they started to hitch up the wagon.

As fast as she could, Adriana hurried through her morning toilette and hastened back to call out to Cleve. But she was too late; they had left. Disappointed, she started to turn away, when she heard Josh's voice nearby.

Adriana could not see him, but as she continued to listen, she became aware that he was directly under her window. When she leaned out to say good morning, she saw him standing against the house, shaking a finger at Amigo.

"You've been naughty, Amigo. You know we're not s'pose to go away from the house alone," Josh scolded. "If Daddy knew you was gone all night, he'd be real mad. I never told him how you've been sneakin' off sometimes these past couple months. But you just wait and see. He's gonna catch you; then you'll be in trouble, all right."

Amigo stretched out, put his head on his paws, and closed his eyes.

"Don't go pretendin' you're sleepin'," Josh said, putting his hands on his hips. "You ain't foolin' me none, Amigo. This morning Daddy asked where you was, and I told him outside. That was no lie, 'cause I knew you were. But you better start behavin' yourself, 'cause I ain't gonna lie to Daddy or Mama if they ask." He knelt down and began to pat his beleaguered pet. "I'll feel real sad if they get mad at you. Don't you know you could maybe run into a wolf or a big rattler out there?" Josh's voice started to crack. "Daddy's only thinkin' of what's good for us."

When Amigo got up and began to lick Josh's face, the young boy put his arms around the dog's neck and hugged him. "I love you, Amigo."

Josh stood up. "I gotta go feed the chickens now." He headed toward the chicken house, and, complete with scampering limp, wagging tail, and utter devotion, Amigo followed him.

Smiling, Adriana turned away from the window.

She made up the bed, dumped the soiled water out the window, and then left the room.

"Good morning," Honey responded cheerfully to Adriana's greeting when she entered the kitchen.

"What time is it?" Glancing at the clock, Adriana exclaimed, "Oh, my, it's seven o'clock already! I guess I overslept. Since we didn't get back until midnight, I didn't expect everyone would be up so soon."

"The day starts early on a ranch, regardless of what

time you go to bed," Honey said, amused. "But you've been ill, Adriana, and need your rest. What can I make you for breakfast?"

Even though Adriana had been raised on a ranch, she had never paid any attention to what time the day began for the *vaqueros* and servants. In retrospect, she realized what an idle life she had led until she met Cleve MacKenzie.

And now here was Honey, on the verge of giving birth, waiting on her like one of the *criadas* on her father's ranch.

"I shall make my own breakfast, and you shall sit down and talk to me while I do," Adriana declared.

"Sounds good to me."

A few minutes later, when Adriana sat down at the table, there was a light tap on the door, and Garnet entered with Andrew in her arms.

"Morning. Hope I'm not too late for coffee?"

"You're just in time," Honey said.

Garnet handed the baby to Honey. "Here, Auntie Honey, you might as well get used to it." She filled a cup and sat down. "Maud and Ben haven't stirred yet, but Flint was up at the crack of dawn as usual. What about the two of you? Have you both recovered from last night?"

"I have," Honey said gaily. "But I can't tell you how exhausting it was for Adriana and me to watch you dance all evening." She winked at Adriana. "My feet and ankles positively ached from the effort."

"I lost some sleep over it, but I made it up this morning," Adriana said with a giggle.

"And it looks like this little guy is still sleeping it off," Honey added.

"Andy would sleep through a stampede," Garnet said. "Nothing bothers him unless he's hungry or has wet linens. He's due to wake up any minute for a feeding."

"Well, I thought everybody would sleep in longer. Where did the men go so early?" Adriana asked.

"Flint found a couple dead calves by that alkaline water hole," Garnet replied. "They rode out to repair the fence around it."

"What happened to the fence?"

"He didn't say."

"We're never going to build up a herd if we keep losing calves," Honey lamented.

When Andrew began to stir, Garnet lifted the infant out of Honey's arms. "What did I tell you? You could set a clock by his eating habits. Isn't that right, Andy?" she cooed lovingly, opening her bodice.

As she watched Garnet nurse the baby, Adriana was reminded of her recent loss and an image of what might have been. She felt a twinge of heartache and turned quickly to Honey. "Are you hoping for a boy or a girl?"

"We keep changing our minds," Honey said, sighing. "I'm leaning toward a girl because that's what Luke would like. Then, in the next breath, he says Josh needs a brother." Smiling, Honey said, "I'll take whatever I get. It took me long enough to become pregnant as it was. I hope I can again; then maybe Josh'll be lucky enough to have both a little brother and sister."

"What about you, Garnet? Are you and Flint planning to have another child soon?" Adriana asked.

"We don't plan them, Auntie Adee; we just let them happen. I hope we do. But if we don't . . . ," she shrugged fatalistically. "Andy here will always have his cousins to grow up with."

"The wisest thing would be to have twins—a boy and a girl," Honey said. "That way everybody would be happy."

"I have a twin brother," Adriana said.

"Really!" Honey exclaimed.

"How wonderful," Garnet said. "Honey was an only child, and I had a brother who died when he was quite young. We have often talked about how nice it would have been to grow up with sisters and brothers. Our husbands were pretty lucky having each other."

"Where is your brother now, Adriana?" Honey asked.

The conversation had stirred up poignant childhood memories she once shared with Antonio, and despite her attempt to hold them back, Adriana felt the slide of tears down her cheeks.

Contrition showed on the faces of Honey and Garnet. "Oh, Adriana, I'm so sorry," Honey said. "I didn't mean to pry." Frowning, she looked helplessly at Garnet.

"Oh, no, dear, we didn't mean to upset you," Garnet offered.

Before Adriana could stop herself, she told them the whole story about her father, Antonio, and Charlie Walden. When she finished, the other two women exchanged grim glances.

Finally, Garnet broke the silence. "I know how we all feel about Walden, and there's no proof that *Señor* Valez is Charlie Walden. But, Adriana, you just said this Valez hit you on the head and then tried to have you killed. If he's not Walden, Valez must have something to do with the gang."

"But why would Walden want to kill me?"

"Because you're married to a MacKenzie," Garnet replied. "That madman tried to hang Flint, and he would have killed me, too, if Flint hadn't rescued me."

"Don't forget; he shot Luke in the back," Honey interjected. "And remember that he led the raid on the Triple M when Kathleen and Sarah MacKenzie were killed. The man is a cold-blooded killer who has no compunction about killing a woman."

"That's what's so confusing to me," Adriana spoke up. "Antonio would never be a party to anyone harming me."

"Well, obviously your brother didn't know about that," Honey said. "But if he's riding with Walden, it doesn't look good, Adriana." She shook her head sadly.

"I know. Cleve keeps reminding me of that." Adri-

ana looked at them with desperation. "I don't know
what to do. I love Cleve, but how can I abandon my
brother? Would Cleve abandon Luke or Flint, any more
than either of them could turn his back on Cleve? I
don't think so."

"Adriana," Garnet said, "trust Cleve. He'll work it
out somehow. I don't believe he'd ever hurt you, dear."

Adriana smiled sadly at her. "But what if Cleve has
no choice, Garnet? Or Luke? Or Flint?"

For a long time the women stared silently into their
coffee cups. Finally, Garnet stood up. "Well, I must get
this little guy home and change him. I . . . I'll see you
later."

When Honey started to pick up the coffee cups,
Adriana jumped to her feet. "Let me do that, Honey. I
want to help you any way I can. You have all been so
kind to me, I want to . . ." She paused, forcing back the
tears.

Honey put her hand on Adriana's arm. "There, there,
dear. If it'll make you feel better, you just go ahead and
cry it out."

"No," Adriana said stubbornly, tossing her head.
"Tears can't wash away trouble, and—"

"At least they get the hurt to the outside," Honey
offered kindly.

"Maybe so," Adriana said with a final sniffle. "But I
don't intend to be spreading gloom all over your
household. You and Garnet are . . . are . . ."

"We are your sisters now, Adriana, and what else are
sisters for?"

Thereupon, in spite of herself, Adriana burst into
tears, releasing both her joy and sorrow.

In the days that followed, no mention was made of
Antonio Fuente.

At the end of the following week, Adriana almost
skipped as she left the doctor's office. He had given her
a clean bill of health, and she could hardly wait to tell
Cleve.

No, she thought, reconsidering. She wouldn't tell him—she'd surprise him. Tonight she'd wear that fancy black nightgown he had bought her, and she'd brush out her hair, because she knew he loved it that way. Then she'd dab on a few drops of that expensive French perfume that drove him wild.

Thinking about what would follow, she trembled.

Watching him in the past two weeks, she'd almost been driven to madness. Funny, how she'd only thought of him as a gambler, a man who lived by his wits and luck. Since they had come to the Triple M, she'd seen a side of her husband she never knew existed. Now she understood where he had developed his muscular chest and legs—certainly not dealing poker in a casino.

She had caught glimpses of him roping steers, driving cattle, mending a fence, and patching the roof on the barn. She had watched him pitching hay and chopping wood.

His black suit, white shirt, and string cravat had been replaced by worn jeans, a cheap blue shirt, and a red bandanna, his expensive Stetson by a dusty, battered, army-issued hat.

Clearly her husband was a rancher—no less at home on horseback than dealing poker at a gambling table.

And as exciting as she found that sophisticated, dark-eyed gambler to be, this rugged, virile-looking cowboy was even more so.

Cleve MacKenzie had a presence she couldn't resist, a sensual magnetism that set her heart to pounding.

She could hardly wait for him to make love to her, and didn't know how she'd make it through the rest of the day.

Hastening over to Jenkins Dry Goods, she found that Ben and Maud had just finished loading the wagon.

"Have you got everything you need, Maud?" Adriana asked.

Maud reread the list Garnet and Honey had prepared. "Yep. We're all set."

"Let's go, *Abuelo*," Adriana said to Ben, climbing up on the wagon seat beside Maud.

"Giddyap," Ben said, flicking the reins.

Adriana saw that calling Ben by the Spanish word for "grandfather" had brought a smile to his weathered face. She felt the kindly, gray-haired man was like a grandfather to all of them.

"What did the doc say?" Maud asked.

"He said I'm fine, but don't say anything to Cleve. I want to surprise him."

Slapping her knee, Maud burst out in laughter. "Dearie, the day ain't dawned yet when anyone could catch that rogue by surprise."

When Cleve rode in later that day, Adriana ran out to the barn to greet him. His face was grimy, his shirt sweat-stained, and he was coated with dust—but he looked beautiful to her.

"Hi," she said as he unsaddled his horse.

He turned and grinned. "Hi, pretty face." He kissed her lightly.

She stepped closer and slipped her arms around his neck.

"You shouldn't touch me, sweetheart; I'm filthy," he warned, but he slid his arms around her waist. "God, Raven," he murmured, his breath rustling the hair at her ear, "you smell good, you taste good—" His arms tightened. "And you feel so good." He kissed her again and then stepped away. "I've got to take a shower bath and get rid of some of this dirt. See you later, sweetheart." He strode toward the outdoor wooden shower stall.

Exhilarated by thoughts of that evening, Adriana wandered down to the corral. As usual, Ole Diablo was isolated in a fenced area. She climbed up on the rail and the horse came trotting over to her.

"*¡Hola, chico mio!*" she cooed when the black stallion nuzzled her. She pulled an apple out of her pocket, and he plucked it off the palm of her hand just as Maud and Ben walked up to the fence.

"I ain't seen the likes of anything like that in my life," Maud declared. "Have you, Ben?"

"Sure beats all," he agreed. "But you best stay away from him. That horse is a killer, gal!"

"Oh, nonsense. He's no killer." Turning to the horse, she began patting him. "Are you, *chico*?"

Seeing a saddle slung over the fence, she suddenly grabbed a bridle that was hanging from a nail, and jumped down from her perch. "I'll prove it to you."

"Now don't you go doing anything foolish there, gal," Maud cried out.

Adriana slipped the bridle on the horse, then slung a saddle blanket over the animal's back. When she heaved up the heavy saddle, Ole Diablo stood motionless. He continued to remain still as she adjusted the stirrups.

"If you try to ride that devil, you're gonna get yourself killed," Ben warned.

"He won't hurt me," Adriana declared confidently.

She paused before mounting and whispered, *"Yo te amo, chico,"* grasping the reins.

Garnet came running down to the corral. "She's not going to try and ride that horse, is she?"

"'Pears like it," Maud said agitatedly. "Somebody get Cleve down here."

"What's going on?" Honey exclaimed, hurrying up to them.

"Mama! Mama! Auntie Adee's gonna kill herself," Josh cried out, frightened by Ben's warning.

With the collective gasps of the concerned spectators ringing in her ears, Adriana put her foot in the stirrup and swung up on the horse's back. She held her breath, waiting for the bone-rattling bucking to begin. Instead, Ole Diablo began to trot around the corral.

"Well, I'll be dadblamed!" Maud exclaimed.

"Sure wouldn't believe it if I hadn't seen it with my own eyes," Ben said.

Honey and Garnet exchanged astonished glances while, awestruck, Josh climbed on the fence to watch.

The grin quickly faded from Adriana's face when Luke and Flint rode up at a gallop. Flint leaped off his horse before the animal came to a halt and vaulted over the fence.

"Stay back, Flint," Luke warned. "Don't rush him, or the animal's liable to get riled and toss her."

Luke climbed over the fence, and the two men began to approach cautiously.

Wearing only a knotted towel, Cleve came running down the path to the corral. "Adriana! Get off that horse before it kills you," he shouted.

"Oh, for heaven's sake!" Adriana exclaimed, dismounting. "What are all of you getting so excited about?" She patted the horse and handed Flint the reins. Ole Diablo snorted.

"Hold him, Flint, while I get the saddle off him," Luke said.

"I don't understand what all the fuss is about," Adriana declared.

Cleve grasped her shoulders and peered down angrily at her. "Don't you have any more sense than to climb on the back of a killer stallion?"

"Will someone please tell me just who this horse ever killed?" she demanded. "He's as docile as a lamb."

"And just what are you doing riding *any* horse in your condition?" Cleve railed.

Embarrassed by his public tongue-lashing, Adriana forgot all about her intentions for that evening. "I'm fine now!"

"Just the same, I don't want—" He suddenly stopped. "You're fine." His expression of anger turned to one of elation. "You're fine!"

She nodded. "You heard me." Embroiled in anger, she realized too late what she had said.

"You mean, we can—"

"Cleve MacKenzie, don't you say another word in

front of your brothers," Adriana ordered, anticipating what he was about to say. "And put on some clothes. There are women and children present." She spun on her heel and headed up the path to the house.

Laughing, Luke and Flint leaned back against the fence. "Hey, Big Brother," Flint asked Luke, "what do you suppose our little brother was gonna say?"

"What do you think?" Cleve replied with a grin.

"We already know," Luke said. As he walked over to his horse, he slapped Cleve on the shoulder. "We've both gone through it, Little Brother."

"Yeah, but you don't know the half of it," Cleve murmured for his own ears alone.

That evening, they all had supper together. Short tempers had cooled, but Adriana had to bear the teasing of Luke and Flint as she sat on the floor in front of the fireplace.

"Don't pay any attention to them," Honey said. "I've had to put up with it for a long time already."

"They don't bother me in the least," Adriana replied. As a matter of fact, if the truth were known, she was enjoying it.

"Say, Auntie Adee," Flint said, "I've got a couple wild mustangs that need breakin'. You think you could handle it and save me the trouble?"

"Why, I'd be glad to, Flint," Adriana said sweetly. "Apparently you *do* have trouble staying in the saddle. I noticed that you almost fell off your horse when you rode up today." Seeing that Josh had been relegated to the floor because of Honey's condition, she pulled him over onto her lap. "Isn't that right, sweetheart," she said, kissing his cheek.

"Yeah," Josh said, settling back against her as she enfolded him in her arms. "How come you almost fell off your horse, Uncle Flint? You told me you could sit a saddle better than my daddy. Daddy didn't almost fall off his horse."

Laughing, Luke playfully patted Flint on the head. "That's right, son. Your daddy's forgotten more about riding than your Uncle Flint ever knew."

"Oh, is that right, Big Brother?" Flint declared. "Well, what about the time when you were twelve years old and we roped our first mustang? Who ended up breaking him?"

Hugging Josh, Adriana leaned back smiling, listening as Flint continued his story. She felt she belonged among them, and knew their teasing was their way of letting her know that all was forgiven.

At eight o'clock, when Honey led Josh to his bedroom, Garnet took Andrew home. Adriana yawned politely. "I think I'll be going to bed, too. You coming, Cleve?"

"You bet, sweetheart," he said eagerly.

"Hey, hold up there, Little Brother," Flint interrupted. "How about a drink before you go? We don't often get the chance."

"Do you mind, Raven?" Cleve asked.

"Of course not."

She excused herself and went to their bedroom. Hurriedly pulling the pins out of her hair, she brushed it to a shine. Then, after donning her fancy nightgown, she dabbed the French perfume behind her ears and between her breasts as a final touch.

Dimming the lamp, she climbed into bed and waited . . . and waited . . . and, two hours later, was still waiting.

By this time, she was pacing the floor. Every other time she passed by the dresser, she'd pick up Cleve's pocket watch and check the time. Exasperated, she finally stormed over to the door and locked it.

Hearing the click of the lock, Flint stood up and grabbed his Stetson. "Well, I've got to get to bed."

"Yeah, me, too," Luke said. "Good night."

Cleve glanced at the clock. He was surprised to see

that the time had passed so swiftly. "My gosh, it's nine o'clock already."

"Nine o'clock? Must be something wrong with that clock," Luke said, stifling a laugh. "I best reset it." He moved the big hand to ten.

"You mean it's ten o'clock, not nine!" Cleve exclaimed. "Oh, God, Raven!"

When his brothers burst into laughter, he glanced at them suspiciously. "What's going on here? Those are the same kind of scurvy laughs I remember from whenever you two pulled some kind of dirty trick on me."

"Dirty trick?" Luke asked innocently. "You mean like handcuffing your brother and sister-in-law to the bedpost? That kind of dirty trick? Turned out it worked to my advantage, though. I appreciated it, Little Brother."

Cleve headed for the bedroom and turned the knob, but the door failed to open. After several more attempts, he realized it was locked. Tapping on the door, he whispered softly, "Raven, let me in. The door's locked." When she didn't answer, he tapped again. "Raven."

Not wishing to disturb Honey or Josh, he went outside. Peeking in the open window, he saw Adriana sitting up in the middle of the bed, her arms folded across her chest.

"Honey, didn't you hear me? The door's locked." He started to climb in the window.

Adriana jumped out of bed, came over, and shoved him away, then slammed down the window.

"What did you do that for?" he shouted, picking himself up from the dust.

Glaring at him, she raised the window. "Why do you think?"

"Honey, I'm sorry. My brothers pulled a practical joke on me, that's all."

"Well, go back and enjoy the joke with them, because you're not getting in here."

"Dammit, Raven, this is ridiculous!" Just as Cleve started to climb in the window, she slammed it down. "Ouch! My hand! My sore hand!" he cried out.

Horrified, she raised it again. "Forgive me, *querido*. Forgive me. Oh, I'm so sorry," she pleaded. "Let me help you."

Cleve heaved himself up on the windowsill, and she grabbed the back of his shirt, pulling him inside faster than he expected.

He landed in a heap on the floor—to the sounds of loud laughter coming from beside the barn.

Flinging herself into his arms, Adriana rained a dozen kisses on his face. "Forgive me, my love. I'm so sorry. I didn't mean to hurt you."

"I know you didn't, Raven."

Sliding her arms around his neck, she kissed him passionately, clinging to him as they stood up.

"Let me make it up to you," she whispered, and began to unbutton his shirt.

"Just a minute, sweetheart." He stuck his head out the window and saw his brothers trying to stay on their feet as they clutched their sides in laughter.

"Thanks, boys. Appreciate the favor," he called out. Then he closed the shutters.

"For weeks I've thought of nothing but making love to you," he murmured, the pressure of his mouth tantalizing the hollow of her ear. "I can't believe I let those guys distract me."

Excitement coursed through her, as it always did from his touch. An arousing scent, part shaving soap and part male, heightened her senses to an even greater awareness of him. She drew a deep, shuddering breath as he slipped the thin straps of her gown off her shoulders, sending a tremor rippling down her spine.

She waited breathlessly for his next move. He released the gown and it slid past her breasts and hips. For an instant, the cool air hardened the peaks of her breasts before he filled his hands with them, pressing moist kisses across her shoulders. Turning her in the circle of his arms, he continued to trail kisses along the swell of her bosom.

In a languorous gesture of surrender, Adriana threw back her head, giving him freer access. Accepting the invitation, he began to feast at her breasts—tugging, stroking, sucking, until his name became an endless purr on her lips.

Her head spun, and her trembling legs could barely support her. Adriana dug her fingers into his shoulders to keep from collapsing.

Drawn by her moans, Cleve lifted his head. She opened her eyes, heavy with passion, to meet his dark, hypnotic gaze.

He raised his hand and lightly brushed her cheek with his fingertips. "I wish I were an artist and could catch your beauty at this moment, my love," he whispered, his warm breath ruffling the hair at her ear.

Then his mouth crushed down on hers, his tongue probing in an erotic exploration. Making no attempt to hurry, he continued to toy with her as their kisses deepened and their tongues dueled. Her need for him became unbearable—a mounting urgency that threatened to erupt if it was not fulfilled.

"¡Querido!" she cried out. "I'm on fire."

"I know; I can feel your heat," he replied, lightly tracing her lips with his tongue.

"Then take me. Take me now, Cleve," she pleaded.

Sweeping her up into his arms, he carried her to the bed and laid her down gently, then stepped back to remove his own clothes.

His eyes devoured her hungrily, his breathing labored by passion. Lowering himself to the bed, he groaned with the delight of feeling her softness beneath him, and he slid his tongue along her silken flesh, tracing her rounded breasts and their taut peaks until she began to whimper.

He continued his tongue's moist and tantalizing exploration to the core of her sensuality. Whimpering from the exquisite sensation, she bit down on her lip to

keep from crying out. She writhed beneath him, burying her hands in his thick hair, pressing his dark head
to the throbbing chamber, her body imploding with
tremor upon tremor.

When the intense spasms ended, her chest ached
from the simple attempt to breathe, yet she wanted
more of the divine sensation.

Cleve shifted to taste the moist sweetness. of her
mouth. With every kiss, every touch, their lovemaking
intensified, taking them to the heights of ecstasy. His
loins felt like an inferno, but he pushed his control to
the limit until it threatened to shatter. Then, capturing
her mouth in a passionate kiss, he thrust into her—and
when he felt her tighten around him, he basked in
erotic glory.

With their bodies joined and their throbbing hearts
beating as one, in that sublime moment of release they
became one soul.

As he slept beside her, Adriana listened to the steady
rhythm of his breathing. Slipping her hand into his, she
realized she was happier than she had ever been before.

Chapter 30

The next morning, Garnet and Honey got out the washboard and tubs to do the laundry. Adriana enjoyed sloshing and rubbing the clothes in the water and had just finished lovingly hanging up Cleve's wet shirts, drawers, and stockings when the three men returned to the homestead.

Seeing the expressions on their husbands' downcast faces, the women exchanged worried glances and followed the silent men into the house.

Luke poured himself a cup of coffee and plopped down on a chair at the table. Cleve went over and stared into the fireplace while Flint leaned against the wall, sipping from his coffee mug.

Putting a hand on her husband's shoulder, Honey asked, "What is it, Luke?"

He looked up grimly. "Taurus is dead. We found his body near that alkaline water hole. He broke through the fence. There were a couple more dead calves, too. All bulls."

Adriana glanced at Cleve. "Taurus was our bull, Raven."

"And it's pretty hard to build a herd without bulls," Flint said glumly.

"Can't you buy another bull?" Adriana asked.

"We'll have to," Luke said. "The bull calves are too young yet to be used for breeding. But there's a lot

325

more we need, too. We have to bring in winter feed for the herd.''

"Dammit! One more year and we'd have been over the hump," Flint said. Frustrated, he shoved his hat to the top of his forehead.

Luke drew a deep breath. "Well, sitting here ain't gonna solve the problem. Reckon I'll ride into town and talk to Stover Kiefer at the bank. Maybe he'll give us a loan.''

"I'll come with you," Flint said.

"What about you, Cleve?" Luke asked. "You coming?''

"No, I'll stick around here. I've got a couple things to go over with Raven anyway.''

After Luke and Flint left, nobody felt like talking, so Garnet went back to her house to break the news to Maud and Ben. Just as she had done ever since they lived in California, Honey sat Josh down for his daily school lesson.

"Feel like a little ride, Raven?" Cleve asked.

"I'd love one.''

"Well, grab your hat; we'll find you a mount.''

Hand in hand, they walked down to the corral. Diablo came trotting over to her. "Cleve, I want to ride Diablo.''

"Dammit, Raven, you know how I feel about that horse.''

"He won't hurt me, Cleve. Believe me. If nothing else, I do know horses. You saw for yourself—he let me ride him yesterday.''

"Yeah, but who knows? He might not feel the same way about it today.''

"Please, Cleve," she implored.

"Raven, if anything happened to you, I'd never forgive myself.''

"Nothing will happen. Diablo is not the devil you claim him to be. Maybe his problem is that he only likes women." She poked him lightly. "Isn't that what you *Anglos* call 'horse sense'?''

"All right, but if he makes one false move, I'll shoot him. Do you understand that, Raven? Are you sure you want to risk his life as well as your own?"

"It's no risk, Cleve," she said confidently.

He grabbed the bridle off the nail and climbed over the fence. The minute he did, the horse snorted and started to paw the ground.

"Let me do that," Adriana said.

Cleve stood nearby, his hand on the Colt at his hip, as Adriana saddled the big black and then climbed onto the animal's back.

"Let's go, *chico mio*," she said when Cleve unhitched the gate.

The stallion stretched out its neck and broke into a gallop. By the time Cleve mounted his dun, the big black had five or six lengths on him.

Feeling that the horse had been confined long enough and deserved the chance to run, Adriana made no effort to rein him in. She galloped across the countryside with Cleve thundering behind her. Turning her head, she waved, but she didn't slow the stallion.

After a ten-minute run, she pulled up near the stream in the shade of a spreading oak and climbed down, loosened the horse's cinch, and led him over to the stream to drink.

"Dammit, Raven! Can't you do anything moderately?" Cleve complained. Dismounting, he released the cinch on his dun, and the horse wandered over to the water. "You don't know this terrain. That horse could have stepped in a chuckhole or something." He plopped down beside her on the ground.

"Isn't that why you MacKenzies only ride dun geldings—'cause they're smart, fast, and reliable?"

"You got that right," Cleve said.

"He's too smart to do that," she said.

Sitting down, she leaned back on her arms. "What an enjoyable ride—and that stallion is marvelous! He has power and speed. And he wasn't even winded! Are you convinced now that he can be trusted?"

"Well, I sure wouldn't turn my back on him." Cleve stretched out with his head on her lap. "Gotta admit, though, he's one hell of a horse. I'm just uneasy seeing you on him."

"Perhaps it's my affection for him that causes his gentleness. Could you be jealous, *querido?*" She leaned down and kissed him.

When she raised her head, he gazed into her eyes. "I'm jealous of any male you're fond of, even a horse."

He sat up and stared across the rolling field of grama grass. "Raven, would you be disappointed if we stayed here this winter instead of going to San Francisco?"

"Of course not."

"I thought I'd give Luke the money I have, so he can replace the stock he's lost and get through the winter."

"If that's what you want, go ahead. I don't mind. I like it here."

Pulling her into his arms, he gently eased her back, and they stretched out. He traced the curve of her lips with his finger. "Are you sure you won't be bored? Winters around here can be pretty lonely and desolate."

"I can't see how anyplace could be desolate with you nearby."

Dipping his head, he kissed her. Currents of desire raced through her as his mouth toyed with hers, biting and nibbling at her lips before he lightly traced the outline of them with his tongue. With a throaty groan of response, she circled his neck with her arms, weaving her fingers into the springy texture of his dark hair. She could feel the raw power in his arms, and her senses responded instantly to the vitality of his brawny body and the heady male essence of him.

"I love you, Raven," he murmured tenderly.

"And I you, *querido,*" she whispered.

He gazed down at her and gently brushed the hair off her cheek. Then he reclaimed her lips.

"Oh, Cleve," she said with a soft sigh. "Sometimes I feel that I can never get close enough to you."

His arm tightened around her. "That's okay, sweetheart, just as long as you don't stop trying."

With a breeze stirring the grass around them, and their horses munching peacefully on a patch of clover, they napped.

Near midnight, Luke and Flint returned from Calico. Cleve went out to the barn to greet them. "Any luck with Kiefer?"

"The sonofabitch wouldn't give us an answer," Flint cursed, flopping his saddle over the top of a stall.

"Don't look too good, though," Luke said. "Kiefer said business has been slow, and a couple of the smaller ranches have been faultin' on their loans. He told us to come back tomorrow, and he'll have an answer for us."

"He ain't gonna give us a loan," Flint fumed. "The smirking little ferret is having fun playing cat and mouse with us. He's hated us since we were kids—the bandy-legged little bastard!"

"Well, don't say anything to the women yet about the loan," Luke cautioned. "We better wait 'til we know for sure."

"Maybe we don't have to worry about what Kiefer is going to do. Let's go inside," Cleve said as they left the barn. "Raven's kept a pot of stew on the stove for you."

Flint yawned. "I think I'll just go home. I've gone to bed hungry before."

"Might as well eat, Flint. It's already hot and waiting. Besides, I've got something I'd like to talk over with the two of you."

Adriana was waiting for them when they came into the house. "Just sit down. The food's hot and ready," she said.

"Where's Honey?" Luke asked.

"She went to bed earlier. Her back was aching, so I promised I'd take care of you when you got home."

With a troubled frown, Luke started to rise from the table. "Is she okay?"

"She's fine, Luke. Just sit down and relax. Maud said

a backache's normal in her condition. After all, that baby's a heavy load. In a couple of weeks it will all be over," she added, filling their coffee cups.

"This is all I need," Flint said, picking up the cup.

"You're going to eat some of this stew, Flint MacKenzie, whether you want to or not," Adriana said firmly, serving him first with a heaping plate.

"Okay, Auntie Adee. I'm too tired to wrestle a she-wolf tonight." He winked at Cleve. "How do you put up with this sassy-mouth female, Little Brother?" He ravenously began to devour the food on the plate.

"And there's a piece of rhubarb pie when you're ready for it," she said as she put a tray of sliced bread on the table.

Later, after finishing his pie, Luke leaned back and patted his stomach. "Thanks, Adee, that sure hit the spot. Now, what did you want to talk about, Cleve?"

Picking up his money belt from a nearby bench, Cleve tossed it onto the table. "Here—it's yours. There's about a thousand dollars there. That ought to buy what we need. If not, maybe that bastard Kiefer will loan us the rest."

Luke shook his head. "Dammit, Cleve, haven't you done enough already? You brought in our first bull and herd to begin with. And you didn't get nothing out of it."

"As long as this brand's a Triple M, I've got a stake in it. You fellows do all the work. This is the least I can do."

Flint shoved back his chair and stood up. "Reckon I best get to bed. Thanks for the vittles, Adee. They tasted mighty good."

Aware of Flint's inability to express his deep feelings, Adriana watched him stop next to Cleve and look at his younger brother as if he wanted to say something. Then Flint grinned and slapped Cleve on the shoulder. "'Night, Little Brother."

"Ain't too often we can catch Brother Flint without some kind of a comment," Luke said, breaking the silence that followed Flint's departure. Luke stood up. "We're all beholden to you, Little Brother." Then the big man hugged his younger brother, who actually stood two inches taller.

"Whoa, there," Cleve said, "you better hold up on that gratitude, because you may want to eat those words. You see, Raven and I had planned on using that money to go to San Francisco after Honey had the baby. Now I'm afraid you'll be stuck with us for the winter."

Luke grinned. "It'll be good to have you home for a lengthy spell."

"You're sure we won't be in the way?" Adriana asked.

Slipping an arm around her shoulders, Luke hugged her to his side. "You see that?" he asked, pointing to three *M*s scorched into the wood above the doorway. "Our pa burned that there when he built this house for Ma. And as long as that brand's above that door, there'll always be room for you here, Adee."

Adriana knew that if she tried to say anything, she'd end up blubbering. Kissing him on the cheek, she turned away and began to clear the dinner dishes.

The next morning, Adriana rode into Calico with the three men. Before falling asleep the previous night, she had thought of another way of solving the situation— her dowry! Her father had never given Cleve her dowry. As soon as the men entered the bank, she headed for the telegraph office.

She was waiting by the hitching post when they emerged from the bank. It wasn't hard to guess from their expressions that their request for a loan had been refused.

Cleve took her to lunch while Luke and Flint went to the tiny newspaper office to place an advertisement for a bull.

"If we're lucky, we'll have a quick response to that ad, and we can get one before winter sets in," Luke said when he and Flint joined them later. "In the meantime, we're losing calves. We've got to do something about that bad water hole."

"How about dynamiting it?" Cleve asked.

"Or burying it?" Flint suggested.

"I think you're both on to something," Luke agreed. "There's a high rise directly above that hole. If we blow that ledge above it, it'll all tumble down and cover the water hole."

"That's it! Let's do it," Flint exclaimed.

"It'll be one hell of a job, but I suppose it would work," Cleve said thoughtfully.

With rejuvenated enthusiasm, Luke jumped to his feet. "Okay, let's get us some dynamite, Brother Flint."

Cleve shook his head as the two men hurried out of the diner. "What's next?"

Adriana smiled, leaned across the table, and grasped his hand.

"Well, I've heard others say it, and I guess they were right, *querido*."

"Right about what?"

"That you MacKenzies can move mountains."

"I don't like the looks of that sky," Flint remarked as they rode back home.

Luke nodded. "Yeah, it looks like we could be in for some rain."

"It sure don't smell like rain to me," Flint grumbled, with another skeptical glance skyward.

Luke shook his head. "Hope it won't stop us from blasting tomorrow. I want to get started before we lose any more cows."

"Ah, quit worrying, Luke," Cleve said. "At least we managed to drive all the cattle over to the south range, and there's plenty of good water there."

Luke continued to fret. "That damn hole's been drying up for years. Thank God it's not deep. Pushing enough dirt in there oughta finish it off for good."

"What the hell!" Flint muttered when a surging,

bitterly cold wind suddenly arose. They immediately felt a drastic drop in the temperature. "Feels like a Norther to me. Told you I didn't like the looks of that sky. We best make tracks." He goaded his horse to a gallop.

Reining up, Cleve grabbed a slicker from his saddlebags and handed it to Raven. "Put this on, honey. And tie your hat down with your bandanna, or you'll lose it," he warned, shouting above the howl of the wind.

They raced after Luke and Flint, but within a couple of miles they had to slow their pace as the wind blowing across the Texas Panhandle began to drive ice and snow before it. The road soon disappeared beneath a white glaze, and the snow became so blinding Adriana could barely see Cleve riding beside her.

"Can't we take cover until this passes?" she called out through chattering teeth.

"We could get a foot of snow before it stops," he shouted back. "Better that we keep going. We're almost home, honey."

Huddled in the saddle, shivering, Adriana tried to protect her face from the sharp ice that stung like shards of broken glass. When they finally turned onto the road leading to the homestead, she wanted to cry for joy.

"Get inside. I'll take care of your horse," Cleve shouted when they reached the yard. She didn't have to be told twice. Quickly dismounting, she discovered the snow was already past her ankles.

A gush of warm air greeted her as she entered the house. She closed her eyes momentarily, savoring the welcome warmth. When she opened them, the distraught look on Maud's face warned her of trouble.

"I don't suppose the boy's with you?"

"Boy?" Adriana asked, removing the slicker. She backed up to the fireplace and lifted her skirt to the heat.

"Josh," Maud said. "He ain't to be found. We've been searchin' for him since the sky took a turn for the worse."

Garnet hurried to wrap a blanket around her shoulders. "You better get out of those wet clothes, Adee," she said as Honey came rushing out of the bedroom.

"Is it . . ." Honey looked hopefully at Adriana. After a silent exchange between them, Honey's shoulders slumped in dejection.

"Gal, get back in that bed," Maud ordered. "You've worn yourself thin searchin' for the child."

"She won't listen to me," Garnet said, throwing up her hands.

"How can I think of lying down when I know Josh is out there in that storm?" Honey cried.

"Told you there ain't nothin' you can do," Maud said. "The menfolk are home now. They'll find the boy, Honey."

Snow swirled through the door as Luke and Cleve entered the house.

"Whew! What a storm!" Luke exclaimed, shaking the snow off his hat. "I tell you, Adee, that damn horse of yours is the most obstinate—" He stopped when he saw their solemn expressions. "What's wrong?" He quickly glanced at Honey. "Jaybird, are you okay?"

"Oh, Luke." Ignoring his wet clothing, she rushed into his arms. "It's Josh. He's been missing for hours." Her words were mingled with sobs.

At that moment, the door flew open and Flint came in. He had to force it shut with his hands and body. Now wearing a heavy sheepskin-lined jacket and gloves, he met Cleve's stare and nodded grimly. "Ben told me."

"Flint!" Honey came rushing over to him, sobbing pitifully. "Everyone knows you can follow an ant in a sandstorm. You've just got to find Josh, Flint."

"We'll find him, Little Sister," Flint said gently. "Don't you fret."

She started to pace the floor. "When I think of him out in that storm . . . he's so little and defenseless. What if—" She broke down in unrestrained sobbing.

Luke grasped her firmly by the arms. "Jaybird, listen

to me. Josh may be young, but he's smart. He'll have enough sense to find some kind of shelter and sit out the storm."

"Even if he does, he's not wearing a coat," she cried. "He'll fre—he'll freeze—"

"Dammit, Jaybird, stop talking like that!" Luke said, trying to disguise his own anxiety. "You know Amigo's with him. That dog's not gonna let anything happen to Josh. The two of them have often cuddled up together to stay warm."

"Honey," Cleve asked, trying to calm her, "can you think of any reason why Josh would leave the homestead?"

She shook her head. "He's always been so good about following Luke's orders. It's never been a problem before."

"Jaybird," Luke said in a gentle tone, "if you won't lie down, will you at least sit down? You're going to make yourself ill. You've got the baby to think about."

He led her over to a chair and seated her. Then he leaned down and kissed her forehead.

Garnet hurried over, carrying an afghan. "Here, Honey, let's not have you take a chill." She tucked it around Honey's legs.

"We're wasting time, Luke," Flint said.

"Yeah. I'll get my things."

Flint nodded. "I'll saddle the horses."

Garnet put her hand on his arm. "Be careful, Flint," she warned gently.

He grinned and reached out to toy with her hair. "I will. And you stay warm, Redhead. I'll be back soon." He kissed her on the cheek and slipped out the door.

Feeling helpless, Adriana watched in silence, until suddenly something dawned on her and she hurried into the bedroom where Cleve was changing his clothes.

He had already slipped into a dry shirt and trousers, and was just putting on a heavy buckskin jacket lined with sheepskin.

"Cleve, I just remembered that I overheard Josh scolding Amigo for sneaking away. Do you suppose he went out to look for the dog?"

"Oh, Lord! If he did, there's a chance Josh might be on his own. Don't mention this to Honey. It will only upset her more."

"Be careful, *querido*," she whispered when he took her in his arms.

"We'll be back soon." Kissing her quickly, he hurried out of the room.

As the men prepared to leave, Maud stopped them at the door and handed them a small bundle of clothing and several blankets.

"Good luck, boys," she said, turning away tearfully.

Garnet kissed each of them on the cheek, then had to forcibly push the door shut behind them because of the driving snow and ice.

"Well, there sure as hell won't be any tracks to follow," Flint declared when Cleve and Luke joined him in the barn. "The wind and snow will have wiped them out."

"You figure we should stay together or split up?" Luke asked, stuffing the clothes and blankets into his saddlebags.

"I think we can cover more ground if we split up," Cleve said.

Luke nodded. "I think so, too. It's only common sense that Josh couldn't have gone more than a couple of miles."

"If he even got that far," Flint added.

"So, let's think about this," Cleve said. "Where would be the logical places he could find cover within a radius of two miles?"

"Well, there's that stand of cottonwood near the south pasture," Luke said thoughtfully. "He and Amigo could burrow against the trunk of a tree there."

"If he had turned west," Cleve suggested, "he'd most likely come upon that deep ravine near Ben Franks's old place. A person huddling against the far side of it would be sheltered from the worst of the wind. Or if he was past it, he might even have made it to Ben's house."

"What about those rocks above the alkaline hole?" Flint asked. "Remember the time we hid from the Comanches in a cave up there?"

"Yeah, I'd forgotten about that cave," Cleve said.

"Dammit!" Luke exploded. "Why would he go? If we only knew that, we might be able to figure out which direction he headed."

"Fellas, Raven thinks he may have gone out looking for Amigo. I guess Amigo's been sneaking out at night."

Luke looked stunned. "Oh, good Lord! I was holding out hope that as long as Josh was with Amigo, he had a good chance of—"

"Luke, who's to say Amigo's not with him," Cleve said.

Flint appeared as grim as Luke. "I don't like this. Last week, I saw wolf tracks near that alkaline hole—" Suddenly, Flint raised his head and stood alertly. "Listen."

"What do you hear?" Luke asked. "Is it Amigo?"

"The wind's stopped."

The men hurried to the barn door and saw the moon filtering through the last of the swift-moving clouds. The storm had passed and night had descended— serene and peaceful. Moonlight glistened on the ice-crusted snow, carpeting the earth as far as the eye could see. Trees, heavy with frost, sparkled in the moon's glow.

"Well, this sure as hell makes things easier," Flint said.

They mounted their horses and, despite the bright night and reflection of the snow, carried torches to light their way.

"I'm heading for those rocks," Flint declared. "I'd bet my bottom dollar he's up there." He rode away.

Luke looked at Cleve. "What do you think? Should we check out the other places?"

"To hell with splitting up," Cleve said. "Let's follow him. I'd trust that old trail mule's instinct anytime."

Shimmering, fiery shadows, squirming like carmine serpents, snaked along the granite walls as the three men rode the narrow path. Under the cautious guidance of their torch-bearing riders, the horses trod slowly up the slippery incline, their hoofbeats muffled by the blanket of snow.

"There it is," Flint said, spying a narrow opening on the face of the wall.

The three men dismounted and surveyed the small gap. "I guess we weren't so big when we hid from those Comanches," Cleve said.

Flint had already dropped to his stomach.

Inside the cave, Josh woke with a start. "Wake up, Amigo. Wake up!" he cried, clutching the dog closer to him. "Di-did you hear that?" he stammered. "S-sure is some-something out there."

Terrified and shivering, he snuggled against Amigo's fur as he stared in panic toward the dim light at the opening. Then, suddenly, a blazing shaft of fire appeared inside the entrance.

"No! Stop!" he sobbed, shielding his eyes.

Having thrust the torch through the opening, Flint stood it on end and wiggled his head and shoulders into the hole. "You better get in here, Luke," he said anxiously. "And bring your saddlebags with you."

By the time Flint had crawled through the hole, Luke was right on his heels. Cleve followed close behind with the saddlebags. They found Josh cuddled against Amigo. The dog was stretched out with his head lying across the body of a gray and white dog. Amigo whimpered when he saw them, but did not move. Even in the dim light of the torches, it was obvious the other dog was dead. Three little pups huddled against the body of the dead dog, and two more pups were lying a short distance away.

Luke crawled over to Josh's side, sat up, and took his son in his arms. "Thank God, you're alive!" he said. The light reflected on the moisture glimmering in his eyes.

"Da-Daddy," Josh cried, hugging his arms tightly around his father's neck.

Luke's voice quivered as he cuddled his son against him. "Josh, son, you had us all so scared."

With tears streaming down his cheeks, Josh pushed back and looked wide-eyed at his father. "You were? Me and Ami-Amigo weren't sc-scared. We knew you'd come, Da-Daddy," Josh said, trying to sound brave through chattering teeth.

Cleve had already pulled a blanket from the saddle-bags, and they wrapped it around Josh.

"Look, Daddy, Amigo must have married up and they had babies, just like Mama and Auntie Garnie." His face puckered in sadness. "But, see there," he said, pointing his finger. "His wife died."

Luke looked over at Flint, who was examining the dead dog. "She's pretty bloated. She must have drunk some of that saltwater. The two little pups over there didn't make it, either."

"Well, let's get out of here. We've got to get Josh home and warmed up."

"What about these dogs?" Flint asked.

"We'll have to take them along, too, or they'll starve to death." Luke slipped Josh's arms into a coat. "Okay, Josh, time to go."

"Come on, Amigo, we gotta go," Josh said.

Amigo rose slowly. Whimpering, he licked the nose of his mate several times, then limped over to them.

"Sorry, boy, but we'll have to leave the others behind," Luke said.

Flint crawled out first; then Cleve handed him the three puppies and followed. After they quickly bundled up the puppies, Flint mounted his horse, and Cleve handed him the pups.

"How do you expect me to carry these whelps and a torch, too?" Flint grumbled.

"I'm sure you'll find a way, stalwart scout," Cleve said, then knelt down for Josh.

Once Luke was mounted, Cleve handed Josh up to him, and Luke settled his son in front of him on the saddle. By the time Cleve picked up Amigo and mounted, Flint had already started down the pathway with Luke close behind. Tucking Amigo into the front of his jacket, Cleve rebuttoned it so that only the dog's head was exposed. Then, holding the torch aloft, he followed.

Their homecoming was tearful and joyous. They ate, drank hot coffee, fed the puppies warm milk, and talked throughout most of the night. Finally, toward dawn, Flint and his family, Maud, and Ben trudged through the snow back to their house.

Except for the puppies in a box by the fireplace, it was late morning before anyone began to stir around the homestead. When Adriana arose, she glanced out the window and saw that the snow and ice had begun to melt. By midday, the temperature had returned to normal, and under the rays of the sun, the melted snow ran in streams.

Everyone spent a lazy day puttering around the ranch or fussing with the puppies—with Amigo standing over them with a watchful eye.

"Cleve, why does Amigo limp?" Adriana asked, watching the dog with his pups.

"I understand he was a stray that had been trampled by a horse," Cleve replied. "Luke was about to shoot the poor little guy to put him out of his misery, but Josh wouldn't hear of it. They nursed the dog back to health. Unfortunately, his leg was too damaged to heal. Amigo and Josh have been inseparable ever since."

Adriana knelt down and scratched Amigo behind the ears. "You're perfect just the way you are, darling."

She received a slobbering kiss and a wagging tail in response.

Chapter 31

By the next day, the snow had completely disappeared. The storm, though not forgotten, was no longer foremost in anyone's mind, because the operation of filling the polluted water hole had begun.

The men set the dynamite charges at the base of the ledge overhanging the hole. When the time came to light the long fuse, everyone watched from a safe distance as Luke put a match to it, then galloped to safety.

The ground shook beneath them as the charges exploded, and to the sounds of their awed gasps, tons of dirt and rock tumbled down, burying the hole beneath them.

When the earth stopped shaking and the cloud of dust finally settled, Josh glanced at the three pups peeking over the rim of the box in the wagon bed.

"Sure wish your mama was here now to see this, but Daddy and Uncle Flint and Uncle Cleve moved her and your two brothers right by that hole. Now you'll always know where they're buried."

The MacKenzie brothers spent the rest of the week knocking away any loose rock that remained above, and firming up the earth below.

"It's hard to believe, isn't it?" Garnet murmured as she and Adriana viewed the scene several days later. "I imagine, when it's covered with grass in a few years, nobody will know the difference."

"Garnet, you just gave me a good idea," Adriana exclaimed.

The next day, accompanied by Josh, Amigo, and the box of puppies, she drove the wagon to a cottonwood grove where they dug up a sapling, then took it to the rubble and replanted it.

"This tree will be the marker where Amigo's wife is buried," Adriana told Josh. "I think we should give this spot a name. What would you like to call it?"

Josh thought for a long moment. "How 'bout Amigo's . . . ah, wife?"

"The Spanish have a lovely word, *marida*. It means 'mate,' Josh."

"*Marida.* Yeah, that's a good name!" he exclaimed. "Hear that, Amigo?" Josh poured a pail of water around the trunk of the sapling, declaring, "I baptize you 'Amigo's Marida.'"

Looking up at Adriana, he grinned, and she was startled by how much the grin resembled his father's.

His young face now glowed with pleasure. "I'm sure glad we thought of that name, Auntie Adee."

As they returned to the homestead, Adriana's heart started to pound in her throat when she recognized the coach parked in front of Luke's house. A driver dozed in the box seat as the three matched pairs of black horses restlessly pawed the earth, flicking at flies with their tails.

Climbing down from the wagon, she cast an anxious glance at the house. "Josh, will you put the pail and shovel in the barn?"

"Wow! Look at that big coach!" he exclaimed. "It's fancy enough for the president of the United States."

Flint came out of the barn and took the reins from her. "I'll take care of the wagon, Adee. They've been waiting for you. Josh, you come along with me."

"How come I have to go with you? Why can't I go in the house with Auntie Adee?"

"Time you learned how to unhitch a wagon," he said.

"Oh, boy!" Josh exclaimed. "You mean you're gonna let me unhitch it?"

"Thank you, Flint," Adriana said.

He nodded.

As she walked to the house, Adriana pulled off her gloves and waved to the half-dozen *vaqueros* lounging in the shade of a nearby cottonwood. *"Saludos, hombres."*

The men acknowledged the greeting and waved back.

As soon as she entered, she could feel the tension in the room. Her father sat stiffly at the kitchen table. Honey was seated opposite him. Cleve stood at the fireplace with his back to the door. Scowling, he turned and looked at her.

"Would you like another cup of coffee, Don Alarico?" Honey asked politely.

"No thank you, *señora*," he replied.

She rose from the chair. "Then if you'll excuse me, I . . . ah . . . have to go and check on my son." She gave Adriana a sympathetic look as she passed her on the way out.

"Hello, *Papá*."

"Adriana," he acknowledged.

"I trust your journey was comfortable," she said, walking over to the pump at the sink to wash her hands.

"Well, now that we have that heartwarming reunion out of the way, will you tell me what the hell is going on, Adriana?" Cleve demanded.

Adriana couldn't remember a time when she had seen him look so annoyed. She could feel the anger he was trying to suppress.

"Cleve, I'd like to speak to my father alone. Would you be offended if I asked you to leave?"

"I certainly would. I'm curious to know why your father and his private army have shown up here at the Triple M."

"I suspect you already know why I am here. It is just as I anticipated," the don said, shrugging his shoulders. "A wealthy wife is easier to bear than a poor one—a fact, *señor*, you have already discovered." He placed a bulging wallet on the table. "I presume this is what you've been waiting for."

"What is that?"

"My daughter's dowry, *Señor* MacKenzie."

"Dowry?" Cleve shouted. "You can take your god-damn money and get the hell out of here."

"I received a telegram from you requesting it," Don Alarico accused.

"I sure as hell didn't send any such telegram."

"I did," Adriana announced.

Cleve turned an angry glare on her. "You did! For God's sake, why, Adriana?"

"Cleve, this is between my father and me."

"Why would you do something like this and sign my name, without even discussing it with me? I don't want a penny of your father's money."

"It's my money—not my father's," she argued. "You know how desperately we need money to keep the ranch going."

"And you think that I or my brothers would consider taking this . . . blood money?"

"Blood money! Whatever do you mean? It is perfectly normal for a woman to have a dowry," Adriana declared.

"Sure! A quilt or some dishes. Not a bulging wallet."

"You pretend not to understand. You know it is the custom of my people, and I have a right to it."

"I know one thing, Adriana. You have no right to embarrass me—and my family—by thinking we'd even consider taking one cent of your money. Whatever made you think I'd take money for marrying you?

Hauling your father up here to give us a handout was not a decision for you to make."

Adriana did not hear the wounded pride in Cleve's words, only the same authoritative dogma she had suffered from her father.

"Are you saying I have no rights? That only you can make decisions in our marriage, and I must be submissive to whatever you wish? You are mistaken, Cleve MacKenzie. The role of a meek and slavish wife is not one I can play. I thought you understood that." She picked up the wallet and shook it in his face. "This is my money, and I intend to keep it."

"Well, I cannot play the role of the village idiot who lives off the dole from his father-in-law. I thought you understood that! I want that money out of here by the time I return."

He slammed the door on his way out of the house.

"Well, Adriana, once again you have acted with your usual willful hastiness," Don Alarico said.

"You are enjoying this, aren't you, *Papá*?"

"As a matter of fact, I am. It pleases me to see that your husband is not weak like your brother, who always yielded to your whims. It appears this *Anglo* you married will not tolerate your rebelliousness any more than I did."

"Nor will I, *Papá*, tolerate his dictates any more than I did yours."

"You disappoint me, Adriana. I gave you credit for more endurance than you obviously possess. I once believed you had some of my strengths." He shook his head. "I will wait while you pack."

"Did I speak of packing?" She stormed outside, leaving her surprised father to get up and follow.

"You going away, Auntie Adee?" Josh asked when she came outside. "Thought you and Uncle Cleve were gonna stay here over the winter."

"Your Auntie Adee's not going anywhere, Josh."

He looked at her solemnly. "That's good, 'cause you

promised to help me with the pups, and you and me's gotta keep that tree watered, don't we?"

"We sure do, sweetheart." She bent down and kissed him on his cheek, then hurried over to Honey and Garnet, who were watching with interest. "Do you know where Cleve is?"

"In the barn with Luke and Flint," Honey said. "What's going on, Adriana? I've never seen him this angry."

She briefly told them about her quarrel with Cleve.

"Oh, Adriana, Cleve's just upset right now," Honey declared. "He's probably cooled down already."

"Sure," Garnet added. "Cleve's the most easygoing of the three."

"Well, I haven't! It would serve him right if I climbed in that coach and left with my father."

"Don't waste your time," Garnet said. "I can tell you from my own experience; it wouldn't work. Twice, before we were married, I tried to leave Flint. But I always came back."

"I once tried leaving Luke, too," Honey added. "I couldn't. Cleve loves you, Adee. You know that."

"Well, he sure has an odd way of showing it."

"Not at all," Garnet spoke up. "He has a beautiful way of showing it. Honey and I have both noticed the way he touches your hair if he passes you when you're sitting down." She sighed. "That's so romantic. I wish Flint would make romantic gestures like that. They say so much—and we all know Flint is a man of few words."

"Well, you've got nothing to complain about," Adriana told her. "Whenever you're not looking, Flint's eyes follow every step you take. He adores you. Isn't that right, Honey?"

Honey nodded. "That's for sure. He looks like a lovesick cow."

"You mean bull, my dear!" Garnet corrected, arching her brow. "Definitely a bull!" Then her face softened in a pleased smile. "So he does, does he?"

Honey and Adriana nodded simultaneously. "You bet he does," Honey reiterated.

Garnet grinned. "Well, it can't be any worse than when Luke and you look at each other, Honey MacKenzie. Goodness! If anyone got caught in the crossfire, they'd get singed from the heat!"

Suddenly the three women were hugging and giggling like schoolgirls—Cleve, Don Alarico, and dowry forgotten momentarily.

"Adriana!"

The sharp call cut off their laughter, and they looked over to see Don Alarico waiting impatiently by the coach, with Amigo and his pups yapping and licking at his boots.

Adriana ignored her father's agitation when she saw Cleve come out of the barn, trailed by Luke and Flint.

"We have something to settle, Cleve," she declared, putting her hands on her hips.

"Fine, but you and I will settle it between us—not my brothers, sisters-in-law, and for damn sure, not your father."

"No, we'll settle it now. What I've got to say, I'll say in front of everyone, because this is for them, too, as much as it is for you—and for my father! I've been around this family long enough to know what you MacKenzies mean to each other: it's one for all, and all for one. I've heard how you men pulled each other out of dangerous scrapes, how Honey and Garnet put their lives in danger to save the men they loved. Well, I'm a MacKenzie, too, aren't I? Don't I have a right to make a contribution, even if it is only money?"

Everyone stood speechless, waiting for Cleve's reply.

Cleve cleared his throat. "I'm sorry I lost my temper, Raven. I've had time to think about it, and I realize how wrong I was."

"So, *señor*, you've reconsidered, and you'll accept the money after all," Don Alarico said sarcastically.

"The name is Cleve, sir. Not *señor*. For God's sake, I'm your son-in-law, and I intend to remain so. Will you please stop addressing me as if I'm some stranger you've just met?"

Cleve walked up to Adriana and slipped his arm around her shoulder. "You've misunderstood what I meant, sir. I was so concerned with my own pride that I didn't think how hard it must have been for Adriana to swallow hers and ask you for money."

"I do not recall being *asked*," Don Alarico said. "It was more of a demand."

"Raven," Cleve said, "I understand why you did it, and I know it was a very difficult thing to do. I appreciate it, sweetheart, and if the money is still important to you, you have the privilege of keeping it and doing whatever you want with it."

"So you'll let me give it to you?" she asked hopefully.

"What do you think, boys?"

"Sounds like her mind's pretty well made up, Little Brother," Luke said.

"What do you say, Flint?"

Flint shoved his hat to the top of his forehead. "Ain't you learned by now, Little Brother? Once they set their minds to something, there just ain't no winnin' with these MacKenzie women."

These MacKenzie women. The phrase raised gooseflesh on Adriana's arms. Grinning, she glanced at her sisters-in-law, and they hurried over, laughing. With arms encircled, the three women hugged and kissed as Amigo and his puppies scampered over to join the circle.

Don Alarico shook his head. "It is difficult for me to understand the ways of the young—much less those of an *Anglo*," he said to Cleve, who had walked over to the coach. "It would appear that I may have misjudged you, *Señ*—ah, Cleve. Nevertheless, I will return tomorrow in the event that my daughter may have a change of heart."

"Well, sir, I doubt that will happen. But come anyway; we'll look forward to your visit. And plan on staying for dinner . . . *Papá*."

Don Alarico's eyes grew wide, but he managed to keep his mouth shut.

Awaking at dawn the following morning, Adriana looked at Cleve as he slept. She loved staring at him while he was unaware; he looked so peaceful.

The events of the previous day had taught her a priceless lesson: any decision affecting their marriage must be shared. Together, they would continue to build on that accord.

With a loving smile, she pressed a light kiss to his forehead, then arose from bed and walked over to gaze out the window. Despite the early hour, she saw Ben Franks preparing to ride away.

Cleve came up behind her. "Good morning, sweetheart." Sliding his arms around her waist, he nuzzled her neck. She sighed as she leaned back against him.

"Where is Ben going so early this morning?"

"Probably riding over to his old house. He likes to visit the grave of his wife, Molly, and if the weather is good enough, he usually goes about once a week."

"Oh, that's sweet," Adriana said, looking up at him. "How long has he been widowed?"

"Ten or eleven years. Remember that I told you he has a daughter in New York? Well, he just wanted to stay here after Molly died."

Seeing another figure cross the yard, Cleve exclaimed "Dammit! I had great expectations of luring you back into bed, but there's Flint! The sun's barely up, and he's rarin' to go. I swear he's part rooster." He released her and turned away. "I better get dressed."

When he was finished, Adriana followed him out of the bedroom, and as they walked into the kitchen, they caught Luke in the process of leaving. He had his arms around Honey and was kissing her.

"Good morning," he said, glancing over at them.

Then Luke turned back to Honey and patted her stomach. "I'm wondering if this baby's gonna decide to be born today," he said, smiling. "Stubborn little critter, isn't it?"

"An inherent trait from his father, I am sure," Honey said.

"Jaybird, I'm gonna make you eat those words when our yellow-haired daughter is born." He kissed her lightly, then grabbed his Stetson. "See you later."

"How's the backache today?" Adriana asked.

Sighing, Honey patted her stomach. "Oh, Adee, do you think this baby will ever be born?"

Chapter 32

Carlos Valez and Antonio Fuente rode up to the hotel in Calico and dismounted. "We'll stay here for the night."

"But why are we stopping so early, Carlos?"

"I have a friend I wish to say good-bye to, my son. I won't be seeing him again. You can remain in the hotel while I'm gone."

"As you wish, Carlos."

"I will return as quickly as possible," Carlos said, as soon as they registered. "This is simply . . . a debt I must repay."

Antonio watched him ride away, then entered the hotel's barroom. Glancing casually around, he stopped abruptly and stared in astonishment when he saw the man sitting at a corner table.

He slowly crossed the room. "Hello, *Papá*."

"Antonio," Don Alarico said.

"I would not expect to see you here in this town, *Papá*."

"I can say the same to you. You have been well?"

"Very well, *Papá*."

"Your sister tells me you have a *patrón*."

"More than a *patrón*, *Papá*. Carlos is a father to me. I love him deeply." Antonio enjoyed the sight of his father's momentary flinch of pain. "We are leaving this country and going to Europe."

"I see. What brings you here? Have you come to say good-bye to Adriana?" Don Alarico asked.

Antonio brightened with surprise and pleasure. "Adriana is here?"

"She and her husband live nearby on the *hacienda* of the MacKenzies. It is called the Triple M."

"I did not know that. Then I must see her before I go. Do you know how I can reach this Triple M ranch?"

"You must follow the road east for about *veinte millas*."

"Then I shall leave at once. Good-bye, *Papá*. It is most unlikely that we will meet again." He started to leave, then turned back. For a long moment he hesitated, then said softly, "*Adios, Papá*."

"*Adios*, my son," Don Alarico said. His expression never altered.

Antonio rode east and eventually came upon a side road with a sign bearing the Flying F ranch name, marked out and changed to the Triple M. He turned onto the road, and after a short ride, he reined up to study the terrain. In the distance he saw a small house that appeared neglected and deserted. Then he spied an old man kneeling by a graveside. A chestnut horse stood nearby. Not wishing to disturb the man at such a private moment, Antonio dismounted and waited in the shade.

After a few minutes, a group of riders rode up to the old man, who stood up. Something about the leader captured Antonio's attention. To his astonishment, he recognized Lattimore and Mel, two of the men who had once ridden for Carlos Valez. It became apparent to Antonio that Lattimore and the old man were having a heated exchange. He was about to ride up to them when, to his disbelief, Lattimore drew his Colt and shot the old man. Laughing, the gang wheeled their horses and rode away.

Appalled by the cowardly act, Antonio galloped up

to the grave, hoping the man was still alive. He examined the body, but the old man was dead.

Torn between caution and curiosity, Antonio climbed back on his horse and followed the gang. After a short ride, Lattimore and Mel broke away from the group. Antonio thought it wiser to stay with them.

As they drew near Calico, a figure rode out of the trees. Shocked, Antonio recognized Carlos. For several minutes, the men talked quietly. Antonio could not hear what they said, but it was clear that Carlos was not surprised to see them.

Fearing for Carlos's safety, though, Antonio rode up to the three men. Lattimore quickly drew his Colt.

"Put that away," Carlos ordered. Instantly, Lattimore slid the pistol back into its holster.

"Antonio, what are you doing here?"

"Carlos, beware of these men. They have just killed a man."

Lattimore snorted, then exchanged an amused glance with Mel.

"Surely you are mistaken, Antonio," Carlos said. His expression had become guarded.

"I saw it myself, Carlos. What are they doing here? Are they whom you came to meet? There are others with them."

"It is my business. Do not concern yourself," he ordered sharply.

"Carlos, haven't you heard what I've been saying? These are dangerous men. They have just killed a defenseless old man!"

"Shut up! I must have time to think." The explosive command came from the mouth of Carlos, but in an accent Antonio did not recognize. Then, in the same strange tongue, Carlos spoke as he clutched his head and rocked himself back and forth. "Now look what you've done, Antonio—you've spoiled it all. Why didn't you stay in town the way I told you to?"

His eyes warm with tenderness, he looked fondly at Antonio. "You will have to come with us, my son.

Tonight we will smoke our pipes, and then tomorrow, as soon as I finish what I came here to do, we will leave this place forever."

Antonio offered no resistance when Mel grabbed the reins of his horse and led him away.

Cleve came riding back to the house at noon, in time to see Adriana saddling Diablo. "Where are you going?"

"Maud's worried about Ben. She said he hasn't returned, so I told her I'd ride over and see what's keeping him."

"I'll ride with you."

Within minutes, they headed west toward Ben's former homestead. When they arrived, the first thing they saw was Ben slumped over the grave of his wife. Cleve dismounted and examined the body.

"Aw, Ben," he said, dismayed. Then he gently rolled the old man onto his back. "He's dead, Raven."

"Oh, no," she said, stunned. Her eyes misted with tears. "I suppose his heart gave out?"

Cleve looked up at her grimly. "No, it wasn't his heart. He was shot."

"What? Who would—"

"I don't know." Cleve got up and studied the ground around the grave. "From the number of prints, it looks like a good-size gang. C'mon—we better get out of here." He picked up Ben's lifeless body and tied it on the back of the chestnut. Then he mounted his dun and they returned to the ranch.

When they rode up to Flint's house, Maud came out the door. "Well, it's about time," she said. Then she saw the body draped over the saddle.

"Oh, Lordy!" she cried out. "Ben!"

Cleve climbed down and put his arms around her. "Cry it out, Maud," he said gently.

"What's wrong?" Garnet asked, hurrying out of the house.

"Ben's dead, Garnet," Adriana said, dabbing at her

eyes. She dismounted and went over and hugged Garnet. "We found him at his wife's grave."

Garnet tried to speak between sobs. "He was such a dear old man. There wasn't a mean bone in his body. His heart must have given out, huh?"

"I'm afraid not," Cleve said. "He was shot."

Maud's head jerked up. "Shot! Who'd shoot him? Ben didn't have an enemy in the world."

"I saw a lot of tracks at Molly's grave."

"You think it's some stray Comanche, Cleve?" Maud asked.

"No. These horses were all shod. It wasn't Indians. Besides, they would have taken his chestnut. Where do you want him, Garnet?" he asked, untying the body.

"In his room, I guess." Garnet wiped her eyes.

"I'll fix him up for buryin'," Maud said. "No sense in taking him into town. You boys can fix him a box."

While Cleve carried Ben into the house, Adriana walked over to Luke's to break the news to Honey.

Later, after the men had constructed a crude pine box, Maud dressed Ben in his finest suit and tucked a small, framed picture of Molly inside his jacket. They placed his body in the coffin and nailed it shut.

"Who'd want to kill him?" Flint asked.

"From the tracks, it looked like a big gang," Cleve replied. "Could be they were just passing through. Then again, maybe not. At any rate, it's a blessing they didn't come upon our women while we were gone."

"Reckon we should get on their trail right away," Flint said stoically.

"This is no time to be leaving our women alone," Luke reminded him. "Especially since this gang might still be around. After we bury Ben tomorrow, one of us can ride into town and tell the sheriff."

Shaking his head, Flint glanced at Cleve. "This is our fight. I'm for settling this ourselves."

"I think Luke's right, Flint," Cleve said. "This is no time to be leaving the women, and it looked like there's too many of them for one of us to be going off on our own."

"Yeah, we've got to let the sheriff handle this," Luke declared.

Shaking his head in disgust, Flint glanced at Cleve. "Big Brother's always the lawman!"

Still feeling a slight stupor from the effects of the opium Walden had forced him to smoke the previous night, Antonio stared at his mentor in disbelief.

Throughout the night, until he had passed into slumber, Antonio had listened to Carlos speak of his plans for their future together as if nothing had happened.

Now, still under the influence of the drug, Carlos boasted of his intentions to raid the Triple M ranch.

"So it is true, Carlos? You are the killer MacKenzie said you are? Your men killed those Rangers, too, didn't they?"

"No! MacKenzie lied, Antonio. All those MacKenzies are liars. It is clear that you and I can never be happy as long as any of them are alive." His eyes were glazed with the effects of the drug. The more he spoke, the more his voice rose in agitation. "These MacKenzies are my enemies. They have plagued me for years. Even killed my brother. I must destroy all of them!"

Am I going mad? Or is Carlos? Antonio struggled with his own sanity. Was this all a hallucination brought on by the drugs? He shook his head as if to shake aside the delusion, but yesterday's images remained clear in his mind: the killing of the old man; being brought here like a prisoner.

"So you came here for revenge, not the reason you told me."

"Yes," Charlie said, "and soon I'll have it." His eyes glowed with madness. In his rising fervor, he was unaware that he had slipped back into the crazed mind and voice of Charlie Walden. "Then I can put this life behind me, and you and I can leave this place."

Picking up a nearby bottle of whiskey, he poured them each a drink. "Here, drink this, my young son. You will see—soon everything will be fine."

Ignoring the proffered drink, Antonio backed away in shock and continued to stare at him in disbelief. "Who are you? I do not know you."

"Of course you do, *mi hijo*. It is I, Carlos," Walden replied, drifting into Carlos's accent.

Stunned, Antonio shook his head. "I believed in you. I thought you were a gentle man—kind and good. And now, I find you are somebody else. Carlos Valez never existed."

"I can be Carlos again. You will see," Walden cried out as Carlos. "I love you, my son. I'll be the kind of papa you never had—*I* never had."

"All just a role you are playing." Still befuddled, Antonio murmured, "Just a role."

"No. Carlos is the real me, Antonio. Charlie Walden is the one who never existed."

"If that is true, Carlos, then let us leave this place now, before there is more killing."

"It is not that I wish to kill them; it is just something I must do. I must kill all of them. I cannot leave any behind. Only then can we get on with our lives."

"Carlos, you can't do this. There are women and children involved."

Carlos snorted. "What does it matter? They are just MacKenzies."

"My sister is among them!"

"That is unfortunate, Antonio, but she has been with them long enough to have become corrupted." Sitting down, Charlie closed his eyes, sipping his drink.

Staring numbly ahead, Antonio said sadly, "As I have become by you."

With horror, Antonio now understood that this person he had come to regard with such love and esteem was in truth a madman—a crazed killer. He had to warn the MacKenzies.

Picking up the bottle, Antonio smashed it over Walden's head. Charlie slumped to the floor, unconscious.

On unsteady legs, Antonio walked to the window. A saddled horse stood a few yards from the house. When he climbed out, the air felt good, and he drew several deep breaths into his lungs. His head began to clear, and he glanced around. Seeing no one, he quickly mounted the horse.

"Hey, what are you doing?"

Antonio recognized Lattimore's gruff voice. A bullet sped past his head as he goaded the horse to a gallop.

The MacKenzies all accompanied Ben's body over to his old homestead, laying him to rest beside his beloved Molly. When the sad task was completed, Maud stepped forward to say good-bye.

"Rest in peace, Ben," she said. "Reckon I could talk for hours 'bout the old days when you first came to these parts, and all the good times we had through the years. We're sure gonna miss our old friend, Lord. Ben was a God-lovin' man, but I reckon I don't have to tell You that. Ain't nobody knows what was in his heart more'n You, Lord."

Honey suddenly put her hand on Luke's arm. Glancing at her, he saw her pained expression. "What's wrong, Jaybird?"

"I think the baby's coming, Luke," she said. "I thought it was just another ache, but the pains are coming regularly."

"How often?" Garnet asked, worriedly.

"About every four or five minutes. Oh!" Honey clutched her stomach as her water broke.

"Oh, God, we better get her home," Garnet exclaimed.

The sudden thud of hoofbeats caused them all to spin around as a horseman galloped up to them. Cleve and Flint's guns had already cleared the holsters when Adriana recognized her brother.

"Antonio!"

"Adriana, you must all get away from here," Antonio shouted. "I've just escaped from Walden and his gang. Hurry! They're on their way here to kill all of you."

"Let's get going," Luke shouted. "Josh, get in the wagon." While Josh scrambled to obey, Luke scooped up Honey and put her in the wagon bed.

Clutching Andrew in her arms, Garnet climbed up beside Maud, who had taken the reins. "Flint!" Garnet cried out.

"Cleve and I will cover you," Flint said. "Luke, you and Fuente stay with the women and children."

"Get moving, Maud," Luke shouted.

Adriana had not mounted Diablo. "Go with them, Raven," Cleve shouted to her.

"No, I'm staying with you."

"I want you out of here," Cleve ordered. He lifted her up and set her on the saddle. "Now get going."

As Maud whipped the horses into motion, over a dozen riders came into view. Flint fired several shots.

"I will not leave you," Adriana cried defiantly.

"Fuente, get her out of here," Cleve yelled to Antonio.

Antonio rode over and smacked Diablo's rump. The black stallion took off at a gallop and followed the wagon.

"Don't stay here too long," Luke warned as bullets began smacking the ground around them.

"We'll give you a start. Just get the women and children to safety," Cleve said.

Luke galloped away.

Flint and Cleve set up a rapid fire, which caused the horsemen to take cover and spread out. After a few minutes, the shots began to come from all directions.

"They're outflanking us," Flint said. "Let's get out of here."

Under a barrage of fire, Cleve and Flint mounted their horses. A bullet grazed Cleve's shoulder but did not slow him as they galloped away.

Pursued by the gang, Cleve and Flint were less than

half a mile from the house when they caught up with the wagon. Maud whipped the reins as the wagon bounced and rocked.

The chase had become a horse race, with the wagon and outriders speeding across the countryside pursued by the gang of outlaws. As bullets whizzed around them, the men repeatedly turned their heads to return the fire.

Finally, they thundered up the path to Luke's house. Grabbing Josh's hand and holding Andrew, Garnet ran into the house while Luke lifted Honey out of the wagon. Antonio swung Maud to the ground, and Adriana jumped off Diablo and made it safely inside. Amidst flying bullets and shouts, the stallion raced down the path to the corral while Cleve scattered the other horses.

Flint sliced the traces and released the team; then Cleve and Flint took cover behind the wagon, returning the fire as the outlaws spread out behind trees and rocks.

"Let's draw some of this fire away from the house," Cleve said. Flint nodded, and, setting up a barrage of rifle shots, the two men dashed to the end of the barn. Flint spun and fired at one of the outlaws who had approached from behind.

"We've got to split up," Flint said. "It's the only way we can keep from being outflanked. Watch your back, Little Brother." He crawled away on his stomach.

Crouching, Cleve dashed from the barn to the cover of a nearby tree. He succeeded in picking off one of the gang. Darting to the next tree, he caught another in his sights.

Luke and Antonio continued firing from the front windows of the house, while Adriana and Maud returned a heavy outburst of shots from one of the bedroom windows. Josh huddled in the corner near the fireplace, holding Andrew in his arms as Garnet worked over Honey, who was in the throes of labor.

"Oh, God!" Honey groaned, as the power of the

contractions increased. "Garnet, they need you. Leave me; I'll be okay."

"Just keep up the good work, Honey," Garnet said. "It shouldn't be too long."

"Is there anything I can do to help?" Adriana asked, coming over to the bed.

"I'm sorry to be such a bother," Honey cried out, then bit down on her lip as her body was seized with pain. "Oh, this is hell," she groaned when she was able to speak. "This baby better look like Luke."

"You better hope not, if it's a girl," Garnet said with a light laugh. She wiped the perspiration off Honey's brow. "Honey, you're doing so well."

Maud had stopped firing to reload her rifle, and Garnet's smile changed to horror when she looked up and saw one of the gunmen climbing through the window.

Adriana turned and fired. Her shot found its mark, and the outlaw fell away. Hurrying back, Adriana closed and locked the shutters. "They're circling the house; we've got to close off the bedrooms."

While Maud hurried to Josh's room, Adriana headed for the other bedroom. Suddenly that door opened and a gunman appeared in the doorway, Colt in hand. He pointed it at Luke's back.

"Luke, look out!" Adriana screamed, and fired. The gunman toppled to the floor, but not before getting off a shot. Luke grunted and fell back, bleeding from the leg.

Antonio hurried over to the body of the outlaw. "He's dead, Adriana."

She drew a shuddering breath; she had killed two men in the course of a few minutes. It all seemed unreal to her.

She was jolted out of her meditation when a bullet ricocheted off the fireplace, narrowly missing Josh as he crouched in the corner, holding the baby.

Hurrying into the bedroom, Adriana managed to close the shutters.

"Goddammit!" Luke cursed, clutching his leg. "It's the same one I was wounded in before."

Maud rushed over to examine the wound. "You got lucky this time, boy. Bullet just nicked you. Tore off a hunk of flesh, but the leg ain't busted." As she tied a bandanna around the wound to stop the bleeding, she suddenly lifted her head.

"For God's sake, Maud, keep your head down or you'll get it blown off," Luke declared.

"I smell smoke."

He nodded. "Yeah, they've set fire to the barn."

"Those goddamn bastards!" Maud raved, shaking her fist. "They're worse than those heathen Comanche!"

Hearing the conversation, Josh cried out, horrified. "The barn! Amigo and his pups are in the barn."

"Oh, God, that's right!" Adriana said, remembering they had put the dogs in there when the family had left to bury Ben. She ran back into the bedroom.

"Garnet, lock up this shutter after I climb out."

"You can't go out there—you'll get killed."

"Adriana, come back here," Honey yelled helplessly from the bed.

Adriana opened the shutters cautiously and peeked out. Then she motioned to Garnet. "I don't see any of them. Just be sure and close these up right away."

"Adriana, don't do it!" Garnet pleaded.

"Amigo and his pups are locked in that burning barn." Adriana climbed out the window and dashed for the barn.

The wait seemed endless to Garnet. Flames had spread to most of the structure, and part of the roof had already collapsed. Suddenly Adriana appeared out of the dense cloud of billowing smoke sweeping skyward. Carrying the box holding the puppies, with Amigo chasing at her heels, she ran toward the house.

After handing the box to Garnet, she picked up Amigo. Garnet grabbed the dog and put him aside, then reached out to give Adriana a helping hand. One of the gunmen spotted Adriana just as she started to climb in the window. His bullet whisked past as she slammed the shutters behind her.

Antonio Fuente looked around at the chaos within the house. Luke was wounded and bleeding; one of the women was about to give birth; and a young boy holding a crying infant was cowering in the corner. Antonio had no idea whether his sister's husband and brother were still alive outside. It would only be a matter of time before the gang either rushed the house or set it on fire, too.

With a glance at the closed bedroom door, he said, "*Señor*, tell my sister I love her dearly." Antonio got up and went to the front door.

"What are you doing, Fuente?" Luke called out.

"If this keeps up, you will all be killed. Maybe I can convince Carlos to listen to me."

"Don't be a fool, man. They'll kill you as soon as you show yourself."

Antonio opened the door and stepped out.

A bullet peeled the bark off the tree above Cleve's head as he ducked for cover. "What's that fool doing?" Cleve mumbled when the door of the house opened and Antonio Fuente stepped outside waving a white neckerchief.

"Carlos, I want to talk to you," Antonio shouted.

"Hold your fire," Charlie Walden shouted.

Antonio walked down the path toward the corral. "Carlos, listen to me. This killing must stop. A baby is about to be born. It is a sign of life—not death. Get on your horses and ride away. I will come with you, Carlos, if you still wish me to."

"Ha!" Lattimore snorted. "That damn traitor must think you're a fool, Walden. He's just stalling for time to let those bastards inside regroup."

Lattimore raised his Colt and fired.

Chapter 33

"**Y**ou killed him!" Charlie cried out in disbelief. *"You killed my son!"*

Without a blink of his eye, he raised his rifle and fired several shots. Lattimore fell to the ground, dead.

"Mel, did you see that? Walden's killed Lattimore!" one of the outlaws yelled from where he was hiding.

"Yeah, I saw it, Macon," Mel responded. "The man's gone crazy."

"What should we do, Mel? Bad enough to be dodgin' MacKenzie bullets without Walden's, too."

"Don't know what you're gonna do, but I'm gettin' out of here," Mel shouted. "Ain't no sense in dying just 'cause Walden's crazy enough to take on these MacKenzies." Mel broke for his horse.

"I'm comin' with you," Macon shouted, and followed him.

"Go ahead, you stinking cowards," Walden shouted. "Charlie Walden doesn't need you. I don't need any of you!"

Clouds of dust ballooned overhead as the rest of the outlaws rode off, following Mel and Macon's lead.

"Looks like you're the only one left, Charlie," Flint called out. "You're not gonna get away this time." Cleve moved in closer to Flint, and they worked their way toward Walden.

Charlie caught a glimpse of Cleve and fired. The

bullet missed Cleve's head and embedded itself in the trunk of a tree.

"Good shot, Charlie, but you missed," Cleve called out.

Flint had worked his way a little nearer to where the outlaw was crouching. Nearby, Flint saw Walden's horse tethered close to where Diablo had strayed. He squinted to get a better look at the dun gelding.

"Naw, it couldn't be," Flint said.

"What are you talking about?" Cleve asked.

"Walden's horse. Remember he stole my horse, Sam, in Abilene?"

To satisfy his own curiosity, Flint gave two short, sharp whistles. Ears perked, the horse turned its head toward the sound, while Diablo continued to munch on the clover patch.

"It *is* Sam!" Flint exclaimed. "My God, it's Sam!" He repeated the whistles. Flailing its forelegs in the air, the gelding reared up, tugging at the restraint until it broke. Then the horse galloped over to where Flint was concealed.

"Sam! You old trail bum," Flint cried out joyously.

Walden fired a shot in their direction, but the bullet careened off the boulder that concealed them.

"What do you figure to do now, Walden?"

Walden spun in surprise at the unexpected sound of Luke's voice nearby.

"Luke?" Cleve yelled. "Everything okay in the house?"

"Everyone's fine, boys. So, Walden—you're outnumbered, outflanked, your gang's run out on you, and you've lost your mount. I'd say you've got a problem."

With rifle blazing, Charlie broke from cover and dashed toward Diablo. Tossing away his empty rifle, he grabbed the reins and jumped on the stallion's back, digging his spurs into the sides of the animal.

Instantly Diablo bucked and reared, tossing Walden over its head. For several seconds, the outlaw lay too dazed to move. Then he stood up and drew his Colt.

In full sight and with weapons pointed at the outlaw, Flint faced him on the left, Cleve on the right, and Luke in front of him.

Walden threw back his head in a maniacal laugh. "So, at last we all meet face to face. Ha! The final reckoning. Which of you MacKenzies has the guts to render the *coup de grâce*?"

"We're all waiting, Charlie," Flint said. "Pick your target. That'll decide it. Oughta warn you: Cleve's the best shot."

Walden laughed again. "Sounds like you're mighty anxious, Flint MacKenzie."

"You bet I am, you bastard! My trigger finger's itchin'."

"You have better cause to try me, Walden," Luke said. "Remember, I killed your brother."

"Oh, yes, Sheriff MacKenzie. I've hated you for years."

"Not as long as I've hated you, Walden. That was my wife you killed when you and those Comancheros raided this ranch."

"And our mother," Cleve said. "Now, I won't shoot a man unless he's got a bead on me—even a piece of swamp slime like you. So try taking that shot. Why prolong your agony, Walden?"

"My agony? 'Pears like the agony's been all yours. I'm kind of enjoying this."

"Yeah, I can see you are, Walden," Luke said. "Bet you enjoyed killing old Ben Franks, too. Any reason why you had to kill the old man?"

"I didn't kill him; Lattimore did. But you just said it—he was an old man." He giggled like a child. "Lattimore did you a favor. The old man had outlived his usefulness." He burst into deranged laughter that caused the three men to exchange glances.

"Ben Franks never hurt a person in his life," Luke said, appalled by the man's callousness. "You really have no conscience, do you?"

"Conscience is for the weak, Luke MacKenzie. I'll leave that for you and your brothers."

"You know what, boys?" Luke said. "Walden's right. We are men of conscience. Besides, if one does the killing, it wouldn't be fair to the other two. Better to let the law hang him. The three of us can share the pleasure of watching him squirm and kick on the end of a rope. Watch the life being choked out of him."

Flint snorted. "Your trouble, Big Brother, is that you're always the lawman. Let's get on with this."

"You want to put down that Colt, Walden, and take a chance on the law?" Luke asked.

"Yeah, Walden, who knows—maybe you'll draw a jury too drunk to find you guilty," Flint said cynically. "But they'll sure as hell find that you're crazy."

"Which is it going to be, Walden—jury or us?" Cleve asked.

Charlie responded with another outburst of laughter. "None of you MacKenzies can kill Charlie Walden." His voice rose in a piercing shrill of amusement. "You're all too soft!" The extent of his lunacy became more evident when he shrugged comically. "Too bad. Too bad," he cried out in a singsong voice. "You've lost your chance for revenge after waiting all this time. Since I know you're all too weak to shoot me, Charlie Walden will have the final laugh."

In the midst of a final outburst of crazed laughter, he raised the Colt to his mouth and pulled the trigger.

The abrupt and violent act left them all stunned. Flint was the first to reach Walden's body. He stared down at the dead man in disbelief.

"It doesn't seem possible, does it?" Luke said, limping up to stand beside him. "All these years . . . only to end like this."

"He cheated us *and* the hangman," Flint said.

They all jerked their heads toward the house when the rapid cries of a newborn infant carried to their ears.

Garnet stood in the doorway, holding the tiny bundle in her arms. "Hey, Luke, don't you want to see your new son? Your wife's been asking about you. You better get up here and put her mind at ease."

Smiling broadly, Luke turned to his brothers. They grinned back.

"The past is settled, Big Brother," Cleve said, slapping him on the shoulder. "Sounds like the future calling."

"I think you're right, Little Brother." Luke limped back to the house as fast as his wounded leg allowed him to, and Garnet placed his newborn son in his arms.

Cleve knelt down at the body of Antonio Fuente. He could tell it was useless, but he checked for a pulse, hoping somehow for a miracle.

He glanced up and saw Garnet, carrying Andrew in her arms, walk over to Flint, who stood looking at the remains of the burning barn. Flint slid his arm around her shoulders and hugged her to his side.

Seeing Adriana running down the path, Cleve quickly moved away from the body and hurried up to her. She ran into his arms.

"¡Querido! ¡Querido!" she sobbed joyously.

Savoring the moment, he held her and let her shed her tears, grateful just to feel her in his arms and know she was safe and unharmed.

He rested his cheek against her head. "It's over, Raven. Walden's dead," he murmured tenderly.

She looked up at him, smiling through her tears. "Antonio? Where is Antonio?"

She looked past him and saw the crumpled body on the ground. Her joy turned to horror, and her arms dropped away from Cleve. Slowly, she walked over to her brother's body and knelt beside him. She gently brushed back the dark hair that had fallen across his forehead, and, picking up one of his lifeless hands, raised it to her cheek.

"*Duerme bien, mi hermano . . . mi amado.* Sleep well."

Cleve put a hand on her shoulder. "Let me take you back to the house, sweetheart."

"No. I don't want to leave him here alone. We have always been together."

They looked up when Don Alarico's coach rumbled up to the corral. The *vaqueros* and the sheriff rode beside it.

"We saw the smoke," Cal Ellis said. "Looks like you had a little trouble here, Cleve."

"Yeah, Sheriff, we had some trouble."

The don climbed out of the carriage and walked over to them. Adriana looked up at him, tears streaking her cheeks.

"Antonio's gone, *Papá*."

Don Alarico knelt down beside his son's body. Cleve turned away and walked back to the fence, leaving them their privacy.

He had known little of Antonio Fuente. Much to his regret, the little he had known about his wife's brother, he had not liked. The sorrow he felt was for Adriana's suffering. But the young man had died nobly and with honor, and Cleve knew he had no right to pass judgement on him.

He waited as others moved around him. Flint and the *vaqueros* were helping the sheriff tie the bodies of Walden and his henchmen to the backs of horses, while Garnet stood silently, holding Andrew in her arms. Whatever she was thinking remained hidden in the green-eyed gaze that followed Flint's every movement.

Cleve was about to go over to Garnet when Adriana stood up. He went to her and put his arms around her. "I'm so sorry, sweetheart."

"I just can't believe he's gone. I'll miss him so much, Cleve," she sobbed.

Garnet came over and slipped an arm around Adriana. "Come on, dear, let's go back to the house. I'll fix you a cup of tea."

Too numb to protest, she let Garnet lead her back to the house.

Cleve walked over to Don Alarico, who sat alone

beside the body of his son. "Is there anything I can do for you, sir?"

Don Alarico looked up at him. Remorse had replaced the don's usual look of arrogance. "I had two sons, and I destroyed them both."

"We all tend to feel guilt when we lose someone we love," Cleve said. "We think of all the things we didn't do or say, that we meant to."

"Or regret what we did say and do," Don Alarico said sadly. "I look at him now, and I think that I don't know him. He is the issue of my loins, yet he is a stranger to me. And I grieve, for I feel the loss. If only I could tell him this."

"I never knew my father," Cleve said. "He died at the Alamo six months before I was born. I used to dream of how wonderful it would have been to have heard my father's voice or laughter just one time. I remember when I was young and I'd see a father holding his son's hand or picking him up in his arms, I'd pretend that it was my father holding me."

Don Alarico stared at Antonio lying peacefully as if asleep. He reached out and touched his face. "*¡Sí, hijo!* Your *papá* never held you very much in his arms," he said, saddened. He glanced at Cleve. "And now, it is too late."

"It's not too late for Adriana, sir. You still have a daughter."

"A daughter who hates me, *señor.*"

"Adriana has a great capacity for loving, sir. I think she would like to love you, if you'd give her the chance."

"I fear she would need a greater capacity for forgiving, my friend, for I have done much to hurt her." He shook his head. "It is hard for so many of our young to understand the ways of our people. Pride and tradition are so much a part of it. My family can trace its roots back to the eleventh century. A Fuente rode at the side of El Cid at Valencia, with Cortez at Mexico City. But what does that mean to our young today?"

"With all due respect, sir, Spain has known much glory in her past, but the time of the conquistador is long gone."

"And with it, our traditions," Don Alarico said sadly.

"By Old World standards, America is a young upstart, not even one hundred years old. But this nation was settled by those wishing to escape Old World traditions, Don Alarico. We fought a revolution to assure it. Your young people see themselves not as Spaniards, but as Americans."

For the first time since meeting the don, Cleve saw a faint smile on his face.

"And the time of the *hidalgo* has passed, too. Is that what you mean to say, *Anglo?*"

"I believe so, sir."

"Perhaps you are right. Still, it does not come easy for the old."

He stood up and motioned to his *vaqueros*. They came over and wrapped Antonio in a blanket.

"Would you like him to remain here, sir?" Cleve asked as the *vaqueros* carried Antonio to the coach.

"No, I will take my son back to the *hacienda*. He can rest beside the mother he never knew."

As they returned to the carriage, he paused and watched Adriana start down the path toward them.

"My daughter is happy with you?"

"I believe so, Don Alarico."

"That is good. And the danger here has passed?"

"Yes, sir."

"Then I shall leave now."

Cleve felt sympathy for this proud man, who had learned a bitter lesson so tragically. Healing the wounds of the past had to begin somewhere. Cleve squared his shoulders and cleared his throat.

"Don Alarico, I ask your permission to wed your daughter, Adriana. I shall love and cherish her to my dying day."

For a moment, the don looked puzzled. Then his eyes gleamed with pride. "You have my permission, *Señor*

MacKenzie. And you honor our family with your request."

The two men shook hands.

"So you are leaving, *Papá?*" Adriana asked when she reached them.

"Yes, but not before I say *adios.* I regret the sorrow I have caused you, and I alone must bear the guilt for the deaths of Pedro and Antonio. Perhaps some day, *mi hija,* you will find some forgiveness in your heart."

"Maybe, *Papá.* Maybe I will. But for now, my heart is too full of sorrow." She started to cry again, and Don Alarico reached for her awkwardly and held her in his arms.

Together, they shed their tears.

Cleve slipped his arm around Adriana's shoulders when they separated, and Don Alarico climbed into the coach.

"Perhaps one day you will return to the *hacienda* for a visit," he said hopefully.

"Perhaps, *Papá*," Adriana replied.

"And until then, sir, you are welcome here any time," Cleve said. "You Spanish have a beautiful saying: 'Mi casa'—"

"*Mi casa, su casa,*" Don Alarico said. "You see, *Anglo,* not all of our Old World traditions should be abandoned." The face of the don broke into an unfamiliar grin. "*Vámonos, vaqueros,*" he shouted with all the authority of his Old World station.

Coach and riders moved away.

"Let's not go back to the house just yet," Cleve said, taking Adriana's hand.

They walked past the corral and across a meadow of wildflowers. After climbing a hillock, they finally stopped. A light breeze stirred Adriana's hair as she stood in the circle of his arms, gazing down on the stream flowing through the valley below.

"It's so beautiful and peaceful here," she said. "It's hard to believe the violence that took place just a short time ago."

His arms tightened around her protectively. "Are you okay, Raven?" he asked gently.

"Yes. I'll be fine, Cleve. Truly I will. There will always be a part of me that will miss him, but deep down, I think I knew I lost Antonio the day he rode away from the *hacienda*. I just didn't want to face the truth. That's why I resented your trying to make me do it."

"Well, I was wrong about him, too, sweetheart."

She turned in his arms. "Cleve, I've got to ask you something," she said earnestly. "And you must be honest with me."

"What is it, Raven?" he asked.

"If Antonio had ridden in here with Walden, would you have killed him?"

"I would have had to, if he tried to kill someone I love, but I would have regretted it the rest of my life."

Her dark eyes seemed to probe the depth of his soul. "Why?"

"Because I love you. I know that if I killed him, eventually you would forgive me—but I would never forgive myself for hurting you."

Her eyes glistened with tears. "I understand. I wouldn't have a while ago. It is strange how much my feelings have changed since we first met."

"Well, I would hope so," he said lightly.

"No, what I mean is that in the beginning I thought you were so handsome, and your slightest touch excited me, but I feel differently now."

"So, I've lost my looks, and I no longer excite you," he teased.

"Oh, no, *querido*," she denied quickly, stroking his cheek. "Now those feelings are greater than ever."

"What are you trying to tell me, Raven?"

"It is I who has changed." She raised her eyes and gazed earnestly into his. "When *Papá* made you marry me—"

"Uh-uh," he responded. "Time we set that record straight: your father never *made* me marry you."

"I realize that, and that's what I'm trying to say. I

married a man I didn't know. Oh, your handsomeness attracted me, and your lovemaking thrilled me. I guess being your wife was a game I played. You flattered me and indulged my every whim. I thought that's what it meant to be married. But I found that isn't really what it means. Marriage is what Honey and Luke share . . . or Garnet and Flint. Two people, yet when they're together, I sense that they are one. I never felt we were, until now."

"Why now, sweetheart?" he asked tenderly.

"Because the events of the last few weeks have forced me to grow up. And now I see beyond the handsome face of the man or the excitement of his touch—I see his soul. And I fell in love." She lightly traced his lips with her finger. "And now your smile spreads to mine . . . your sadness binds my heart. We have become one."

She cupped his cheek in her hand and gazed into his eyes. *"Yo te amo, querido."*

"I love you, too, Raven." He kissed her gently, tenderly, then pulled her tighter into his arms. "God, how I love you!"

She stood in his tight embrace, drawing strength from his arms and body—and his love.

Finally, he asked, "Could you be happy here on the Triple M, Raven?"

She smiled serenely against his chest. "Yes, I can't think of anywhere I'd be happier."

"What would you think of us staying here? I don't mean just for the winter. While we're waiting for that new bull to arrive, we could get a house raised and practically finished."

"Oh, Cleve, are you sure this is what you want? I thought you liked city life—gambling, moving from town to town."

"I did at one time. I don't anymore. I'm holding my excitement in my arms right now. I've found what I'd been searching for since I left here."

He relaxed his hold and looked into the warmth of

her eyes. "But what about you, Raven? What about San Francisco? New Orleans? You may find that the Triple M's a poor substitute. Ranch life can get pretty boring, day in and day out. Are you sure it's what you really want?"

Her eyes sparkled with the gleam of defiance that he had faced so often in the past.

"Try me and find out."

Night had descended by the time the MacKenzie men walked down to the small fenced-in plot containing the few wooden crosses.

Flint and Cleve stood back when Luke and his son hunched down, and Josh laid a small bouquet on his grandmother's grave.

"Well, Ma, reckon it took longer than we thought it would," Luke said, "but it's all over now. And Josh has the brother you hoped he would, Sarah," he said, as the youngster laid the other bouquet he carried on his mother's grave.

"Reckon you and Sarah can rest peacefully now, Ma," Flint said.

"And we're all home—this time to stay, Ma," Cleve said.

Luke and Flint looked at him in surprise, slow grins spreading across both their faces.

"You mean that, Little Brother?" Luke asked.

Returning their grin, Cleve nodded. "Raven and I talked about it this afternoon."

"Well, I'll be goddamned!" Flint declared, whacking Cleve on the shoulder. Then he quickly doffed his hat. "Oh, sorry, Ma."

"You better say you're sorry, Brother Flint," Luke declared. "We just told her she could rest in peace, and you'll have her rising up to wash your mouth out with soap."

"Hear that, Amigo?" Josh said, turning excitedly to his companion. Four canine snouts, which led to four wagging tails, were pressed up against the outside of the fence. "Uncle Cleve and Auntie Adee's gonna stay. Betcha that means pretty soon I'll have another cousin to play with."

Josh turned to Cleve. "Is that right, Uncle Cleve?"

"Wouldn't doubt it a bit, Josh," Cleve said, swooping the boy up onto his shoulders.

Laughing, they all left the graveside.

Luke suddenly stopped and cursed, "Dammit! Take a look at that. What is Honey doing out of bed? She just had a baby!"

Cleve glanced up at the house and saw Honey and Garnet standing outside. Honey's golden hair and Garnet's long, flaming tresses gleamed in the moonlight. At that moment, he realized that in his mission for revenge, he'd given little credit to the courageous women his brothers had married. They had embraced their husbands' enemy as their own—and each had faced death defending that conviction.

A dozen memories swirled through his mind: the vision of Honey standing with a Colt in her hand, protecting his wounded brother; Garnet holding Walden's gang of cutthroats at bay to prevent them from lynching Flint. He recalled the women's fortitude as they forded rivers, fought off Indians, and ate dust while driving a herd of steers from Texas to Abilene, Kansas.

A myriad of images flashed through his memory: their faces alive with laughter, streaked with dust and tears, Honey strumming a guitar by a campfire, Garnet racing past on horseback during the bedlam of a cattle stampede.

And through it all—even as chaos reigned around them—they had borne their children, bringing forth the immortality of the men they loved.

Those two MacKenzie women were as remarkable as the men they married, Cleve thought with pride.

When he saw a slim, dark-haired figure step out of the house and stand beside the others, his heart swelled with love. His Raven belonged with them. Her courage and loyalty matched theirs, and today she had borne her baptism of fire for the man she loved—as Honey and Garnet had done before her.

As if reading his thoughts, Luke said, "You should have seen Adee in that gun battle. She sure proved herself to be a real MacKenzie today."

"Yep," Flint agreed. "She sure did."

When Adriana broke from the others and ran toward him, Cleve put down Josh, quickened his step, and moved ahead of Luke and Flint.

Grinning, Cleve reached out and grasped the hand to his future, to the promise of love, of contentment—of life.

Hand in hand, they walked back to the house.